Praise for Mary Ann Ma

"Marlowe makes a name for herself in this hilarious and sexy debut. . . . It's filled with frisky sexy scenes set to the backdrop of rock music . . ."
—*Booklist* STARRED REVIEW

"Fun, flirty read about a magical romance . . . a light-hearted pick me up. Eden and Adam's chemistry was so electric, I rooted for them the whole way!"
—*FIRST for Women*

"This love potion romance, which pairs up the lead singer for a rock band with a biochemist who's also an amateur singer/songwriter, is light and fluffy."
—*Publishers Weekly*

"The chemistry between Adam and Eden is instant and electric, and watching them bring out the best in each other gives the story warmth along with the heat. . . . "
—*RT Book Reviews*

"Frisky, Flirty Fun!"
—Stephanie Evanovich, *New York Times* bestselling author of *The Total Package*

"Sexy, engaging and original. I completely fell in love with Eden and Adam. An amazing first novel."
—Sydney Landon, *New York Times* bestselling author of *Wishing For Us*

"Marlowe is a deft, compelling writer with a modern, confident voice . . . A smartly-written, entertaining debut!"
—Robinne Lee, author of *The Idea of You*

Books by Mary Ann Marlowe
Published by Kensington Publishing Corporation

Some Kind of Magic

A Crazy Kind of Love

Dating by the Book

Crushing It
(written as Lorelei Parker)

Published by Mary Ann Marlowe

Kind of Famous

KIND
OF
FAMOUS

MARY ANN MARLOWE

Published by Mary Ann Marlowe
www.maryannmarlowe.com

ISBN-13: 978-1-7334018-0-7 (Paperback)
ISBN-13: 978-1-7334018-1-4 (ebook)

First Paperback Edition: April 2020

Printed in the United States of America

To all the fans on the music forums
I've run, participated in, or lurked on
Some of you know who I am

The world is mine
I'm breaking through
Expectation
Adulation
The horizon line
Is nearly in view

—Walking Disaster
"No Holding Back"

Chapter One

I could find a Walking Disaster song lyric appropriate for any occasion.

Humming, *"The world is mine/I'm breaking through,"* I spun the revolving door into the marble lobby of the high rise in Times Square. Today, this song was my anthem.

I'd finally broken through, and the world would be mine.

Well, at least a job in the music industry would be.

Standing in honest-to-God New York City, I felt like a tourist gawking at the big city, but if the shoe fit. It wasn't like I'd never set foot outside of central Indiana, but before I took this job at the *Rock Paper*, most of my traveling had been concert related, and my career had been dullsville. As an extreme music fan, my true passion had been a very expensive hobby.

That all changed today.

Today, I became a legitimate New Yorker. I still couldn't believe I'd landed this job at this magazine. I closed my eyes to breathe in the air actual rock stars may have exhaled. Cigarettes, coffee, and crowd musk formed a uniquely Manhattan cologne.

Halfway across the lobby, my phone rang out a popular Walking Disaster song. The call could only be from Ashley, aka DeadFan on the fan board. Online, we all had our aliases. People knew me as Pumpkin39. Pumpkin because of my flaming orange hair. The rest because of my March 9th birthday.

Oh, yeah. In my spare time, I ran the biggest Walking Disaster fan site on the Internet. My obsession with music was about to become my real-life career.

I swiped the phone to answer, as I strode purposely toward security. "Ash? Is there a problem?"

It wouldn't matter if the site had gone offline. She knew I wouldn't have time to put out trash fires on my first day at work.

"Just called to wish you good luck! I'm so excited for you."

I patted my hip for the lanyard then slid my shiny new ID badge over the electronic sensor and took my place among the many other career-oriented people waiting for the elevator. I adopted a professional, non-fan-girl tone. "Thanks for calling. Is everything okay?"

That was a mistake. Ash could talk a mile a minute. "Yeah, though there was some drama this morning over a bad review. You know how they call people bad fans for agreeing with criticism? A fight broke out, but I handled it. I think."

I zoned out a bit as she chattered on, but my attention perked up when she said, "I wanted to tell them how you're about to start work at the very magazine where that review was posted."

The elevator dinged its imminent arrival, and I switched the phone to my other ear so I could better enunciate my response. "Do not under any circumstances tell anyone where I'm working." I'd already explained all of this to her.

"Oh, I know. They'd all go nuts, expecting you to share state secrets or whatever."

That was only half of it.

The elevator doors opened, and the crowd jostled me as people got off. I whispered as loud as I dared. "And if my boss, or anyone here, happened upon your posts, they'd figure out pretty fast you were talking about me."

Maybe it wasn't lethally uncool be a fan forum admin, but I wasn't ready to find out.

She sighed. "Got it. It's still exciting."

I stepped onto the elevator. "Ash, I need to go. Please only text if there's a real emergency, okay?"

"Sure thing. And good luck, Layla." Before I could hit End on the call, her tinny voice came through the speaker. "If you meet anyone famous, let me know!"

Muffled chuckles on the elevator made it clear they'd all heard.

There were days I started thinking I was too old to run a fan site for a band who didn't know or care that I spent my time promoting them, all for free and out of the goodness of my heart. Not that they needed the publicity. Walking Disaster was one of the most successful bands of the past several years with no sign of slowing down.

Once upon a time I felt proud of what I'd accomplished, but nowadays, I never mentioned to anyone in real life that I ran a fan forum. It sounded interesting when I was nineteen. At twenty-eight, announcing that I was anonymously famous in a very remote corner of the Internet would be met with understandable pity.

Still, I shot a glance around the elevator on the off chance a celebrity hid in our midst. It would be entertaining to bask in Ash's jealousy if I could report back a Dave Grohl or Ed Sheeran sighting. Despite how unlikely.

Even the remote possibility humbled me.

I rode to the ninth floor with trepidation and giddy expectation, but an anticlimactic silence greeted me when I entered the floor for the *Rock Paper*. There were a few people scattered about, but the overhead lights hadn't even been completely turned on.

Somewhat relieved I wouldn't have to interact with anyone right out the gate, I found my assigned cube sandwiched between a pair of identical desks on either side. Another matching set ran parallel across the narrow aisle. I tried to ignore the implication of so much conformity, accepting the necessity of efficiency. Still, I had a romantic notion of the music industry. Mainly, I liked to ignore the *industry* part of that phrase. I'd been around long enough to understand the compromises and little deaths that everyone, even the most artistic people—the ones who made the rest of our jobs possible—had to endure.

I dropped into my chair and slid paperwork out of the manila envelope they'd given me, searching for my login credentials. When I noticed nobody had delivered the company-issued laptop, I bent forward to check under the desk and peeked around the cube walls in case they'd left it with my neighbors.

Nothing.

In the cube cattycorner to mine, a head of brown curly hair bobbed in a jerky rhythm. As self-assured as I came across on my website, I had a hard time talking to people in real life, but I'd need to get over my anxiety working in the real world, so I mustered up my courage and knocked on the strip of metal along the top of the wall. The cube's inhabitant didn't look up. I tapped again before I noticed she wore headphones, something I'd be doing as soon as I had a laptop and assigned projects.

I walked around to her side of the dividing wall and touched her shoulder. The girl jumped out of her seat with an embarrassed laugh. "Oh, my Lord. You scared the dickens out of me."

Her chair spun, and when she looked up, I found myself face to face with Josie Wilder. My eyes grew wide, and I took a giant step back because I knew her well—although she didn't know me from Adam. And I shouldn't have known her. Josie was a relatively obscure photographer, not a celebrity in her own right. However, through a spiderweb of connections, she'd earned a bit of notoriety in my small corner of the universe. She was the girlfriend of Micah Sinclair, whose sister was Eden Sinclair, whose husband was none other than Adam Copeland, lead singer of Walking Disaster, the band my fan site idolized. True story.

I'd never expected to run into my own celebrity fixations. Not at work. Certainly not on my first day.

"What are you doing here?" I blurted out.

She tugged her headphones out of a tangled lock and shook out her curls. "Boyfriend's on the road, and I was going batshit insane in that empty house. I thought I'd file these photos here."

Right. Of course. I knew she freelanced for the *Rock Paper*, but I envisioned her working on a tour bus, at a concert, somewhere exciting. The juxtaposition of my imagination and this office-space reality threw me.

A second later, the detonation of the word *boyfriend* went off, and I realized she meant Micah—rock star in his own right. My eyes popped open even further if possible.

She tilted her head, eyes narrowed slightly. "Have we met?"

I stood flummoxed, unsure whether to reveal that I'd seen and loved her concert photography, or if I should praise Micah's music, or if I should confess my involvement in the whole fan community. But I really didn't want her to read my awkwardness as recognition.

Thankfully, despite my extreme social ineptitude, my solid Midwestern upbringing prevailed, and I stuck out a hand. "Hi. My name's Layla Beckett. Sorry for the rude greeting. I'm new here, and I'm still a bit lost." I clamped my lips together to shut up.

Jo had more grace than me and didn't seem to notice that I was genuinely starstruck. "I'm Jo. It's a pleasure to meet you." She took my outstretched hand. "You're new? What will you be doing?"

Her slight southern accent surprised me. I'd seen dozens of pictures of her, but I'd never once heard her speak.

"Social media. Web content. That sort of thing." I tugged the sleeves of my cardigan over my hands, shrinking into myself, wanting to stick my head in a hole. "I'm hoping to get more experience with development, though."

Jo's bright smile seemed sincere. "Social media, huh? I used to work as paparazzi and had to practically live on Twitter."

I bit my tongue to resist saying, "*I know.*"

"Now, I try to avoid social media altogether. You must know how to navigate the mine fields pretty well, I bet."

That's not why I was hired, but she was right. I'd never gotten sucked into an online war or been baited by trolls, except when I felt like it. I'd put out a lot of dumpster fires and quelled potentially damaging fan uprisings in my years at the helm, but I only got into a fight if I knew I could win it.

She didn't need to know all that.

"Twitter can be a nightmare, but I try to see it as another tool. There are a lot of potential clicks that shouldn't be ignored."

Jo laughed. "Spoken like a social media master."

"It's kind of ironic honestly. I suck at the social part, but I guess I'm good at it online."

She laid a hand on my shoulder. "You could've fooled me." Her gentle encouragement made me feel less like a dork.

Several of the cubes had become occupied while we chatted. More people were entering through the glass doors separating the office from the elevator bank.

I remembered why I was bothering her. "Do you happen to know where the IT guys sit?"

"No, sorry." Jo followed my gaze. "But let me show you around."

She led me to the kitchen and then the mail room. Everyone wore T-shirts with concert logos, skinny jeans, and Converse tennis shoes. Jo had on a knit shirt and an infinity scarf, but otherwise, she fit right in. My heels made me stand out in more ways than one. I'd completely overdressed for the job.

But Jo put me at ease. I couldn't help notice that faces lit up whenever she approached. She had good energy, and I genuinely liked her. Even though she probably had more friends than she needed, I hoped she liked me, too.

As we moved back toward the cubes, she gave me a quizzical look, and I realized I was smiling at her dreamily. "It was really nice to meet you. Thank you so much for showing me around. I'm just so happy to be here."

Her smile matched mine. "Yeah, it's a special place. The job I had before—" She shuddered. "You don't even want to know."

I knew more than a casual observer ought to. "It must have been a toxic environment."

She grimaced with secret knowledge. "You can't begin to imagine."

That southern accent came and went like a subtle breeze, reminding me that she wasn't who I'd always imagined her to be. "If you don't mind me asking, where are you from originally? You have a slight accent. Georgia?"

"Yeah. Atlanta." She exhaled. "Most people who ask me where I'm from are trying to figure out if I'm even American."

"What? Why?"

She gave a little shake of her head in response, and I let it go. The answer came to me as an afterthought. It was common knowledge her father was Indian, but it had never occurred to me to ask about that. I just hadn't read that she'd moved here from the south.

It would have been fun to divulge that information on the website. Fans loved gathering tidbits of hoarded knowledge. But I wouldn't. I still hadn't decided whether or not to mention to anyone besides Ash where I'd started to work. The demand for insider information would become unbearable if I let slip even this small detail. They'd want to know what she smelled like. People generally had no boundaries.

Jo paused by my desk. "And you? Where did you come here from?"

"A super small town outside Indianapolis you wouldn't have heard of."

"Oh, wow. This must be a big change for you then."

"You have no idea."

"No, I remember how overwhelming it is." She tucked a curl behind her ear. "Thankfully, one of my good friends had already settled here, so he gave me a place to stay and helped smooth the transition."

And then, you moved in with a rock star. "Lucky for you. I still need to tackle my housing situation."

"Where are you staying?"

"Actually, I've got a hotel somewhere in Brooklyn. It's on—" I searched my mind for the street "—Flatbush Avenue?"

"Oh, yeah? That's not far from where I live."

That didn't surprise me. I knew Adam Copeland lived in Brooklyn. Not because I'd stalked him, but because the people on my website sometimes did. I encouraged people not to pry into Adam's personal life or pester him on his off hours although I understood how hard it would be to refrain from asking for a picture and an autograph if you saw him sitting in a coffee shop. I honestly wasn't sure if I'd have the will power to practice what I preached, but I hoped I could honor his privacy just like I would want if I were in his position.

It was all academic. Sitting in my apartment in Indiana, I'd never had to make that decision.

Jo was about to change that.

She took a step away, but turned back, nose scrunched adorably. "Hey, Layla, maybe you could come over for dinner tonight."

She was speaking English, but nothing she said was computing. "You want me to come to your house."

"I know how hard it is to be alone in a new place. And honestly, I could really use the company."

My eyes continued to blink, but my mouth couldn't formulate an appropriate response. My brain was busy screaming, "*Worlds collide!*"

Part of me—the one that spent too much time creeping on these people—urged me to jump at Jo's invitation and see what her life was really like.

Another part of me—the fan forum admin—balked at even considering this invasion of her privacy.

A third deeper, darker part of me—the one that hid online behind a fake persona—wanted to retreat to my empty hotel room and catch up on a day's worth of fan forum chatter that was already piling up. I'd been cramping all day, thanks to a particularly painful period that was mercifully coming to an end, and the idea of burrowing under covers alone in my jammies with a hot cup of cocoa appealed to me a lot.

Online, people thought I was cool and connected. Online, I could delete my social gaffes.

But when would I ever have a chance like this again?

So I stood there debating with myself, probably with my jaw agape, drool threatening to spool over my dumbstruck lower lip until Jo nudged me. "Well? I promise we're not ax murderers. Micah's not supposed to be home until tomorrow, so it would be just the two of us. You'd like Micah, I'm sure. You're not allergic to cats, are you?"

"No." I still wasn't sure if that was an answer to her first or last question.

"Then it's settled." She grabbed a pen and scrawled down a number on a Post-it. "Here's my cell. Give me a call when you're ready to leave work. I have something to do downtown, but I can swing back up and fetch you. Okay?"

As I stuck the Post-it to the back of my phone, frequent scene of my crimes, I vowed I wouldn't break her trust or treat her like an exhibit at the zoo.

Talking Disaster Forum

Hipster101 wrote:
I'll have more pictures to post later. And Jayhawk was there. I think he shot some video.

Jayhawk wrote:
Yeah I shot the whole show. Trippy to see Theater of the Absurd opening last night.

Sailor8 wrote:
Ooh, @Hipster - any pictures of Micah or Noah? *Fingers crossed*

Hipster101 wrote:
eye roll I took pictures of the band, yes. They aren't Glamour Shots.

Jayhawk wrote:
Were any of you around back when Walking Disaster opened for Whiplash? And now Theater of the Absurd is . . . I predict big things.

Insidious wrote:
@Jayhawk - Yeah, but one of these things is not like the other. Of those three bands, one's not touring . . .

Pumpkin39 wrote:
For good reason, Sid.

DeadFan wrote:
Adam's staying home with the baby after all!

Sailor8 wrote:
Hey @Pumpkin39, do you have any secret insider knowledge about the next tour?

Pumpkin39 wrote:
As if. I wish I did. I'll know as soon as you know.

Jayhawk wrote:
Can we get back to the Whiplash tour? Did you hear about some tension between the bands? There were some rumors that something went down after the show involving Noah possibly.

Chapter Two

Just as I was beginning to think I'd imagined the manager who'd interviewed me over Skype, Byron rolled in and ushered me into a conference room where he introduced me to the team: a couple of guys who identified themselves as Ajit and Dave. I quickly discovered I didn't corner the market on social awkwardness. Dave barely made eye contact with me, and Ajit snort-laughed when I dorkily blurted something about having a case of the Mondays.

Joining a team of developers at a rock music magazine should have been the most thrilling and intimidating part of my day. I was a self-taught programmer, hired to propose new functionality for others to code, and I worried the legit geeks would ferret out all my technical blind spots.

But my awe at meeting Josie overshadowed the excitement of a new job, and since it soon became apparent that I didn't have enough knowledge yet to follow along, I began to daydream about the pending dinner with Jo. Would we gossip about the workplace? Would she share secrets about Micah?

Before long, Byron asked if anyone had anything else, then dismissed us with a last request to Ajit to show me how to set up my workspace. An hour later, I had my laptop, some basic software, and a connection to the Internet.

Ajit said, "Don't worry. It always takes time to ramp up. We'll have you walking through code in no time."

A frisson of joy passed through me, and I didn't bother to correct his assumption that I'd been hired as a developer.

I itched to jump on the forum to share my incredible morning. The fans were the only people on earth who would understand how mind-blowing all this was, but I couldn't yet. Not only would that be unethical and hypocritical, I wasn't ready to deal with the curiosity such a confession would invite.

Still I wondered if I could at least text Ash and squeal with her.

As if she'd read my mind, my phone rang out a riff of Walking Disaster's "Expulsion"—Ash's text message ringtone. Since I had no other pressing tasks, I slid it open.

Help! There's a revolt on the board. They've decided to stage some kind of search and destroy mission against that reviewer. I've tried to intervene, but they're ignoring me

Shit.

My fingers flew. *Just lock the thread. Or delete it.*

The phone rang out again. *Layla, please. Just pop in?*

I gritted my teeth. I'd put her in charge because she promised she could handle any drama in my absence.

Glancing around to make sure nobody could spy on my laptop screen, I opened the fan site and logged in, smiling at the rotating banner up top. A picture of Adam from the early days loaded, giving me a twinge of nostalgia for the rush I'd felt building my community alongside the rocketing success of the band.

I quickly found the thread in question since it now had a fire icon to the side, indicating it was literally a "hot topic."

I clicked on the last page to jump right into the fray. The last message, written only a minute earlier, told me all I needed to know.

Di$a$ter, who had no life off the boards, had written: *All right. I've set up a fake email account so I could register. Let's all go and let Gabriel Sanchez know he can't mess with WD.*

I rolled my eyes at how childish these people could be and at myself for letting this still be such a huge part of my life, but I began composing my trademark level-headed response to the incredibly short-sighted attempts to salvage the already solid reputation of the band from one bad review.

Guys, are you shitting me? You do realize that this is one review among dozens. The reviewer has a right to his opinion, and you only give the fan base a terrible reputation by flooding the comment sections. It won't change the mind of the reviewer. It may in fact cement it. I'm going to lock this thread now.

If I come back and find you're continuing this nonsense, I'll have to start banning accounts. I don't want to do that. I know you mean well, but please knock it off, you knuckleheads.

This was my life. My weird alternative life.

The fan reaction didn't surprise me. Fans assume the world revolves around all the arcane knowledge they've collected over the years. After a while, a fan community is nothing but inside jokes, memes, and long-held grievances. The name Gabriel Sanchez would be added to the ever-expanding list of people who were dead to us.

Of course, I didn't reveal that I currently sat at the very magazine they were battling. Hopefully Gabriel Sanchez wouldn't know I had anything to do with the fans. If I ever crossed paths with him.

The reality of that possibility hit me.

I stood and scoped out the other cubes wondering if Gabriel might appear in the flesh. It would have been funny to tell him to his face what my posters wanted to say in blog comments, but I didn't see anyone matching his bio pic, so I settled back in at my desk disappointed.

Confident I'd put out the distant fire, I couldn't resist a quick run through unread threads.

Most of the action was about Walking Disaster's new album and some chatter about concerts for other bands. I zeroed in on a discussion about a show Jo's boyfriend Micah's band had opened. The forum members would have lost their shit if I'd casually mentioned I'd be dining at their house that evening.

As it was, I was losing my own shit.

Once I'd caught up, I put my phone in airplane mode to avoid the distraction, but as soon as five o'clock approached, I reconnected. For a wonder, Ash had only texted me twice, and the second said: *Never mind. I straightened it out.*

The immediate temptation to check on the earlier forum drama lost out to my promise to contact Jo. After so much time dealing with brand-new coworkers, I considered bailing. I could unwind alone with my hundreds of anonymous friends, vague-posting about my brush with fame and hinting about the night that might have been.

But I knew I needed to wean myself from virtual society and make real-life friends, so I sucked up my courage and dialed Jo's number, worried she'd forgotten about me anyway.

My pulse sped up as she answered. "Layla?"

In my mind, a million hearts exploded at the sound of her voice. It was official. I had a girl crush.

She instructed me to head down to the street, and fifteen minutes later, a town car with its own driver whisked me away like I was a movie star. As we rode across town, Jo told me about an art show she was putting together. I found myself straddling a line between showing enthusiasm while not veering into outright familiarity.

When she asked me about my day, I babbled as if she really wanted to hear all the technical mumbo jumbo, all the while saying, "*Shut up!*" in my own head. But it was easier to ramble about work than anything else, and she was sweet enough to listen.

We pulled up at her place. The front steps were identical to others up and down the street, punctuating one long row of townhouses. It looked like Sesame Street to me.

"Is this called a brownstone?"

"Yeah. That's right."

She dug out her keys and entered the abode, dropping her bags in the entry and moving quickly to the kitchen where she sat down and pricked her finger with a stick. "Don't mind me. I'm diabetic. I just need to test my blood sugar real quick. Then we can eat."

I knew all that. Of course, I did. I'd been peering through her virtual window for years. The worst of it was, I knew less about her than I did about her boyfriend Micah. And I knew less about Micah than I did about his sister, Eden. And I knew less about all of them combined than I knew about Eden's husband, Adam Copeland.

One degree. I was one degree of separation from Adam Copeland.

Ten years ago, that would have driven me to fan-girl frenzy. Five years ago, I would have begged Jo to introduce me to Adam at the expense of her friendship. Even two years ago, it would have given me an intense thrill to get invited this far into a world I'd been watching like a scripted TV show for so long.

It *was* exciting. Of course, it was, but compared to my former psychologically questionable levels of fanaticism, my response to the current situation bordered on intellectual curiosity more than hysteria. Somewhere, sublimated deep in my brain, I was blowing my mind. But Jo was so nice, and her house seemed so ordinary. Her life was just . . . *normal*. And she'd taken me in as a friend.

All in all, I felt like I was being pretty damn cool.

As she packed away her testing kit, she said, "I've got these premade dinners in the freezer. I can heat up this incredible Thai peanut shrimp. You're not allergic, are you?"

I shook my head as I climbed on a stool at the kitchen island, trying not to gawk at everything. "That sounds great."

She grabbed a couple of Tupperware boxes of premade dinners that looked homemade. She turned the oven on and said, "If you'll excuse me, I need to change. I'll just be a jiff."

"No problem."

Alone in her kitchen, I looked around. What would they say on the forum if I snapped a picture and told them where I was? I couldn't do that, though. It would open such a can of worms. They'd want me to dig through drawers, basically destroying any chance of maintaining a friendly relationship with Jo. One glance at the boards, she'd know without a shadow of doubt who'd betrayed her.

I considered texting Ash, but she might get jealous or blab.

There was one person I could talk to who'd never spill. She'd been trying to call me anyway. I slipped through the sliding door out into the backyard and dialed my mom's number.

A little cat showed up and rubbed around my ankles while the phone rang and finally picked up.

"Hello, Pumpkin!"

Yup. That's where the nickname originated.

"Hi, Mom."

"How was your first day? Meet anyone interesting?"

I dropped onto a chaise longue facing out toward the fence on the far side and stared up into the dark sky, unable to make out a single star in the not quite black night.

"I'll say."

"I want to hear, sweetie, but you'll have to tell me quick. Your dad and I are on the way to Phil and Debby's." Something dinged in the background, and I could hear Dad say something. I wished they'd FaceTime. I missed them, and it made me a little homesick to hear them going about their normal Monday night without me.

I glanced back into the house at the empty kitchen and petted the cat. "You wouldn't believe where I am right now."

"Let me see. Times Square?"

"No, Mom. I was there today. It's crazy over there."

"Oh, I know. Your dad and I went there a couple of years ago. Remember?"

I remembered. It was an anniversary trip. "I do, but I'm actually in Brooklyn at someone's house."

"Ooh. That's interesting. Is it a coworker's house? I hope it's not some stranger's house. You haven't been meeting people in bars, have you?"

I snorted. "No, Mom. This is actually someone I already knew, but she didn't know me."

"Hmm. A mystery. Is it one of your friends from online?"

"Something like that."

"Oh, you'll have to just tell me. We're here."

"She's a friend of a band I follow. Her name is Jo. She's really nice."

"That's great, sweetheart. Here's your dad. He wants to say something."

The phone audibly passed between them, then my dad's voice filled my ear. "Hey, Pumpkin. You're settling in okay?"

"Yes, Dad. Better than expected."

"The offer still stands if you want me to come help you find an apartment."

I did want them to come out and smooth my transition, but this was my life to create. "Thanks, Dad. Not right now."

"Okay. Take care, Pumpkin. We love you. Here's your mom."

"Layla, don't forget to call Max. He said he's been trying to message you on Facebook."

I groaned. I had a couple of different Facebook profiles but constantly forgot to log into the one my brother knew about.

That was the one where I was still "friends" with Liam, an overly intense guy I'd dated in college. Anyway, I knew already why Max wanted to contact me.

"So, have they finally set a date?"

"Call him, Layla."

My brother Max and his girlfriend had been best friends forever. Just like my parents before us. It was inevitable they'd get married sooner than later. I felt a pang of jealousy. Maybe if Liam hadn't been so pushy, or maybe if I hadn't found it easier to control relationships on the Internet, I might have had the courage to go to bars against my mom's warnings. I might have met someone by now.

Impossible to know.

"I'll call him later, Mom. I should be getting back to my hostess."

"Call us again soon. We love you."

"Love you, too."

Once they hung up, I stared at the Chrome icon on my phone for a heartbeat. On any given night, I'd be Jonesing to read the boards, if for no other reason than to clear my Unread Posts notifications. Not tonight. I needed to interact with real humans. Jo was about as easy an introduction into the real world as any. She'd practically forced me to socialize.

I stood and took one long breath of the warm spring air. When I turned around to go in, I nearly dropped my phone from shock.

Chapter Three

Sitting at the kitchen island were three men I'd recognize anywhere. Closest to the door sat Micah Sinclair, lead singer for the band Theater of the Absurd, Jo's hot-as-fuck boyfriend. On his right, the unmistakable red hair of his drummer whose name completely escaped me. My eyes were drawn immediately to the pretty-boy lead guitarist, Noah Kennedy. My heart tripped over itself.

A few years back, Theater of the Absurd went on tour, opening for Walking Disaster in Europe. That's when fans started threads to discuss their music, learned their songs, and picked favorites among the band.

I confess I'd ranked the guys' hotness over the years. I'd gone through a phase where Micah was my number one pretend musical boyfriend from his band, and I wasn't alone. As the front man, he got the most attention, plus he's simply beautiful with his blond hair, blue eyes, and broad build. Once he'd fallen into a serious relationship with Jo, it became a bit harder to even joke about him in fake romantic ways. Not that it would stop me from drooling over a photo. I mean, they're just pictures.

But that was no photo, leaning over the kitchen island with that thousand-kilowatt smile.

Then there was Noah, a bit mysterious, sometimes distant with fans, but onstage, he exploded. I'd seen him shred a guitar at a show, and I could still remember what color pants he'd had on that day because his ass was one of those works of art that people had made a point of photographing whenever possible. Jeans, red leather pants, or the rare suit slacks all worked in service of his perfect butt. And it was sitting on a stool five feet away from me. All that separated us was a plate-glass door.

The other guy—I wanted to say Shawn—had the other two entranced with some story he was telling. His hands shot dramatically forward and up and down and back, in circles, in swoops, like he was drumming out the narrative. His face lit up so that I desperately wanted to hear what was so funny. Micah and Noah leaned in to listen, both so engaged, it made me hesitate to interrupt.

On the other hand, I was dying to actually meet these guys. What a day.

With a good shake of my hair to maximize volume, I slid open the glass door, and three heads turned my way.

Micah said, "Well, hello."

I swallowed hard. My brain fritzed, and I stood there, frozen.

Jo popped up from the base of the fridge. "Oh, here you are. Someone came home early. Let me introduce you to my boyfriend and these other clowns." She flipped her hand toward Micah. "This here is Micah Sinclair. This is his house, actually. I'm just a guest, alas."

Micah grabbed her upper arm and reeled her in for a kiss. "Liar. You'd be out on the streets if you didn't live here."

She pushed his chest away. I admired her restraint. "Stop. We have guests."

"I thought you were a guest." He chuckled at himself.

Jo simply rolled her eyes to the ceiling. "Excuse him. He's literally the worst. Meanwhile, over here, we have the insufferable Shane Morgan."

Shane! Right.

Shane tipped an invisible hat and said, "My lady."

He still wore a mischievous smile leftover from the anecdote he'd been sharing before I walked in.

"Finally, this brat is Noah Kennedy."

Noah winked, and I melted a little.

"Gentlemen, let me present my newest coworker and a brand-new resident of our fair city, Layla—" she faltered "—shit, I've already forgotten your last name."

"Beckett. Layla Beckett."

Noah immediately sang my name, and it should have thrilled me to hear those words coming out of his beautiful lips. I couldn't help it though. I judged people who went for the obvious joke the minute they met me, as if they honestly thought it was original and clever. People often asked me why I didn't just go by my middle name if I didn't like being a punchline. Except my parents had saddled me with the middle name Prudence. Their love of music spilled over into their kids' names. My brother had scored with Maxwell Jude.

I schooled my face into a placid mask of indifference until Noah flashed the charming smile I'd seen in pictures on the forum. "Awesome name. Really."

Maybe he realized his faux pas. His comment smoothed some of my ruffled feathers. "Thanks."

My mind searched for anything I knew about Noah, besides how perfect he looked. I'd read about some fan encounters with him, but I usually ignored them unless they got graphic, and then I nuked them without much thought. Of course, Micah had a worse reputation with women before Jo tamed him. But fans claimed Micah was a sweetheart. Noah on the other hand came off as rude. I wanted to give him the benefit of the doubt, since Lord knew, fans could be demanding.

Noah waved his hand toward me then Shane. "Can you imagine the children these two would have?"

Shane's head rose as he realized Noah was talking about him. A blush crept up his pale skin to the roots of his hair.

"Red's turning red!" Noah laughed.

I trained my eyes on Shane, willing him to look my way. His milky skin had a definite reddish cast to it, but I couldn't tell if it was from anger or embarrassment. I'd heard every red-haired taunt in the book, and although Noah probably thought he was gently ribbing his friend, Shane's tense jaw and gritted teeth belied years of buried hurt with layers of insults heaped on top.

Finally, with a flick of the eyes, he glanced over. I pegged him with what I hoped was a penetrating gaze, a telepathic communication to say, "*I know.*"

A small smile lifted the corners of his mouth, and he breathed in and exhaled. "You're right, Noah. We'd have gorgeous kids. Look at her."

It was the first time he'd been completely still. His hands settled onto the counter, and all the mischief and mockery drained from his face, leaving behind an open sincerity that sucker-punched me. Time slowed, and I brazenly stared at him, as if he were another photograph posted in some fictional *Hot drummers* thread. He might not have the glitz of Micah or the glam of Noah, but next to them anyone would appear ordinary. Overall more boyish than his two pretty bandmates, Shane had a rugged build, wide shoulders, and a tight muscle running up the side of his neck. That cord could have spawned a photo thread of its own. I followed the set of his jaw to his mouth, dragged my eyes over his plump lower lip, took in his slightly crooked nose and high cheekbones, and studied the small gauges in his earlobes.

By the time I'd made the circuit back to his arresting eyes, I'd concluded he was very easy to look at. And he didn't seem to mind looking at me either.

My lips curled to match his. And quite possibly, my cheeks now matched my own hair.

With the unexpected arrival of the boys, Jo abandoned her dinner plans in favor of ordering a bunch of pizza, apologizing to me for the switch, as if I would've been eating anything other than takeout back at the hotel. While she made the call, I excused myself to go to the bathroom, freshen up, check my teeth, and freak the fuck out privately.

My brain hadn't yet absorbed the new reality. These people lived in photographs and videos. They existed as anecdotes from fans who'd made it backstage, onto the bus, or into the hotel. I couldn't wrap my head around the everyday banality of them.

Once I'd returned to earth, I casually strolled into the kitchen and climbed onto the stool beside Noah, pretty, pretty Noah. Sailor8 on the forum would cream her pants to be close enough to touch his wavy blond hair. She'd demand I sniff him and report back my findings, but that wasn't about to happen. I was working undercover, and I didn't want to blow my disguise.

As we waited, Micah set plates and glasses on the kitchen island. He and Jo moved around each other like choreographed dancers, putting out silverware and drinks. All the while, she interrogated the guys on their tour.

"How was it traveling with Whiplash?"

I wanted to gush about what a great score it was for them to open for such a huge band, how it would expose them to even more fans. I waited for them to rave about the amazing opportunity, but they all sort of awkwardly looked in different directions until Micah said, "Noah doesn't want to talk about it."

He didn't laugh, so I couldn't read if he was teasing or serious.

Jo shot a look at Noah. "Oh, right. Sorry." I was curious to know what had just passed between them, but she changed the topic abruptly. "How long are you home?"

There'd been something in the forum about tension on the tour. I was dying to ask them to fill me in on the mysterious subtext only I couldn't decipher.

After a heavy pause, Micah said, "We have to head back out on Sunday."

Jo sagged. "Okay, then. I'm glad you got home early."

She reached her arms around Micah's neck and gave him a proper kiss right there in front of us all.

Noah whistled, and the weird vibe seemed to dissipate with the teasing camaraderie. He suddenly cut his gray eyes over to me, catching me studying his perfect profile. He flashed a wicked charming grin. "So, Ginger Spice."

I bit the inside of my cheek at the unintended slight. His bratty reputation seemed well founded.

"Where did you say you're from?"

"I didn't. I'm from Indiana."

Noah drummed his fingers on the table for a moment, lips twisted, like he was trying to remember where Indiana might be. "July. We were in Indianapolis in July."

"Uh-huh." I wasn't sure how best to respond to that piece of information.

Shane's face lit up. "Oh, yeah. Maybe Layla was there."

"Yup. I totally was." I laughed.

"Sure," said Noah, sarcastic, as though reading my response as polite good humor, which suited me just fine until Shane's mouth squeezed together in disappointment.

"No, I really was."

The admission of my fan status was worth it if only to watch Shane's face brighten again. His expressions changed like a chameleon, like a mood ring. And those eyes. Noah's were a fascinating swirl of gray cold mist, and Micah's were the clear aqua of island seas you find in travel brochures. Shane's were the dark blue of the midnight sky. A black ring encircled the universe of his incredible eyes, and, as I lost myself in those depths, he let me drink my fill.

Noah turned all the way to face me, elbow on the counter, blocking my view of Shane entirely. "So, where did we play then?"

Never did I expect I'd be sitting here having to prove my fan cred to a member of a band I was slightly overinvested in.

Without missing a beat, I said, "You played the Lawn at the White River State Park." Savoring the pearly white grin spreading across his face, I added, "Chain Smoke opened for you."

Noah swung his head back to face Shane. "Is that right?"

It was. My interest in Theater of the Absurd was genuine. Not nearly as ardent as my love of Walking Disaster, but I could hum a few bars.

Micah started laughing, and that distracted Noah enough to lean back so I could see Shane clapping his hands.

"Well done."

I hugged myself a little. I could have died right then. Hanging with these guys had made me feel truly special, and that was something I could take with me when this night ended. I wished I could snap a picture, get an autograph, or just tell someone about this, but I forced myself to behave like a human and focus on the experience.

The pizza arrived, and once Jo placed the boxes on the counter, we helped ourselves. Jo chose a piece covered in veggies, while Micah and the two guys demolished a meat lovers. Fearful I might lose a limb if I ventured too close to the pepperoni, I hesitantly reached for one of the veggie slices.

Chewing on his food, Noah honed back in on me with a lift of the brow. "So, you're a fan then?"

The question confused me. Had my confession ruined any chance of being treated like one of them? I told the truth. "I don't know what the right answer here is."

Jo cut her pizza with a fork and knife and pointed an impaled corner at me. "The proper answer is always yes. They want to hear you're a huge fan."

I snickered. "In that case, yes. I'm a huge fan."

Fishing the depths of my sincerity, Noah said, "Name one of our songs."

Shane laid a hand on his shoulder. "Man, ease up. She just said she came to a show. What difference does it make?"

Noah's eyes slid off me and over to Micah. "Just curious if she's a normal fan or a super fan." He set me in his sights again. By the way he'd said *super*, it sounded synonymous with *creepy*, and I didn't want to fail his test. "Five bucks she can't tell us what instrument Shane here plays."

Now, that was a trap. He wanted me to confess knowledge no casual fan ever knew: the name of the drummer. If anyone had asked me to name their drummer this morning, I would have drawn a blank, but it was stupid to point to the guy and ask what he played when I just told him I'd been to a show. Process of elimination would rule out guitarist.

If I pretended to guess, if I lied and said, "*Bassist*," I felt like I'd be letting Shane down.

I nervously glanced to Jo for help, and she laughed. "Noah, she's not a super fan. She's a music fan. She works at the *Rock Paper*. She's gonna know her bands."

Micah shook his head with a look of parental disapproval. "Noah, you can be such a dick."

Shane had watched this whole exchange in silence, but now he said, "I play drums, Layla."

For that little kindness, it was worth blowing some cool points. I shot him my flirtiest smile. "Yeah, I knew that. You're a force of nature."

He beamed. "Hurricane Shane. That's me."

Noah's shoulders relaxed, and he seemed to give up his cat and mouse game. I had no idea what he was after. Did he suspect my interest here bordered on stalker? Did it matter? Would they treat me differently if they knew what I did in my spare time? If they knew I could sing some of their songs by heart?

It wasn't like they were Walking Disaster. I wasn't sure I could be so cool if Adam Copeland or Mark Townsend were sitting at that counter.

Not to mention, Jo was right. I knew my bands. Rock trivia wasn't a game I played to lose.

Fortunately, the heat of the conversation lifted while everyone concentrated on eating. I might have been imagining things, but I felt as though Shane glanced my way surreptitiously a few times. When dinner came to an end, Noah said, "Let's hit the road, man. I'm beat."

Shane thanked Jo for dinner, punched Micah on the shoulder, then shoved a hand in one of his pockets and said, "It was nice to meet you, Layla."

A swirl of sunrise played along his jaw, and I suddenly didn't know what to do with my own arms. I shoved my hands under my thighs and sat on them. "You, too."

As the guys headed out, I started gathering my things together, wondering if I should call a cab.

Jo laid a hand on my arm. "Micah and I think you ought to stay here."

I was speechless. "Uh."

"We've got a cozy guest room upstairs for when my mom visits. You could take a little more time to scour craigslist for something affordable but not sleazy."

"I don't know." It felt incredibly invasive. Micah had just come home, and he clearly wanted some privacy with his girl-friend.

Micah spoke up. "I can send my driver over to pick up your things. You'd be safer and more comfortable here."

"Come on. I'll show you." Jo led me to the top of the stairs. I peered into a master bedroom with an enormous king size bed, but she crossed the hall, explaining, "I work in here sometimes, but I'm done for the day."

The guest room had a queen bed and a desk. On the wall, above a laptop, hung a picture of Micah sleeping like a god on a divan, covered in nothing but a blood red throw. I stared at it. "I think I've seen this before."

She chuckled. "Yeah. My old boss published that in an effort to show him in an unflattering light." She cocked her head. "But I like it. Plus, it embarrasses my mom."

I didn't know anything to say, but my lack of response was bordering on rude, so I forced myself to smile and tell her, "Thank you. This is incredibly generous of you."

"Nonsense. You'd do the same I'm sure."

True. But would she have been so neighborly if she knew about my hobby? Would she invite me into her home if she knew I was the equivalent of an Internet peeping Tom?

Talking Disaster Forum

CaliforniaDreamin wrote:
I see tummy! *swoon*

AdamsWife wrote:
OMG, I love that one, CD! He's so casually sexy, you know?

NewDawn wrote:
Hi. I'm new here. That photo brought me out of lurker mode to say, meow.

mAdam wrote:
Welcome to the forum, @NewDawn! I cannot disagree with you. That's one beautiful photo . . . of one beautiful man.

NewDawn wrote:
Hee hee. Love your username! I think I'm going to love reading back through this thread.

WeedGirl wrote:
Holy shit! That photog sure knows how to capture Adam's lips.

Pumpkin39 wrote:
That's one of my favorites. Wouldn't mind trading places with that microphone. :)

CaliforniaDreamin wrote:
We even got Pumpkin to comment. Score! Hey, Pumpkin, you think you could maybe get this one into the banner rotation?

Pumpkin39 wrote:
I dunno. You know how the music nerds object to the objectification . . . But I'll see what I can do.

CaliforniaDreamin wrote:
Bows down. We'd love you forever!

WeedGirl wrote:
Marry me, Pumkpin! You're the best.

Chapter Four

Alone, waiting for my things to arrive from my hotel, I slipped my shoes off and propped myself against the fat pillows in decorative shams.

I was exhausted, but I needed to get online soon, or I'd be so far behind I'd never catch up. I trusted Ash to keep order, but there was usually something to attend to, so I booted up my laptop and turned on my phone's hotspot.

The front page of my site held the blog—curated content where I could post recent tour videos, new album releases, links to reviews, or write my own personal commentary about anything, band related of course. Usually. Sometimes I posted on other topics, but I kept it at least tangentially related. I could, for example, post a recap of my day, along with a picture of Micah Sinclair's guest room. Fans would eat it up, and the hit count would explode, which would bring me more money since I'd monetized the site.

But I had no intention of exposing myself to that level of scrutiny. Tonight, I only wanted to make sure nobody had disrespected my order to stop talking about invading the comments section of Gabriel Sanchez's review. I wasn't surprised to find an inordinate number of private messages from people responding to my edict. I already knew these would fall out into a Neopolitan of three predictable flavors.

The yummy chocolate would be the do-gooders who'd observed the dramatic review revolt thread with consternation. They'd pat my back and tell me Adam should send me free tickets to his shows in heartfelt gratitude for all the hard work I did. I'd never ascertained what these suck-ups thought they'd get for praising me to high heaven. I was a nobody with a website. It wasn't like I could get them backstage passes.

The banal vanilla would be the remorse-filled hooligans who'd been reprimanded and wanted to let me know how truly sorry they felt for crossing the line. There was no need for prostrating themselves at my altar. I rarely banned anyone.

Then there was the rebel strawberry: cantankerous rabble-rousers who intentionally broke the rules. Mostly, when confronted, they simply stopped without any further communication. Some special snowflakes thought we were friendly enough to have a spirited debate about free speech on the Internet, or worse, disliked me enough to argue vociferously against my reign of terror.

It made me laugh a little. I was just a grownup kid who went a little fanatic about a band and wanted to chat with others who understood my obsession. I did like these people, but they could drain my energy. I responded briefly to each message, then went into the forums.

While nobody fanned the flames of the Gabriel Sanchez invasion, the conversation about that review had run hot all day. To be honest, the new album hadn't impressed me as much as I'd hoped. I planned to give it some time, but it felt too studio, too polished. They'd necessarily gotten more commercial over time.

I expected I'd come to love the album eventually, but I never believed I had an obligation to love everything Adam ever did, nor did I ask the fans to be blind or uncritical. I only asked them to be fair.

Still, I actually agreed with the rebellious posters who took issue with Gabriel's review. He'd essentially shredded the album for sounding inherently different from the old music, as if the band wasn't allowed to go in a new direction. Earlier in the year, he'd torn Theater of the Absurd apart for the exact opposite reason, which was completely unfair. Theater of the Absurd had pushed the envelope since their first album, both in their performances and in their song architecture. They'd pulled from bands like Of Montreal, The Shins, Radiohead, and others to make melodies that sometimes took me a while to appreciate. It pissed me off a bit that Gabriel wrote them off so easily. Like he cared more about his reputation than about their career.

Especially after meeting the guys and realizing they really were just people.

Obviously, I came at things as a fan, not a critic, but I always thought one should be a little bit of both. Fandom without criticism was idiotic worship. Criticism without fandom was pointless and miserable.

I added my own opinion to that effect to the thread. I loved that I could be an administrative jerk to my posters in the morning, but by evening, I could count on them to argue with me on philosophical questions without hesitation. That's what kept it fun for me to engage with them.

Still, the power to delete the Adam/Micah slash fanfic (no matter how hot) at any moment set me apart. Loved or hated, praised or feared, I would never really be one of them. Maybe that was why Ash still called me in to be the bad guy. She'd made too many friends to do the dirty work.

I opened the popular photo thread where the fan girls shared their favorite pictures of smoldering hot Adam Copeland. On a good night, they'd find new pictures to share, but on a slow night, like tonight, they never tired of recycling through the oldies.

I didn't mind the view myself, and to better connect with the community, I threw in a comment of my own. After a few minutes, someone replied to my comment, but they appealed to my role as admin, asking me to turn the picture into a new banner. Maybe it was my imagination, but sometimes I thought they humored me like the kid their mom made them hang out with. They might have been sincere, but I'd never be quite sure.

I opened my photo editor and dragged in the photo, thinking about how I'd let this kind of exchange pass for friendship for far too long.

Back home, my only real friend had gotten engaged to my brother. At my last job doing social media for a pharmaceutical company, I couldn't connect with the ambitious sales reps enough to make any friends. I shared more common interests with Fergus, a sixty-year-old customer service rep who still played in a band. Close, but no cigar really.

As for romance, sometimes I'd get set up on a date with someone's single friend. That was a whole other hell.

It didn't help that I pretty much lived on the Internet where I could interact while remaining in perfect anonymity. There's an immediate intimacy that you reach with people you only know through words, through their thoughts, their likes and dislikes. Online, we pretended to be who we wanted to be, or maybe we shared our truest selves. It never mattered if someone was twenty years older or younger when we both agreed that Walking Disaster's third album was arguably the most technically proficient, but their second album had more heart.

But I couldn't go to bed with a shared opinion, and I needed a social life.

Yeah, if I'd put forth any effort, I could have made better in-real-life friends with the fan forum people. I did occasionally crash their get-togethers when they'd meet before a show for dinner, but I'd never tell them who I was. I mean, I'd tell them I was a lurker named Layla, never revealing that I was the site admin, Pumpkin. I liked being one of them for a little while.

I had a lot of experience pretending to be myself.

Three knocks sounded on my door. I set my laptop down at my side and flung my feet off the bed just as the door cracked open a fraction.

"Is it okay to bring your suitcases in?" Micah's familiar voice through the narrow opening brought home how totally out of place I was.

I hopped up. "Come on in."

He rolled my larger suitcase behind him while lugging both my smaller duffel bag and cosmetics case in one hand. His bicep flexed, and I swallowed down unbidden thoughts about a guy who'd been no more than pixels to me until very recently. Except for when I saw him on a stage commanding a crowd of thousands, he'd never been flesh and blood until tonight.

Without noticing my cartoon-like popping eyes, he set all the luggage up against one wall, dusted his hands, and faced me. His chest swelled at his job well done, then he exhaled, shoulders dropping. "And now you can finally settle in for the night."

I wasn't sure if I should move toward him, hug him, shake his hand, or what, so I wrapped my arms around myself and said, "That was really nice of you to bring my things over." Heat rushed up the skin along my chest and neck. I could talk to normal guys as well as I could talk to anyone else, which honestly wasn't saying much, but while I'd felt fairly invisible in the group setting, this one-on-one thing left me tongue-tied and awkward, like I had too many limbs.

Micah, bless him, took it in stride. "Hey, it's no problem. We gotta watch out for each other, right?"

Jesus, what a nice guy. "Mmm-hmm," I squeaked. My lips folded into my mouth, and I couldn't think of an actual word to speak.

He slipped toward the door and backed out, saying. "Let us know if you need anything. And make yourself at home. Help yourself to anything in the kitchen."

"Thank you!" I yelled after him as the door clicked shut.

Fuck. I shoved my palms against my eyelids and relived the last five minutes in mortification.

Once I'd convinced myself it wasn't that bad—I hadn't asked if I could have his babies or anything—I went through my suitcase, then headed to the bathroom armed with pajamas, my toothbrush, toothpaste, and a couple of extra-long super overnight sanitary napkins that I planned to tape together front to back to make damn sure I didn't bleed all over Jo's mom's guest bed. Day five of my period wouldn't bring a tsunami, but I didn't want to risk a last-minute menstrual monsoon and leave here with their bed looking like the scene of a murder.

Clad in comfy clothes and as protected from disaster as possible, I settled back in and grabbed my laptop, ready to do a little snooping on my new world order.

I clicked open the *Other bands* sub-forum and hunted down the Theater of the Absurd threads. There was a topic specific to Micah that would have pulled back a few years' worth of tours, meet and greets, and albums. Everyone wanted to talk about the charismatic Micah. There'd been plenty of stories about his hookups, too. Those had often come straight from the gossip magazines—and the very pages of the newspaper Jo had been working at when they met. I would have loved to hear that story directly from her sometime. The unfiltered version.

But it had been a long time since I'd paid much attention to what anyone wrote about Noah. Or Shane. If I ever had.

While I couldn't find a topic devoted to Shane, I'd apparently created one for Noah at one point. I opened the first page and scanned through the posts. The boy was seriously so pretty he'd inspired a massive collection of photos—onstage, with girls, walking to the bus. I was surprised to find a couple of posts I'd made at some point, appreciating the beauty. The forum had a long, forgotten history sometimes. Between collected pictures, fans shared personal anecdotes about meeting the band. Some days Noah was charming and flirtatious. Other days he was impatient and moody. I'd laughed when Jo had introduced him as a brat. It was the perfect description from everything the fans reported.

The number of Shane photos paled in comparison with those of Noah or Micah. Hidden behind the drums during the shows, he hardly stood out in stage shots. Although he was incredibly cute, next to the preternatural beauty of Micah or Noah, he might come off as a bit ordinary. But he wasn't completely forgotten, and his name caught my eye in a few posts here and there.

It was like he'd always been there, hidden in plain sight.

I hadn't set out to stalk him so much as to refresh my memory on things I'd already read at some point. I wanted to try to reconcile my preexisting expectations with my newfound experience. They seemed to line up, but my brain was struggling to find a path from screen fantasy to flesh-and-blood humans.

Woven through the anecdotes, I found more such tales of meet and greets where Shane endeared himself to fans just by being his good-natured self. I smiled remembering exactly how easygoing he'd been compared to Noah, how talking to him had come so easily compared to Micah.

In the Whiplash tour thread, I found a picture of Shane, from the week before, posing with fans. He didn't seem remotely aware of the camera, didn't stop and flash a perfected smile. I pulled the screen wider and really looked at him. His lips were frozen as though he were perpetually saying the word *you*. His eyes twinkled, and the girl standing with him smiled so bright, either the photographer had just said, "*Say Penis!*" or else Shane had told her something to make her laugh. I'd put my money on the latter.

How had he gone unnoticed all this time?

Feeling like I'd found what I hadn't even known I was looking for, I shut down my laptop and crawled under the fluffy duvet to dream about one of the best days I'd had in a very long time.

Talking Disaster Forum

CubbiesFan wrote:
Noah and Micah were surrounded by a throng. Robin noticed the drummer leaning against a back wall and suggested we chat with him. We had a great conversation with him.

RobinHood wrote:
Cubbie was so nervous to talk to any of the guys. We were dumb enough to basically say, 'Hi, you're the drummer, right?' I don't recommend this, btw, but he didn't seem to mind. He even called us out on slumming it with the off-brand musician. He told us he'd forge Noah's autograph if we didn't want to wait. Then he went into a hilarious impression of Noah. Cubbie got a couple of pics. I liked this one best:

<ShaneMorganToTAandMe.jpg>

CubbiesFan wrote:
We finally did meet Noah. He was a bit of a disappointment.

RobinHood wrote:
Noah was a dick. He clearly didn't want to be there. Not sure why he even showed up to the meet and greet.

McBoatface wrote:
Did you get any pictures of him, though? From behind maybe, heh heh.

Di$a$ter wrote:
Major eyeroll. Why do you even pretend to be a music fan?

RobinHood wrote:
(Check the Noah thread, @**McBoatface**.)

Chapter Five

In the morning, Jo was sweet enough to wake up and make sure I ate breakfast before I headed into the office. She even called her driver to transport me. What were they doing to be able to afford these luxuries? Granted, Micah's band had been on a steady rise, thanks in large part to his own personal celebrity. They weren't headlining arenas, yet, but opening for a band like Whiplash had to be a sign things were going well. They toured constantly, playing festivals and other mid-sized venues.

For the first time, I really wondered what it would be like to date a touring musician. Gone a week here, home a few days there. How on earth did Jo manage with that schedule? I knew she often went on the road with other bands to get concert photos. It must have been a rare day they were both home at the same time. I pitied her a little bit for the lifestyle they shared.

Just a little bit.

On the ride into Midtown, I considered the flipside—the enviable aspect of dating a famous musician. For starters, it didn't suck to take a car to work as opposed to getting jostled on the subway. And I doubted the average person, like me, could afford such a nice townhouse in Brooklyn.

Apart from the money, the life of the vagabond musician fascinated me. I'd watched with longing as forum denizens followed a tour from city to city. I'd driven to shows, even flew to a few, but my finances never allowed me the freedom to float around the country.

I chuckled at the realization that I'd spent a decade doing exactly that from the comfort of my own sofa. I liked to think I kept everything in the right perspective though.

As I exited the town car, my phone notification went off. A quick glance revealed that Ash only wanted to say: *Thanks for yesterday! I think I'll be okay today. Hope you're enjoying your new job. Let me know how it's going!!*

Tempted as I was to share everything that had happened, I couldn't imagine she'd be able to keep from namedropping on my behalf in a private message somewhere. I'd spent enough time with fans to know secondhand knowledge held its own currency. Ash wouldn't be able to resist spending it.

I understood it all too well. I wasn't immune to the desire to tell the world where I'd spent the night. I'd momentarily enjoy some notoriety while they all asked me questions and expressed their jealousy over my situation. It wouldn't be real fame. Just attention.

I'd already achieved a kind of celebrity on my own website. They all knew me, and yet nobody knew me.

My phone went off again once I got through security. As I waited for the elevator, I checked my texts. I didn't recognize the New York City number. The only person I knew here, besides Jo, was my manager.

I braced myself against bad news and swiped to open it.

Hi, Layla! Jo gave me your number. I hope it's okay. Just wanted to tell you it was nice to meet you. —Shane.

I pressed my knuckle against my lips to contain the giddy smile erupting. The elevator arrived, thankfully, giving me a moment to compose my response. I wanted to wait a beat to pretend I wasn't a total screen-obsessed addict.

Did his text leave an opening for a response? Should I keep to a short *Me, too?* Or exactly as long as his?

While I debated these quandaries, I added him to my contacts and thrilled at my growing coterie of quasi-celebrities I could call if I wanted. First Jo, now Shane. I knew it was silly, but I loved how easily they befriended me. I wanted to tell everyone online what nice people they were.

When the doors opened onto my floor, I intended to sit down and reply, but the minute I stepped through the glass doors, Byron emerged from his office.

"There you are, Layla. Can you come down the hall for the morning scrum?"

I glanced wistfully toward the kitchen. I needed a cup of coffee before I could use my brain, but Byron waited. So much for easing into the morning work.

Byron motioned for me to precede him and take a chair.

"Okay, now that everyone is here, let's get started." Byron opened the floor to a discussion of defects and other concerns, but my mind drifted back to that text message. My phone sat in my pocket, and I resisted the urge to pull it out and re-read the words Shane had sent. I tried to imagine him composing it. Where had he been so early in the morning? At breakfast? By default, I pictured him where I'd last seen him: sitting at the counter at Jo's.

Maybe he'd been out on the street or at a coffee shop.

Maybe he'd been in bed.

My stomach went into freefall.

Why had he texted me? Should I read anything into it? I'd seen the way he looked at me. I didn't think it was far-fetched to imagine he liked me for some reason.

I thought maybe I liked him, too. He'd been kind and funny, in a goofy kind of way. And shy. Adorably shy. So unlike Noah.

Noah was like an impossibly perfect diamond—shiny, pretty, eye-catching. Micah gave him a run for his money in looks, but he was taken. If Noah hadn't been so rude to me, if he'd flirted with me, would I have missed Shane?

If Noah was a diamond, Shane was more like the sunrise, not just because he was all reds and oranges, like me. Always in the background, Shane was easy to take for granted. But like the sunrise, his complex beauty revealed itself when I stopped to look.

I could never say any of that to him. I'd have to keep it light and hope he wasn't just being polite.

"Layla, I believe you had some ideas you'd like to share about automating the Twitter posts?"

Oh, yeah. Work.

I cleared my throat, nervous that they'd find my ideas weak or poorly conceived. "To start with, I'd like to create automated tools to pre-craft social media posts so authors will have an easier time sharing their articles on other platforms."

I stopped talking and waited for any kind of reaction.

Nothing.

After a beat, I lost confidence in my own proposal and added, "It's just a first step. Lots of blogging software already has similar functionality."

Dave frowned and breathed in. I expected him to tell me he didn't understand or say it wasn't feasible, but he surprised me. "Yeah, our web presence is pitiful, and this seems simple enough. Could you write it up and set up a meeting? We can hammer out the requirements later this week and design within the month."

"Sure."

He gave me his full attention. "Let me know any other ideas you have."

"Will do."

Meeting adjourned, I bounced to the kitchen, eager to get some caffeine and settle in to write up the requirements for the proposal. While the coffeemaker sputtered out a dark, sludgy liquid, I sensed a presence behind me and spun around to find myself face to face with a dark-haired, dark-eyed, well-dressed Gabriel Sanchez who I recognized instantly from his byline. I started to speak, but my throat produced a sound eerily like the over-used coffee machine.

He must have taken my reaction as some kind of insta-lust because his lip curled into a mischievous grin. "Well, hello. And who might you be?"

I stuck my hand out. "Layla. Layla Beckett."

Gabriel wrapped his hand around mine. His smile grew and he showed his perfectly white teeth. "Layla? Should I get down on my knees?"

I grimaced but forced out a pitiful laugh. "Heh."

"I'm Gabe. Or you might know me as Gabriel Sanchez. I'm one of the head writers." He leaned against the counter, looking as casual as one could in the middle of a brightly lit half kitchen.

The temptation to take a picture and post it in the forum overwhelmed me, but I mastered my face to get my surprise under control and managed to play it cool. "What do you write?"

That was the wrong tack to take with him. He straightened up and pressed his lips together briefly. "I hope you'll figure that out soon enough."

Nervous words spilled out. "I'm getting up to speed."

If he had been any other writer, I might have casually mentioned I'd read all his reviews, and it would have been mostly true. I'd done my homework before coming to work here. I wanted to know the names of all the staff writers and freelancers. But I hadn't needed to research Gabriel Sanchez. I had a guilty obsession with his reviews because he'd become increasingly hostile to the bands I loved most. Particularly Walking Disaster.

Ever since the magazine had hired Jo, Gabe seemed to go out of his way to pan anyone remotely connected with her. I secretly doubted the magazine cared enough to make such elaborate plans, but try telling fans their opinions amount to ridiculous conspiracy theory.

He retrieved a mug from the pantry and slid it over, taking the opportunity to edge closer to me. "How are you enjoying it here?"

"Fine." I added a packet of sugar to my mug then stepped around him to give him free access to the machine. "There's so much to do. The work is interesting so far."

"And what work is that?"

"I'm the new social media manager."

He dropped a French Roast packet into the machine and punched the start button. "So, you schedule the tweets for all the current articles?"

I stirred my own coffee. "That and I'll be helping writers like yourself make sure links to your articles automatically post elsewhere."

He crossed his arms and his tailored shirt creased ever so slightly. He came across as some old European effete—both effeminate and masculine all at once. He was lithe and radiated grace and charm. "Maybe you could tweet the review of Walking Disaster's latest album I put up earlier this week?"

"Oh! I was just setting that up." It wasn't exactly true, but I really wanted to talk to him about it and couldn't think of a better way to recover from failing to admit I'd heard of him.

"Thanks."

"No problem. It's literally my job."

"And did you read it?" His brow rose, as though he anticipated my praise.

"I may have scanned it." I narrowed one eye and lied. "Looked like a well-argued review."

He sneered. "Several crazy fans disagree."

"Oh?" I studied the floor tiles to hide any expression that might give me away.

"But you liked it?"

"I mean, I can't speak to your opinion on the album, but the writing was quite good." There. Honest, yet hopefully misleading.

"Thank you. I appreciate that."

His coffee finished belching out, and he poured in some creamer.

I awkwardly lurched for something to say to break the weird tension. "So, you really didn't like that album, huh?"

"Like or dislike? That's a simplistic way to look at it. Reviews are more nuanced than that."

I bit my tongue. "Mmm-hmm."

"It's a question of expectations. The band has made solid, if derivative, efforts in the past, but this new album goes in a direction that doesn't offer anything new."

"I see."

"You do?"

"So, you think the value of rock music is what it brings in originality."

"Well, no, that's not what I mean exactly."

"Oh, I must have misunderstood you, then." Even though I sort of agreed with him, I never got tired of arguing about music.

"What I mean is that they've diverged from the sound that made them really stand out in the market."

"Ah. So, you *don't* like that they've done something new."

He shifted with an exasperated sigh. "You're twisting my words."

"Am I?" I tilted my head at him as though I really didn't understand. "You want them to stay in their lane while creating something groundbreaking at the same time."

His eyes disappeared briefly into his palms. "You are purposely misrepresenting my words."

At that moment, Ajit entered the kitchen. He stopped when he saw us, apologized, and turned on his heel. I saw the scene from his point of view. Gabe held his hands up in frustration, and I was horrified to discover my finger pointing at him in righteous indignation.

I laughed to diffuse the situation. "I didn't mean to get into an argument."

"Indeed." He licked his lips. Why did someone so arrogant have such pretty lips? "We are getting off to a bad start."

"I'm sorry. Shall we start over?" I held out my hand. "My name's Layla."

"Gabriel." He took my hand and didn't let it go. His hands were soft, softer than mine. Like calf leather or a newborn puppy. "I wonder if you might be free tonight. You're new to the area, right? There's a decent steak restaurant around the corner from here."

My eyes must have turned into softballs. I hadn't seen that coming at all. "Oh, uh. I actually promised a friend I'd do something with her."

He grunted. "I see. Well, maybe some other time." He stood and straightened his slacks. In the entire office, he was the only person dressed professionally. Besides me. I could have worn jeans and a concert T like everyone else here, but all my T-shirts were a dead giveaway for my band preferences, and while I wasn't ashamed of them, given the circumstances, I didn't think I should broadcast my feelings. I could only imagine the previous conversation with Gabriel if I'd worn a Walking Disaster T-shirt circa 2017.

"Sure. Maybe." I hoped I'd simply misjudged him. He might be stiff and lacking in humor and boorish, but perhaps underneath all that—

"Won't you ease my worried mind?" he sang.

Nope. Underneath all that, he was an oaf. I plastered a fake smile on my face. "Yup. That's the one."

"Oh, I guess you must get tired of that."

Captain Obvious. "A little."

"I apologize, then. The song's been stuck in my head since you introduced yourself."

"Understood." I hoped I didn't sound mad. I just wanted to part ways without him thinking I was a huge bitch. I'd worked with and dated guys like him, and it was always a tightrope walk between being nice enough to keep them from treating you like a she-devil and being mean enough to discourage their attentions. As cute as he was, his demeanor made my gut clench.

Gabe's eyes slowly trailed off me, and he walked toward the hall. "It was nice to meet you."

Back at my desk, I spent the rest of the morning trying to write up how the developers might implement my proposed design. I only took a short break to grab a sandwich at a shop and surfed the forum while I ate, cracking up at some in-fighting over something as obscure as the interpretation of a homophone in a song lyric. Then I went through the latest month's *Rock Paper* articles to set up staggered automated tweets to promote them. That took longer than I would have liked, proving that they needed to create a better system for controlling their social media.

Once I'd set up the last tweet, I stretched until my back cracked, then reached for my phone to text Jo.

I suddenly remembered Shane's text with the same wide-eyed *oh no* as if I'd forgotten my purse in the middle of Grand Central. I'd intended to wait thirty minutes or an hour to appear sane, not an entire day. I hadn't wanted to give him the impression I didn't care. Damn.

My fingers flew. *It was great to meet you, too. I hope I see you again soon.*

I wondered if he'd be at Jo's again. The night before had probably been an anomaly.

When my phone remained silent, I texted Jo to let her know I was heading back and that I'd be fine taking the subway.

She texted back: *Wait for the town car!*

Standing near Times Square, waiting to be picked up by my own personal driver—okay not my own, but still—felt like a million bucks. I had so many things to share and nobody to share them with.

Except Ash. She knew where I'd taken a job. Surely, I could at least tell her about meeting Gabe. That wouldn't be unexpected, I rationalized.

I typed: *You'll never believe who I met!*

Smiling stupidly, I stared at my phone, waiting for her to write back and ask, composing the response in my head. Should I blurt it out or make her guess? How would I answer if she correctly guessed Micah Sinclair?

The town car arrived before any response from Ash, so I pushed my phone back in my pocket and climbed in the back seat, disappointed twice. Once in myself for having given in to the temptation to over-share. And again, for my confession falling on temporarily deaf ears.

Talking Disaster Forum

Topic: Walking Disaster - Music - Albums - Horizon: New Dawn - Page 14

Walker wrote:
Next stanza:
Every hour, a new day's begun
Next rotation. another generation
And with the rising dawn
We welcome a brand-new sun

Gropeland wrote:
Thanks for transcribing the lyrics, Walker, but I'm going to tweak a line. I suspect that instead of: *We welcome a brand-new sun,* it should actually be: *We welcome a brand-new SON.* Think about it.

Walker wrote:
That makes no sense. The whole song is about the sun. The line before is: *With the rising dawn.* Rotation is about the earth turning, right? A new day is the sunrise. So, sun makes the most sense.

Di$a$ter wrote:
Are you stupid? The word generation is a dead giveaway that he's referring to his progeny here.

Walker wrote:
In the next stanza, which I'm transcribing now, he goes on to talk about the afternoon, etc. Why would he be talking about the course of the sun in the afternoon if he's talking about his kid?

Gropeland wrote:
You're in denial, Walker. This entire album is Adam's meditation on what it means to have a kid. Have you ever had a kid? You start to think about your own place in the universe, your own parents, your own mortality. Obviously, afternoon refers to what stage of life Adam is at. The title of the song, "New Dawn" has to do with a beginning. What's beginning? He's starting a family. You are aware of symbolism?

Pumpkin39 wrote:
Guys, don't be jerks, okay. Did it occur to you you can both be right? That's the beauty of art. If you want to read more into it, you're free to do that. Only Adam knows for sure, so let's keep the discussion civil.

Chapter Six

When I arrived at the townhouse, Jo threw open the door but immediately ran upstairs, yelling, "Sorry, I've got to finish this. Come up."

For some reason, this welcome made me feel more at home than if she'd ushered me in with a polite greeting. The apartment was quiet and rather dark, like nobody had been home all day. I looked around for signs Micah was around somewhere before climbing the stairs to find Jo sitting in the guest room at the computer.

I sat on the edge of the bed while she clicked a picture and started typing, cursed, deleted, and typed again.

"Ah! I have to tag all these pictures before we go. Are you ready?"

"Where are we going?"

"Cookout. You should change into something more comfortable."

I scooted onto the floor and opened my suitcase, wondering if I should reveal the depths of my fandom in the form of a Walking Disaster T-shirt or wear one of my nice for-work knit shirts.

Jo kept her eyes trained on her screen. "How was work today?"

"Interesting." I pulled out a pair of jeans. Nothing controversial there. "I met Gabriel Sanchez."

I watched her from the corner of my eye and swore her hand froze on the mouse for an instant. She blinked and continued to work. "Oh, yeah? What did you think of our local Lothario?"

"Lothario?"

With a flourish, she exited the program she'd been working in. Her attention freed, she lavished it on me, changing her position to face me with a knowing look. "There's no way he didn't hit on you."

I laughed. "How'd you know?"

She shook her head gently. "You're too pretty to have passed by him unmolested."

Her choice of words made me grimace. "Ew."

"He's mostly harmless." She snickered. "Except with his pen."

"Pity. He's kind of cute."

"To be fair, I hold a slight grudge against him on Micah's behalf." Her forehead wrinkled. "You should have seen the steaming pile of dog doo he flung at Micah's band last month."

Actually, I had.

"But you wouldn't believe the vitriol his fans came back with."

No, I would.

"I'm sure you don't care about all this foolishness."

Oh, yes, I did.

I'd read the particularly brutal review he'd written about Micah's last album. "You'd think he'd be a little nicer considering you work there. Did you claw his eyes out?"

"I leave that to his fans." She covered her mouth as if to hold in a cackle. "They get under his skin."

Interesting. "He gets upset when fans retaliate?"

"He gets insulted. Like his opinion is final."

How obnoxious. "Doesn't he just write worse reviews?"

She leaned in. "Gabe's an ass, but he thinks he's objective."

Her glee over the fan support made me instantly regret having squelched the revolt. Maybe they were right and I was wrong. A little fan pressure might make Gabriel Sanchez think twice about writing a shitty review.

I mulled this over while deciding between a navy blue short-sleeved V-neck sweater and a white silk button-up blouse, neither appropriate for a cookout. But neither had the name of a band plastered across them.

"Do you want to borrow something?"

I held up my wardrobe choices. "I have jeans, but my shirts are either too dressy or too . . ." I didn't want to confess they were too fan girl. If I were hanging out with anyone else, I'd throw one on, no problem.

She pointed across the hall. "My dresser is on the far wall. There should be a T-shirt you can borrow in the bottom drawer. Or if you want something a little nicer, check the closet."

I thanked her again for her hospitality and proceeded to invade her privacy even more. Her openness constantly impressed me, given her own history and that of anyone around her. The press could print the ugliest stories about her. Yet, she trusted me. It meant a lot.

She'd been on the road with so many bands by this point, it didn't surprise me to find a varied collection of her own concert T-shirts in the drawer. I picked one up and smelled it, immediately feeling weird about that. Fans always joked about that, asking "What does Adam smell like?" when someone got lucky enough to meet him. Sadly, I knew the answer to that. For some reason, he supposedly smelled like jasmine.

Micah supposedly smelled like citrus. I was in Jo's drawers, and all I could smell was laundry detergent.

"Did you find anything?" she hollered.

I glanced at the shirt in my hands. In giant gold letters, it read *Not throwing away my shot!* I laughed because it brought up visions of my mom singing along with the *Hamilton* soundtrack in her car.

"Yes!" I hollered, pulling it on. I clicked a photo and texted my mom.

"Good. Because we need to be going." She walked into the bedroom. "Ah. You found my favorite shirt."

"My mom would love this."

"Yeah? I'm a huge theater geek myself." She pulled the bedroom door closed so she could look in the hanging mirror. "Shit. I need to fix my hair and makeup. Do you need a minute in the bathroom?"

I still didn't know where we were going, but a cookout sounded casual, and casual sounded familiar, and familiar made me think it involved her friends, and her friends included Shane.

"Yes. I'll just be a minute."

I gave myself a lightning fast makeover. Slightly dramatic eyeliner, subtle foundation, a bit of cheek shading, and a lip color that worked well against my bright hair. I surveyed my work and decided it was the best I could do on short notice.

And then, I took care of nature. The tail end of my period didn't require ShamWow! levels of absorbency, but I was spotting, so I made sure to load up with some backup protection. It reminded me to take today's sugar pill from my birth control pack.

"I'm ready," I called as I went downstairs to wait.

Five minutes later, Jo practically tumbled down and grabbed her purse. "Let's go!"

As the car rolled up, I asked, "So, where is it we're going?"

"It's not that far. Just over in Brooklyn Heights."

Before I could ask anything more, she picked up her phone. "We're heading over now. Can you meet us?" Pause. "Love you, too."

She hung up. "Micah's been rehearsing since noon."

"It must be nice when he's home, though."

"Oh, yeah. I never thought I'd get involved with someone who's never around. We make it work. There's video chat, and I join him when I can. We definitely cherish the few times the fates convene so we're all in town at the same time."

I wanted to ask what she meant by "all," but she said, "It's just up here," and unfastened her seatbelt. The car halted in front of a building similar to the one she lived in. We climbed the steps, and Jo knocked once, then just opened the door. "Hello?"

"We're back here!" called a voice.

We followed it through a living room into a kitchen that opened onto a backyard. An older woman sat at the kitchen table with a baby asleep on her lap. "Shhh!" she somehow yelled.

Jo leaned down and whispered, "Hello, Joshua. How's my good boy?"

The woman said, "Fussy. He just fell asleep. If Eden would quiet down."

Eden?

Micah came in from the back patio, kissed Jo, laid a hand on my shoulder with a "Hey, Layla," and disappeared into the house.

Jo waved me through the sliding door onto a deck to where Shane stood in the yard, hammering what looked like croquet hoops. Before I could drink him in, Eden stood and put a hand on her hip. "No, I think they're supposed to be farther apart."

I whipped my head to the patio table where I discovered a black man with a killer afro holding hands with a Latino man with short-cropped hair. When the latter glanced up at me, I felt like I'd seen him somewhere before. He smiled, and I blinked at the intensity of him just sitting still. He might have been an actor. Another movement caught my eye, and I looked left.

There, at the grill, stood Adam motherfucking Copeland.

The oxygen expelled from my lungs, and I forgot how to get it back. The entire diorama caused my brain to blow a fuse.

Jo stepped beside me and touched my arm. "Guys, I'd like you to meet Layla Beckett. She's just started working at the *Rock Paper* with me." She took one look at me and laughed. "By the expression on your face, I guess I don't have to tell you this is Adam Copeland and Eden Sinclair." She stage whispered, "It's okay to be starstruck at first."

Adam smiled. At me. "Nice to meet you. Layla, is it?"

I nodded like an idiot. Shane dropped the croquet mallet and waved.

Jo said, "You already know Shane."

The baby made a fussing sound, and Eden said, "Excuse me," and ran in.

Jo gestured after her. "That's little Joshua. And Eden's mom, Peg."

Peg emerged from the kitchen, patting her hair into place. Inside, Eden sat with the baby latching on.

I focused on this ordinary activity so I could breathe and gather my composure until I realized I was ogling Eden breast-feeding her child.

Jo nudged me out of my stupor. "These are our friends Zion and Andrew."

I raised a hand and said, "Nice to meet—"

Right then, out of all possible moments, my phone rang out a riff from Walking Disaster's very first radio hit clear as day.

I snatched it from my purse and silenced it. When I looked up, every pair of eyes locked on me, like the enemy had breached the fortress.

I could explain. I could tell the truth.

"It's my friend, Ashley. She's a huge fan of yours."

Adam flipped over a burger. "Your friend is, huh?"

Then it occurred to me that I'd stepped in a giant turd sandwich with that excuse. "I mean, I am, too. Of course."

He chuckled. "I'm just messing with you. If you want to give her a call, I'd be happy to tell her hi."

"You'd do that?"

Good Lord. She'd love me forever.

"Of course." His eyes actually sparkled. "Where would I be without fans?"

But I couldn't let him call her. If he talked to her, there was no way I could keep her from posting that on the forum. I wouldn't have time to explain to her why she couldn't. And there was no way she'd be able to contain that geyser of information.

She'd kill me if she knew I was even considering telling Adam no.

What if he was calling my bluff? What if he thought I'd made her up to hide my own lurking fandom?

I could prove I wasn't lying if he called her. Problem solved.

But Ash would blow my cover. Problem not solved.

Fuck.

She was going to kill me.

"That's really cool of you, but she's at work right now. That's why she's texting."

His eyebrows quirked for a split second, but just as fast, he flashed his blindingly beautiful smile which nearly caused me to swoon. "It's okay. Maybe later. Like I said, it's fun to connect with real fans." Maybe it was my imagination, but he seemed to laugh at that.

Then, thank God, Shane bounded up the steps and rescued me from my one-woman festival of foolishness.

"Hey, Layla." He held out his arm for a side hug, and it was the most comforting gesture he could have made.

When I reached around his back to return the squeeze, I got a good sense of how muscular he was. It was like hugging a rock. A cuddly rock. It shouldn't have surprised me, given how physical drumming was, especially for the upper arms and back. I'd seen pictures of sweat flying off his hair in a dramatic arc as he attacked the set but now regretted never encountering any shirtless pics.

He drew back almost reluctantly, and I tried to take a gander at the tattoo snaking up his tricep into his sleeve without creeping him out. Self-conscious of my lecherous interest in his muscles, I cast around to look at anything else, but my gaze fell right back on Adam, and I felt like I'd fallen into a Dr. Seuss book. Nothing made sense, and I couldn't process it at all.

Adam flipped the burgers while telling Peg, "I think the Huggies fit tighter than the Pampers, though."

I forced myself to look toward the sliding door as Micah stepped through, yelling back in the house, "Why exactly did you bring over Mom's croquet set?"

Eden stuck out her tongue and slid the door closed with her foot.

Shane inched closer. "It's great to see you again."

My head turned toward him, the only part of my body following the proper script. I nodded in response, but I'd barely registered the question, and as soon as my eyes made the circuit back to him, they drifted right back over to Adam. Adam Copeland, grilling in his backyard. Adam Copeland, talking about diapers. He wore short sleeves, and I could see the beginnings of his Zoso tattoo on one shoulder. When Peg moved away, he hummed a little tune to himself, with a satisfied little grin on his face.

"I felt the same way as you the first time I met him."

I twisted back to look at Shane for real. "Huh?"

"Adam." He raised his hand, and Adam glanced at us, but he didn't acknowledge that we stood a couple of feet away, openly discussing him. "Before we went on tour, Adam came out to hear us perform. I'm glad nobody told us he was there until after or I might have blown the whole set."

"And then?"

His eyes narrowed against the setting sun, and his long lashes burned in gold and orange. "He came over and introduced himself as if we didn't already know who he was. Did you know Adam used to be a drummer?"

The nonsequitur threw me. I swallowed. Yes. I knew that. Was that something I shouldn't have known? I just nodded like I was listening, not like I was admitting to arcane trivia.

"Well, he was. And even though we're both musicians, even though we both have drumming in common, I couldn't think of a word to say to him."

Adam spoke up. "That's not how I remember it."

Shane shrugged one shoulder. "True. I'm a chatterbox, but I was still nervous. So, you know. It's okay. You could ask him for a picture if you wanted to be a fan for the night. Nobody will think less of you."

I loved that he'd chosen to acknowledge the weirdness of the situation rather than profess something trite like *Adam's just an ordinary person*. I mean, duh, but that's a bit like saying a million-dollar mansion is just a house. It helped a lot that everyone here understood, and I felt myself relaxing thanks to Shane's candid confession.

As for the picture. "Thanks. I'm good." What would be the point? I couldn't share it on the forum. Was I going to make it my screen saver? Or print it out and hang it on my wall? Maybe I could recover some cool points by declining the photo opp. I had no idea. These were uncharted waters.

To change the topic, I asked, "Where's Noah tonight?"

Shane's goofy grin faltered. "Oh, I, uh, told Micah not to invite him." He rubbed the back of his neck. "Sorry."

I snorted. "Why did you do that?"

His shoulders drooped an inch. "I didn't want the competition."

A shiver skittered down my spine. Did he mean what it sounded like? That blush started to creep up his neck, and I figured he must. "I don't know what you mean," I lied. "But I'm glad you're here."

His eyes shot up and locked onto mine, and that charming little smile melted my heart. His lips were even prettier than Gabriel's, prettier than Noah's. His blue eyes were framed in a fan of those gorgeous eyelashes, and he had the smoothest, freckly skin. My breath caught. Was he thinking what I wanted him to be thinking?

He stepped a bit closer and said, "So, maybe—"

My heart tripped.

"Jo?" Zion stood and laid a hand on Jo's shoulder. While Shane and I were flirting right beside her, she'd slumped forward with her head in her hands.

Micah crossed the deck in two steps, kneeling at her feet. He called in a voice both controlled and urgent. "Eden?"

"On it," she hollered from inside. She came out two seconds later with the baby cradled in one arm, a bag slung over her shoulder, and a juice box in one hand. She handed the baby to her mom, the bag to Micah, and the juice box to Jo in one smooth series of moves. The juice box disappeared under Jo's mass of hair spiraling down around her bent head. Micah slipped out a device and punctured one of her fingers.

Adam brushed past me and laid a plate on the table next to Jo. "I think she was angling for the first hamburger. Congrats, it's all yours." His joke was tinged with obvious concern, and he didn't move until Micah nodded.

"She's fine. It's just low." Micah rubbed her arm. "What happened?"

Jo sat up and reached over to pinch off a hunk of hamburger bun. She popped it in her mouth and talked while she chewed. "Just didn't remember to eat."

"Since when?"

"Earlier. I got to working on my portfolio. It got late, and then we were coming here anyway, so I pushed it."

Micah still knelt before her, holding her hand gently, but his tone bordered on angry. "Are we going to have to go back to setting an alarm?"

"No, Micah. I'm fine." She picked up the hamburger, shaking it at him like proof, and then nibbled at it.

"This time, yeah." He exhaled in apparent relief. "Why don't you come lie down for a bit?"

"What? And miss the croquet?"

Eden said, "If you want to go back home, I understand."

Jo looked to Micah for some telepathic advice. Then she shot me a glance. "No, we just got here, and Layla surely wants to stay."

I started to tell her not to worry about me. I mean, I owed her so much for everything she'd done, and besides, I didn't belong at this party.

Shane broke in. "I can get her back to your place." Six heads swiveled his way. "If you need to leave, I mean."

"Layla?" Jo laid the decision at my feet.

Oh, Layla, would you like to climb into a town car and be shuttled back to hang out with Micah Sinclair and Josie Wilder? Or would you like to stay at a party in Adam Copeland's backyard with a cute red-haired boy with incredible blue eyes?

If anyone had told me either of these options would have been available to me tonight, I would have told them they were writing fan fiction.

I glanced at Shane, and he met my gaze with such intensity, I forgot for a second what the question was. I took a step toward him, relishing how the corner of his lips rose. If I stayed here, I could coax out a full smile.

"Layla?" Jo touched my hand, and I remembered that she was my hostess. I should do what she needed.

"Whatever's easiest."

Wrong answer. Jo pursed her lips. "Are you fine with Shane bringing you home?"

"Oh. Yes. Of course." I clenched my fists tight. Could this be my life?

"Good. I'm sorry to abandon you like this, but you'll be in good hands." She stood with Micah supporting her elbow. "Don't hesitate to knock when you come back. Micah will be up no matter when."

They gathered their things and left me standing with total strangers that I knew way too much about.

Talking Disaster Forum

Lore wrote:
Has anyone noticed this picture in the DailyFeed of Eden out with baby Joshua? Is it my imagination, or is the little stuffed monkey tucked in with the baby the one we sent in the basket?

DeadFan wrote:
Oooh. I think you may be right! Here's a picture of the basket we shipped.

PeaceAndLove wrote:
It's gross how you guys fawn over that whore.

RobinHood wrote:
Whoa. Look what the cat threw up. Think you can sneak in here because Pumpkin's been occupied?

PeaceAndLove wrote:
You know Eden's the reason the new album isn't getting good reviews.

Nefertiti wrote:
PandL's right. Eden's the band's Yoko Ono. It's only a matter of time before she ruins everything.

RobinHood wrote:
Oh, hello, @Nefertiti. Back to share your bullshit stories about sleeping with Adam?

Nefertiti wrote:
I gave him a better night than he's had in a long time stuck with that train wreck that trapped him.

DeadFan wrote:
You guys. Do you want me to lock the thread?

PeaceAndLove wrote:
Sure @DeadFan. You scare the shit out of me.

Pumpkin39 wrote:
I'm giving you two options. 1) Follow the rules of the forum and respect everyone including my posters, the musicians, AND their significant others. Or 2) Leave. If you go for some third option, believe me I'll delete your accounts and block your IP.

Chapter Seven

*O*nce the chaos of Micah and Jo leaving subsided, I asked Eden to point me to the bathroom, mainly as a pretext to check my texts, though I also wanted to take care of my lady linens. Sitting on the toilet, I read Ash's message. It was unintelligible, so as soon as I flushed, I dialed her.

"Hey, Ash. What's going on?"

As usual, she spilled it all out without taking a breath. "Some old trolls hijacked an archived thread and started saying major shit about Eden. I don't want to lock it because everything that was there before is innocuous. What do you want me to do?"

I sighed. "I'm kind of busy right now."

"Can you at least take a look?"

Crap. "Sure."

"Thank you." She paused a beat, then with renewed excitement. "Oh, and I just saw your text from before. Who'd you meet?"

There was no possible way I could drop any of this on her and still escape this bathroom in any reasonable time. And as I didn't want anyone to suspect I had a bad case of the runs, I told the smallest truth. "That reviewer, Gabriel Sanchez."

"Oh, right." She sounded disappointed. "But that was kind of to be expected, right? I mean, eventually, you'd have to run into him."

"True." I zipped up my purse. "I need to go. I promise I'll look into this as soon as I can, okay?"

"Thanks, Layla."

I took a deep breath and held it. It was entirely frustrating that my one night in the vicinity of these ridiculously out-of-reach people would be ruined by my ridiculously out-of-touch hobby.

When I stepped back into the kitchen, Eden sat at the table, bouncing the sleeping baby gently in one arm while she tapped on her laptop one-handed. She bent to lay Joshua in the car seat, then stood. "I'm sorry. In all the chaos, I never asked you if you'd like a drink. You wanna come help yourself?"

"Sure." I followed her around to the refrigerator which was crowded with beer bottles. I grabbed a Stella. "I hope you don't think it's rude, but I need to check something on my phone real quick."

"Of course. Make yourself at home."

I found the thread and started reading backwards. The ironically named PeaceAndLove spewed some bullshit, and she'd brought another friend with her to stir the pot. These jealous girls behaved as if Eden had stolen Adam away from them personally. Poor Ash had tried to squelch the trash talk, but she was too timid to bring the hammer.

I was not.

My blood pressure went up when I had to deal with hateful people, like I was going into an actual battle or confronting them face to face. I was good at it because I knew I was safe and they couldn't hurt me. That was one reason I was so careful to remain anonymous. I could don my bad-ass persona when I needed to without fear of repercussions. They could hate my alias all they wanted, and it never made me feel bad.

Out of necessity, I'd gotten fairly proficient at typing tomes on my phone. When I was angry, my fingers flew. I posted my crackdown and then began deleting the offending posts back through when the drama started.

"That must be important?" Eden's voice drew me out of my alternate reality.

"Oh. Yeah." How to explain? "A friend wanted me to back her up in an argument."

I stopped what I was doing and watched so-called fire-breathing Eden putting glasses away.

I'd been so mesmerized by Adam, I'd completely failed to process that I was hanging out with another musician, who to be honest was more infamous than famous. When her scandal hit the tabloids a few years back, fans speculated about her relentlessly. She had a career of her own—and her own fans—but to Walking Disaster fans, she was Adam's wife. There were plenty who still thought she was a gold digger, unworthy to lick his boots.

The running narrative was that she was a harpy—rude to reporters, rude to fans. I kept a close eye on the forums whenever the topic of Eden came up—and she often did. I didn't want to censor people, but I liked to remind them that Eden wasn't a fictional character. She didn't deserve to be raked over the coals by the very people who should show the most support for her. They could criticize her music all they wanted, but when they started to attack her personally, it crossed a line.

She reached into the fridge and brought over a can of Coke, then she tucked a blanket around Joshua. A little monkey that looked a lot like the one fans had sent peeked out from under the baby's arm. When she stood, she arched her back, hand on her waist, striking such a quintessential exhausted mother pose, I had to smile.

"You seem tired."

"Oh, yeah. We're just getting out of the crying-all-night phase. Now he weighs so much, it's like carrying around a sack of flour all day."

I watched the baby's face change from little pouts to gaseous grins. "He's precious."

She fell back into her chair. "Thanks. Luckily, he takes after Adam."

Adam and Eden had the exact same coloring—dark hair, fair skin—so from where I sat, the baby took after them both. "He's going to be a little heartbreaker."

She smiled. "I hope not."

Sipping on my beer, I peeked outside to where the real heartbreaker stacked burgers onto a plate, laughing at whatever Shane was saying to him. Shane had such an open expression, good-natured, honest. I loved that he was laughing at his own story. What could they have been talking about?

"You're handling this all really well. Have you spent much time around musicians?"

I turned my phone to airplane mode and dropped it into my purse, determined to experience the present. "Not really. I spend a lot of time listening to musicians."

"My best friend fell apart when she first met Adam."

"How so?"

The ghost of a smile crossed her lips. "She gushed all over him and made him take pictures with her. She posted them all over Facebook."

"Oh." I laughed a little nervously, hoping not to show her the cracks in my facade.

"You're not losing your shit, so I figured either you're not much of a fan or else you've spent some time among musicians. And since it's not the latter—"

"Actually, no. I'm a fan. I'm a huge fan," I confessed. "I'm just not that kind of fan, I guess."

Her eyes narrowed. "What kind of fan?"

"I'm in it for the music."

"Oh, one of those." She snorted. "I've read comments like that on the message boards. 'True fans' I think they called it."

My stomach twisted. Had I said too much? "You read the message boards?"

She shot a glance at the baby. "I don't have time for that. I have though. Curiosity."

I wondered what that would be like, if I would want to read about myself. "That must be weird."

"Most people are well meaning. The fans are opinionated, but supportive of Adam."

"And you? How do they treat you?" Not that I didn't know the answer. I wanted to hear her point of view.

She straightened the placemats within her reach. "Considering the circumstances, they're forgiven for the occasional barb. Plus, there's a forum admin who has been amazing at keeping things about me pretty quiet. I appreciate that."

I couldn't make my eyelids stop blinking in overdrive. She couldn't know who she was talking to. It was pure coincidence. I forced myself to remain calm. "How nice."

"It is. I've seen what goes on in Micah's fan forum, and it can get pretty ugly."

That was an understatement. I knew the admin, Jaclyn, aka State of the Absurd. She didn't keep her fans to the same level of decorum as I did. Her main rule was *Don't get me sued.* Otherwise, the board was a complete free-for-all.

She chortled. "But it fits Micah somehow."

Exactly how I was supposed to respond to Eden's comment on this topic eluded me, and I absently reached over and touched a heavy book sitting beside her laptop. My eyes focused on the title. "Molecular and cell biology?"

Her face lit up. "It's for a class I'm taking."

"You're in school?" Why was this new information?

"Yeah. I got my degree in biology. I actually used to work in the field, but I had the wrong job, and I wanted to give music a shot, so I just dropped out. But lately, I miss it." She sat up a little taller. "And then I met Jo and wished I could find a way to help her, and it all came together. So, I've gone back to grad school." She said the last like an announcement, like she was still coming to terms with the decision.

"I didn't know you—" *Shit.*

Her head tilted. "Didn't know what?"

I thought fast to cover the near confession that I'd have any reason to be aware of her scholarly pursuits. "That you could juggle school with a newborn."

That was plausible.

"Well, it's easier than touring with kids. And just between you and me—" she leaned closer "—my music career ain't going so hot. Right now, I'm taking a few classes at night. Plus I have Adam here, so—"

"Night classes?" Her solution to her complicated life struck me as so genius yet practical that the revelation about her music career hit me like a secondary shock wave. I wondered if it was too late to back up and give her some sympathy. And pry. Was she quitting music altogether? I didn't want to watch her detractors gloat over that possibility. But she'd sworn me to secrecy, not that I'd go on the boards and gossip about her. Especially not now. Not after she'd morphed into a flesh-and-blood person.

She must have taken my remark as skepticism or judgment. She laughed. "Yeah, I know. Sounds sketchy, but it's a Master's program at Long Island University. The Brooklyn campus is within walking distance from here."

"No, it's not that." She'd planted a seed. "It's just that I'd love to get a degree in computer sciences. I never thought about taking night classes."

"Give me your email address, and I can shoot you a link to my school. Maybe they have a program for you there."

Wheels in my head started turning. I knew I could do what Dave and Ajit did. A degree would help me prove it.

Adam tapped on the glass, and Eden stood. "Food's ready at last."

I would have given anything to be able to set up a live feed of the next hour for everyone else to be a part of. For the rest of my life, I'd be able to re-experience the time I hung out in Brooklyn on a warm night as the sky turned periwinkle and Adam Copeland asked me if I was done with the ketchup.

As much as I wanted to remain present, I shrank back, intending to observe the scene from a safe distance, quietly.

But Andrew, sitting to my right, had other plans.

"Layla, right?" He passed me a casserole dish of baked beans.

I scooped some onto my plate, nodding. "And you're Andrew."

"I am." He batted his eyes, and that feeling I knew him redoubled. "You work with Jo?"

"I just started yesterday." My gaze lingered. I was dying to figure out where I might have seen him. "And what do you do?"

He gave me a saucy little shrug. "I'm a singer."

I tried to picture him in a club, at a microphone, holding a guitar, on an album cover, under a spotlight. Nope. I'd never seen him. He must have shared a resemblance to someone else.

"And Zion?"

Zion didn't break concentration with the hamburger he was meticulously assembling. "Photographer and editor at the *Daily Feed*."

"Oh, how interesting. I've read that paper before."

They peddled gossip about celebrities. They'd manufactured the stories that vilified Eden when she started dating Adam, and then they ran a scathing article on Micah last year, dragging Jo down into the muck with him.

I wanted to ask how an editor at that paper was welcome here.

As if reading my mind, Andrew added, "That's where Jo used to work."

I'd known that but forgotten. Everything sort of clicked into place, and I stilled my tongue, thinking the rest of the questions swirling in my mind as nosy and impolite. Instead, I chose to recede and mentally record everything.

With an end to the ordinary business of passing around the condiments and complimenting the chef on the grilled burgers, everyone tore into their food. I'd experienced this scene hundreds of times in my own Indiana suburban backyard. I tried to pretend like this was normal, nibbling on my burger, eavesdropping on the banter between Adam and Eden or the bickering between Eden and her mom.

"Leave it, Mom. He's fine."

"He's going to catch a chill. That blanket's too flimsy." Peg turned to Adam. "You talk to her. She's always been so stubborn."

Eden threw up her hands. "It's seventy degrees out here."

The baby, slumbering in the bouncy seat, appeared perfectly content.

Zion cut his eyes at Andrew. "You really want to have to worry about whether or not a blanket is necessary on a night like this?"

Andrew grimaced. "When you put it like that."

Peg raised an eyebrow. "Are you thinking of having children?"

Zion showed us his palms, like a stop sign. "*We* are not. Andrew is."

Andrew sighed. "Think how fun it would be. We could dress him up in little outfits and sing to him."

Adam laughed. "If that's all you want, you're free to come play with Joshua."

It felt like such a nice extended family. Even when they argued or teased, there was so much love. I envied them this community.

Conversation remained light through dinner, and when we started pushing empty plates back, Peg stood to clear. I jumped up to help, but she dismissed me with a wave. "Stay."

Adam didn't pay her any mind and loaded the condiments in the crook of his elbow and snagged a couple of empty bottles with his fingers. He returned with fresh beers and set them down in front of Shane, Zion, and Andrew. He tilted one toward me. "Layla?"

I'd already had two, but in what world would I say no to Adam?

Peg came around to give Zion and Andrew a hug. She patted Shane on the shoulder, then knelt by the baby, whispering, "I don't want to bother him."

"Are you heading home?" Eden had pulled her feet clear up into her chair, one knee hugged up against her.

"Your dad's all alone."

"Despite what he thinks, he doesn't need a passport to enter the state of New York."

Peg stood and bent to kiss her daughter's forehead. "Will you come to church on Sunday?"

Eden closed her eyes with a heavy sigh. "Mom. We were just out there last week."

"And so?"

Adam laid an arm around Peg's shoulder. "We'll come next week, okay?"

She turned into him and let herself be pulled into his hug. She didn't even seem to realize she'd be the instant envy of my fan forum if I posted a pic of that online right now. She gave him a final pat and asked, "You're going to synagogue this week?"

Eden answered for him. "Just like always."

"Good. As long as you're going to worship." She grabbed her purse and waved once more to everyone. Then she was gone.

Adam sat beside Eden and took her hand in his, his thumb gently stroking hers. The ring on his fourth finger glinted in the last gasp of sunlight, and I imagined his skin under that strip of gold was fish-belly white from lack of exposure. Lots of girls would be disheartened at his devotion to Eden, but I loved it. I wanted my heroes to prove they were worth looking up to.

"Are you raising Joshua both Jewish and Christian?" Maybe the beer had loosened me up.

Eden pulled herself back up to the table. "Jewish mostly. I mean, it can't hurt him to spend time at my mom's church, but I'm converting."

"Really?" That was new to me. Twice in this one night, I'd come to realize that I didn't know nearly as much as I thought I did about her. In a way, it made me glad. Maybe my obsession wasn't as bad as I'd thought. On the other hand, maybe I'd been fantasizing about fictional people for the past decade.

"My mom doesn't know yet." She smiled. "But I think she'll be glad I'm no longer straight-up heathen. And Adam will score another point with her." She shook her head. "He can do no wrong. Saint Adam."

Adam chuckled and laid his other hand on her arm. "Honey, we don't have saints."

The sun had fully set, and the purple-black sky shed no light on the company. The stillness blanketing the backyard seemed to drive everyone into their own thoughts. Conversation stalled while we sipped beer and listened to the crickets chirp. Eden sauntered into the house and returned with citronella candles.

Now faces floated, eerie, golden, and unfamiliar. As the beer settled into my veins, I relaxed and convinced myself we were all just regular people sharing a moment in time.

Adam and Shane started reminiscing about some inside joke, which led Shane to share a story about when his band first started out.

"Noah's been drinking, so he's over on the edge of the stage, playing his guitar and flirting with this girl at the same time. I'm back behind the drum set, you know. No girls coming around behind the stage to flirt, so I'm living vicariously through Noah, as usual, watching all this unfold."

Adam snickered. "Ah yes, I remember the celibate life of the drummer well."

Eden shushed him. "What happened?"

"You have to imagine this place. It's this hole in the wall country bar with a massive pool table dead center. The barflies are all back there—" he flapped one hand toward the distant imaginary bar "—ignoring us. The pool sharks are ignoring us. There's this one girl yelling out cover song requests over and over and sort of swaying and dancing in front of Noah."

We all sat rapt. Shane in motion mesmerized me. A kaleidoscope of dramatic expressions crossed his face while he regaled us with his tale, all of them more adorable than the last.

"Noah turns back to grin at me like the arrogant prick he is, so he doesn't see the man approaching as fast as a bullet. Micah's center stage singing his heart out, eyes shut tight. Rick's on the side, all honey badger and not giving a fuck about any of this, and I'm behind the drum set. I start to stand and yell a warning, but before I can, Noah turns around and his face meets the guy's fist coming right at him."

"Oh, my God." I'd never heard this story before. Why would I have?

"Yeah, so the place erupts in a riot of pool sticks, and I start grabbing up my drumkit and packing it away as fast as I can because I can't afford another one. Micah's trying to extricate Noah from the fracas, and Rick just stands there and lights up a cigarette like we're on a break."

"Fucking Rick," said Adam.

"Moral of the story—don't flirt with the girls at the bar." Shane snorted. "Or count on Rick to have your back."

Adam shook his head, commiserating. "Beats that time we were playing some bar slash restaurant, and in the middle of our set, these patrons at a booth erupted in the Happy Birthday song. Seriously. Midway through one of our songs. Come to find out, some lady there is celebrating her eightieth birthday." He widened his eyes in remembered disbelief. "I can tell you, we felt like edgy rock stars that day."

I listened silently, absorbing everything and trying not to draw attention to myself—a fly on the wall—until Shane remembered I was there. "I'm sure this isn't interesting to Layla."

"No. It really is." I couldn't even begin to express how I could sit there the rest of the night, hearing them talk about anything at all. "My dad used to play in a small band, and he would take me to gigs with him sometimes. Not to bars, but I remember he once played a subdivision club house."

Shane laughed. "That would have been an improvement from some of our early gigs."

As an afterthought, it occurred to me I could have name-dropped an actual musician instead of recalling my dad's adventures in rock. I'd grown up with Dylan Ramirez an aspiring pop star who now went by the stage name Dylan Black. But whenever I saw him back home, he was still just that ordinary guy who lived out on the farm and dated my best friend in high school. Other than the few times he performed at the local beer hall, I couldn't honestly say I'd had much experience with his music. Meanwhile, I'd been my dad's mandatory audience.

Adam focused on me with inky black eyes, like he saw me, like I mattered. "What was that like for you?"

It meant everything to me that he asked. "Weird. Kind of boring, though."

Eden bent to pick up the baby. "Yeah. People don't realize what a snoozefest a musician's life can be at times."

She was right about that, and I didn't understand why I found rock bands so intriguing, but I hadn't wanted to participate in my dad's music at all.

"I'd bring my homework or a book to read while they set up. The funniest thing would be the older ladies who came to get away from their bridge games or whatever they did on a

Tuesday night. They'd gush to me about how excited they were to see some live music. All I could think was that they were coming to see my dad's band play 'In The White Room' which I'd heard approximately seven thousand times in our basement at home." I heard myself and realized who I was talking to. "God, that sounds so rude when I say it out loud."

Adam raised his bottle toward me. "You were a brave soldier."

"Does he still play in a band?" asked Eden.

"You know, not really. It was a hobby, and now he practices alone or plays solo at the local bookstore cafe. He always wanted me to learn guitar and become a family band of two."

"Did you?" Shane crossed his arms on the table and leaned in, giving me his full attention. "Learn guitar, I mean."

It was a bit unnerving. Nobody ever listened to me talk for so long unless it was in writing.

"I tried. My dad sat me down with a ukulele, then moved me to a half-sized guitar. If I was forced to, I might be able to strum 'Horse with No Name.' "

They all laughed at that. I guessed everyone started out with that two-chord song.

"I guess I'm more music fan than musician."

"She saw Theater of the Absurd in Indianapolis." Shane beamed. "She's one of our fans."

"Oh?" said Eden. "Have you ever seen Adam in concert?"

"Actually, yes." Twenty-seven times. Twelve times in Indianapolis, from the smallest clubs to Market Square Arena. Three times in Chicago. Twice in Columbus. The rest were one-offs in various cities where I happened to be—like when I arranged to go for training in DC the same week they played there. That wasn't bizarre, was it?

"You really are a music fan," said Adam.

I was tempted to ask him about his new album, what he'd meant by certain lyrics, how he felt about the negative reviews, whether he'd ever read the fan forum.

Before I could formulate a coherent question, Shane asked, "Who's your very favorite band, Layla?"

His question snapped me out of my crazy, and I shot him a coy smile. "Do you really want to make me choose between the two best bands?"

Eden chortled, which apparently disturbed the baby. With Joshua fussing, Eden gently hoisted him onto her shoulder, patting him, and took him inside. I began reaching for the empties, intending to gather them and follow her into the kitchen, but Adam laid a hand on my forearm—he actually touched me—and said, "Sit. I'll get that."

He wrapped his left arm around five empty bottles and grabbed Eden's empty glass in his right hand. It amused me that he'd always been this one guy in my mind: sweaty, sexy, singing. Yet, here he was, quiet, almost shy, domestic, and incredibly sweet. He was amazing with fans, so it didn't surprise me that he'd be genuinely nice, even in private, but I didn't expect him to be so mellow. So down to earth.

Shane cleared his throat, and I realized I'd been staring at Adam as he disappeared into the house. "Oh, sorry. I guess I am still a little starstruck."

"Understandable." He tore tiny pieces off a napkin. "So, I think we should probably be going soon."

"Oh, yeah. That's fine."

"Would you mind walking? It's such a nice night, and it's not terribly far."

I remembered the car ride over. It wasn't far, but it wasn't near. A couple of miles at least. It was a nice night, and it would mean more time in Shane's company. "I'd love to walk."

Zion and Andrew came around to give me a hug. I hadn't realized how tall Andrew was until he was towering over me. Imposing, really. I made a mental note to do some digging and try to find his music later. "It was great to meet you, Andrew. What did you say your last name was?"

"I didn't. But it's Larraine."

Andrew Larraine. I'd search for him on YouTube later.

"And it was very nice to meet you, too, Layla . . ."

"Beckett."

After we said our farewells, Shane led me through the sliding doors, where Adam met us. "Heading out?"

When I picked up my purse and lifted my hand to wave, he pulled me in for a hug. "It was great to meet you. I hope to see you again."

I breathed in to test out the jasmine theory and smelled baby powder, lighter fluid, and Downy. Beyond that, a faint musky man smell.

Eden didn't come down to send us off, but I imagined she had her hands full with the baby. I couldn't expect her to yell down the stairs if she didn't want to wake a drowsy child.

With that in mind, I walked softly through the living room and waited to get outside before I said another word.

Chapter Eight

Out on the steps, lit only by the sconce by the door, the magical sense of normalcy returned. The soft stillness transported me to the Indiana suburbs. I used to spend nights just like this, riding bikes or rollerskating down the sidewalk in the silence of spring moonlight, loving how the only sound in the world was the *clack-clack-clack* of my wheels over the cracks. There was a familiar comfort in the dark.

Shane skipped down the steps, then slowed until I caught up. We made our way down the quiet street side by side. Sort of.

He lurched away from me and back, like he had too much energy for a slow walk and needed to avoid the straight line from A to B. It put me in mind of a bouncy kid running in circles while a parent plodded forward. I had no intention of rushing. I was too curious about this guy I'd never been curious enough about before.

KIND OF FAMOUS   77

"That was lovely," I said, by way of small talk.

"Mmm-hmm. They're great people."

As we passed by other houses on the row, my mind kept returning to the larger-than-life rock star whose home I'd been invited into as if I were simply one of his friends. What was life like for Adam in his regular environment? Did his neighbors all know him? Could he walk down the street without being harassed or did he keep to himself mostly?

"You're awfully quiet." Shane's gait had settled into a leisurely stroll, his hands jammed in his pockets, his Converse sneakers gliding along.

"Just processing."

"You're an introvert, aren't you?"

Was I? I pushed a lock of hair behind my ear, self-conscious of his attention. "I'm not really used to being around people. Especially not famous people. It's a lot to take in."

"It is. I can't speak to being around people in general, but you'll get used to Adam and Eden. They're not arrogant about the fame, but they're realistic."

"Realistic? You mean, like how they straight up asked me if my mind was blown?"

"Imagine that they have to deal with that reaction from every single new person they meet." He shook his head. "Micah, too. It could make anyone get a swelled ego. They work hard to keep things normal at all times."

"What about you?" I elbowed him. "Don't you have to deal with it?"

"Me?" He chuckled. "I have to show my ID when we go to our own afterparties."

I burst out laughing at the image of that. "You're joking."

"Sort of." He gently tugged on my arm. "We need to cross here."

He steered me toward a side street then let go. Hoping I hadn't misread his cues, I wrapped my hand around his upper arm, part of the way, anyway. His bicep was huge and rock hard. At my touch, his shoulders hunched up a little, and he inched closer to me.

"So, what do you do in your spare time? Do you have any hobbies?"

Without meaning to, he'd lobbed a grenade. I evaded it. "I love to read."

"And listen to music, right?"

I made a valiant effort to duck that bomb. "Yes. I love music."

"You never said who your favorite band is."

"Who's yours?" Another bullet dodged.

"Can I say my own band?" He raised one eyebrow at me. He looked so cute, I nearly stumbled.

With my eyes sharp for any actual land mines ahead of me, I flexed my atrophied flirting muscle. "That would be rather arrogant, don't you think? How about your favorite band you have no friends in?"

At a busy intersection, Shane rested his weight against the light post, his face lit by the Starbucks. "You've eliminated a large number of current bands, so I'll have to go back in history."

"That sounds fair."

As soon as the flashing hand gave us permission, we crossed over, and the landscape around us transformed into what could have been downtown in any other city. All the buildings were taller and statelier than I would have expected so far from Manhattan. Cars flew along beside us now.

Shane kept the conversation going. "So, I'm a drummer, right?"

"Right."

"When I was a kid, my parents took me to see The Police on a reunion tour."

"Wow. How was it?"

"Stewart Copeland had this incredible drumkit. I mean, it looked like a middle school's entire percussion section surrounded him." I'd let go of his arm when we'd crossed the street, and now his hands flew passionately to somehow paint the picture of his words. "He attacked those drums like a madman. It was insane."

"Is that why you took up drums?"

"No, I'd been playing in the school band, but that sort of woke me up to the possibilities. I'd never paid that much attention to The Police before that honestly, but after that, I collected it all."

"So, are you all about John Bonham?"

He'd picked up the pace since we'd started talking about drummers, and he practically bounced on his toes now. "John Bonham, Neil Peart, Keith Moon. If you hang out with me for long, you'll get sick to death of The Who."

I laid a hand over my heart. "I could never get sick of The Who."

"I think I might love you." He spun around and walked backward long enough to ask, "Your turn. Who's your favorite band?"

Kaboom. I had one more trick up my sleeve. "Right this minute? Theater of the Absurd."

My accompanying smile was meant to be equal parts coy vixen and flirtatious scamp, but his lips pinched together for half a beat. It was so subtle, I might have missed it, but I'd been tracing those gorgeous lips with my eyes. When they pursed together, he looked for the first time like I'd said something wrong.

Maybe I'd dodged right into a different grenade

"Kidding." Shit was that worse? "I mean, like I said before, I'm obviously a fan, but I've seen Adam's band more often than yours." Truth at least.

He turned to walk forward, the frenetic energy lost, like a popped balloon with the helium leaking out. He side-eyed me. "You've seen us more than once?"

Wow, I was digging a grave. "Well, yeah. You put on an amazing show."

He nodded. "Damn straight we do."

I hoped it meant I'd hit the right balance finally.

We'd been walking for what seemed like forever already, but it was probably only twenty minutes. In front of a Macy's, I stopped to tie my shoe, and he asked, "Do you want me to call a cab?"

Had I made him want to bail. "How much farther?"

"Thirty minutes, maybe?"

And the cab ride would likely be five minutes, and then we'd say goodnight, and I might never see him again. "Let's keep walking."

For the next few blocks, he moved us to a safer conversation topic. "Favorite musician from before we were born."

That was territory I could navigate endlessly. "My dad would want me to say Clapton. Hence the name. But hands down Bowie."

His smile returned. "Bowie is a huge influence on our music."

"I know." It came out. I couldn't help it. Talking music was my jam. Talking music with a musician? How often would I get the opportunity?

We turned onto Flatbush Avenue, and he peppered me with more questions.

"What was the best concert you ever saw—" he held up a hand "—without any band members you've shared a beer with."

He was a quick study. I scrunched my lips up as I ran through my mental Rolodex. "I'm going to have to say Of Montreal."

His eyes went wide. "You know them?"

"Uh. Duh." My eyes rolled. "Kind of a music freak here."

"If your music collection got destroyed, what would be the first album you'd buy again?"

I burst out laughing. "Would you believe this has happened to me? An entire disk drive *and* the backup drive lost."

"Oh, shit. Worst nightmare."

The first album I'd downloaded, not bought—I figured it wasn't stealing if I'd bought it once before—was Walking Disaster's eponymous album. But I applied the same rules as before. "The first album I replaced was Muse, *Black Holes and Revelations.*"

"Excellent choice."

"You?"

"Metallica, *Master of Puppets.*"

"Ah, Lars Ulrich, huh?"

"You know your drummers!"

"A few."

He paused for a second and then he said, "Come this way."

We turned right onto a street marked Sixth. The traffic and noise fell away. Store fronts gave way to a never-ending row of townhouses, trees, and quiet, maybe a back way to Jo's.

Conversation stalled as if it had fed off the life of the busy city behind us. He'd once again put me at my ease, but ever since I'd said something wrong before, he hadn't invaded my space. I decided to come right out and ask the question that troubled me. "So, do you have some kind of no-fan dating rule or something?"

"Me?" He looked genuinely shocked. "I can't afford to have any kind of no dating rule."

His honesty made me chortle.

"I'm going to sound really lame here for a minute." He scratched his chin like he was deciding whether to speak. "Can I ask you something?"

"Sure."

"What did you honestly think of Noah when you first saw him?"

I decided to play along. "I thought he was pretty." I waited a beat. "Pretty arrogant."

He smiled, but he stared at his feet. "Women usually have their eye on him. It used to be Micah, but Micah's no longer eligible."

Was he really asking me to sympathize that Noah and Micah got more tail?

"Ladies don't fall all over you, Shane?" I pouted dramatically, like he was telling me some problem I'd care about.

"No." His hands opened and closed as he weighed his words. "I mean, yes, they do, but I'm not the end game."

"What are you saying?" I tilted my head so I could better look into his eyes. "Girls use you to get to Noah? But that's—" awful, hurtful, disgusting "—inconceivable."

That little smile curled up the corner of his lip, and he relaxed, shooting me a tentative glance. "So, that's where I'm at with dating fans."

"Oh, I see." I didn't.

"Can I hold your hand?"

The abrupt question made my breath hitch. I nodded, and he slipped his fingers between mine. It sent an unfamiliar twist to my stomach. Was it excitement? Or fear of the unknown?

We walked in silence for ten minutes. Was he as aware of the contact between us as me? A car passed, and the headlights on his skin revealed a flush I recognized. At a nondescript corner, he said, "Mind if we make a slight detour?"

I wouldn't have known if he'd lured me completely off course. I shook my head, and we turned onto an even darker street.

He sighed. "I'm going to prove I have no game here, but I have to apologize about Noah."

"Why?"

"I was serious before when I said I wanted to remove the competition. That was a douchey thing to do to you."

"To me?"

"Look. Girls always chase Noah. When he's around, I don't even rate. Normally, that's fine because I don't want a shallow night with a super fan after a show anyway."

His confession took me by surprise, and I felt a little bad that he needed to make it, a bit hurt too at the unintended slight at who I was.

"Shane."

He kept his eyes fastened to the sidewalk before us. "I could tell there was something about you, and I didn't want to take the chance that Noah would get there first. I'm sorry both for taking that choice away from you, but mainly for assuming that you'd make that choice in the first place."

I squeezed his hand. "Honestly, I'm not remotely interested in Noah. I swear. He lost me when he teased you."

"He did?"

"I mean, Noah's a pretty guy," I confessed and laughed at his sudden intake of breath. "But you're more interesting. By far."

He cut his eyes at me for the first time since he'd started his little speech. "Yeah?"

We stopped short of the next cross street beside a brick building with a paint-chipped green door.

"Hell yeah." With my free hand I gestured up at him. "Not to mention, you've got much prettier hair."

That brought a full grin. "You oughta know." He lifted his finger, and I swore he was going to muss my hair like he might a little sister, but as soon as his palm lay against the side of my head, he froze.

The moon shone bright, but his eyes remained dark as the deepest ocean. He blinked twice and ran his thumb down my cheek to my chin. I confess that I'd had some illicit fantasies about the guys in the band, but I'd never felt the one-two punch to the gut that I got when his hand slid around the back of my neck and he pulled me forward to press his lips against mine.

He drew back, slowly enough that his lips continued to touch mine for a lingering moment, and I opened my eyes before he did. He looked like he'd tasted ice cream for the first time and wanted to savor it. My mind reeled with questions, and I had this crazy thought that I wished he were more famous so I'd have read something about him on the Internet before, so I'd know who he was and what I might be getting myself into.

If he were like Adam, I'd know to grab hold of him and never let go. If he were like Noah, I wouldn't want to give him the time of day.

But those lips.

A tiny smile lit his face. "Should I apologize again?"

With that, I threw caution to the wind and twisted both hands into his T-shirt. He laughed when I pulled him back into a less hesitant kiss, but his laughter stopped when my tongue brushed his, and he spun us around so he could press me up against the metal door behind us.

It had been a long time since I'd been physical with a man. Way too long.

Shane's lips teased mine, and I felt like I'd lived in a desert my whole life, never knowing that water existed. Suddenly I'd fallen into a deep pool. It might turn out to be an oasis, or I might drown, and I didn't care. My fingers traced his cheek, then brushed his neck, and his body responded in shivers. He lifted the edge of my shirt and explored my lower back, creeping up my spine until he reached my bra.

I'd lost track of where we were. Everything was him. His mouth on mine. His hands on me. His skin. His . . . I gasped. He pressed harder into me, and I ground back, need flaring inside me.

He took the first step away. "Layla." The fact that his voice came out ragged and breathless only made me want to tear his shirt off and spend the next ten hours licking every inch of him while he said my name.

"Shane." My own shaky voice gave away my physical discomfort.

"I'd really like to take you up to my apartment. Now." He adjusted his pants. "Unless you still want me to take you back to Jo's?"

My body screamed: *Take me anywhere.* "Where do you live?"

"Right here." He stood back and pointed to the edifice behind me. Confused by what he was saying, I jerked my head from the metal door back to him, and a telltale blush crept up his cheek. He looked away.

Had that been his plan all along? Did I care?

Was he looking for a one-night stand?

It wouldn't be the first time I'd hooked up with a guy. Blind dates that turned into a second and third, leading eventually to a kind of inevitable night in his bed, followed by an awkward morning and a silent phone. I'd grown immune to the disappointment, but at least I'd gotten the sex out of it. Back when I'd gotten any sex at all.

Shane's interest had seemed genuine, but now that he'd led me back to his place, I put the odds on never seeing him again, whether or not I slept with him. Of course, I wanted to see him again, but if I had to look back on tonight with regret, I'd prefer it at least come with the fond memory of his bed.

That may have been the lust talking, but damn I needed him, in me, on me, under me.

One impossible-to-ignore wrinkle might foil my get-fucked-quick scheme. I was wearing a potentially pink pantyliner, and visions of Shane encountering that drew me up short. I didn't want our first time to be that awkward. Even if this was a one-night stand, I still didn't want to feel embarrassed about it tomorrow.

I stared at him, memorizing the planes of his face, the curve of those lips, wanting to say *yes, yes, yes*. It was taking an effort to refrain from crushing my face against his. It was the tail-end of my period after all.

He twined his fingers with mine and pressed his forehead against mine, his features obscured in shadow. "What do you want to do?"

His body crashed back against me, and it was so unfair.

How could I say no?

"I could pick up a bottle of wine. Or a six pack." His lower lip disappeared under his front teeth with a wince. "Or soda. Or nothing."

My mind churned, looking for any rationalization that would allow me to puddle his pants at his ankles. But that image brought with it *my* panties on the floor, sporting spots. It wasn't that I was a period prude, but it wasn't exactly the first impression I wanted to make with a near total stranger.

I sighed. What I wanted to do and what I ought to do were not always the same. Not just because of my crimson cave. The truth was, I barely knew the guy. I couldn't even tell him why.

That realization decided me.

My mom had passed on a bit of wisdom to me. She said, "Layla, if you can't talk to a boy about sex, about your body, then you're not ready for sex with him."

Knowing I had to say no, I felt three stabs of disappointment. First, the immediate frustration of needing a man, any man, now that my sexuality had been awakened. Next, the appalling realization that I'd always regret not banging the drummer, like some rocker-collecting groupie. And third, the dismay that I might lose an opportunity to get to know a genuinely nice guy if I didn't latch on when I had the chance.

But none of these would seem like compelling reasons in the cold light of morning.

So, I gave him another kiss, and reluctantly told him, "Not tonight."

As if we'd suddenly been reverse polarized, he dropped back a step. "Sure."

I hadn't meant to reject him outright, but before I could think of something that might take the sting out, he turned and walked in the direction we'd come from. I fell in beside him, wondering if I'd wrecked any chance with him, which in turn made me a bit angry at how shitty it would be if he pouted or treated me like I'd wronged him because he didn't instantly get what he wanted.

I'd had experience with guys like that. Guys who thought I owed them something because they'd bought me dinner. Guys who sent me hostile messages when I suggested I wasn't as interested in them as they were in me.

Despite what he'd said before, I supposed Shane got whatever he wanted from girls out on the road all the time. And that in turn made me sad because I hated to think I'd misjudged him so much. I'd pegged him for one of the good guys. Had it all been a bunch of lines? Had he lied to me?

Before I could work up a strongly worded feminist manifesto to unload on him, he said, "Can I still hold your hand?"

It took me aback. The question sounded so shy, so unsure, even though he'd had his tongue in my mouth five minutes earlier. Instead of pointing that out, I said, "I'd like that," surprised to hear the same shy, unsure tone in my own voice.

We were an awkward pair.

Rather than snatching me like a teenager, he slid his hand down the inside of my wrist and across my open palm until his fingers clasped mine. It was at once so hesitant and confident, so seductive, that I nearly changed my mind about going to his place.

For another block, we walked, together yet apart. I was aware of the contact between us, but there was a divide. I didn't know how to cross it.

As if life wanted to bring metaphors to life, a traffic light forced us to wait for the signal to continue. He dropped my hand and spun to face me. "I'm sorry for coming on so strong. I tend to rush into things when I know what I want."

"Oh?" I focused on keeping my eyes from bugging out.

"I'm like a kid seeing the best toy at the store and demanding to have it now."

"Toy?"

He pressed his fingertips against his closed eyelids with a shake of his head. "Bad analogy."

The white hand beckoned for us to walk, so we crossed the street and passed a coffee shop I was sure I'd seen before. Was that where I'd seen Micah and Jo in the tabloids?

Another tree-lined street, another row of townhouses, but things began to look familiar. We were close to Jo's now. As we closed in on the steps to her house, Shane slowed. He took a breath and looked me straight in the eyes. "Can I just speak plain? I mean, is it too soon to tell you what I really think?"

A shiver shot down my spine. "No. Tell me."

"Okay, but if I freak you out, just pretend we're cool for at least as long as it takes for us to get to Jo's. I don't think I can bear an outright rejection."

I lay my hand on his chest. "Do I look like I'm freaking out?"

"You look like you've stepped through a portal into another dimension and your normal rules no longer apply."

"Huh?" His analogies were more confusing than the plain speak he'd promised. I tightened my fingers in his to lend courage. "Okay. Go on with your plain talk."

"There's a lot going on here, and I'm chasing after the puzzle pieces trying to make sense of the big picture."

"Explain."

"So, you're new to town, right? And you haven't figured out what's up and what's down. You don't even have a place to live." He didn't wait for me to agree. "Part of me wants to warn you not to trust that stranger you only just met. That you shouldn't be here with me on this dark street. That you should not under any circumstances go up to my apartment."

I opened my mouth to protest, but he held up his hand.

"However, you happen to have exceedingly good judgment." He flashed a sheepish grin. "I mean, I'm a nice guy. I have no intention of taking advantage of your apparently trusting nature."

"How do you know *I'm* not the sociopath?"

"I'm getting to that." He scratched his neck. "I don't know why I felt immediately drawn to you. Maybe it was because you sided with me against Noah's stupid teasing. Maybe it's simple physical attraction. Maybe it's love at first sight."

My heart hammered in my chest. Was I starting to freak out?

"Shit. I'm not good at this." He clasped my other hand, and we stood there on the sidewalk, looking like we were exchanging vows.

He really was not good at this. I squeezed his hands and waited.

"What I'm trying to say is that I don't know what you expect, and I can't predict the future, but I'm interested in getting to know you."

It was a bit unnerving that he came on so strong, so honest, but at the same time I found it endearing that he was floundering. Then it hit me. "Are you nervous?"

He snorted. "Of course, I'm nervous. Do you know how rare it is to connect with anyone?"

I did. But how could he know that we had a connection? We were practically strangers. I nodded anyway.

"I don't want to screw this up before it's even anything."

It occurred to me that this wasn't about him. This was about me. I lay my head against his chest. "Hey. I like you."

He wrapped his arms around my back. "I like you, too."

The front door opened, and Jo peeked out. "Layla? There you are. I've been trying to call you."

I pulled back from Shane and gave him a serious eye fuck, wishing it could be more. He lifted my hand and planted a kiss on my knuckle. Somehow that small gesture nearly killed me. I was going to literally die because I couldn't have this man tonight.

"Goodnight, Layla."

"Night, Shane."

He turned to go but spun back. "Can I call you?"

"Yes!" I bounded up the steps and into the house, and Jo crossed her arms like she wanted to hear the whole story.

Talking Disaster Blog

ON REVIEWS AND REVIEWERS
—Pumpkin39

Yesterday, on the forum, several fans organized an attack against a review of Walking Disaster's latest album. Those of you who know me won't be surprised that I asked you to resist the urge to defend the band against the unnecessarily harsh words of the reviewer Gabriel Sanchez. (Yes, I share your outrage, even if I didn't share your solution).

You'll be happy to know that I have since had a change of heart. While I don't normally condone pissing off reviewers who may simply continue to pan future albums out of animosity toward the fans, in this one case, I concede that you all were right.

And in that light, I'm unlocking that review thread. I won't be participating in this particular crusade, but if you feel like unloading your disgruntlement on Mr. Sanchez's article, feel free to strategize and high five in the forum.

Chapter Nine

Jo closed the door behind me. She'd already changed into her pajamas, and her hair was up in a ponytail.

"Well?"

"I'm sorry. I turned my phone to airplane mode back at Eden's, and I guess I forgot."

She waved me off. "No need to apologize. I worried a bit since Eden said you'd left over an hour ago. I thought maybe you'd decided to spend the night elsewhere." She gave me that look again, like she expected a tell-all account.

"Nah. We just decided to walk and—"

"You *walked*?" She shook her head. "That explains a lot then." She headed toward the kitchen. "You want something to drink?"

What I wanted was to flip my phone back on and find out if I'd missed anything important, but I chided myself. *Live in the moment.* "Sure."

In the kitchen, Micah sat at the island writing in a notebook on a page covered in black ink, most of it scratched out. He glanced up. "Hey, Layla."

The thrill of having him recognize me hadn't worn off.

"Hey, Micah." I scooted up and tried to read his handwriting. "What are you working on? A song?"

He set the pen down. "Would you rather hear unreleased songs or covers?"

"Uh."

Jo laid a hand on his shoulder. "You want to give her some more context, babe?" She reached in the refrigerator and said to me, "Juice or water?"

I thought back to Eden's fridge full of soda and beer, and the difference reminded me of how Jo had left earlier. I wanted to ask her how she felt now, but I didn't want to pry either. "Water's fine."

Micah leaned on his elbows, pen twirling in his fingers. "We've got a festival coming up, and I'm still working out the setlist. We only have a few days left to rehearse before we hit the road, and I can't decide between a few songs."

I craned my neck. "What do you have so far?"

"We've already got a couple of our new songs on here, so it makes sense to do a cover. I'm just not sure if we should waste the slot on someone else's music."

He showed me the notebook, and I understood how it must feel to be an archaeologist handling an artifact from an ancient civilization. I would have died to get my hands on this setlist after a show. But to be a part of the process? To potentially shape the resulting list? This went beyond expected fan experience. I'd found my way to the inside somehow.

"Layla?"

"Sorry. I was just thinking about other shows I've been to. The thing is, if I'm really into a band, I want to hear new songs because it's like a secret that you're sharing with us for showing up. But I always love covers."

"Yeah?" He tapped his pen on the list. "Why?"

"Seriously?" Cover songs were always a hugely popular topic. Fans fantasized about which songs they wanted Walking Disaster to cover, and the list was endless. "It's just fun to hear one favorite band interpreting another."

"But if you've paid money to see a show, wouldn't you rather hear the band's own songs?"

"You'd think." I combed through my knowledge of fan behavior and tried to articulate something more meaningful. "To be honest, a lot of it comes down to identity."

"What do you mean?" He leaned in, really listening now.

"Fans want to think their favorite artists are fans of each other."

He chuckled. "Validation?"

That gave me an idea. "Have you ever covered any of Adam's music?"

As far as I knew, neither band had ever covered each other.

Micah scoffed at the suggestion. "Cover Walking Disaster? That would be—"

"Incestuous?" Jo piped in.

"But Eden's covered both of you, right?" Was I showing too much of my hand? Eden's style wasn't remotely similar to either band, and she'd recorded acoustic versions of their music. Micah had a whole acoustic solo career. Maybe he did WD covers on the side that I wasn't aware of. "It would be really interesting to hear your take on some of their older songs."

Micah rubbed his chin, scratching at the golden scruff that hadn't been there a few hours earlier. He drew a line under something he'd scrawled. I wished I could make out his illegible handwriting. I wished I could sneak a photograph of his notes.

He looked up from the paper. "You ought to come out to our rehearsal tomorrow."

My heart skipped a beat. "What? I mean—" Fuck I wanted to say yes. "I have to work."

"Ah. That's too bad." He seemed legitimately sad, and it fed into my own sense of tragedy. Life was unfair.

I mentally slapped myself. How could I pity myself when I was sitting across a kitchen island talking music with Micah Sinclair? And not just talking, but actually advising him. How easy it was to want more, but I needed to count my lucky stars.

"Thanks for asking though." I bit my lip and finished with more honesty. "And for letting me help with your planning. That was a pretty cool moment for me."

He grinned. "Awesome. And you did help. A lot. So, thank you."

I jumped down from my stool, chest swelling with pride and gratitude, and headed upstairs to log into my erstwhile life and try to figure out where I fit in there now.

Upstairs, snuggled up in the covers with my laptop, I had so much to catch up on, but I didn't go straight to the forum. Instead, I cracked my knuckles and logged into my blog. I clicked on New Post, then began typing an article for the front page apologizing for putting the ban on efforts to organize a skirmish against a poor review. As long as I stayed out of it, there was no conflict of interest. Fans would do what fans would do.

I added a link to the thread and unlocked it as promised. Fuck Gabriel Sanchez and his ignorant review.

Then I clicked on my bookmark to the Theater of the Absurd fan board and dug around until I found a thread dedicated to Shane. Holding my breath, I opened it up and was rewarded with a lovely photo someone had dug up of him laughing, eyes crinkled, teeth flashing, oblivious to the camera. I wasn't surprised his thread was far shorter than those for Micah and Noah. On my board, our thread for WD's drummer, Hervé, only attracted the drumming enthusiasts. Then again, Hervé's dominant physical trait was a walrus mustache. Shane was boyishly adorable.

My curiosity wasn't sated at all though.

I shot off a private message to Jaclyn, aka State of the Absurd. We'd virtually known each other for years, and I figured she'd be honest.

Jaclyn—
What's the DL on Shane Morgan? Asking for a friend.
—Pumpkin

I didn't expect to hear anything from her right away, so I hunkered down into the soft, fluffy blankets of Micah Sinclair's guest bed, taking a moment to marvel at where I was. I wanted to squeal like a crazy fan girl. At the same time, I wanted to shrug like a nonchalant insider. Could this be my real life? Would these be my friends now?

I didn't want to relax into that level of expectation, because I knew that would make the retreat back into obscurity that much more disappointing. Would I be content to simply run my fan forum from a place of anonymity after this? I wasn't sure.

And if they knew who I really was, was there any way I'd be accepted into their inner sphere like this?

Talking Disaster Forum

Topic: Walking Disaster - Reviews - Horizon - The Rock Paper - Page 9

Di$a$ter wrote:
Testing one, two, three. Is this thing on?

Attention boys and girls. Operation Bollocks is back on. Forward march!

DeadFan wrote:
Did you guys see Pumpkin's post above?

Di$a$ter wrote:
Check the blog, DF.

DeadFan wrote:
blushes

Sorry. I saw this thread lit up and wondered. Carry on.

Insidious wrote:
Ha ha! They don't validate your email address, so I've been spamming the comments with my pithy wisdom all day under a variety of creative monikers.

Di$a$ter wrote:
=D

Walker wrote:
LMFAO Sid. I'm heading over. Doubt it will do much good, but I've been spoiling for a fight since I read the word "derivative."

RobinHood wrote:
Give him hell, guys! *popping popcorn*

Chapter Ten

*W*ednesday morning, I got ready as quietly as possible, hoping to sneak out without disturbing Jo or Micah. I was starting to feel bad for taking advantage of their hospitality. If they fed me and sent me off to work in a glorified limo again, it would only compound the guilt. I could grab coffee and breakfast on the go.

I hadn't realized how hard it would be to find a place to live. The sheer number of ads on craiglist overwhelmed me, and I didn't know the neighborhoods or how to vet potential room-mates. I planned to ask around at work and do some intense research. Later.

Once I was out on the street. I woke up my phone to locate a subway stop. The notification light blinked, and I groaned, wondering what Ash wanted so early, but the text was from Shane. With a goofy grin, I clicked through.

Good morning. This is Shane. I just wanted to tell you that I really enjoyed talking with you last night.

At the corner, I entered the coffee shop and got in line. While I waited, I texted back.

Hi! I tapped the phone, trying to think of something more interesting, but all I could come up with was: *I had a nice time, too. Hope to see you again soon.*

No response came while I moved up the line. I placed my order then pulled up my own website to see what nonsense had transpired during the night after those two trolls had stirred the pot. But all was quiet.

I clicked on the Private Messages link and opened an administrative request from Adamant to help Scott, aka MetalNation, figure out why he couldn't log in. Scott's email address was included. I grumbled in annoyance. I'd instructed everyone in the Admin Info thread to contact Ash about this kind of shit for now.

My order came up. I grabbed the coffee and pastry and moved to a table where I opened Scott's profile and discovered that his email address on record didn't match the one they'd sent and updated it. Then I wrote back to say:

Tell Scott to request his password again.

The next message was from some user I'd never heard of: Sandman. The subject of this was: *Your blog post.*

I sighed.

Sometimes people would contact me to respond personally to an article I'd written or an opinion I'd posted instead of just commenting right on the blog or forum. Stifling a yawn, I opened it.

If you want your band to be respected for their music, you might reconsider sending your army of mouth breathers to infest a well-respected reviewer's opinion piece. You give the band a bad name.

That put Bon Jovi in my brain, and I hummed "You Give Love a Bad Name" as I hit Reply and set about typing a jaunty rejoinder.

KIND OF FAMOUS   99

Thank you for taking the time to share your opinion regarding my blog post. Perhaps you'd like to post in the comments section, as that is what they are there for. Unlike the reviewer you refer to, I welcome dissenting points of view.

I actually started out thinking our fans shouldn't vociferously disagree with a bad review. Then I had a second thought: It's entirely possibly the reviewer is deaf and/or musically ignorant.

I do appreciate your feedback, but in the future, bear in mind that I have 14,000 registered users and can't always respond to every private message.

Have a good one.

And send.

That probably would merit a scorching reply, but half the fun of the Internet was kicking ass. After all, I hadn't taken my fight to him. Unless of course, that had actually been Gabriel.

Wait.

I opened the original message again and hit the moderation tools link on it. The user's IP address showed up, with an option to block or ban the user. I clicked a link to open another website that would locate the origin of the poster.

New York City. Interesting.

It wasn't definitive by any means, and likely far-fetched. Still, who else would go out of their way to defend Gabriel as a "well-respected reviewer"?

I finished my coffee and muffin as I quickly read through the rest of my messages. Then I remembered I hadn't checked back on the TotA site for a response from Jaclyn. As I walked, I pulled up her board to find a message from her.

Pumpkin!

It's been too long! How are things? I have to admit, I'm curious to know why you're interested in our sweet drummer boy, but I won't pry. Much. :)

Not sure what you're hoping to discover. I'm sure you've already read his bio on the blog. We've got some collected vids of him drumming. He tends to favor the DW Design Series for his toms and bass drum, and Zildjian cymbals . . . but somehow I don't think that's what you're after.

If you want to know something specific, like about his temperament or whatever, feel free to ask. I won't pretend to be the resident expert, but I'm happy to share what I can.

Jaclyn

What could I ask her discreetly? What would I think if she had started digging for intel about Walking Disaster's bassist Mark Townsend out of the blue?

I stopped at the corner so I wouldn't run into anyone as I typed a quick response.

Jaclyn,

One of my friends told me she met Shane recently and thought he was super cute. She wondered if he was seeing anyone and whether there were any red flags. I did poke around your forum a bit, but I don't think she's looking to dig up his whole dating history.

Pumpkin

She could at least point me in the right direction. With her lax moderating, anything terrible about Shane would still be on her forum somewhere. And the Internet was forever.

But all I wanted to know was whether he was someone to steer clear of. I didn't want to learn about his every past girlfriend. Not via a fan forum at least. Jaclyn might not value privacy, but she and I had different philosophies on what constituted boundaries. And here I was breaching one.

I dropped my phone in my bag and headed toward the nearest subway station. I felt like I'd already put in a day's work, and I hadn't even arrived at my real job yet.

The subway took forever, so by the time I made it to Midtown, I was a bit later than I'd intended. The office bustled with activity as I set up my workstation. On my way to grab a second cup of coffee, I craned my neck to peer into the corner office where a long-haired hippie sat at his desk, talking on the phone. The placard beside the door read: *Lars Cambridge.* The editor and head honcho of the *Rock Paper.* An enormously influential man. A legend really. Goosebumps ran down my arms just knowing he was behind that door, probably making magic happen.

Would I ever get to meet him? I concentrated on breathing normally so I wouldn't alert everyone in my vicinity that I was a freak and a total fraud. How had I ended up in the coolest place on the planet?

As soon as I sat back down at my desk, Byron called my name from the meeting room.

"You coming?"

I furrowed my brow. Crap. I needed to put a reminder on my phone. Not a great way to start the day. I undocked my laptop and carried it with me into the meeting room intent to listen and learn.

On the overhead screen, Ajit had pulled up a web page covered with graphs. "There was an unusual surge overnight. Nothing too concerning, but I got an alert and went to investigate."

Dave leaned in. "Around what time?"

"Sometime after midnight. Load average was coming down by the time I logged in."

I watched the interchange between the two developers, wondering if there was any chance an invasion of trolls in a comment section of a review could cause the servers to experience heavy load. I'd managed to optimize my own website to handle that kind of traffic. Surely a large music magazine was prepared to handle a fan war.

"This might be off base, but—" I hesitated. I wasn't a real developer. "I'm wondering if you've captured the SQL and tuned the queries. What you described of the increased load last night—"

Ajit interjected. "That was actually going to be my first avenue of investigation."

I sighed with relief. He hadn't laughed at my suggestion.

"Would you like to sit with me while I look over the snapshots?"

I grinned at his invitation. I loved troubleshooting. "I'd love to."

As the meeting came to an end, Byron asked me how my requirements doc was coming, reminding me my responsibilities lay in product management. The truth was, I was happy with that, too. My own site was a one-man operation, and I could do anything they asked of me, coding, testing, writing, marketing, provided they gave me time to learn.

"I should have something ready by tomorrow."

He nodded, and I near sashayed back to my desk, so happy to have a purpose, I forgot to check my phone until lunchtime. When I did, I discovered another text from Shane.

You should skip out early and come hang out with us at rehearsal.

I stared at the words, wanting to say yes. Regretfully, I had to turn him down. *Really wish I could.*

That was no lie. I didn't want to play hookie from the world's best job, but it killed me to miss out on an even rarer experience to witness a band while they jammed out on their own music. It was like I'd scored tickets to a great concert yet envied the people with a backstage pass.

Except this time, I literally held a backstage pass I couldn't use.

Poor me.

One glance at the office where Lars Cambridge worked reminded me that I had enough going on right here. I checked my lack of gratitude and conjured up the excitement of knowing that just sitting here constituted a dream come true.

Shane's next text made me laugh. *Dooo it!*

Rain check? God, I hoped there could be a rain check.

When do you get through? Time is both dragging and fleeting at the same time. How is that possible?

Adorable.

I wrote back: *I leave at five.*

I turned back to my work, grinning like a maniac, until a voice harshed my mood.

"What's got you so happy, Red?"

Sigh. Gabe peered over the cube wall. Thankfully, I had my requirements doc pulled up, so he didn't catch me wasting company time on my website.

"What's up?" I didn't bother to stop my fake typing.

"Are you free for lunch?" He moved into my cube, nearly touching my chair. "I enjoyed our conversation yesterday about my review."

"Did you?" My eyes flitted up to check for traces of sarcasm. My recollection had been that we'd argued.

"Especially since all of a sudden, I'm being viciously maligned online." Such drama. He needed a fainting couch.

I was tempted to say, "*So, you can dish it out, but you can't take it?*" Instead, I faced my Word doc, masking my reaction. "Are you?"

"Come out and cheer me up. We could talk about what you liked about my writing."

I felt a little guilty for having kicked a hornets' nest his way, but if he'd been the one PMing me during the night, then he could suck it. "I don't think I'm your girl."

He pouted. "Why are you being so mean to me, Layla?"

Considering I'd known him only two days, that was a good question.

"I'm sorry. I'm going to work straight through lunch." And go read these vicious comments. "Maybe another time?"

"How about after work then?" His eyebrow rose slightly, like I wouldn't be able to resist his invitation.

I tilted my head, trying to find a way to say no without pissing him off. Who knew if he was the kind of guy who might retaliate after a rejection? On the other hand, I didn't want to keep giving him a flimsy pretext every day either. I wished I had more experience dealing with people face to face or knew how to handle men pursuing me.

The best I could come up with was: "I promised Jo I'd spend the evening with her. Sorry."

"One of these days you'll run out of excuses."

My stomach knotted up, but I smiled to keep things light. "Thanks for asking. I've really got to finish this doc."

I put my head down and focused on doing just that.

The afternoon flew by, sitting in with Ajit and occasionally Dave, presenting my ideas and learning more about the system. Before I knew it, five o'clock had rolled around, and I texted Jo to let her know I was getting ready to leave work.

She texted back: *I'm going to make up for abandoning you last night. Save your appetite. I'll send the car over now.*

My imagination took off, and I wondered if I'd get to spend another evening with Micah's band.

And Shane.

I flashed back to that kiss, and my stomach went into free fall. His texts this morning proved that his interest wasn't fleeting. As did a new one that came in while I was heading to the subway: *Can I come over tonight after work?*

I had to assume it would be okay with Jo. He'd been over once before. And I wanted him to. I wanted to get to know him better and figure out who he was. So, I said, *Yes*, then squeezed my fists together and held back a squeal of excitement.

The Rock Paper

Review of New Horizons - Discussion

Big Fart:
I feel embarrassed for you.

Sabe Ganchez:
New Horizons is the best album I have ever heard. Every single song has a unique hook. This album will be huge.

FanPop:
You need a hearing aid.

Sage Fanchez:
You're not entirely wrong that the sound deviates from past albums, but you forget that WD's music has been ubiquitous for the past few years. They've mastered the rock-pop chart sound, and this album pushes them out of their comfort zone. It's a reinvention that might take adjustment, but if you listened to this album more than one time, you'd recognize it for the genius it is. Maybe critics spend so little time just enjoying music that they forget it's meant to be broken in, lived in, experienced. It's not a piece of fruit.

AnonyMouse:
U suck!

Vencor:
If this is any indication of your music understanding, you need to quit your job.

Chapter Eleven

Micah sat on the patio, strumming his guitar, but I couldn't hear him through the plate glass, especially with Jo sorting through the refrigerator.

"I hate to say this." She closed the door. "I should have planned for another person, especially since the guys are always dropping in unannounced."

"It's okay. I can find something on my own." I felt like a jerk. "I should have asked you before inviting Shane over."

"No! It's fine." She held up a hand. "We'll just have to order in again. Or go out." She sighed. "I'm glad he's coming over."

A knock sounded on the front door, and my heart fluttered. I'd taken the time to shower and fix my hair and makeup, like I was going on a date. My period had officially tapered to nothing, hallelujah! I'd dug up a shirt that I'd intended for work that flattered me without looking too corporate. I'd paired that with a short skirt, hoping Shane would like me in something flirty.

Shane hollered, "Hey," as he made his way to the kitchen.

At the same time, the sliding door opened as Micah returned, asking, "So, what's for dinner?"

Jo leaned on her elbows against the island, one eyebrow raised at Shane. "We could order in or—"

Shane rubbed the back of his neck. "Oh. No. Uh—" He ducked his head a little, eyeing me with a coyness that reminded of how we'd left things the night before. "Would you want to go out to dinner with me?"

I shot a glance at Jo, unsure what the protocol was for ditching one dinner invitation for another. She shrugged. "Whatever you want to do is fine by me." Her little grin told me what she really thought.

Jaclyn had never gotten back to me with any more information about Shane, and I didn't delve any further into her fan forum, but if Jo thought it was a good idea for me to go with Shane, then I'd trust her intuition. Or at least that was my rationale for doing what I wanted to all along.

"Yeah. That would be great."

Shane bounced on his toes. "I know just the place." He slipped out his phone. "I'll call an Uber."

Turned out, we only went a few blocks, but I was starving, so I appreciated that he hadn't asked me to walk.

We got out next to a Japanese restaurant at the base of a four-story building with a massive set of fire escapes across the edifice. Unlike Micah's street, this wasn't one of those quaint blocks with the perfectly positioned steps and the tree-lined sidewalks. In fact, the entire street level was dominated by shops.

Shane directed me to a hole-in-the-wall Chinese restaurant. I was a little horrified at first, but as soon as we walked through the door, the smells made my stomach growl.

"What is that? Can I order that?"

We circled half a dozen different things on the menu and then grabbed a table under a blinking fluorescent light.

The atmosphere was a perfect place to talk to him like a real person. If he'd taken me somewhere swanky, I would have felt out of place. Somewhere intimate, and I would have felt awkward. But here, in this take-out Chinese restaurant with three sticky tables and an abundance of individually wrapped duck sauce packets, I could say, "So, how did you start playing with Theater of the Absurd?"

He took me through the early years when he and Noah had started a Black Keys cover band that wasn't working out. They'd picked up Rick to add bass, but things hadn't clicked until Micah had responded to their ad, and then it was magic. "Micah brought song-writing chops, guitar skills, and the front-man charisma we'd been lacking."

After years of hard work, they went from playing small clubs to opening for some of the biggest bands in rock.

The food came out as Shane was explaining how they often fought now, but he believed they were on the cusp of truly breaking out. I couldn't help but agree.

We dug into sesame chicken, moo goo gai pan, fried rice, dumplings, Kung Pao shrimp, hot and sour soup, and a couple of egg rolls. It was way too much food, but I discovered the source of the delicious smells (the sesame chicken), and while we ate, I gushed about his band's better-known songs, not wanting to reveal I knew the deeper tracks too.

"And the rhythm on 'Close Enough' always makes me bang on my steering wheel when I'm driving."

"The thing people never realize," he opined, waving his chopsticks like magic wands, "is that a band without a drummer might as well be an orchestra."

I laughed. "It's true."

"And yet, it's always the damn guitarists who get all the glory. Now, is that fair?"

"Not remotely."

"You understand. But have you ever noticed how few spreads there are of world's hottest drummers?"

I chased a piece of chicken around, then gave up and stabbed it with the chopstick. I'd never gotten the hang of eating with them. "That would be a short article. Unless they put you on every page."

"Naturally."

I snorted. "You really do have it so hard."

His eyes narrowed. "For you."

I waited a beat for the curl of a smile, an arched eyebrow, some sign I should snicker at the joke, but his features conveyed no irony. What could I say to this boy, throwing himself before me without fear after knowing me for a couple of days?

It was crazy. What did he even see in me? I couldn't match his reckless abandon without second guessing at every step. It was too soon to tell him about the men who'd come before him, leaving their individual scars, with fears that had nothing to do with him, fears that he tripped with his too intense interest in me.

But it wasn't too soon to confess about the fandom. That was a much easier part of me to share, and one I'd have to cop to eventually. We were well beyond cool points.

"Shane."

I opened my mouth to go on, but he must've picked up on my hesitation. He hid his sincerity behind the goofy grin I'd originally expected. "I was supposed to say, 'That's what she said.' " He picked up his plate and stood. "I really blew that."

He laughed as he carried the empty trays to the trash. I stared at a glob of rice that hadn't followed the script, escaping the threat of capture from inept chopstick handling.

Right when he returned, my phone exploded in vibrations and that Walking Disaster song. I really needed to change my ringtone.

"Sorry," I said, as I reached back to grab my phone. Seeing Ash's message irritated me to no end. I swiped the notification off the screen without reading it and muted the damn phone before tossing it into my bag.

His eyebrow rose, curious.

"Not important." I wanted to get back to the more serious conversation, the one he'd aborted with a joke, but Ash's interruption had broken the moment. Besides, it was getting late for a work night. "I should head back."

He nodded and held out a hand to help me to my feet. Out on the sidewalk, I waited for him to suggest an Uber, but he spun around on one foot in a complete circle, like he was stalling for time. "I could walk you back to Micah's."

The prospect of accompanying him through the dark Brooklyn neighborhoods again gave me a warm fuzzy. I reached out to take his hand, but he immediately roped me over and put an arm over my shoulder, just cuddling me into him as we started walking. It felt comfortable to press into him, and I allowed myself to slide a hand up his back, just under his shirt hem, hooking my thumb into his belt loop. Here we were, out on a busy sidewalk, two near strangers, and our touch created an intimacy I craved, opened a doorway I wanted to walk through.

He sighed into my hair. "Layla."

And in that moment, I didn't want him to walk me back to Micah's. I wanted him to whisper my name somewhere private. "Maybe we could go somewhere else?"

His breath tickled my ear. "I could show you my apartment."

My chest rose and fell. "How far away is it?"

"It's right here."

Whoa. Déjà vu.

We turned the corner, and I saw that paint-chipped door where we'd kissed the night before. I hadn't recognized his building from the busier avenue.

As if the location released muscle memory, he lifted a finger and ran it across my forehead, tucking a strand of hair behind my ear, before he leaned in and placed a kiss on my cheek. "We could pick up a bottle of wine."

I shook my head, fearing something in the outside world might waylay us or detour me from breaching that door. "I want to see your place."

Now.

His hands trembled as he punched in the security code. My own knees grew weak in the stairwell. Two flights up, he unlocked another door and gestured for me to lead the way.

The transition from public to private was exhilarating, intoxicating, and frightening all at the same time. I held my breath and stepped into his lair.

I'd expected a cookie-cutter apartment like I had back at home: beige carpets, efficient square rooms, and cream walls. Instead, I encountered a fairly open space with hardwood floors, exposed brick, and a unique decor. The vibe it gave was at once cozy and charming, and yet trendy and fun. Smoke-brown wooden floors shone where they weren't covered by large area rugs and colorful furniture.

"This isn't like Micah's place at all."

He followed me in and tossed his keys onto a distressed console table. "Thank God."

His face held all the delight of a parent watching a child on Christmas morning. He knew this place rocked.

To my left, beside the entrance to the kitchen, a bright red spiral staircase wound up through a hole in the ceiling to another level. My curiosity got ahead of my logic. "Oh, I have to see what's up there."

He chuckled. "Be my guest."

As I climbed up, intending to merely peek my head in and then come right back down, I sensed him behind me. As soon as my eyes crossed the threshold, I saw his bed looming before me, and my breath caught.

With Shane blocking my way down, I had no other option than to fully emerge onto his second floor.

The loft had soft brown walls and a loaded bookshelf running across one entire length. An open door revealed a small office with a desk and a papasan chair.

Nervous now about the implications of where we were, I stepped over to the window to check out the view, staring stupidly when the black metal of the fire escape grate met me. I wrapped my arms around my elbows and said, "It's quiet here."

He was behind me in another moment, hands on my shoulders.

I shivered. It had been one thing to throw caution to the wind in the heat of the moment out on the street. But here, with his bed mere feet away, possibilities gave way to probabilities.

When I turned to face him, his expression matched my thoughts. I bit my lower lip, wishing I could stop the questions running through my mind. "Maybe we should have stopped for that bottle of wine after all."

My attempt at a laugh came out shaky, telling him everything I'd been trying to hide.

He exhaled. "Come here." He sat on his neatly made king size bed. His whole place was so tidy, as if he'd been expecting company. As if he'd been expecting me.

"Were you planning on bringing me here?" I blurted out.

"Not planning. Hoping? To bring you to my apartment I mean. Not necessarily up here. I don't mean to rush into this. I just . . . like you."

His nose wrinkled at the quasi-confession, so cute. The image of him straightening up for me endeared him to me. The speed with which he shared how he felt terrified me.

"Would you mind if we just talked for a bit?"

His crooked smile put me at ease. "Most people tell me to shut up."

"I love listening to you talk." And staring at him when he did. I loved the way his features changed so dramatically as he spoke about things he felt passionately about. I loved that he could go from animated to totally still, and somehow his intensity never abated. He gave off all the potential power of a lit stick of dynamite.

But my mind was urging me to beware. His interest in me was too much, too fast. What if I changed my mind?

My history with men had never been successful.

Back in college, when Liam hadn't taken my rejection well, he'd persisted for months, nearly stalking me, trying to make me change my mind. He hadn't done anything illegal or violent, but it left me leery of fanatic devotion. Ironically.

And yet, Shane drew me to him, like the moon pulls the tides. I liked that he didn't play games. I liked that he didn't play it cool.

It scared me in equal measure.

He scooted onto the bed and fluffed the pillows against the backboard. "This okay?"

I propped myself beside him but slid down flat and turned on my side. He did the same, and we faced each other in what felt like a bizarre sleepover.

His mouth was maybe six inches from mine. "What should we talk about?"

Our bodies didn't touch, but I felt as though we did. Something like an electric charge built up in the space between us. "Maybe get to know each other?"

His hand found mine, but he didn't twine our fingers. Instead, he followed my arm until he reached my shoulder and then took a sharp detour to the hair falling over my neck. With a strand twirling between his fingers, he answered. "I'm an open book. Ask me anything."

It was hard to think of words with him looking at me with those dilated eyes, with his shallow breathing, with his tongue running along his lower lip.

"Um, how old are you?"

He smiled. "Oh, good. You didn't research me ahead of time."

If he only knew. "Why? Is there something you don't want me to know?"

He shook his head. "Like I said, I'm an open book. But you can't learn everything about a person from a Wikipedia entry."

Wikipedia! I hadn't even thought to check there. "You have a Wiki page?"

"Not much of one. It would have told you I'm thirty-one."

I peered at him, memorizing the planes on his face, the curve of his lips. I wanted to watch those lips move. "Where are you from originally?"

"Outside DC." He met my eyes, and I knew he felt the desire I was failing to combat.

He let go of the strand of hair he'd been examining and used his fingers like a comb, tickling behind my ear, my neck, along my collarbone.

My brain shut down.

I didn't want to ask him questions or think or glean facts that didn't matter. I just wanted to give in to feeling.

I touched his wrist and traced the length of his arm. His gaze locked with mine.

"What else do you want to know, Layla?"

Nothing. I didn't want to know anything else. "Can I kiss you?"

He didn't respond in words. His eyes softened, and he moved an inch closer. I rolled toward him the rest of the way.

This time when our lips met, we were closer in spirit than in body. He kissed gently, coaxing, like we had all the time in the world, and this deserved our full attention. He shifted slightly, and his hand slid up my spine, urging me closer, until we lined up perfectly, legs against legs, chest against chest. My fingers worked their way under his shirt. I needed to feel his muscles. Every touch brought another adjustment from him until our legs were completely intertwined, our arms wrapped around each other, and our mouths inseparable.

But feeding one need only birthed another. We were as close as we could possibly get, except for the thin layer of clothes that might as well have been a hundred feet thick.

The same thought must have occurred to him because he grabbed the hem of my shirt and tugged. I sat up to help him slip it over my head. Then he spent an eternity exploring the edges of my bra, touching my skin, inching down the lace until he'd exposed my very hard nipple. He devoted his full attention to licking me as he unhooked my bra and slid the straps down my arms. My entire body melted from the delicious magic in that tongue.

A groan escaped my throat, and he pushed me back against the pillows, kissing my lips, my neck, my breasts, hands now exploring my stomach along the waist of my pants.

He was getting ahead of me. "Take your shirt off," I rasped.

With one arm, he had it over his head and tossed onto the floor, revealing a mess of tattoos I hadn't known he had. I traced them, but where one ended, another began. I didn't know why, but they made me even crazier for him. And those muscles. I'd never been with a guy who had such prominent biceps, but his chest was worthy of a Pinterest board—sculpted and hard. I shoved him over so I could devote myself to running my fingers along every pronounced bulge in his six pack. I was overwhelmed with desire to see the rest of him.

"You are insanely hot, Shane."

Seriously, if he'd been drumming shirtless all this time, Noah would have been chasing after his castoffs. Who knew? How was this all mine?

I threw my leg over his waist, savoring the feel of his hands as they slipped around my back.

"Layla, you are—" he took a sharp breath "—I can't think of words that haven't been ruined. Beautiful seems so inadequate."

I froze in place. I'd had men tell me I was beautiful. That was never an issue. I'd never actually felt it though.

Until now.

My body thrummed with pulsating energy, all of it co-alescing like nuclear fission onto an ever-increasing heat at my center. I needed him, and if I didn't have him, I would detonate.

I ground against him, dry fucking him like he was my own personal sex toy.

"You're killing me here," he grunted.

Unable to contain the combustion, I reached down and unsnapped his jeans. Leaning back a bit, I slowly opened the zipper and wiggled the denim down until his erection pressed up through the fabric of his boxers. I couldn't stand the suspense and tore down the boxers, too.

The exact word I thought at that moment was *glorious.* He was smooth and cut, long and thick. And so damn hard.

I couldn't resist touching him. His eyes closed, but his lips fell open as he made guttural sounds. I moved back further so I could drag my tongue across the shaft and wrap my lips around the head. His back arched, and I loved knowing that I was bringing him pleasure that wracked his entire body. His fists bunched up the sheets on either side of his hips.

With a last kiss on the tip, I sat up and worked his pants the rest of the way off, laughing because he still had on his shoes.

I slipped my own shoes off and let him undress me the rest of the way.

"One second." He rolled over and opened a side table drawer, which brought on uninvited thoughts about who might have shared this bed before.

"Shit." He sat up and began digging around, shoving aside envelopes and pens. "Dammit."

He jumped up. "Be right back."

He walked his sexy ass into the bathroom where I heard more violent rummaging. Finally, he emerged victorious and set the condom on the side table. The second he hit the mattress, I grabbed his shoulders and drove my lips into his.

"Whoa." He lost his balance and knocked me sideways. He chuckled at the mishap, but I touched his extended cock, and he lost all his mirth.

He licked his lips, then ran a hand down my hip and up my inner thigh. As if to mirror my thumb stroking his shaft, he slid one finger across my need, intensifying the friction with every stroke.

Unable to bear it any longer, I fell back and pulled him down with me. "Shane," I begged.

He grabbed the condom, rolled it on, and returned to kissing me. He whispered, "I can't get close enough to you."

With one beefy arm planted on the bed, he positioned himself to enter me. I tilted up, throbbing to the point of pain. He hesitated until I groaned, "Yes, Shane."

As reverently as he'd kissed me, as slowly as he'd worshiped me, he drove in, inch by incredible inch, until I felt him deep inside me. All thought fled when he dragged himself back out and plunged in again, faster, asking, "Does it feel good, Layla?"

"So good." It came out on a sigh. "You?"

"Exquisite."

He worked up to a steady rhythm that built pleasure on pleasure, and then he leaned down to suck on my lips, slowing his pace, and caressing me as if I meant more to him than his ultimate orgasm. I'd learned to take care of my own needs during sex, so his focus on me surprised me, delighted me really, and invited me to lavish attention on him, too.

My hands roamed across his strong triceps and clutched his broad shoulders. My fingernails raked his back, and he bent down to bite my lip. All the while, he moved in and out of me, with increasing urgency, but with admirable control. He watched me and when I closed my eyes and moaned, he said, "Is it good?"

While I loved how careful he was to make this about me, what I needed was for him to let go and really fuck me, so I wrapped my foot around his back and gave him a literal kick of encouragement. He got the message and sped up his pace, drilling deep, hitting me again and again in the spot that had me nearly crying from the overwhelming explosion of raw pleasure.

"There," I cried. "Yes." I couldn't say more for fear of losing my already tenuous grip on the relentless journey to outer space.

He breathed my name, and everything broke. My center burst into light and color and sugar and joy. I released an earth-shattering moan and began to sob all at once.

Shane pulled out. "Are you hurt?"

"No. No." I didn't sound convincing at all. My voice quivered with emotion, and tears leaked down my temples. I wrapped my arms around him and pulled him to me tight. "You just sort of sent me somewhere I'd never been."

He dropped beside me, panting, and I worried he'd stopped before he'd finished. I threw my leg back over him, but he laughed and said, "You're kidding." He ran a hand across his sweaty forehead. "I won't be ready to go again for a long while. You just took everything I had."

The proof was in the reality of post-sex condom cleanup after which he came back to bed and tucked up beside me. I laid my head against his chest, and his arms encircled me. I didn't want to move from that spot ever again. I couldn't remember ever feeling so safe and loved and cared for at any other time in my life.

Chapter Twelve

Sometime in the night, I awoke to the sound of my phone's ringtone on the lower floor. I lay on one side of the bed with the blanket tucked over me and Shane's arm laced under mine. I wanted to stay in the warmth of his body, but I had an urgent need to pee. I slipped out from under the covers, careful not to jar Shane. He snorted and rolled onto his back. In the dim light, I could make out his inky chest rising and falling.

Although that body he'd kept under wraps made me go weak at the knees, what really sucker-punched me was his gentle face as he slept. I knelt down and put my chin on the mattress just to gaze at his sweet lips that were quick with an awkward analogy or a surprising compliment or a goofy joke. And they knew how to kiss. His nose was a bit crooked, but that only made him more interesting to look at. His skin was smooth like milk, except for the dusting of freckles, like my own. Thankfully our similarities stopped there, or I might start to worry we'd come to find out we were secret siblings. His hair was red, but not orange like mine. He was ginger; I was pumpkin.

What I liked best about him was absent while he slept. What endeared him to me was how his pretty blue eyes saw me. How his pretty lips spoke to me.

I stood and stretched. There was a bathroom upstairs, but I didn't want to wake Shane—especially not that way. I found my clothes and carefully wound back down the spiral stairs to the lower floor. I'd spied a half bathroom on our way in and located it easily. I peeked in his cabinet to find travel-sized soap, toothpaste, lotion, mouthwash. I squeezed some toothpaste on my finger and gave my teeth a pitiful scrub.

Then I went into his kitchen to snoop around. His stainless-steel fridge was stocked with the usual, though his choices amused me. He had a penchant for brands I'd never heard of— probably from some local store that imported only the finest from the hills of New Zealand or from local organic sustainable farms. His milk came in a glass bottle. He had both jalapeno and raspberry-chipotle-flavored bacon, like he subscribed to some kind of bacon-of-the-month club. I giggled at his imagined bacon fetish.

Glass bottles labeled *Antipodes* appeared to be water, and I hoped it didn't cost $200 an ounce because I took one and cracked it open. I also plucked a brownish pear from a bowl and went to dig my phone out of my purse. I passed another bookcase on my way to the inviting overstuffed sofa in the living area. I perused one shelf, charmed by his assorted collection. No leather-bound editions here. *Brave New World*, *Lord of the Flies*, *1984*, *Slaughterhouse Five*. They were so dog-eared, he'd either bought them at a used bookstore and left them here for show, or he'd read the shit out of them.

I had to question for a moment if his entire apartment was staged. The pretentious food in his kitchen, the implication he read widely, the character in every piece of furniture, the perfectly chosen paint colors—all wrapped in a deceptively shady exterior. I took a bite of the perfectly ripe brown pear, pondering the mystery, and realized that the apartment was a little meta-phor for Shane himself. The best of him was happening on the inside. My little secret.

The battery on my phone was running on fumes, but Shane had left a cord on the small side table. Thankfully it was the right kind, so I plugged it into the port and sat down to find out who'd been trying to reach me.

The most recent text came from Jo: *I assume you're with Shane. Could you text me and let me know so I don't worry?* —*Mom*

Aw. Crap. I should have let her know where I'd gone. It was sweet of her to put the onus on herself for worrying rather than on me for being a rude guest. I quickly texted: *I'm so sorry. Shane and I got to talking. I guess I fell asleep here.*

I paused before hitting send. Should I tell her when I'd be back? I didn't know myself. Would I be able to get into her place in the morning to change for work? I hadn't thought this out at all. I figured if she responded to my text, I could make a plan.

The next text was from my actual mom, approving of Jo's *Hamilton* T-shirt from Monday night and checking in to see how things were going. I didn't respond right away because I didn't want her to wonder what I was doing up at—I checked the time—six in the morning.

It surprised me it wasn't earlier. I glanced out the win-dow and noticed the sky had brightened considerably. The sun would be up soon, and I'd need to decide what to do about my morning commute. A change of clothes would have been nice, but the clothes I'd worn out would suffice. They weren't the same as I'd worn to the office the day before. I could take the subway directly from Shane's. I pulled up the MTA map on my phone, and, using GPS, found the nearest stop.

Once I had a plan in place, I curled up onto the sofa to check my website and see if anything interesting was going on. My first stop was to check if Jaclyn had replied to my private message, although given that I was sitting on Shane's sofa in my underwear, it had become an academic question. Unless I learned he had contracted an infectious disease, there wasn't much she could tell me that would unravel my own current opinion.

But in fact, her assessment matched my own.

Pumpkin,

You piqued my curiosity. We've all been so fixated on the Noah train wreck, I haven't paid much attention to our dear Shane, lately. He doesn't typically pick girls up on tour, though, and I can't find any indication that's changed. I know I said I wouldn't pry, but I can't control what my curiosity does, and I'm deducing the following.

Your friend didn't likely meet him on the tour, and your timing suggests she met him since he got home, which would mean this week, probably at Noah's or Micah's. Micah's makes more sense considering Noah's in a foul mood and not up for hosting. So, the friend could be someone Jo knows, either through her work or from her aerobics classes.

Since you're being coy, I'm guessing it's someone who works with Jo over at the Rock Paper, who wouldn't want to scream her interest in Shane from the rooftops because it would undermine her credibility or something.

My next thought was that the friend might have met him for something work related, like an interview, but who'd want to interview a drummer? (Rim shot!)

Am I close?

Don't worry, her secret is safe with me. I'd love to know if I'm in the right ballpark though.

But you just want to know if he's free and/or a total creep.

Alright, so he's not currently seeing anyone. His dating history is scattered on the boards if you want to dig around. I will tell you is that he's both particular and intense. The boy knows what he likes and he goes after it. Your friend shouldn't take it personally if he doesn't notice her. If he does notice her, she'll already know it. He's kind of obvious.

What else? Dude's sweet and loyal (sounds like a dog, sorry). The only thing she should watch for is Noah who's on the war path. Don't let your friend get into their dog fight. Yes, that's twice now I've reduced them to animals. I love these guys, but they can turn into cave trolls when they get all up in their feels.

I pinched the bridge of my nose, trying to parse out her meaning. What the hell was going on with Noah? And what did that have to do with me? Did Jaclyn think Noah would try to hit on me out of some strange competition? Or did she think Noah would be mad at me for stealing Shane away? Neither situation seemed remotely plausible.

Instead of writing Jaclyn back with questions I couldn't formulate, I went to check out my own forum, scanning through my private messages to clear out any personal requests.

Di$a$ter had sent me a link to some concert video, adding: *Just in case you haven't seen this.*

I opened the YouTube link. Concert video loaded and started auto-playing. Shit, it was loud.

"*Hello, Boston!*" yelled a sweaty, scruffy Adam. "*This one's for you!*" Then the very recognizable opening chords to "Light My Way" rang out. I hit the X again and again until finally the window closed.

It was too late; I heard footsteps above me. Shane's bare feet and legs appeared on the spiral staircase, followed by his box-er-clad self. Every inch of him was solid as a rock. He wouldn't pass as a body builder, but I'd bet he'd sink in a pool full of saltwater. I bit my lip, hoping he'd come straight over so I could put my hands on that body. He did cross to the sofa, but after leaning in for a kiss, he straightened his back and stretched. The waistband on his boxers edged down, revealing his hip bones.

I gaped at the line of auburn hair inviting me like a trail of breadcrumbs. I remembered my way back there.

He caught me ogling him, and his yawn broke into a laugh. "Morning, Star Shine. Hungry?"

"Star Shine?"

"Yup." No further explanation. "Do you like cinnamon? I have these amazing pastries." He didn't wait for an answer and went into the kitchen. I heard the refrigerator door open, then a clattering of pans. He hollered, "Do you drink coffee?"

"Of course," I yelled back.

A few minutes later, he was back empty handed, pushing in next to me on the sofa. "Did you sleep well?"

"Mmm-hmm. You?"

"The best night I can ever remember." I had a feeling he wasn't talking about sleep.

On a sudden urge, I climbed across his lap and straddled him, twisting my fingers in that mop of cinnamon hair.

"Oh, hey," he said. "This is shaping up to be a pretty great morning." His hands slipped under my shirt, up around my shoulder blades, and he drew me into him. Those lips. They were everything.

I broke away from his kiss. "What are you doing today?"

"Rehearsal mostly. You?"

"Work. All day."

His fingers never quit moving, working their way down my sides, to my thighs, then up to my stomach and across my breasts, where he lingered. "Do you think you can get the day off? You should call in sick and come with me."

Oh, the temptation.

As much time as I'd spent supporting Walking Disaster, I'd never once scored so much as a meet and greet.

Way back when they first started out, Adam played pretty small venues, and back then, I could have met the band members by hanging out at the merch table after the show, or even volunteering to work it for free. Since I started running the fan site and they blew up so huge, I'd never gotten closer than tenth row at Bankers Life Fieldhouse, and those tickets had cost me a couple hundred dollars on a scalper site.

For the second time, Shane was offering me something way more valuable than a meet and greet. Experiencing a real rock band's rehearsal—not my dad's band—would be, as they say, priceless.

It would kill me to decline. And yet . . .

"It's my first week. They might frown on that."

"Can't you take vacation?"

I shook my head. "Haven't accrued any yet."

"Can you work remote?"

"Theoretically." At the hopeful look on his face, I added, "I haven't really tested it out, and I don't know if my manager would like me to up and decide not to come in."

"You work for Lars, right?"

"Ultimately, yes. He's not my manager."

"I'm friends with Lars. He runs a music magazine. He understands the importance of accruing music experience. You know he'd want his staff members to spend a day watching a world-class band practicing."

"World class?" I raised an eyebrow. "Which band would that be?"

He pinched my side, gently. "You're asking for it."

"Ouch!" I batted his hand away. "You need to stop tempting me. If I lose my job, I'll have to go back to Indiana."

"Give me your phone."

I reached over and hugged it to me. "No way."

He dragged his teeth across his lower lip, and I thought for a half a second about calling in sick after all. But before I could dive back into him, a timer buzzed, and he lifted me off him with ease and set me down on the sofa. Then he disappeared into the kitchen and returned with cinnamon croissants and two mugs of coffee. He sat on his ankle.

I picked at the pastry and popped a corner into my mouth. "Mmm. Oh, Jesus."

"Try the coffee. It's real Kona."

Of course, it was. I took a sip and stopped scoffing. "Holy God. Why does this taste so good?"

He shrugged. "It's Kona."

Because obviously.

I couldn't tease him about it though. So far, he'd proven he had impeccable taste, and I wanted to savor every mouthwatering bite and every delicious sip.

As if he thought the food could coax me to play hookie, he pressed me with puppy-dog eyes. "Stay here this morning. Come in with me to rehearsal and shoot video for Lars. If I know him, and I think I do, he'd love that."

"Don't you think it's nepotism or at least a conflict of interest if I use you to get content for the magazine? I mean, isn't that like sleeping with your source or some other journalism taboo?"

He leveled me with his blue eyes over his coffee. "Layla, everyone uses their connections in this business. It's not a big deal." He twisted his index finger around mine. "Lars wouldn't hate for you to hang out with your favorite band."

His cocky grin proved his confidence in the belief that that favorite band, for me, was his.

He wasn't entirely wrong. I was becoming a raging fan of one member. Speaking of members . . . My imagination went wild with the things I wanted to do to him, but, sadly, I had a different kind of job to do.

Chapter Thirteen

We finished our amazing breakfast together, chatting about inconsequential topics. He asked me about my job. I asked him about the things in his apartment and fridge. When I got up to get ready—as much as I could, given that I had no fresh clothes—he announced he'd be coming into town with me and began the process of commandeering an Uber.

That prompted me to ask, "So, I noticed you don't have a driver?"

He scoffed. "Uh, no. I'm not a special snowflake like Micah." His goofy smile flat-lined. "You're okay with an Uber, right?"

I hadn't meant to imply I'd come to expect a higher standard of living. It was an innocent question. "Of course. This is way better than the subway."

We descended back out into the real world to find a Toyota Corolla awaiting us. Shane slid in beside me, wasting no time to wrap an arm around me. The constant intimacy might start to chafe, but for the moment, the security it gave me outweighed any future discomfort. Shane didn't play games, and so I didn't have to either. I laid my head on his shoulder and said, "You're just about the nicest guy I've ever known."

"Nice?" He cleared his throat. "That isn't your way of telling me I'm homely."

I lifted my head and shot him a serious side eye. "Are you fishing?"

"Just a little."

"Looks aren't everything, Shane."

He clutched his heart. "Shots fired!"

"You really think I don't find you attractive?"

"Do you?"

As we crossed over into Manhattan, I swiveled toward him and said, "Shall I count the ways?"

His eyes lit up. "Please."

I ran my fingers through his hair. "You have the perfect coloring."

"Narcissist," he laughed. "You have to like my coloring."

"I don't have to, but I do."

"Continue."

I touched his nose. "Your nose gives your whole face character."

"Character. Oh, God, not that."

"It's good."

"Character and nice are two words that people use as euphemisms."

"Whatever." Tracing his bottom lip, I said, "Your lips are sinfully sexy."

He kissed my thumb. "That's more like it. Go on."

"You're the worst."

"Now that's not even a euphemism. Foul."

"Shall I continue to praise your beauty, or shall I move on to your drool-worthy body?"

"Drool-worthy? Really?"

"Oh, hell yeah. Has nobody ever lusted for you?"

He moved closer, with a mischievous grin. "I don't know. Do you?"

"Isn't it obvious?"

Our lips connected, and we didn't speak for several blocks. There was no satisfying us though, and I could tell he was as frustrated as I was by our situation. Kissing him was pure heaven, but heaven couldn't exist without hell, and hell was made of hot, burning fire. And the flames licked my sinful desire.

He drew back, dragging his teeth across my lip with a deep sigh. "Do you really have to go to work? I could spring for a hotel. We could be there in minutes."

"We could do that." I gave him a peck on the cheek. "After I go to work."

He groaned. "You're going to be the death of me."

The cab finally arrived close enough to Times Square, and we got out. Shane followed me into the lobby.

"Well? This is it." I gestured toward the bank of security turnstiles, indicating the end of the road for Shane.

"I want to see where you work." He walked over to a desk and secured himself a guest pass.

I was about to drag a bona fide rock musician up to a rock music magazine. Maybe nobody would recognize him.

We slipped into the office mostly unnoticed. I pointed out the cube where I worked and shrugged. "It's an office. There are meeting rooms over there and a kitchen if you want something approximately like coffee. Oh—" I spun around "—and that's Lars Cambridge's office, but I've never—"

Shane's head shot that way. "One sec."

He walked straight back to Lars' office and tapped on the door frame. I heard a voice say, "Shane!" and then the door clicked closed.

Right then, the air pressure seemed to change in my cube, and I turned around as Gabe said, "So, you brought us a second-rate drummer, I see."

"What can I help you with, Gabe?" I had a brief panic that he'd somehow figured out I'd been the one to send a hoard of pitchfork-wielding commenters to his review. But that wasn't possible.

He craned to get a better view into Lars' office, where Shane stood behind the glass pane, hands flying the way they did when he got animated. I took a second to admire his under-appreciated ass. Honestly, I couldn't understand why all the girls in the office weren't popping up like meerkats to get an eyeful.

Gabe draped one arm over my cube. "You didn't strike me as a fan of their music."

I waited for him to tell me why my taste in music was *pedestrian*, but he surprised me with a curve ball. "So, listen. I've got a pair of tickets to *Kinky Boots* and wondered if you'd like to join me."

"Tonight?"

"If you're free. It's a good show."

"So I hear."

I'd never been to a Broadway musical, and it sounded like fun, but the audacity of the short notice made me balk. Not to mention, I was somehow involved with someone else. But how were Shane and I involved? Occasionally, in the past, I'd assumed things were exclusive just because I'd shared a bed with a guy only to never hear from him again. I couldn't read Shane's mind, but I thought we had the start of something.

If I'd never met Shane, would I have said yes? Gabe was pretty, and his dark eyes might have caught my attention, but I distrusted him somehow.

"So, you'll come with?" His whole body relaxed.

I clenched my fists to turn him down, knowing it might push me into *that bitch* territory. I winced. "Sorry. I've got other plans."

He nodded and inched closer. "I realize I sprung it on you at the last minute. Surely you'll be free later this week?"

How did people navigate social obstacles like this? "I don't—"

Gabe's eyebrow dipped. "I'll let you get back to work." With a small bend at the waist, like he was literally bowing out, he backed out of my cube, slowly, as if he expected me to stop him and tell him I'd changed my mind.

When he turned to go, I stood there glowering after him.

"What was that about?" Shane leaned against the cube wall, almost the same way as Gabe, except instead of adorning it like a gentleman, he made the wall look like a prop in a fake office. His bicep dwarfed the narrow width of the bar running along the top. I hoped he wouldn't bring the whole thing down.

"Nothing. He writes some of the reviews for the magazine."

Shane's head shot up, and he scanned the office. "That guy writes reviews? Shit. I should have introduced myself."

"Oh, he knows who you are."

"Really?" He grinned. "Cool." With a smug nod, he modestly added, "That's to be expected at a magazine that focuses extensively on rock music, I guess."

I didn't let him know that Gabriel had referred to him as "a second-rate drummer."

Out of the corner of my eye, I saw Ajit slip into the meeting room. With a sigh, I said, "I need to get to work." I bit my lip unsure whether Shane intended to pull up a chair and hang out with me all day.

"Oh, right. I guess it would be unprofessional to kiss you here?" He snagged a pen off my desk and tore a corner of paper from my notepad. Leaning forward, he drew a picture of what appeared to be a pair of lips. "Just pretend that's me kissing you goodbye. I'll see you later, right?"

"Yes." Definitely. I was into seeing him later. I was relieved he still wanted to see me. "Later."

As soon as he'd left the office floor, the charge went out of the room, like when the power shuts off all of a sudden and sounds you hadn't noticed before become noticeably absent. The absence of Shane was palpable.

I followed the developers into the meeting room, ready to answer any questions they might have about the changes I'd proposed, only then remembering I'd left my laptop at Jo's.

Crap.

I could get through this meeting, but after that?

Byron broke in before we'd even started. "Layla, do you have Chatter turned on?"

The office used an internal chat program that I had, in fact, not opened up yet, seeing as how I was computerless. "No, sorry."

"Lars is looking for you. Can you go see what he wants?"

My stomach flipped.

Lars Cambridge was summoning *me*?

I swallowed down the immediate panic that he'd figured out I was just masquerading as a competent addition to his magazine and had decided to let me go.

Maybe Shane had mentioned me to him. I gathered my things and left them at my desk before smoothing out my clothes and heading in to see the head honcho.

I'd seen pictures of Lars, but they must have been out of date. The man seated at his desk was weathered like the distressed shiplap I saw in hipster bars. As I entered his office, he gave off the impression he was watching me over a pair of aviator sunglasses, though he wore none. He waited, like he was curious to see what I might do, while I decided between standing or sitting. At last, I took a chair across from him, and he said in a gravelly voice, "Hey there."

"Hi. I'm Layla Beckett. Byron said you sent for me? I'm the new social media admin."

"Social media," he said, though it hung in the air like a question, like he didn't understand the term, or maybe like he could see straight through me to the social anxiety that made my role ironic.

"And web content?" I wasn't sure why I answered him with another question. His narrow eye slits unnerved me. "I'll be helping to configure the software to take advantage of auto tweeting and shares to Facebook, among other things."

His sharp intake of breath seemed an acknowledgment of his sudden comprehension. "Right. Good. It's incredible how much the world is changing."

Lars could best be described as "one cool cat," but he didn't seem to want to chat about the philosophy of his magazine or impart any on-the-job wisdom to me. In fact, he seemed like he'd just smoked a giant bowl and wanted nothing more than to mellow out.

What I did learn from him was that there was no way I would ever be the most underdressed person at the office. If someone had told me he'd been transported directly from the late seventies, I would only wonder why his clothes appeared to have experienced every minute of the ensuing decades. Lars was worn in. I was beginning to think nobody was at all who I thought they would be. Crazy

He continued to watch me through his stoner lids, and it was like we were playing a game of chicken. Finally, I blinked. "Did you need something?"

"Got an interesting visit today." He tore a rectangular piece of paper from a small pad and tapped it on the desk. "You know Shane Morgan, I think?"

"Indeed, I do." So, Shane had gotten me noticed. I wasn't sure how I felt about that.

"He tells me you're a big fan of the band. Said you'd probably get a kick out of hanging at rehearsal with them."

I coughed. "Well, yes. Who wouldn't?"

"You'd be surprised." He glanced at the paper, one eye narrowed further if possible, as if making a decision. Then he turned those slits on me. "Can you write?"

"Write what?"

He leaned back, lifting the mysterious paper off the desk, where it hung between his thumb and forefinger midair. "Articles, blogs, that kind of thing."

"I—" I took a deep breath "—actually yes. I've written my share of blog articles."

His tongue darted out and took a slow tour of his upper lip before he sat back up. "Where exactly?"

"Fan sites?" I offered this information as if I expected it to be met with derision.

"Fan sites." He sat there for a moment, considering. "Can you be more specific?"

And there it was. I knew I'd eventually have to come clean about my moonlighting, but I hadn't expected it to go this way. "Lars, if I were to tell you I ran a fan site for a band, would that be a problem?"

He laughed, though it sounded more like a rock tumbler. "If that were a problem, I'd have fired half the staff years ago. Why? Do you?"

"Yeah. It's not a big deal."

"For Theater of the Absurd, right?"

"Actually, no." The paper he held descended. "Though I am a fan of their music."

His head bobbed an affirmative. "Curious. Who is it, then?"

Could I tell him? "It's kind of embarrassing."

"The Backstreet Boys?"

I burst out laughing at the dated reference. "Why would you think that?"

One shoulder rose in the world's least committed shrug. "You said it's embarrassing."

I wondered if he'd ever heard of any recent pop bands. He obviously kept up with rock music. But I'd been raised by parents who wanted me to appreciate the full spectrum of music, from classic rock to the cheesiest of boy bands. Appreciate. Not necessarily love.

"I actually do like them, full confession. Just not enough to devote time talking about them online."

"So, who then?" The paper fell to the desk as he leaned forward on his elbows, fingers steepled. "I can keep a secret. Come on. Now, I'm dying to know."

For the first time I saw the whites of his eyes, and I froze.

Could I trust him? Was it a secret I'd be able to keep forever? Ash wouldn't stay mum about my dual life indefinitely. And once the forum knew, how long before the connection trickled back upstream? Even Jaclyn had nearly identified me from the little bit I'd shared with her. I bit my lip, nervous now. Was I actually about to confess my alternate identity?

Yes. Why not?

Straightening my spine, I exuded the confidence I didn't feel and then exploded my protective barrier. "It's actually Walking Disaster. The site's called Talking Disaster."

His eyes widened to nearly normal. "That's you?"

My surprise matched his. "You know it?"

"Well, yeah. We get trackbacks from your site, and I've clicked around. Lots of energy there." His weathered face cracked out a whole smile. "This is a fortuitous turn of events. You have exactly the youthful vibe I'm hoping to tap into."

At the words "youthful vibe," I nearly chortled, but I wanted to be absolutely clear on one point. "So, there's no conflict of interest or anything, right?"

"Conflict? More like a confluence of interest. Just think about the traffic we could get from the pool of subscribers you've collected."

"They'll definitely click over if I drop a link to interesting content."

"They trust you." His eyes drifted back to the forgotten paper lying on his desk, and he slid it over. "This is the address where Shane said he'd be rehearsing all morning."

I picked it up. Something had been scrawled in black ink. I could sort of make out the numbers, though if it were a Captcha code, I wouldn't feel one-hundred percent confident I'd be getting it right. But I had Shane's phone number, so I politely took the paper, folded it over and tucked it between my thighs.

"Thank you. Can you tell me what exactly you're hoping for?"

"One of their new songs. Shane promised he'd let you record something they're working on."

"Wow." Shane hadn't played with an empty hand. My first reaction was stunned delight. Spending my day immersed in rock band pheromones was the closest thing to heaven next to Shane's bed. A small red flag of warning stirred, but I pushed it down.

"It's free publicity for them. And I'd like to see what you can do with it."

As badly as I'd wanted to meet Lars, I suddenly wanted nothing more than to be out of his office and on my way.

"Go talk to Kate about video equipment."

With that invitation to leave, I bolted. Uneasiness pricked at the back of my head, but this opportunity excited me. As I walked down to see Kate, I took out my phone and texted Shane for clearer directions.

Chapter Fourteen

Shane's text directed me to an area in Brooklyn I'd never been, but not too far from where he lived. When I emerged from the station, he waited at the exit, scrolling through his phone messages.

I tapped his forearm, and he blinked against the sunlight, a smile breaking out to compete with the brilliance of the afternoon. His freckles splayed out like a galaxy across his cheeks and the bridge of his nose. The glare forced his eyes to narrow so that his beautiful eyes were imprisoned by those long cinnamon lashes.

Neither of us moved or spoke for a full minute. Just as I'd been inventorying him, he'd been studying me in the new light of day. I gave him a wry grin and sighed happily. "Should we go?"

"It's not too far. Let's walk." He crooked his elbow out, and I snaked my hand through.

For the third time in as many days, we strolled together on a Brooklyn sidewalk, and once again, he reeled me closer to him and wrapped an arm around me, high-school boyfriend style.

"I missed you this morning, Star Shine."

The admission hit me with a mix of conflicting emotions. Just like Jaclyn had said, he was a big, dopey puppy—adorable, but overwhelming. If he'd been any other guy, his intense attention so early on probably would have freaked me out.

But Shane wasn't any other guy. Time and time again, he revealed himself to be different than I expected.

I nudged him and teased him with my own choice of nickname. "Missed you, too, Cuddle Rock."

He snorted. "Cuddle Rock?"

I shrugged and cast my eyes up at him. "Yup."

His mouth turned down in a poor attempt to conceal a burgeoning smile, and I chuckled.

Maybe I'd been a social hermit for such a long time, I no longer knew how to handle sustained human contact. I was a castaway on a deserted island, and romance was a ship headed for adventure. Right now, I needed to get my sea legs and steel my nerves for the possibilities ahead.

As if he were reading my mind, he pulled me closer, and my disquiet melted away. It was impossible to resist his charms, so I stopped trying. Instead, I leaned into him and relished his arms enveloping me as we strolled together.

I wondered how often one of the band invited a girl to hang out. It was an instant aphrodisiac. Surely they'd used band practice to get chicks at least early on.

"Thanks for getting me out of work. Or at least getting Lars to let me go on a field trip."

"It was a little selfish on my part." He kissed the top of my head, and not for the first time I felt like I must be dreaming.

After a couple of blocks, we stopped in front of a building that looked like an abandoned mechanic with three metal garage doors covered in graffiti. Shane produced a key and unlocked a red door that opened with a grinding creak. Previously muffled noise burst out as a guitar solo mixed with an erratic bass line.

"This is where you rehearse?"

How many of their fans had figured that out? Anyone could hang out here and wait for them to appear. I scanned the immediate area, but the only person hanging around was a lumpy, pale guy across the street, leaning against a tree, earnestly reading his phone. Just as Shane held the door open for me, Mr. Potato Vampire lifted his eyes and met mine. It may have been my imagination, but I got the sense he was recording us.

When I got inside the entryway, I asked, "Did you see that guy?"

"Which guy?"

"Across the street. Looked like he just came up from some underground lair."

Shane peeked back out. "Oh, that's just Jim."

"Jim? Who's Jim?" My voice rose to compensate for the cacophony coming from farther in.

"Nobody, really." He leaned against the wall. "He's this guy who runs a fan site out of his basement or something. He snoops around sometimes."

"A fan site?" My stomach felt sour.

"I guess you call it that. He's not a very good fan."

That made me laugh. "What's a good fan?"

"Well, I mean, he doesn't say very nice things about us, or anyone really. He's not exactly a jerk or anything, but he kind of likes to sensationalize things a bit."

If there was a sensational Theater of the Absurd website out there other than Jaclyn's, I'd never come across it. "And he follows you around?"

Shane scratched his chin. "I don't know what he does, honestly. His site isn't about us so much as whichever bands he can glom onto. It's insane what people will do to get a little closer." He curled his nose, obviously disdainful of that level of overinvestment.

I wondered if anyone might think I'd taken my job only to get closer to Walking Disaster. Obviously, I wasn't rejecting these invitations, but band access had turned out to be a side benefit to an already golden opportunity.

Surely, I wasn't the same as Jim.

"So, why's he here?"

Shane shrugged. "Probably spying on Noah."

As if that answered the question. I lifted my phone and opened a browser. "What's the name of his site?"

"Fan something. I wanna say *Fan Blog*, but that sounds pretty lame. I honestly don't read it, but he usually introduces himself with a laminate badge like he's official."

I Googled, but as I suspected, the name was too vague. I decided I'd ask Ash later and shoved my phone back into my bag.

Shane pushed off the wall. "I mean, he's got to be pushing thirty. You'd think he'd have a job or something."

I coughed. "Yeah. You'd think."

He took my hand. "Speaking of jobs, can I show you around my workplace?"

We followed a fluorescent-lit corridor into a cavernous space that had clearly once been a garage, converted with soundproofed walls, guitars lining the floor, a huge set of drums in one corner, and various other instruments and amplifiers scattered around. My dad would have fainted at the sight. The three aluminum doors that fronted their rehearsal hall had been boarded up, and a makeshift stage stood where the hydraulic lifts had been.

"Wow." My jaw dropped.

Shane waggled his eyebrows, aware it was a cool-ass space. The whole thing was such a turn-on, I entertained illicit fantasies about doing him on one of those amplifiers.

Sadly, we weren't alone.

Noah, Micah, and bass player Rick, now standing still with silent guitars, made for a quintessential garage-band tableau. Micah smiled and waved his pick in greeting. Rick set down his bass and lit a cigarette. Noah shot us a glance, then absolutely shredded his guitar with what sounded like a ghostly shriek.

Shane dragged me back into the corridor. "Let me take you on the rest of the tour, such as it is."

Back the way we came, an office had been transformed into a temporary kitchen with a refrigerator and a microwave. Farther in, what was once a waiting room held a sofa and some other rickety furniture. On the table sat a duffel bag.

Shane palmed his forehead. "Oh yeah, Jo thought to send along some of your clothes and your laptop."

"That was super nice of her."

"She also said you're welcome to stay there tonight still."

"Oh, I—" hadn't thought that far ahead.

"But I was kind of hoping—" Red crept up the side of his neck in an endearing display of shyness. Oh, to have five minutes with him alone on an amplifier.

"Let's see where the day leads, yeah?"

"Yeah." He backed toward the hallway. "If you really need to work, we can set you up in here. The fridge is filled with snacks and drinks. *Mi casa es tu casa.*"

I blinked rapidly. If he'd manipulated my day job just to stick me in the corner, I was going to lose my shit. "Uh. Lars expects me to record your new songs. If that's okay."

He brightened. "Of course. That was one of my better ideas, yes?"

I relaxed, laughed, and agreed. "Do I have time to change?" I ran Vanna White hands over my day-old outfit.

"Yeah. They'll be tuning their guitars forever. If you want to hide in the waiting room until we play our new stuff, I'll understand. Or you could come watch for a bit." His lower lip disappeared between his front teeth, and it suddenly registered that he was nervous to have an audience of one: me.

"Are you kidding? I plan to catch every second."

Noah's voice exploded from the other room. "Kind of need a drummer in here."

Shane gave me a quick kiss, and I said, "Go on."

As he turned, I swatted his butt, and he took a step without peeling his eyes off me, which resulted in him tripping over my computer bag. He recovered with a little flourish, and I wished I could have a few more minutes alone with that adorkable boy.

Once he'd closed the door, I dug into the bag Jo had kindly packed and stripped off the day-old duds. I appreciated slipping into fresh-smelling clothes, even if I had to exchange a nice blouse for a T-shirt. At least she'd packed another skirt as an option.

Out of all the possibilities, she'd selected my well-worn Theater of the Absurd shirt, and I had a brief moment of panic picturing her discovering my disproportionate amount of Walking Disaster merch. What would she make of that treasure trove?

When I found the bag of makeup, my toothbrush, and a tube of toothpaste, I decided that Jo would be my forever friend even if I never saw her again after this week. I prettied myself up and shook my hair out. I felt human again when I walked out into the rehearsal hall.

Noah wolf-whistled when I crossed the room and said, "Hey, Ginger Spice." I couldn't believe I'd thought he was the attractive one just a few days earlier. I ignored his taunt and settled cross-legged on the sofa, studying the camera with feigned interest.

Shane hollered over, "I know this can get boring, so let me know if you need to take a break."

That made me chortle. "You have no idea how not boring this will be for me."

Micah's voice reverberated low through the amps as he pressed his mouth to the mic. "Love the T-shirt."

I rolled my hand with a regal bow of my head.

"Super fan." Shane grinned, and I knew he meant it as an endearment.

Noah shook his head. "Did she promise to fuck you if you brought her here?"

Shane rose off his stool, eyes narrowed. Crash cymbals wobbled. "Noah, I'm giving you one warning. Don't start."

Noah laughed. "I guess that answers that." He lifted his guitar strap over his neck and turned his back to Shane.

I had no idea what was going on between them, but I didn't think I'd ushered in the tension. This was the *Behind the Music* moment when the narrator announced, "Backstage things were falling apart."

Micah strummed a chord and said, "Come on. I don't want to be here all day."

Shane settled in behind his drumkit, and once in place, he ruled all he surveyed.

Chapter Fifteen

The minute I was settled in with my camera, Shane smacked his sticks together four times and yelled, "We are Sex Ba-Bomb!" Then he attacked his set in a passionate but undisciplined drum solo.

The other three looked at him with varying levels of disgust, waiting until Shane stopped.

In the sudden silence, Noah asked, "What the hell was that?"

"Improv?" laughed Shane.

"It's from *Scott Pilgrim*," muttered Rick. "Great movie."

Micah imposed order on the chaos. "We were planning on the Black Keys cover? But Layla suggested we try a Walking Disaster song. Maybe we could give 'Expulsion' a go?"

At the mention of a cover, I checked the camera battery and flipped my phone to airplane mode just to be sure it didn't interrupt.

Noah groaned, but Rick just said, "Cool. It's been a while since that song was a hit."

"You can play it, Noah? Right?" Micah's taunt did the trick. Noah played the opening riff, then sucked on his teeth like a baby.

After a little more discussion, Shane gave a real count off and kicked off a rhythm at the same time Rick started a bass line. Noah's fingers flew across his guitar while he lifted a foot in a step he never took. Micah strummed his guitar and then cupped the microphone with a pick lodged between his thumb and forefinger. Then he began to sing the first verse.

Chills.

Sure it wasn't a real concert. When they performed for an audience, they more than brought it. They'd made a name for themselves for their surprising and interactive live shows. When I saw them at the amphitheater outside Indianapolis, Micah jumped off the stage and went back to the vendors and bought a beer—while he was still performing the song. Shit like that made them unpredictable and fun to watch.

This was a whole different world. If I wanted to, I could have walked right over there and touched them. They could see me. Micah winked right at me, and I wanted to squeal.

I was a sucker for lead singers. Often beautiful, but always charismatic, they made everyone in the audience want to be them or have them. Micah was no exception. He'd always been a favorite of mine, although nobody could hold a torch to Adam for sheer sex appeal.

Noah went to town on a crazy lick and reminded me why I'd crushed so hard on him for so long. There's nothing sexier than watching a man seduce the hell out of the neck and body of a beautiful piece of wood. My whole life, I'd been a guitarist girl.

But there was a drummer hiding behind all of the glitz, and when all was said and done, I wanted to go home with him.

I'd somehow become an insider for the time being, and my mind followed that trajectory to the possibility of one day getting this kind of access to Walking Disaster. It wasn't likely, but the possibility was there, when it hadn't been before. Like

I'd gotten five of the six lottery numbers and just needed a little more luck for that last one to click into place. If I played my cards right, I could maybe even get backstage passes. I could be the envy of every fan girl on the interwebs.

I let those asshole thoughts have free rein until I hit the limit of my imagination, which involved revealing myself to my fan site family as someone with legit connections to the band and not simply a girl with a website who hid behind anonymity and fear.

Contact fame wasn't my true end desire, but the temptation lurked. What I really wanted was right here. I got to be a private audience of one and hear this incredible band put on a show for me.

I didn't want to normalize this experience because I knew I was nothing more than Cinderella at the ball, and at midnight, my life would revert to normal. All these Prince Charmings would stay in their castle. I didn't have a glass slipper to lose.

I pulled my knees up under my chin and listened, head bobbing to the beat. Speaking of the beat, I zeroed in on Shane who kept the rhythm so perfectly, he disappeared into the background. Occasionally he'd do something fancy with the high hat, but mostly he banged and banged and banged.

Like he had the night before. *Ba-dum-cha.*

He made eye contact with me for a moment and twirled the stick around his knuckle, catching it in time to bring it down again. I clapped my hands together, and he grinned.

If only he'd done it shirtless.

At that thought, my heart beat in the wrong part of my body. *Pulse. Pulse. Pulse.* The term *heartthrob* suddenly made perfect sense. The discomfort was almost too much to bear.

Once the song came to an end, I made sure the camera kept rolling. The song they'd played was cool, but fans would worship me if I could share the interactions between songs. Fly-on-the-wall stuff. I wouldn't miss that for anything.

Micah said, "Noah, tighten up the solo after the bridge."

Noah kept his eyes on the neck of his guitar as he plucked the strings. "In due time. I'm not in much of a mood to jam today."

"Not asking you to jam, Noah. I'm asking you to work out your shit before you get here."

Noah didn't respond or bother to even acknowledge Micah further.

"And Rick, you've got to bring some more energy. I couldn't even hear you through the second chorus."

"Noted," was all Rick said before he sat on an amplifier and lit up a cigarette.

"Shane." Micah turned his back to me, but his voice carried. "You were on point, but I imagine that's because you're performing for someone." Shane shot me a glance with a cheeky eyebrow waggle. "Keep it up."

Noah shook his head. "Of course, he's on point. He's hoping to get laid."

I hit stop on the video. I didn't like where this was going.

Shane just laughed. "Projecting much?"

"Fuck off, Shane."

"Say please."

Micah held up a hand. "Can you guys flirt later? We've got a setlist to figure out."

Noah said, "Whatever."

They worked through a couple more of their regular songs and a cover of "Little Black Submarines," which was one of my favorite Black Keys songs.

Unlike at their shows, Micah stayed planted at the mic, playing and singing like your run-of-the-mill front man. The energy was low, like they were going through the motions, like they'd forgotten some of this would be posted on the *Rock Paper* e-zine.

Micah said, "Layla, are you ready to record?"

Then I realized he must not have known I'd been recording the entire time. I wasn't sure what to do with all that video.

They hadn't told me not to capture it. "Yeah. Are you going to do your new music now?"

Noah's eyes widened dramatically. "She's not going to record our new songs."

"Why not?" Micah clearly didn't take any shit from any of them. Of them all, he probably had the least to lose if the band fell apart. He had his solo gig, and he had the highest profile of all of them. He could probably replace any one of them and the band would continue on. Micah *was* the band.

"Look. I get that she wants to hang out and take pictures to show her friends. I get that Shane's all gaga over her. But come on. Isn't it enough that she's getting a personal concert? Do we have to let her leak new music?"

"Noah, stop being a dick. You never gave a shit about fans leaking bootleg. What's the difference? Are you worried you didn't put on your makeup today?"

I snorted and covered my mouth when Noah shot me a nasty side eye.

"Okay. Fine. Let's start with 'Sugar Rush.' "

Micah heaved an exhausted sigh. "Good." He shot a glance at Rick then Shane. "Ready?"

Shane answered with a "One, Two, Three, Four!" Then they all came in at once.

The song was heavy, grungy, with a throwback sound. Jane's Addiction, maybe. Noah brought the electricity, playing his guitar like he'd been injected with a dose of adrenaline. He prowled the stage area and even moved out in front, toward me, pursing his lips in a kiss he might have blown. He smoldered into the camera, and I could almost feel the hearts exploding all over the Internet.

While he kept hogging all the attention, I leaned a little to my right and framed Shane in the view, zooming closer to capture his relentless attack across all the drumheads. I pulled back and focused tight on Micah since the majority of fans would want to examine his every expression. While he could go as bananas as Noah, Micah had the ability to completely disappear into a song, too. When he did, it was like the song consumed him. He'd gone there now. His eyes closed, and he made love to his guitar.

I gave Rick some air time, then zoomed back out so I could record Noah strutting around like he was the star of the show. If I didn't know better, I might have thought so. His ass looked mighty fine in those jeans. He made sure I had ample opportunity to immortalize his posterior for posterity. But he'd been so ugly to me, I'd rather kick him than kiss him.

They played three more new songs and finally took a break. Micah sat on the sofa beside me, dripping sweat everywhere. Shane paced in a semi-circle a few feet away, like he was waiting his turn. Noah took off for parts unknown, and Rick just sat on an amplifier with another cigarette.

"Can I see how they came out?"

I handed Micah my camera. "I got some earlier songs, too," I confessed. "And the covers."

While he played back a few seconds of video, Shane moved closer, and I lifted my eyes to his. He crossed his arms, tapping his fingers against his biceps, still drumming, and my gaze lingered on muscles that glistened from his exertion. I bet my hands would slip right along his body right now.

Micah interrupted my dirty thoughts. "These are great."

Relief. "So, I can share?"

"Yeah. I don't care what you share, but Lars will only want one of the new songs. The rest is miscellaneous stuff for the diehard fans."

He was right about that. I didn't feel right posting their banter, though. Not without Micah's permission. "I caught some of your arguments. Should I delete that?"

"If the fans don't know Noah can be a turd, they're not paying attention."

He handed me the camera back. "So, which new song did you like the best?"

"Wow. They were all so good. Um—"

He chuckled and looked up at Shane. "She's diplomatic." He touched my arm. Micah Sinclair touched my arm. "Seriously, though. We don't need to be coddled. Did you have a favorite? Or were they all shit?"

"No! They were all fantastic."

His eyebrows rose a half an inch, and his clear blue eyes pierced me. Damn, Jo must melt every time he looked at her. It would have been unnerving enough even if I hadn't seen those eyes on the glossy cover of a magazine. But he was waiting, so I gave him my honest opinion. "I loved them all, but I liked the second one best, I think. Does it have a name?"

"The one that went—" and he sang a little of the chorus "—*Hit me like an aftershock?*"

He was singing a foot from me. The corners of my mouth felt like helium.

"That's the one."

Micah nodded. "Cool. Then that's the one we'll play at our next show. It's called 'Aftershock.' "

I felt dumb. "Of course."

He stood and thanked me. "Feel free to post those other vids over on Facebook or on our message board if you want. Shane can point you to it."

I became aware for the first time that I'd been gaping at Micah right in front of Shane. As soon as Micah was out of earshot, I said, "Sorry for the fawning, but super fan and all." I hoped that would cover for enjoying the eye candy far too much.

He twisted his lips into an inscrutable expression. Reluctant acceptance? Judgment? Displeasure? He sighed. "It's fine. I've seen worse."

"Yeah?"

He sat beside me. "Oh, God, yes. There's a girl who used to come to all our shows, and at the end, she'd somehow manage to get Micah into a bear hug. I don't know how it started, but Micah's too nice and afraid of turning away any single fan."

"Wow. He just let her hug him?"

"I'd stand behind her making signs at Micah asking if he needed a rescue, but he'd shake his head." He shrugged. "Eventually, Micah just stopped coming out after shows because of shit like that."

"So, I passed the test?"

"He probably didn't even notice. It's the way things are in Micah world."

Shane had noticed, and I felt like a jerk. "Well, right now, I'm fawning over a certain drummer. By the way, you are incredible."

His face lit up. "Good?"

"Very." I dragged my teeth across my lower lip. "And fucking hot."

He quickly glanced at the empty studio, then leaned in to steal a kiss, just a peck. He started to pull away, but like gravity, he drew me toward him, and my lips caught his. I could feel him smile, and so did I, essentially wrecking what might have turned into a passionate makeout.

"Maybe we could sneak out. Go back to my place?"

Whether he was teasing or not, his would-be plan was foiled when Micah came back in, trailing Noah, and said, "Hey, can we finish this up so we can break for lunch?"

Shane stood, adjusting his pants. "I need to walk around for a minute before we start back up."

I turned airplane mode off, and my phone notifications started coming in one after another. I had a missed call from my mom and voice messages from Ash. I groaned. "Ugh. I'm gonna have to check on this."

"Do you want to go back to the waiting room? You won't miss much. We'll just be going over shit Micah wasn't happy with."

I weighed my options. I really wanted to sit through the rest of the rehearsal, but if Ash was calling me, things had gone south according to her DEFCON meter.

With a wistful look at the guys setting up for another set, I took my phone and headed to the breakroom.

I played back the messages from Ash. She rambled on incoherently about trolls, and I couldn't piece together what she was freaked out about. Trolls were easy to deal with. It wouldn't take but a minute to call and tell her how to handle it.

I hit call, and her voice poured through. "There are a bunch of people suddenly commenting all over your reviews, all disagreeing with you and calling the fans idiots. I didn't notice right away because—"

"It doesn't matter, Ash. Give me a minute to log in."

I had to go back out to the rehearsal room to grab my laptop bag. Shane had settled back behind his drum and was tapping out a beat while Noah noodled around. I waved at Shane. He responded with the most famous drum beat from "In the Air Tonight."

I laughed with my fist over my mouth. He settled into another rhythm, and it took me until I got back to the kitchen and Micah kicked in with the rhythm guitar for me to recognize their song "Close Enough."

I remembered his words the night before.

"I can't get close enough to you."

My thighs turned to liquid at the memory. I wanted to think he'd played that on purpose, just for me, and I preened a little. Over the speaker, Ash asked, "What the hell is that? Where are you?"

The closed door provided no respite from Shane's relentless drumming.

"Um." I'd forgotten about Ash. I would have loved to confess it all, but besides her inability to keep a secret, she'd want to know everything, and that could take a while. It was too much to explain, and she'd be mad I'd kept the secret. I'd deal with it later.

"I'm at a bar." My nose scrunched up as I processed that terrible excuse.

"At noon?"

"Co-workers took me out for lunch."

"Why are you calling me then?"

"Uh." Fuck. I couldn't think of anything.

"Is that band covering Theater of the Absurd?"

"I hadn't noticed." I opened the hotspot on my phone. "Hold on. I'm almost online."

Ash kept talking. "The usernames are all one word, like Unforgiven and Puppets."

"Aren't those from Metallica songs?"

Had we done something to piss off Metallica fans? With everyone so bored, waiting for anything to do, a fan war would be like throwing a spark into dry kindling. I didn't have time for it. A few trolls, we could handle. An assault? I already dreaded the expended energy putting out the fires.

But I couldn't understand why they'd want to attack us. "Do you know if Metallica fans are prone to start feuds?"

"No idea. They hit about ten of your blog posts, but most of the comments are on your review of the new album."

"Did they go to the forum?"

"Not yet."

Not yet, but if this was the start of a board war, they would.

"I've got the blog up now." I scrolled through hundreds of comments, kind of laughing at how lame they were.

There's no way you listened to this album. Did the band pay you to write this?

This is a shit album. You're a shit reviewer.

I scanned the rest without reading. "When did this start?"

"The earliest one I found was from around seven-thirty. The last one came about an hour later. They're all roughly a minute apart. What's weird is they're grouped. Like they hit one blog post, then moved on to the next."

I shook my head. I couldn't believe I was missing the band's rehearsal for this stupidity. The comments weren't going to hurt anything. Most of them were on old blog posts which had been buried by time. If anyone was reading my archived reviews, they must be bored. Or vengeful.

"I think we should just leave them and pretend we never saw them. That will piss off whoever it is." I disconnected my hotspot.

She snorted. "Won't they just come back and do more?"

My turn to laugh. "What's the worst they can do? Drive traffic to the blog? Make me an extra twenty-five cents this month?"

"You're always so levelheaded, Layla. I should have known you wouldn't panic."

The music in the other room came to an abrupt halt, and I felt a stab of disappointment and regret for choosing to take care of business rather than enjoy the last few minutes of my fly-on-the-wall experience.

"Thanks for helping out, Ash."

"No problem. Traffic's down anyway. People are getting restless though. It will be good when the guys are on the road and we can get back to discussions about setlists and sharing vids."

"For sure."

The door cracked open, and I closed the lid on my laptop before anyone could catch a glimpse of my dirty little secret.

Shane said, "Rehearsal's over," a little too loud, like he'd suffered temporary hearing loss.

"Rehearsal?" came out of the speaker, and I shook my head at Shane.

His eyes widened. "Oh, sorry. Didn't know you were on the phone. I'll be outside." He shut the door behind him, leaving me to clean up another toxic spill.

I tried dodging yet again. "Sounds like we've got a plan then. Let me know if our friend comes back."

"Layla, where—"

"I've got to go. Talk to you later."

"Okay. Thanks again."

It was becoming painfully obvious I was going to have to confess to Ash and then pass the torch to her entirely. She could run the forum easily without me. She just needed more confidence. Surely someone would agree to take over the blog for me. I couldn't keep it up if for no other reason than I'd just wasted twenty minutes investigating a trivial issue instead of watching a rock band rehearse.

The blog troll would have to stew a little longer. Shane waited for me.

Shane.

That one thought pushed all others out of my head, and I packed up, curious if lunch would be with all of the band or only him, finding myself not caring either way as long as I could enjoy the swoops in my belly whenever he looked my way or touched me. My hands trembled as my imagination took those small gestures to their logical conclusion and I pictured him on his back under me again.

Rock n' Roll. Literally.

Chapter Sixteen

Shane leaned against the wall with one leg bent, looking so hot in the setting sun, it was a wonder he hadn't scorched the earth. The orange light made his hair look like he'd caught fire. Did these guys really just wander around here at all hours of the day and nobody accosted them?

Right now, there were probably a couple of fans online arguing about their favorite Theater of the Absurd song lyric, and I'd just lived the dream. It was giving me a serious sense of cognitive dissonance to compare the reality of these guys against years of my own imagination.

When Shane saw me, he pushed off the wall. "Freedom at last."

I couldn't help but chastise him a little. "You know the rest of the world has lunch breaks that last about as long as you work."

He grabbed my hand, twining our fingers, like it was no big deal, like we'd been a couple for longer than, oh God, less than twenty-four hours. Barely more than twelve. My head spun with how quickly things were changing.

"Speaking of food, the guys went on ahead. I told them we'd catch up."

"Pity," I joked and squeezed his hand.

"We don't have to." He slowed. "I don't need to spend another minute with Noah."

"He obviously thinks I'm in the way, anyway." I stopped altogether and faced him. "He's so—"

"It isn't you." He hooked his arms around my back and pulled me into him so my face was inches from his. "I swear. He's got something going on. He's also a total prick. But not usually quite so deserving of a swift kick to the nuts."

"You sure?"

He pressed his lips against my forehead. "Positive, Star Shine."

I pushed him away so I could see his face when I asked, "Are you ever going to tell me why you keep calling me that?"

"Maybe." His coy expression left no doubts he planned to milk the mystery a while longer.

"Fine." I turned my back on him and started down the sidewalk.

Shane caught up, laughing. "I promise I will, but do you want to go eat with the guys or not?"

I'd barely eaten anything since the croissant at breakfast, and my stomach churned. "Yeah, let's."

He ushered me into a local fast food burger joint that gave off a dodgy vibe, but seeing a crew of rock musicians casually hanging out in such a dive made my entire year. I never thought about where they might eat, but if I'd been forced to imagine it, I might have pictured somewhere that had silverware. Or catering.

A couple of teenagers at a booth had their phones out and were taking their own selfies with an impressive photobomb in the background. Micah signed an autograph for a mom wearing a baby in a front-facing sling while Noah sat with one foot up on the Formica bench and his arms draped across the back, a half dozen leather wristbands hanging loose.

They were kings of the greasy burger bar.

I made eye contact with the gawkers, feeling both self-conscious and exceedingly cool when I slid in next to Shane. A waiter brought out a mess of bacon burgers, and the guys continued to squabble over some decision they hadn't ironed out regarding which cover song they wanted to focus on. Micah wasn't happy with their rendition of the Black Keys song, and since I'd recorded both covers, he asked if they could be leaked out to fans to find out which was working enough to take on the road.

They all looked at me like I had some kind of say in their plan. Micah said, "Do you think you could?"

Shane reached over and blatantly stole a fry from Noah, which didn't go over well. Noah smacked Shane's hand and then hunched over his food like a caveman.

"Damn, Noah. Can you try to remember who your friends are?"

"Fuck off, Shane. Am I supposed to just put on a happy face and act like everything's okay?"

I watched the two of them, afraid to say a word. I couldn't help but speculate on what could be eating at Noah. My brain ricocheted from testicular cancer to creative differences to a pregnant groupie to a bad review to a hike in his tax rate. I had to sit quietly. It was none of my business.

That immediately changed when Noah gave me one nasty look and blurted out, "How about when you catch *your* girlfriend fucking some other guy, I'll come and tell *you* to cheer up."

There was too much to unpack in that statement. First, Noah's anger suddenly made more sense. If his girlfriend had cheated on him, no wonder he'd been such a grump. I felt pity for a split second until I understood the implied insult hurled at *me*—as if Noah believed I would one day do the same to Shane. My instinctive response was to defend my honor, but even as my mouth opened, I heard the echo of the word *girlfriend* and clammed up with a quick look to Shane for some idea how to react.

I could see my input going over like a lead zeppelin, but I didn't know any way around this particular Yoko Ono moment.

"Don't drag Layla into your shit." Shane placed his white-knuckled fists on the table. "Apologize. Right now."

Noah's lips, which I used to find so beautiful, curled into a sneer of disgust, and he spit out, "I apologize, Layla. You're obviously *not* using Shane as an entry-level rock star to work your way through the band."

The sarcasm dripping off his words could have burned a hole through the floor.

My jaw dropped open, and I finally found my tongue. "How dare you?"

Whatever thrill the band vibe had given me, Noah had just completely torn the scales from my eyes. "You know, you're right about one thing. I did consider myself a fan of your music, and even of you, Noah. But you're not who I thought you were. And I'm not who you think I am." I grabbed my bags. "And I'm leaving."

I stood and headed toward the door, unsure where I was going, but I wanted to get there before the tears stinging my eyes started to fall.

Shane said, "God dammit, Noah," and ran after me. He put an arm across my shoulder, and that, more than anything else he might have said or done, made me feel like I wasn't alone. He was on my side. "Fuck lunch. Let's go on back to my place."

Out on the street, once we'd cleared the view from inside the hole in the wall, I grabbed his forearm and twisted him to face me. "What was that?"

His cheeks sported splotches of red from his own anger. "Noah's been out of control all week."

"Why is he taking it out on you? Or me, for that reason?"

"It's not about you. His girlfriend dumped him last Saturday night." His eyes narrowed, and he added. "For Samuel Tucker."

I gasped at that. "The lead singer of Whiplash?"

"The very same. Noah met the girl on one of our tours. I don't know what he expected."

If that was true, she'd done the exact thing Shane said fans did to him, climbing Noah to gain access to another musician. Samuel Tucker was a much bigger deal than Noah. Whiplash played huge arenas.

Damn. What a cold-hearted bitch. Poor Noah.

"I'd warned him she was a fame fucker. And then two days after she proved me right, I met you. I think he's jealous you're so obviously not working an angle. That's why he's mad at me. You got caught in the crossfire."

"And so now he's suspicious of any fan girl?"

"Pretty much." He shook his head. "Unless he pulls his shit together, one of us is going to have to go."

"What about the band?"

He scowled. "Fuck the band."

That didn't make me feel better. Of the two of them, Shane was probably the more easily replaced. After all, Noah wasn't a household name, but he was known to any serious music fan.

"Oh, Shane."

"Come on, Star Shine." He dropped a little kiss on my forehead. "If you come home with me, I'll confess the origin of your nickname."

That did the trick, and I let him lead me the few blocks back to his apartment.

Once inside, he ran up the spiral stairs and returned with the last thing I expected to see him carrying: an acoustic guitar.

"This is going to be brutal, but I'm going to let you in on a little secret: I sometimes write songs."

"You write songs?"

His cheeks reddened. "I'm trying. What people don't realize is that Micah doesn't just make money from the band. He writes more songs than we can record, so he sells his music to other artists. Most of the money he makes now is from song-writing credits. I don't expect to ever achieve what he has, but he's an excellent role model, and he's pushed me to be more courageous with my art."

I didn't know any of that, but it explained why Micah had the private car while Shane had the Uber service. Still, I wasn't interested in the business side of the music industry.

"I just want to hear the song."

I dropped on the sofa, feet crossed under my knees, eager to hear what Shane might play for me. I braced myself for what I would say if he sucked. It was one thing to tell someone as competent as Micah that one song was better than another, but Micah was a professional songwriter. Shane's effort might need some gentle encouragement. I was prepared to blow smoke up his ass. I loved the fact that he was letting me see this side of him, after knowing me only three days.

That fact kept blowing my mind. It seemed like we'd always known each other.

"Okay, so let me warm up a little." He began by strumming some chords, then a single string. He adjusted the tuner for a bit, and then he started walking his fingers on the neck in a way that was far beyond my abilities.

"Show off."

He blushed. "Just a little."

"You're raising my expectations."

"I was hoping to raise more than that."

I snickered. "That's what she said."

Finally, he stopped fiddling and assumed the guitarist position. "You're not allowed to laugh. In fact, flat out lie if you hate it." He took a deep breath. "I can't believe I'm about to do this."

He strummed a melody that sounded incredibly familiar, then sang the first line from Layla.

I threw a pillow at him, and he ducked so it bounced off his back. He sat up, laughing. "Sorry. Couldn't resist."

"You just lost any chance you had of me taking pity on you."

He grimaced. "Crap. No pressure."

"It will be fine. Play."

"So, by way of introduction, Micah recently challenged me to write a love song, but I didn't have a girlfriend, and my exes would inspire a different kind of song. I've got a pocketful of sad songs. Those are easy to write."

My heart picked up a beat at the notion of this guy sitting on the floor playing a love song for me that nobody else had ever heard. Was I dreaming?

"Without further ado, then."

He strummed a C, then an E, an F, then back to C, standard chords. The strum pattern was more interesting, kind of down, down, pause, up, pause, down, up, down. He played this pattern through twice, then coughed and laughed. "Shit, here goes."

His face lost all traces of humor, and his eyes closed. And there he was, a man with a guitar. Sexiest thing alive.

His voice cracked on the first line but smoothed out. "Another tequila sunrise/misty and gray."

If I'd worried about his ability to play or sing, those fears were assuaged right off the bat. He wasn't doing anything super fancy, but he handled the guitar like someone who'd spent enough time with it to instinctively know how to slide between frets without missing a note. His voice was a bit scratchy, a little bit bluesy, but low and warm. His sexiness quotient kept going up, up, up. I leaned back and listened to what he was saying, what his song meant to convey.

Empty house
Empty bottles
And the sun sets
On another lonely day

So much for the love song. He was painting a depressing picture of hungover heartbreak.

> *Hope glints against the darkness*
> *Pinpricks of light*
> *Fill the night sky*
> *Moonage daydreams*
> *And her star burns bright*

I covered my mouth with my hands to stifle a gasp. I loved the Bowie reference, and the unexpected turn from pessimism to hope took me completely off guard. His eyes opened, and he sang the chorus, baring his soul, wide-open.

> *Constellations turn*
> *Turn around in flight*
> *Stars shine*
> *Shine against the night*
> *Wish I may*
> *Wish I might*
> *Find my one true love's light.*

Tears brimmed in my eyes, as the revelation of what he'd meant by calling me Star Shine hit me. He strummed a few more chords, then dropped into a minor key, and sang, "This is where the bridge will go." Then went back to the chorus, but he was laughing now. He sang it again, then stopped. "I haven't really finished it."

He set the guitar to the side, and I took the opportunity to rush him. His chest shook as I climbed into his lap, wrapping my arms around his neck.

"That was incredible."

"You think?" His eyebrow dipped with suspicion, like I might be humoring him.

"Amazing. Really. You need to finish it."

He nuzzled into my neck, and his lips brushed my skin, lighting me up like the stars in his song. He whispered in my ear. "Maybe I will now that I know how it ends."

I didn't know what to say. How could he think of me as the one he was searching for? Was he just looking for a body to fill the void, the empty house?

"Shane."

"Don't panic. I know we're just getting to know each other. I'm really not this impulsive." He adjusted his position and created space between us. "Normally, I wouldn't even be able to be so honest with someone like this, but I keep finding new reasons to think that maybe this is stronger than I thought it could be."

"What do you mean?"

He ran his tongue along his lower lip, and I followed it with my eyes, jealous. I wanted to suck on that lower lip, but he was clearly contemplating. I didn't know if he was hesitant to extrapolate or if he was searching for the right words. Finally he said, "When I first saw you, I knew I wanted you. Physically, I mean. I considered myself a lucky guy when you felt the same way."

My heart beat a bit faster. I'd wanted him right away, too. "Mmm but you get sexier every minute."

"The more I learn about you, the more I like you. The more I think you might be the girl from my song."

My pulse traveled south and was now drumming out an urgent need.

"You think you created me with your art? Be careful, you know how that usually works out."

"How's that?"

"She'll wrap herself around you and never let go."

His arms snaked around my waist. "That would be terrible."

There was mounting evidence he was being sarcastic, and I adjusted myself so I could feel that evidence in just the right place. Face to face with him, I gave into my growing need to be as close to him as physically possible and pressed my lips against his. He sighed and slid his strong hands inside my shirt, holding my back, drawing me to him for a lingering kiss.

When I looked down, my eyes landed on the bulge in the center of my view, and I reached down and unsnapped his jeans. Just like that.

"Layla," he sighed.

I slid down the zipper. Shane's boxers beyond didn't provide much in the way of camouflage, and something monstrous lurked beneath the white fabric. I had a wanton desire to wrap my lips around that part of him.

I lay one hand on his thigh and nudged him onto the sofa, where he fell back. He didn't need any more encouragement than that to weave his fingers in my hair. His hooded eyes mirrored the desire I felt.

There he lay on the sofa, partially naked, totally panty-melting. I got down on my knees. Yup, just like the song.

It was time to get to know his penis in greater detail. We'd only had a brief introduction, and I couldn't stop thinking about what I'd seen the night before.

He watched me without protest, as I grabbed the waist of his jeans and boxers in my fists and tugged them down. I was glad he didn't try to tell me not to worry about him.

They say it's not what you have, but what you do with it, and I've always believed that, but Shane's cock was simply beautiful.

I stared in admiration. "Damnation."

As if he didn't already know it, he said, "Yeah?"

"Oh, yeah." I wrapped my hand around the base, excited myself by how hard he felt. "I want to watch you lose your mind."

As I ran my palm along the shaft, he sank down further into the sofa with a soft moan.

I dragged my thumb through the precum pooling in the hole in that perfect head, then followed with my tongue, licking, sucking, stroking. His eyebrows scrunched together, making him look more like someone in terrible pain than pleasure.

When I'd brought him close to the edge, I reached under and tickled his balls, loving how they tightened.

Everything in his body arched.

I picked up the rhythm, my mouth sucking his corona, my tongue licking the sensitive skin beneath, my right hand and thumb stroking up and down his shaft, and my left hand now gently kneading his completely hard balls until he cried, "Layla, I'm going to . . . Oh, God."

His face went slack, like he was in free fall, and when he blew, it was impressive.

I licked him until he dropped his hands on my shoulders and tugged at me to climb into his lap.

"Fucking hell, Layla."

I climbed up next to him and nestled my head on his shoulder. "Yeah?"

"Oh, yeah." He sighed. "A girl who can do that? I might have to hang onto forever."

Between the song he'd played just for me and watching him fall apart so sweetly, I wanted him more than I had the night before, but when his hands roamed down my thighs to the edge of my skirt, I stopped him.

"I need to—" I didn't know how to be delicate about how gross I felt, having gone to work in dirty clothes that morning. I blurted out. "Can I use your shower?"

His grin turned wicked. He practically carried me to his upstairs bathroom where he slowly peeled my clothes off, then his own. Under a spa-like shower head, he reverently shampooed my hair, between soapy kisses. He lathered up his hands so they slid across my neck, my shoulders, my arms, my stomach, and my breasts. His fingers found where I needed him. Kissing me slow and sweet, he stroked me until my knees began to wobble.

I feared I might collapse before he'd gotten me there, but he shut off the water and wrapped me in a perfectly fluffy towel that he probably bought from the Argonauts, then carried me to his bed, where he laid kisses down my body right back to the spot that was craving his tongue. And what a talented tongue he had. I groaned out his name as he slid a finger inside me while his mouth sucked and licked me until I was chasing after the pleasure he was giving me.

And the one thought that put me over was the certainty this wasn't casual to him. Shane was someone who could be in my life, like this. I could be his Star Shine.

After I fell apart, Shane lay beside me, not talking for once, just sharing the post-sex haze that felt an awful lot like love.

Then his stomach growled, and I kissed his nose, and we rolled off in search of clothes.

We ordered in and sat across from each other at his tiny kitchen table, him in boxers that barely hugged his hips, me in a pair of his sweatpants that swallowed me whole. His borrowed T-shirt smelled of him and threatened to fall from my shoulder. As we ate, he reached over and lifted the slipping neck back into place, followed by a touch here, a caress there.

And we shared secrets.

Some secrets.

Chapter Seventeen

$\mathcal{F}$or the second day in a row, I went to work wearing a day-old outfit and a two-day old grin. Dreamy-eyed, I rode the elevator, replaying the night before—and the early morning before I had to leave.

The words Shane whispered in my ear.

The way he touched me, gently and then desperately.

My hand drifted up to my neck where I was certain a hickey was forming.

Once I got to my desk, I dropped my laptop onto the charging port and went for a cup of coffee. As I passed Byron's office, he called my name. I stepped through the door, and he acknowledged me with a quick nod but kept typing furiously. When his fingers finally stilled, he motioned to a chair.

"I understand you had some fun yesterday."

Five days in, and I was already going to be reprimanded. "Lars sent me. It's part of the whole 'web content' side of this job."

He sucked in his cheek. "Hmm. Yes. I'm not really seeing how all that fits in with your day-to-day responsibilities. We're still waiting for your requirements doc."

"Right." I kicked myself for not sending that over the day before. It was all but done.

"And will you be able to attend our daily stand-up today?"

I narrowed my eyes at him. "Of course."

He turned back to his computer, so I left and went to get the coffee I'd need to wake up. Shane had kept me up way too late.

In the breakroom, while I waited for the machine to finish sputtering, two ladies I hadn't met came in, midway through a whispered conversation.

"But then he said, 'Why don't we just get dinner instead?' "

"I bet he didn't even have tickets to the show."

"And that was the only reason I said yes."

They glanced over and caught me staring, so I quickly left the room, wondering if they'd been discussing Gabe and his promise of *Kinky Boots* tickets. If so, Jo wasn't wrong. He really was the office Lothario. It would be a relief to know his constant attention wasn't specific to me.

Armed with a steaming cup of Joe, I dug up my doc, scanned it for thoroughness, then emailed it over to Byron and cc'ed the developers.

Then I started splitting the videos I'd recorded, hunting for the new song Lars wanted. He'd set me up with permissions for the *Rock Paper* contributors' section, so I started a new blog post and uploaded the video file.

I'm a huge fan of Theater of the Absurd. Yesterday I had the amazing opportunity to sit in on band practice and soak up the experience. The guys generously allowed me to record them performing their new song 'Aftershock' which sounds like a definite hit. Judge for yourself.

I centered the video below my paragraph, then saved it to draft and emailed the link to Lars with the heading: *Is this what you had in mind?*

My name was going to appear on an article on the freaking *Rock Paper.* How was this my life?

Freed for the moment, I texted Jo to apologize for abandoning my stuff at her place, promising I'd come and get it, but then what?

As if she read my mind, she texted: *Are you sure? You're welcome to stay here. Or I could have Micah swing your things over to Shane's.*

I couldn't impose upon her indefinitely, and moving my stuff to Shane's felt presumptuous and impetuous.

I'll check craigslist today. I've put it off too long.

She had a better proposal: *Call or text Zion before you do that. My old room is still vacant.*

I stored his phone number in my contacts and made a mental note to call him after lunch.

Then I got back to work for real. I went to the morning meeting where Ajit had no problems with my designs. During lunch, I lined up all the Tweets to send out for the latest articles. Once we got the new features in place, this chore would become obsolete, but there was no reason to ignore the potential click stream.

My Chatter app blinked in the taskbar with a message from Lars. *Can you come by?*

When I opened his door, I could hear the music from my video playing. Lars bopped his head along with the rhythm.

"I love this. It's exactly the kind of fan-sourced video feel I wanted."

I breathed a sigh of relief. "Thanks."

"Did you get any other videos? Anything that might add to the insider experience?"

"Yeah. I have a lot of video. Too much, really."

"And could you put together a bit of a narrative? I was hoping to really capture that excitement of a real hardcore fan getting to hear her favorite band in such an intimate context. Don't hold it back."

"You want me write like a fan, not a *Rock Paper* reporter?" It went against everything I was trying to present here, but he was right that it would appeal to the band's fan base in the same way as Gabe's review hadn't.

"I want you to pick out the videos that you think best encapsulate your experience, and let your readers feel like they were there, ya dig? Like a—"

"Fly on the wall."

He nodded. "Exactly. Can you make that happen?"

"Absolutely."

I returned to my desk in a stunned haze.

No sooner had I packed away all the super fan thoughts about Walking Disaster than I had to manufacture over-the-top enthusiasm for a totally different band. What I felt for Theater of the Absurd did qualify as serious fandom. I had all their albums. I'd covered them plenty on my blog since they were considered a "Related Artist."

But until Monday, I hadn't known the name of the drummer.

Meanwhile, I could hold a ten-minute conversation about whether or not Walking Disaster's drummer, Hervé Diaz, had gotten liposuction after the most recent tour. I'd even unearthed video from when Adam drummed for the band, back before they'd changed the lineup and the name of the band from The Pickup Artists. I could discuss the stylistic differences between Adam and Hervé. My level of fandom for Walking Disaster bordered on obsession, and although I could tell you I wasn't a crazy person, anyone who wasn't a part of our community might say otherwise. I knew too much.

Did Lars expect that level of excitement for Theater of the Absurd? Or did he even know that level existed?

I could only do what I could. In addition to the new song I'd already added, I uploaded the two covers, since Micah had asked me to, plus a couple of their old songs and some of the less explosive bantering to my post. Then I set about bragging and gushing, like the biggest fanatic that ever fanned.

I hit save to draft and forwarded the link over to Lars for his approval. I didn't think I could enthuse any more than that. On the plus side, maybe it would make Shane think I loved his band the most. On the minus side, it was going to make him wonder if I might be a little overinvested. Particularly in his bandmates. I knew what Lars wanted. I'd been doing this too long not to know what a fan experience sounded like.

With a free moment, I finally placed a call to Zion.

"Hey, it's Layla!" My phone anxiety threatened to shut me down. "We met the other night? At Adam's?"

"Oh, Layla. How are you?" His enthusiasm didn't match my own.

"Um, so, Jo mentioned you might have an extra room to rent." I chewed on my lower lip, fighting against the awkward hesitation. "I was wondering if you're looking for a roommate."

"Right. Jo said you might call."

I waited a beat, tapping my fingernails on the desktop. "Of course, I can check craigslist if you'd rather not room with a total stranger."

"No, don't do that." An exhale followed. "You met Andrew, right?"

"Yes. The other night."

"It's just that he's got his stuff all over the apartment right now."

"Oh. I understand." My face flushed with the sting of rejection.

"He'll be going out of town in a couple of days though, and he normally stays at his own place anyway, so if you can maybe tread water for a few days?"

"Of course!" My heart sank. I was sure Jo would let me stay a bit longer, but this was no way to live. I should have let my dad come help me find my own space. I was practically homeless.

"Can you swing by next week?"

"Yup." What else could I say? "Thanks, Zion. I appreciate it."

"Sorry I can't be more hospitable. Timing."

"No worries. I'll be in touch."

As I hung up, I got a response from Lars. *Perfection. Let's post it on Monday.* My mood rebounded. I was on an emotional trampoline lately.

Publishing under my own name meant my online family wouldn't recognize it as me, the persona they knew as Pumpkin. It was petty to want their praise and congratulations on top of everything else, so I swallowed those feelings. I was plenty lucky with what I'd been able to do.

Speaking of which, I made a quick perusal of the fan forum, made sure the drama on the blog comments had stopped at some point, and then checked my private messages. That Sandman guy was back.

So, I went to the comments section like you told me to. I see that I'm not alone in my disregard for your shallow opinions. Maybe you'll figure out that reviews should be left to the professionals.

I should have left it alone. He wanted attention, but I could never resist sparring with the assholes. Not to mention, I'd been involved in a lot of shenanigans over the years, and my spidey senses were tingling.

One time, a competing forum started stealing our best concert photos and claiming them as their own. It became a huge drama. Our posters created hundreds of fake identities, or "sock puppets," so they could flood the other site with accusations of theft. It brought home how unregulated and deceptive the Internet could be. Nobody was who you thought they were, and people would go to weird extremes when their passions were inflamed.

Remembering that incident, I opened the admin center on the blog and started checking the origins of those new comments. Every single one originated from the same IP address. The same as Sandman.

He was a one-man show.

I returned to my private messages and composed a reply.

Gee, Mr. Troll. That's a subtle way to try to make sure I see all your sock puppet posts. Please grow the fuck up.

It made me feel kind of nauseated once I'd actually typed it out. It felt good to write it, but sending it was a whole different matter.

My cursor hovered over the Send button, but my phone rang out the chorus to "Close Enough" I'd chosen for Shane's notifications, and I Xed out of the message without sending. Instead, I picked up my phone, smiling at Shane's text.

Guess where I am?

I responded: *Middle Earth?*

Before my phone could explode in sound again, I lowered the volume. Shane's next text came in muted, vibrating.

Oh, good. For a second I worried your phone was off and all this was in vain.

All what?

I'm here.

You're joking.

It's 5. I know you're free. We're invited to Jo's for her birthday dinner. Let's go find her a present.

I shut down my laptop and threw it in a bag. I was on my way to the elevator in minutes. Just before the doors shut, a hand shot in and stopped them. Gabe stepped in.

"Got any plans, tonight?" He inched closer. The space was so confined, I'd back into a wall if I moved. I didn't relish the idea of being trapped by Gabe.

"As a matter of fact, I do." I straightened my spine, hoping my demeanor might make him back off.

Thankfully, the doors opened, and I quickly strode over the polished marble floors through the turnstile to get some distance. Shane crossed the lobby toward me. I heard Gabe say, "Mmm-hmm. I see," as he continued out into the late afternoon traffic.

Pretending nothing had happened, I flashed Shane my brightest smile, which only grew bigger when he leaned forward and scorched me with the kind of kiss I'd only dreamt about.

"Come on, Star Shine. There's a cool Broadway store around here somewhere, and I know Jo loves T-shirts from musicals."

He slipped his hand in mine, and we headed out. I'd been in New York City less than a week, and everything felt like a fairy tale.

Chapter Eighteen

We arrived at Jo's around seven. Shane added our contribution to the pile of presents stacked on the coffee table. An actual chef worked at the kitchen island while Micah, Zion, Eden, and Adam observed. Baby Joshua slumbered in his car seat.

My eyes goggled at the sight. "You have your own chef?"

Jo waggled her eyebrows. "Yeah. Micah's been learning to cook, but it's easier to learn from a professional than attempting to grab recipes online. Pratosh comes by on special occasions."

Everyone rearranged themselves so Shane and I could sit next to each other. I ended up right next to Adam, so close our arms might have brushed if I'd been so bold.

Even though I'd seen Adam a few days before, my shock and awe had reset back to wide-eyed bewilderment. It was Adam fucking Copeland after all. I'd seen him on TV. He'd been on the cover of the *Rock Paper*. It would take me more than a week to adjust to casually rubbing elbows with him, literally.

Shane's arm snaked around me. I leaned into him, and everything seemed normal again. When he pressed a kiss to the top of my head, I reached up to clasp hands with his, draped over my shoulder. He pulled me tighter, and I melted a bit. How could someone's body feel like a second skin in so short a time? How could he turn me on while simultaneously putting me at ease?

Micah caught my attention when he started cutting up veggies like a sous-chef, asking questions about the spices and other culinary techniques.

Jo explained to me how they'd found Pratosh. "Micah figured we could get some authentic Kerala cuisine. Kerala is the part of India where my dad lives. Do you like curry?"

I nodded. "I think so."

While they worked, Zion said, "So, Layla, why don't you stop by on Wednesday? The room should be ready for you by then."

Jo said, "Oh, I'm glad you guys were able to work that out! Not that I mind having you here, Layla. I just think—"

"Wait, what?" Shane's voice rose.

I faced him. "I'm talking to Zion about renting his extra room. I can't keep living out of a suitcase in Jo's guest room."

"You could move your stuff to my place for now." He scratched his chin and held his breath in a way I read as a mirror to my normal awkward posing.

"That's really nice, Shane, but—"

"I mean, until Zion's ready. I'll be gone in a couple of days anyway."

It did make a certain sense. I'd imposed on Jo long enough, and I'd assumed or at least hoped I'd be going home with Shane again tonight. "Okay."

His face brightened, reminding me of the night when I'd first seen him sitting in this very kitchen. When I'd first locked eyes with him, like he'd been my destiny. And here we sat now, not even a full week later, with expectations, with history. He waggled his eyebrows, happy again. "Good. Now that that's settled . . . Where's the food?"

Diced chicken sizzled in a wok. Soon, Pratosh began ladling it out, and Micah popped a bottle of champagne.

"Hope y'all don't mind, but this is non-alcoholic." He poured and passed out six flutes. Raising his, he said, "Happy birthday, Jo!"

Everyone chimed in. "Happy birthday!"

As we ate, conversation went from hopes for Jo's success in the next year, to the amazing food, to touring, and landed on the topic of writing music, which Shane eagerly joined in. Zion, Jo, and Eden started a side conversation on their end of the counter, so I sat between Adam and Shane while Micah cross talked.

"It's the meter that kills me," Shane said. "Do you just write without regard to meter and fix later?"

Adam took a drink of water. "Depends. The structure can change a lot as a song morphs, so I try not to get too bogged down in lyrics at first."

I started to lose my grip on normalcy. *The* Adam Copeland was discussing his songwriting process a half a foot from me. I'd spent one third of my life trying to get into that man's head, analyzing song lyrics with other fans, speculating how they related to things going on in his personal life or in the world around him.

"You write the music before the lyrics?"

He frowned, thinking. "Sometimes. It's more that I don't get married to any particular lyrics until we've hammered out the melody. Like with 'New Dawn,' there's a line that goes, *we welcome a brand-new sun.*" He sang it, and I leaned forward, wanting to ask him if he was singing about his son, but he went on. "The original lyric went something like, *in the light of the rising sun,* but I had to re-tool it a bit to fit the music. I'm kind of happy with it."

My eyes fell on his mouth as he spoke, and I could superimpose a decade's worth of images on those lips, from photos, to music videos, to concert bootleg. I'd seen thousands of photographs of those lips. I'd watched them make love to a microphone. I'd watched them smolder on the jumbotron, sitting in the audience, too far away to see them for real.

The reality of those lips curled up, pursed, or moved with the words he spoke with that voice I'd heard nearly every single day for ten years.

I hadn't started my fan site to drool over Adam. In fact, I'd started it to learn how to build a website. When the band blew up, and people flocked to my site, I learned how to put up ads so I could earn revenue. Traffic increased. I made it my mission to be a one-stop source of photos, videos, news articles, tour info, and community. And in time, the site consumed my whole life.

My whole life devoted to this one man.

What did Adam think of what I did? Did he approve? Did he even care? I wanted to ask. Did my fan site make him proud?

"Layla? Hello?" Shane tapped me on the shoulder, and I pulled my gaze away from Adam and refocused my eyes. All the guys were watching me.

Adam said, "The salt, please? I didn't want to reach over your plate."

"Oh, sorry." I passed it over, wondering how long I'd been mesmerized into a complete drooling idiot.

Shane covered for me. "You have to bear in mind, Layla's still a bit starstruck."

Adam laughed, but I didn't think he was mocking me. He struck me as so realistic and even modest about who he was. Charisma rolled off him in waves, effortlessly. He lived in the vortex, but he didn't let it consume him.

"Layla?" Shane chided.

I'd done it again. I blinked my eyes a few times. "I'm sorry. It's just a lot to process."

"Take your time." Adam kept on eating as if we were talking about the weather rather than me nearly professing a devotion that I'd spent half my life cultivating.

"She's actually a cool fan," said Shane. "Lars sent her out to check out our rehearsal, and she recorded everything without rushing the stage."

"Do people do that?" I remembered thinking about doing that very thing.

Shane dragged a piece of chicken through the brown sauce. "They do at concerts."

Micah blotted his lips with a napkin. "We used to be able to go out into the audience for part of the show, but it's getting harder to do that."

"For you, maybe." Shane's dig had a bitter tinge.

"You should send Rick out," Adam joked.

Shane guffawed at that suggestion, and we all laughed. From what I'd gathered about Rick, he was the kind of musician who clocked in and performed proficiently but hadn't signed up for the rock star life. And the rock star life had left him alone. I barely remembered he was a part of the band.

Adam turned to me, his dark eyes like pools of ink. I reminded myself not to fall in again. It wasn't lust or love. Just plain-old circuits misfiring. I knew he was just a man, but I'd built him up to be a rock god, and my brain couldn't make sense of it.

He cleared his throat. "You should come to our rehearsal. I mean, if you wanted to."

I nearly fell off my stool. "Are you serious?"

"It's a cool idea to release some behind-the-scenes stuff to the magazine. I could talk to Lars."

Cue a volcanic eruption of fan babbling. "Oh, my God. I know Lars would say it was okay because he's been talking about how he wanted to put up more fan-driven content to generate the kind of excitement that would bring more traffic." I bit my lip to shut myself up.

Adam exchanged a glance with Shane. "What do you think?"

Shane put a hand on my shoulder that felt like he was saying, *Mine*, though I wasn't sure if the message was intended for Adam or for me. I measured my breathing and tried again, slowly. Normal. "I mean, I'm sure he'd use it."

Shane squeezed my shoulder. "Yeah, you should ask him. I think Layla's going to be gushing about us in an upcoming blog. I can't wait to read that."

I flashed back to what I'd actually written. If Shane expected gushing, he wasn't going to be disappointed.

Adam nodded. "What about your friend? The huge fan of ours? Maybe she'd like to do it."

"Ash? She lives in Portland." Not that I'd let anyone else take my place.

Shane narrowed an eye. "Your best friend lives in Portland?"

"She's not really my best friend. We met online."

He looked at me like I'd said we met on Mars but let it go. "Hmm. Do you think you know enough about Adam's music to do it?"

I coughed. Was he joking? "I'll be fine. Swear."

"What about next Friday then?" Adam's eyebrows rose, and I studied him for another moment. "Shane won't miss you since he'll be gone."

Shane hugged me into his chest. "That's exactly why I'll miss her."

"She could come with us," offered Micah, and my composure began to seriously falter. "If she wants."

I thought of Byron. I could get Friday off maybe. The weekend was mine, but an entire week to follow a single band? I doubted even Lars would find any benefit to that. "Maybe one day."

Micah jumped up and saved me from further embarrassment by lighting the candles on the cake. As we all sang "Happy Birthday" to Jo, I took a snapshot in my mind of this amazing moment.

I had nobody to tell.

After Jo opened her presents and the party broke up, I excused myself to gather my belongings.

Upstairs, alone with my thoughts and my things, I appraised my situation. Was I making the right move? Jo would let me stay another night, but it was her birthday, and I was willing to bet she and Micah were eager to have some privacy. They weren't shy about showing their affection in public, and I was sure they were unabashedly physical in private.

I could go home with Shane and keep my things with Jo, but what was the difference between sleeping over at Shane's with or without my stuff?

Funny how'd I'd been worried about a one-night stand a day ago, and now I was parsing out the legalities of shacking up.

Plus Shane would be leaving on tour, and I could move out before he got back. Once I'd settled on a course of action, I carried my suitcases to the top of the stairs.

Shane bounded up and grabbed them for me. He'd already called an Uber, and it stood waiting out front.

As I babbled out my thanks and goodbyes, Jo gave me a hug and whispered in my ear, "If you change your mind before you find a place, please give me a call."

Eden slid one arm around my back in a side hug. Joshua cradled in her other arm. "Either way, when they're on the road, feel free to come hang out with us."

Jo shot a glance at Micah who was wadding up gift wrap cast offs. "I can always use the company when they're gone. Come on Friday, and we'll marathon all the rom coms Micah doesn't like to watch."

Eden nodded. "Ooh! I'm so there. Can we rent *Guardians of the Galaxy*?"

Jo snorted. "That's not a rom com!"

"It's not? But it's got Chris Pratt!"

It cracked me up that Eden was married to a man thousands of women fantasized about and still had her own celebrity crush.

I told them, "I'll definitely be there," still in shock that this had become my life.

Shane called for me, and I climbed into the cab ahead of him. He didn't immediately scoot over next to me, so I slid against him and nudged him. "Hey."

"Hey."

"Are you mad at me?"

"Of course not."

I tilted my head to look him straight on. "You're annoyed, though. I'm sorry I keep losing my shit."

"I'm annoyed at myself, not you."

"It's not me, it's you? Should I be worried?"

He cut his eyes at me finally with a little sigh. "No. It just stings to watch your girlfriend fall under the spell of your friends. I get it, mentally, but it's tough to watch."

Girlfriend? There was that word again. I guess I was.

"I'm sorry. I have to confess I'm a bigger fan of his than I let on." It was a relief to unload some truth.

"No shit. That much is obvious."

"He's kind of a big deal. You said so yourself."

"I would have thought the novelty would wear off." He looked out the window. "Like I said, it's me, not you. I've seen it happen before. Too many times."

"Seen what?"

"The gravitational pull."

"There's no gravitational pull. I'm just starstruck."

"Your eyes turned into saucers." He shook his head, but at least he chuckled, and I felt less chided than mocked. "I expected to see them spinning like a hypnotized cartoon cat."

"I did kind of space out there. It's surreal for someone like me. I'm from central Indiana. I've never met anyone. I'm suddenly thrust into your world. Give me a minute to catch up."

"Adam said it best. Take your time. I'll try not to die of jealousy every time you make googly eyes at my best friends instead of me."

I wasn't making googly eyes. Okay, maybe I was, but how could I explain that it was more like meeting Jesus than Fabio. I was in awe, but I had no romantic feelings for any of those guys. Sure, I could objectively appreciate their glorious gorgeousness, but Shane had nothing to worry about. At least not on that score. Shane was real. Those people were all make believe.

"Trust me. You don't want me to look at you like that." I clasped his hand and attempted to adopt a come-hither gaze.

It must have worked. The rest of the tension seeped out of him, and he leaned over to brush his lips against mine, but his anxiety must have transferred to me. I couldn't put my finger on what was bothering me. Maybe I was just out of sorts from moving my suitcases yet again. Maybe it was the speed at which things were changing. It felt like something lurked in the closet. It was time to have a conversation about where things were going with this relationship. But not in the back of an Uber.

I pulled back. "How long until we get home?"

"Home." He smiled. "I like it when you say that."

I didn't have the heart to correct him with "temporary home" right then.

The driver stopped in front of the Japanese restaurant. Shane grabbed my bags from the trunk and carried them up the stairs. Once inside, he said, "I should probably give you this," and handed me a bronze key. "That one's for the door, and I'll text you the downstairs key code so you'll always have it."

His trust in me was humbling really, but more evidence we needed to have a real discussion from the onset. So instead of dragging him up that spiral staircase to his inviting bed, I sat on the sofa.

"Shane, we need to talk."

"Uh oh. Should I be worried, now?"

I planted my palms on my knees and shot him my serious face. I needed to put my people management skills to some kind of real-world use for once. "Just come here, please."

He shuffled over, acting as though he'd been called to the principal's office. With sagging shoulders, he finally dropped down beside me. "Okay. Do your worst."

"Now, see, it's that attitude that is going to make this hard."

"Crap. You're starting to scare me."

I exhaled. "Don't you worry we're rushing into things? I met you on Monday. It's Friday, and I'm more or less moving in with you. We didn't even talk about it beforehand."

He looked confused. "Did you want to stay at Jo's? Did I push you to do something you didn't want to?"

"No. That's not it." All at once, I started to laugh at how ridiculous it all was, and the words flowed out. "This shouldn't be happening. You and I are impossible. Who's ever heard of any serious, long-lasting relationship starting so fast? We're flying on instinct and emotion, and we barely even know each other."

His face brightened. "Oh, that's all you're worried about? I thought maybe you'd figured out you don't really like me and want more space. Or a restraining order."

"No. That worries me the most. What is wrong with me, Shane? How have I let this happen? I was in Indiana a week ago."

"Lucky for me, you're here now."

"What are we going to do about it?"

"About what? I don't understand the problem."

"Do you usually move this fast?"

He shook his head. "No, but I've never felt like this before about anyone. It's like I'm caught in a riptide. I don't know how to slow it down, and I don't really want to. Do you?"

I couldn't say I did, but the lack of caution worried me. "How are we going to know if it's right? That we aren't making a huge mistake?"

"We don't know. We just live it and see." He took my hands. "Doesn't it feel right?"

"It feels—" I tried to find the word for what I was experiencing "—intoxicating."

He inched closer, until his forehead pressed against mine. "Perfect."

It should have scared the shit out of me. Maybe the reason his intensity didn't freak me out like it had with boyfriends past was simply because I was feeling it too. We were in the same boat while the current carried us down the rapids, and as long I didn't fall out, then I wouldn't drown. But where was the river leading?

And what if I decided I did want out eventually?

Shane stood and held out a hand. "Let's go upstairs."

His eyes sparkled with mischief, and I was tempted to follow him anywhere, but that sense of warning hadn't dissipated. Maybe it was too much novelty, homesickness, or just stupid hormones messing with my brain chemistry.

I decided it might help to touch base with my normal by checking in with Ash and catching up with any fan site drama before I went to sleep, so I said, "I've got something I need to do for a few minutes on the computer. Do you mind?"

"Oh. Of course not. I have a book to read." Despite his words, his forehead furrowed, but then he leaned over and kissed me on the cheek. "I'll be upstairs, okay?" He stood, took a step back, and added, "Waiting." Two more steps. "Upstairs." Another few feet. "In bed." He made it to the stairs. "Most likely naked."

"With a book." I rolled my eyes. "Don't fall asleep, please."

"Not a chance."

He took his sweet time walking around the steps, and when his feet finally disappeared, his shirt came fluttering down. Followed by his pants. And his boxers.

God.

I closed my eyes and breathed in. I had my private messages open and was about to find out what Vencor had written.

But then Shane yelled, "You ever going to come up here? I've only got on my socks."

I had to laugh at him, and the dark cloud dissipated. The computer could wait a few hours.

Chapter Nineteen

I found him, exactly how he'd said, naked, reading a book, in nothing but his socks. He'd neglected to mention the heavy black hipster glasses that made him look borderline ridiculous, but given my proclivities, it pushed him over to the side of delectable. I crawled on hands and knees up him and trapped him beneath me. He peeled my T-shirt off. I did the same with my pants.

I rolled one of his socks off. Then the other. His toes curled, and he giggled like the Pillsbury Doughboy. I ran a finger along his arch, and he yanked his foot away.

"You're ticklish."

"Am not," he lied.

"No?" I dragged my fingernails along the back of his knee, and he hissed.

"Do that again."

I did.

His calves were slender but toned, covered in red hair that would match my own if I hadn't shaved. But I had, because it was nearly summer, and I'd been wearing skirts. And banging a drummer.

Speaking of which, when I got to his thighs, which were substantially thicker than his calves, like he did squats for a living, and maybe he did when he half crouched in front of that drum set, I ran my tongue along the inside of his leg. His groan satisfied me.

"Will you please hurry up, Layla? You are going to drive a man insane."

I pushed his knee to the side, knocking his legs apart, and despite his griping, he let me. His erection stood out like a neon marquee, demanding my attention, but I zeroed in on his taint, just below his balls. When I licked him, he cursed, and I smiled. I did it again.

"Layla. My God."

His balls drew up tight, and I took one in my mouth. Then the other. His back arched. I wrapped my hand around his cock, wondering for a humorous second if his dick had done squats as well because, phew, Shane was a handful. I loosened my grip enough to slide up his length while I focused my mouth on the nether regions. The guttural sounds coming from him now were making me moan.

"I'm going to come if you keep that up. And you're going to regret it."

I never would. But he made a fair point. I retreated and slithered up beside him. "You are delicious, Shane."

He kissed me while his hand trailed down my torso to my own wet heat. "You want me."

"I want you."

"Because you like me."

"You know I like you."

He grinned. "We're perfect together."

I couldn't disagree at the moment. Instead, I threw my leg over him, and he gasped as I centered him beneath me.

"Layla." He swallowed. "The condoms are in the drawer. Or maybe the bathroom. Somewhere."

"Do we need one, Shane?"

His fists grasped the sheets, and his eyes closed. "We should use one."

"I'm on the pill. I'm clean. You?"

"Last I checked, yes. Same. But are you sure?" His eyes were liquid night. "I don't mind using one."

His breathing was shallow, and I made a decision to trust him. He was so hard, all I had to do was settle onto his tip and then sit slowly down onto his hips. He said something unintelligible, and I lifted back up.

"Jesus." His head tilted back, and I took control of him, touching his chest and the muscles along his abs, watching them ripple as I settled into a rhythm. He met me with his thrusts, his hands gripping my hips, helping me up and down.

I fell forward so I could press my lips on him, and as we started to kiss, I slowed, so we could experience this moment together. Skin to skin.

His eyes locked onto mine, and we stared into each other's souls as I rocked against him, as he rolled into me, an easy beat. Excruciatingly up, deliriously down. He stretched me out and hit that spot deep inside me, again, again, again, until I felt nothing but waves of pleasure. And they built and crashed over me with a sudden intensity.

I groaned out his name, aware that he hadn't come yet. My forehead fell onto his chest and he flipped me onto my back, still hard, still pumping in me, sweat dripping from his hair, falling onto my forehead, and he picked up the pace, slamming into me harder, faster, uncontrolled, and I went over the brink again, grunting out an animal cry. The word *yes* escaped my lips more than once, and I wrapped a leg around his back, urging him to completion.

One, two, three more thrusts, and he cried out as he released.

Panting, he dropped beside me, and we lay side by side, staring at the ceiling.

He was the first to speak. "You sure you can't come with us on tour?"

"You want a groupie on your tour bus?"

He rolled toward me. "There won't be any groupies on the tour bus. And I'd get us a hotel."

"I wish I could."

"Okay. But I don't know how you're going to live without all this while I'm away."

I laughed. "You've got me there. You really are Hurricane Shane."

His silly grin melted my heart. "That's me."

Nobody warned me that we'd be working on Sunday, but as soon as we'd had time to eat and grab a cup of coffee, Shane was on the phone with Micah, and the next thing I knew, I was carrying a million round boxes from the rehearsal studio to a trailer. While Shane broke down his drum set into a reverse thousand-piece puzzle, Rick rolled amps out. Noah was nowhere to be found, and Micah only arrived when we were closing the trailer. I was going to shake my very tired fist at him before I realized he was there to drive over to his townhouse and load up his own things. We walked over and arrived as Micah was carrying out a black guitar case. Then he disappeared inside.

He must have unearthed eight more guitars from his basement.

He passed by, head down, hauling gear. It had never occurred to me that they had to do this every time they went on tour. "When do they get roadies?"

Jo handed me a bottle of water and led me out of the way of the traffic. "There will be people at the venues to help them set up. They're picky about making sure they have everything."

A bus rolled up, and Noah climbed down. "It is a gorgeous day to get on the road."

Everyone's spirits were up. At least for the guys. They seemed like they'd bottled up energy while hanging around at home, practicing and preparing. Now they were kinetic and ready to burst.

Jo hollered at Micah. "Where will you be tonight?"

"Not sure. I'll check in a minute."

"Excuse me." I squeezed past Micah, suddenly too curious about that bus to remain a mute spectator. I'd heard about bands' touring buses and everything that goes on in them. I'd never personally set foot on one.

They'd shut off the engine, but the door was left open, so I climbed in, expecting to find a decadent sex cave. Maybe it needed a few rock stars to transform it into something more than a glorified mobile home. I'd been on the normal kind of buses, with the carpet-covered seats paired two-by-two to the back. I wasn't expecting anything like that. I was still surprised by black-and-white diamond lamination on the floor. Leather sofas ran along either wall facing tables fixed to chrome poles. Farther in, a flat-screen TV graced the back wall.

"Layla?" Shane stuck his head around the front divider and stepped in.

"Just checking out your digs. Not too shabby."

He rolled his eyes. "Not for a short trip maybe. Thankfully, we've got hotels every night this week."

I pictured the parties in those hotel rooms, the groupies, the sex. "Will you call me while you're gone?"

He moved closer and slid his hand around my back. "Every chance I get. You won't find it annoying?"

"Maybe avoid work hours?" I could just imagine Gabe's look if I sat at my desk, flirting over the phone. "After you're done performing, you could tell me about the show?"

His breath tickled my ear. "Or I could tell you what I'd rather be doing."

"Break it up, you two." Fucking Noah had arrived. "Shane, say your goodbyes. We need to hit the road."

I turned my attention back to Shane. He wore a short-sleeved Henley with the first three buttons undone, and I peeled it open to take a gander at his chest. "I'm gonna miss this."

He dragged me into a bear hug. "You could come with us."

"Stop. I have to earn some money."

"So, grab a train and come up to Boston Friday."

"To the festival?"

"Why not? You could hang backstage. You wouldn't have to fight the crowds. Think about it."

I wanted to. Backstage . . . My God, that sounded amazing. "I don't know. My boss was already mad I missed a day last week." Not to mention, Adam had invited me to his rehearsal on Friday.

"Just think about it. Maybe it will work out."

Micah climbed up the steps. "Are we just waiting on Rick? Oh, hey Layla. Did you decide to come with us?"

The image before me—three of the band members from Theater of the Absurd—standing in their tour bus suddenly struck me as surreal. This had never even been anything I'd ever fantasized about. Backstage, sure. Tour bus? Never. It was so crazy, the awe snuck up on me.

"Let me get a picture of you guys before I go. I can add it to my blog post. I bet fans eat up this kind of stuff."

It might have been my imagination, but I could have sworn Noah rolled his eyes. Micah said, "Yeah, sure. We're not going anywhere until Rick gets here anyway."

Shane joined them as I got out my phone, praying the lighting would cooperate. "Say cheese!"

Not a single one of them said cheese. Noah brooded. Micah flashed his normal perfect smile. But Shane gave me bedroom eyes and sexy-times lips. I exhaled wishing we could be alone on that bus for a few minutes. I snapped a bunch of pictures in quick succession, planning to find the one that flattered Shane the most and use that one. I had no doubt that anyone who hadn't noticed how hot he was wouldn't miss it in those pictures.

"Got it! Thanks!" I tucked my phone away, then glanced around awkwardly. I had no further reason to be there. "I guess I'll just—"

Shane took my hand and led me off the bus where he pressed me up against the side and kissed me like we were in private. I relaxed into him, wishing I could stay with him the rest of the day, then stay in his hotel the rest of the night. But it wasn't meant to be.

Rick chose that moment to appear. "Come on. We've got to be in Albany by six if we want time to check sound."

The bus started up with a raucous rumbling.

Shane placed a foot on the first step. "I'll call you later."

"Take care."

He tipped an invisible hat. "And I'll be watching for your blog post!"

The doors shut, and I backed away onto the sidewalk, waving at Shane through the windows as the bus pulled away, and the wild part of my life went with it.

I took a deep breath. It had only been a week, but it was going to be so weird to stay at his apartment with him gone.

Almost as if she read my mind, Jo came over and draped an arm over my shoulder. "You know you're always welcome here."

I shook my head. "I appreciate it, but it's fine."

Honestly, though, I felt keenly alone, like I'd lost a part of myself I hadn't known existed until Shane exploded into my life and then just as quickly disappeared. I wanted to ask Jo how she managed the intense loneliness when Micah toured, but she'd think I was insane to have succumbed to a Shane addiction in the span of a week. How was she able to let Micah go time and time again and trust he'd return as in love with her as when he left?

The Rock Paper

In the Rehearsal Hall: Theater of the Absurd

By Layla Beckett

As a fan of a band, you feel lucky when a new album drops and you get to queue it up, close your eyes, and listen for the first time to brand new tunes.

You feel like you've won the lottery when you score tickets to see that band in concert and hear the songs you've been singing for months.

You hit the jackpot if you win a meet and greet and get to ask the band you love for an autograph and a picture.

Then, if all the stars align, you might get a once-in-a-lifetime opportunity to combine all of these experiences into a private concert for one.

I don't even know how to describe the day I just spent with a band I adore as they performed never-before-heard new songs, never recorded or even performed in concert.

Lucky doesn't cover it.

I've been following Theater of the Absurd ever since they broke on the scene while touring with Walking Disaster. Once on my radar, I made it a point to buy all their albums, falling in love with their off-beat rock music. Whenever I had the chance to see them in concert, I jumped at it, and like so many fans, I couldn't get enough of their surprising onstage antics. The first time I saw Micah bodysurf across the audience, I knew I'd be a fan for life.

I never expected I'd ever meet the band. I'm just a Midwestern music fan. Never scored a backstage pass. Never went to a meet and greet. I've always been in it for the music, but I'd be lying if I didn't confess a certain idol worship of the guys who bring this music to life.

Today my lucky stars converged, and I got the chance to meet them, hang out with them, and watch them banter, fight over setlists, cover a couple of songs, and perform unreleased music.

And as the ultimate treat, I get to share my score with fellow fans.

Here are my impressions from the day.

Micah Sinclair is as hot as you think he is. He's also incredibly generous and as easy-going as you'd expect a Libra to be, but it was impressive to watch his leadership skills in action.

Noah Kennedy loves to play to the camera. He has a reputation for his fiery personality, and he didn't disappoint. Between sets, the give-and-take between Noah and Shane could get blistering.

Shane Morgan is my secret favorite. He's a madman on the drums as you ought to know already if you're a fan. You'll also be aware that he's kind and funny. I can attest to how hot he is in person, and all I can say is: Hands off, ladies. I saw him first.

Rick Walters hangs back and does his thing, which is to show how to play a bass guitar righteously. I really loved watching him at work, but I don't think we exchanged two words the entire day.

As it was a rehearsal and not a live show, the guys were more subdued than I'm used to, but it made for a more intimate experience. It was awesome just to focus on the music which as always blew my mind.

Videos with new music, including two covers and some between song banter are posted below the fold.

Chapter Twenty

As nice as it had been to get chauffeured or taxied to work, the subway presented a certain amount of novelty for this Indiana girl. I didn't mind riding in and watching all the different people around me, most of whom seemed considerably more bored than I was.

Even the thrill of emerging into Times Square hadn't worn off yet. I still couldn't believe I had the most amazing job at the most amazing music magazine in the most amazing city in the world. I breathed it in, foul-smelling gutter garbage and all.

Once on my floor, I nestled into my cube and prepared for the morning scrum. My plans for automating Tweets had gotten provisional approval. Ajit anticipated no problems implementing the proposals. He wondered why they'd never coded it before. The meeting went smoothly, signing off on estimates and deadlines.

I was in a fine mood as we broke up and I headed back to my desk where I discovered an email from Lars telling me I was free to post the blog I'd set up. Holding my breath, I hit submit.

And just like that, my name was on the front page of the *Rock Paper*.

The adrenaline from that experience came rushing back as I clicked through and watched one of the videos. Would I get lucky enough to do it again? I composed a quick email.

Lars,

Thank you for this opportunity. I wanted to let you know that Adam Copeland loved this idea so much he invited me to their rehearsal on Friday. Please let me know your thoughts. I'd need to clear it with Byron of course.

Layla

There. I wanted to get that on the books. My stomach swirled with excitement. My God. Walking Disaster in a small room. Just me and them. Could I make a request? I wished I could post about it to the fan forum and solicit opinions on what to ask them to play.

I wished I could tell the posters anything about this at all.

As I stood to go grab a cup of coffee, Gabe stepped out from between the cubes, blocking my path.

"Now I understand why you found my review too critical."

"I never said your review was too critical. I only questioned your assumptions and conclusions." I tried to move around him, but he put his hand over the nearest cube wall, and I realized I'd be doing the limbo to get through him.

"This is a well-respected music magazine, Layla. Do you know people read us to get an objective opinion about the music from reviewers whose expertise they value?"

"Yes. I know that, Gabriel. I think I even complimented you on your writing. If you recall."

He moved an inch closer. "Yet, it's funny what passes for journalism when you lose that objectivity."

I stopped looking for ways to get past and met his eyes. "I'm sorry?"

"I read your article this morning. If you can call it that." His jaw clenched. "You basically just gave free advertising to your boyfriend. And 'hands off, ladies'? I don't think I've ever read that printed in a music magazine in my life."

Was he truly offended as a writer? Or just jealous? I rolled my eyes. "Are you fucking kidding me, Gabe? This very magazine once printed a fifty-page spread of the pretty boys of rock. You know who was in it? Micah Sinclair."

"The fact that you know that is troubling."

"The fact that you find it troubling means you don't know your audience."

He glowered at me, then moved out of my way. As I passed, he hissed, "Maybe I should write a balanced point of view of that new song you just posted." His threat registered, and I paused long enough for him to know he'd made an impact. "The drumming sounded . . . what would we say? Maybe like a poor attempt to copy The Who?"

I tried not to laugh. Shane would no doubt find that insult rather amusing. Complimentary even. I flung the back of my hand dramatically across my forehead. "Oh, no. Please don't compare him to Keith Moon."

Then I shot him a death glare and stalked back to the kitchen in a much shittier mood. I muttered to myself, "*Douche!*" I let it go and focused on cramming the little coffee packet into the machine. I slammed the flap closed a little too hard. As the coffee sputtered out, sending lava-hot drops onto my skin, a Walking Disaster notification ringtone exploded.

I grabbed my phone to silence it and quickly check what the emergency was.

Ash had texted: *Is that where you were last week? OMFG. Why didn't you tell me?*

Crap. I should have given her some warning. Now I was going to look like I didn't trust her. Or worse. Like we weren't close enough friends to share that kind of news.

I texted back: *It was top secret.* I lowered the volume on my phone, knowing she'd want more intel, and sure enough, it vibrated seconds later.

How did it happen?

I befriended Jo. That was the truth at the end of the day.

Congrats! It's amazing. Can I post it to the forum?

It's a public article, isn't it?

Then I sent a follow up because I didn't think she'd realize I couldn't be connected to my own self. *Don't mention that I'm Pumpkin, okay?*

Aye aye.

I shoved my phone in my back pocket and finished making my coffee, but I'd barely set it down on my desk before I heard my name.

"Layla."

I craned my neck around to find Lars standing in his doorway. He waved me into his office then leaned against his desk, motioning me to a chair. I worried I was in for round two of Gabriel's harangue

"Really loved the article. You totally captured the spirit I was aiming for. I've read fan blogs that had that same genuine enthusiasm, and already, I've seen a lot of positive responses in the comments section. I followed the trackbacks to some of the sites where the link was dropped. Fans wish they could have been you."

I beamed, relieved and proud. "That's great, Lars. Thank you."

"You say you landed a similar gig with Walking Disaster?"

"It was Adam's idea actually."

"Oh, was it?' He rubbed his chin. "Hmm. It got me to thinking. This seems to be something that bands might find useful."

"I can see that. It's free publicity for them." I realized Gabe had said the exact same thing moments before. But how was that a bad thing? "Micah said it's a great opportunity to connect with fans, but also to float some experimental songs and get honest feedback. Plus, it's interesting content for you."

I shifted in my seat because my hands suddenly wanted to talk for me, like Shane was rubbing off on me.

"That's why I suggested it in the first place." I didn't correct him. Instead, I waited for him to piece together the bits of information and draw the conclusion I was hoping he was leading toward.

He paced to the back side of the room, then back to the floor-to-ceiling window and looked down over Times Square in silence. I continued to wait.

"What if—" he spun around "—what if we made this a series? We could pitch it to other bands as a way to cultivate some of the content we share, but it would give us a unique insider view. We could even call it something like '*Inside Access.*' "

I winced. "Or '*Fly on the Wall*'?"

He nodded. "Yeah. I like that."

It was definitely something I would have loved to read myself. "What fan doesn't want to hang out and watch a band do its thing?"

"Any specific bands you'd like me to reach out to?"

I could have rattled off dozens. "Pretty much anyone. I don't think I could tire of that experience."

"Awesome." He went back to the chair behind his desk, and I sensed our meeting had come to an end.

I stood and thanked him, then went back to do the less glamorous part of my job, scheduling tweets and setting up FB content. I started to daydream about sitting in with Walking Disaster and meeting all the other guys in the band.

Talking Disaster Forum

DeadFan wrote:
Some lucky fan. Can you even imagine?

The Rock Paper: In The Rehearsal Hall - Theater of the Absurd

WD40 wrote:
What's Noah playing? Is it a Gibson?

MusicArt wrote:
Micah's so subdued. It's kind of weird to see him standing in one place like that except when he's solo.

RobinHood wrote:
Who's Layla Beckett?

CaliforniaDreamin wrote:
Could just be someone who works for the magazine they sent over to fabricate some fan buzz.

CakeOrDeath wrote:
I bet you're right. The whole thing did feel a bit forced. Like she'd wikipediaed some random info about the band. Libra? How is that relevant?

Jayhawk wrote:
Oh my god. This is amazing video! New music! I'm going to hang out over on the TotA fan forum tonight and hope that there are more videos.

LowRider wrote:
Y'all know that's probably just one of the girlfriends, right? Did you notice the picture from the tour bus? Doesn't one of their girlfriends ride along sometimes?

Jayhawk wrote:
@LowRider - who cares?

Sailor8 wrote:
Micah's girlfriend usually takes credit for her photography. Rumor has it Noah's broken up with his girlfriend (hoping it's true!) and Shane doesn't have one. Rick's married. His wife never travels with them. Looks to me like someone just got lucky. (And why is it never me?)

Chapter Twenty-One

*W*ith a pillow plumped behind me, I sat in Shane's bed and read through the reaction to the blog I'd posted. Over on the TotA forum, the posters were having a field day discussing the new song and debating which cover they preferred. It was fun to wallow a bit in their thrill of seeing it all secondhand. I was already starting to forget the first-hand awe of sitting right there.

My phone erupted in the FaceTime ringtone, and I rolled over to grab it and accept the call.

"Hola, Cuddle Rock." I attempted a seductive grin, but it was awkward to do so at a device.

Shane appeared on my screen. I guessed he must be in a hotel in yet another college town. Their schedule up until Friday was basketball arenas and small theaters. Friday, they'd arrive in Boston for a major festival.

"Layla, I've got a question for you." There was a bit of scruff covering his chin. I'd never stopped to investigate if he tended to go unshaven during a tour. I smiled to myself as I considered all the fun things I had yet to learn about him.

"Uh, huh?" I grinned anticipating some flirty banter.

"When's my birthday?"

My breath caught. "Oh, shit. Was it today?" He'd told me he was thirty-one when we talked about it, and I never did go look up his statistics. "I didn't know."

"No." The muscle in his cheek twitched. "Do you even know what sign I am?"

I hadn't figured out where he was going with this, so I attempted a stab. "Uh, Taurus?"

He snorted. "Close, but no."

"I don't know. When's your birthday?"

"April 6. I'm an Aries."

"Okay. I don't follow astrology. Is that supposed to mean something?"

" 'Micah Sinclair is as hot as you think he is. He's also incredibly generous and as easy-going as you'd expect a Libra to be, but it was impressive to watch his leadership skills in action.' " He was reading my own blog back to me.

"Yeah?"

"You don't know my birthday, but you know Micah's sign? Do you know Noah's, too?"

"No. Why would I?"

He sighed. "Why do you know Micah's?"

That was a valid question. Why did I? I searched my mind, trying to remember where I'd come across that detail. Probably on the forums. "I don't know. Maybe I read it in an article and it stuck."

The jealous routine was beginning to piss me off. I knew he had an inferiority complex about the other guys, but I thought we were past that. I tried a different tack.

"Did you see what I said about you?"

"Yeah." His tone still sounded upset, but less belligerent at least.

"And did you know I'm currently in your bed? Alone?"

He raked his fingers through his hair. "Yes. I know. I'm sorry. I hate being on the road right now. I wish you were here. I miss you, and I'm on edge. And Noah's been—"

"Could you stop listening to Noah? He's an asshole." I exhaled. It would have been easier to be mad at him if he was totally off base, but I had made that blog sound a bit unhinged on purpose. "Look. Lars wanted me to build enthusiasm, really push the fan-with-inside-access angle, so I did. That's all. Okay? I truly love your music, and I really am a fan, but I don't have some sinister angle, Shane. I'm here for you."

His facial features relaxed. "Okay. I'm sorry."

"Forgiven. Now. Tell me about your show tonight."

I settled back into his deliciously comfortable bed. He'd invested in sheets I didn't even know they made—ten-thousand count or something. They were almost as thick as blankets, but so soft. His blankets were another story. Everything Shane picked out showed the greatest care. I sank into the pillows and listened to him give me a first-hand account of the concert from a real musician's perspective. I loved hearing all the stories that no concert-goer would ever know—the squabbles, the jokes, the mistakes.

When he asked me what I was wearing, I showed him the tank I'd pulled out of his drawers. It smelled like heaven, and I loved stealing his things. Then he held the camera back so I could see he wasn't wearing a shirt. And although the rest went off screen, it would appear there was nothing below that.

"You're making me miss you more, Shane."

"Come see us on Friday. You can take the train up. Take a day off."

If the idea had appealed to me in the abstract, the promise of seeing him Friday instead of waiting until he got home a few days later made me consider the idea for real. It was only a couple of days, but Shane was so intense that his absence in his apartment felt like a body part was missing.

"I'll try. Okay?"

First thing Tuesday morning, I shot an email to Lars to ask him if it would be okay to postpone the rehearsal hall with Walking Disaster for another week. I came right out and confessed I was thinking of taking the day off to go to the Boston festival.

Once I'd gotten my mug of coffee and scanned my few emails, I pulled up Talking Disaster to catch up on the chatter about the blog post.

"Ah, I see. You're checking out reactions to your own stuff. How very vain."

Gabriel stood inside my cube, peering over my shoulder.

"Ugh. Gabe, why are you harassing me?"

"Harassing? I thought we were having a friendly exchange."

"Hardly."

He leaned down. I could almost feel him against my hair. "You do know that site is the source of the infestation on my review last week?"

On a hunch, I clicked the link to my blog page and scrolled to the last review I'd written. I opened up the comments section and scooted out of the way so he could get a better view of the dozens of sock puppet posts.

"Have you seen this?"

He laughed. "Yeah, serves her right. Did you see where she told people to troll my review?"

"I did." I swiveled my chair all the way around to face him, although he was so close, our knees might have brushed. I cleared my throat, and he backed away a few paces. "Did you have something to do with those comments?" I tried to match my tone to his, as if I found the retaliation impressive when, in reality, I thought it was entirely cowardly to hide behind a fake name.

I was ninety-nine percent sure he was Sandman, but I wanted to coax the admission from his own lips.

"Maybe." He smirked. I had him. He wouldn't be so cocky if he knew who I was. And I itched to prove it.

"Explain."

He looked around and lowered his voice. "I just wanted to give that irritating beast a taste of her own medicine."

I let him feel his oats for a minute before I dropped the punch line. "Yeah, well that irritating beast didn't really give two shits about your payback."

He snorted. "How would you know how she feels?"

"Because she's sitting right here."

His eyelids went into defib. "What are you saying? You—"

"Yes, me."

"You're responsible for that attack?"

"Hardly an attack, Gabe. Those people had valid opinions."

"Did you read what they wrote? It was vicious."

"No." I'd glanced at them once, but it had never occurred to me to follow up on their comments. Who cared what they said?

"Well, you really should. It was pretty hurtful."

I couldn't feel sorry for him. "Gabe, you write caustic words about musicians, but you can't take it when people respond in kind? I honestly expected you'd have thicker skin."

"At least now I know why you keep shooting me down."

"What?"

"I get it. I mean you run a fucking fan site." He grimaced. "That guy's a musician, and I'm not. It's exciting, and he gets you even closer to the band you worship. But you have to know, that's not a realistic basis for dating a guy."

"You're not even close to the truth."

He ran his tongue over his teeth and lodged it in his cheek, not impressed by my answer. "You're blinded by proximity to fame. Is that why you got a job here?"

I closed my eyes. He wasn't worth it.

"Or maybe I have it backwards. Maybe you have your sights set on a more ambitious prize. Did you think you could impress Lars with your inside connection?"

My head jerked up at that. "You think I'm using Shane to impress Lars?"

"Honestly, I might respect you more if you were. It would be less clichéd than sleeping your way through the band."

I winced. "You're way off base, Gabe."

"Why? Are you going to pretend you really like the guy? That's almost more pathetic. Do you even know how many short-lived relationships that drummer goes through? Have you done any homework? You really don't have a clue."

He was shooting with blanks if he thought he could convince me Shane was a womanizer.

"I need you to leave my cube right now, Gabe."

"History has a way of repeating. Does he have any idea what you do in your spare time?"

I spun my chair back around, pretending to shut him out.

"He doesn't, does he? I know that guy, Layla. He's not going to take it well. It would be a pity if he found out."

"Shut up, Gabe." It was killing me that he might be right. I'd have to tell Shane about it, and he wouldn't take it well. Handing the reins to Ash was becoming an inevitability.

"Come on, Layla." His tone turned gentle, like we hadn't just sprayed each other in verbal venom. "It's almost lunchtime. Why don't we forget about all this and go get a bite to eat?"

My fists clenched together, and I spun around so fast, my hair whipped across my face. "I'm about two seconds away from punching you in the nut sack."

He flinched. "Jesus. Ask a girl out and get threatened with physical abuse. Nice, Layla."

I shot him one more death ray glare, and he held out his hands in a whatcha-gonna-do-about-it gesture, like he really didn't care either way. Yeah. Sure.

At least he avoided me for the next couple of days. I put my head down and worked on proposals, spoke up in meetings, and made an effort to stay away from lurking on the forums at work at least. At night, alone in Shane's bed, I might have started following the tour on the TotA forum. But anything I read came from people seeing the band in a way that had grown foreign to me. They were reading into their every behavior for signs and meaning that didn't exist.

Noah was still the primary source of gossip. Ever since his breakup, speculation was that his more than usual grumpiness was due to his heartache over this loss. Plenty of posters saw this as their big opportunity to land in his bed. If they could only get close enough to him to offer.

I wanted to post: *Don't bother, ladies. He truly is an ass.*

On Thursday, I got the news I'd been crossing my fingers to hear. Lars called me in to tell me they'd set up the rehearsal hall with Walking Disaster for the following Friday, and that I was free to take the next day off to head up to the festival.

Everything I could have ever dreamed of was happening.

Chapter Twenty-Two

As much as I loved concerts, festivals weren't really my thing. They reminded me of the Indiana State Fair when I was a kid. Hot, dusty, and crowded. Worse, they seemed geared more toward socializing and partying than appreciating the music.

As I dragged my carry-on from Boston's T station to the park, I remembered why I avoided these things. Way too many concertgoers crowded the main entrance. I studied the map with mounting anxiety. Multiple bands would play simultaneously on three outdoor stages plus inside an arena. The fear of missing out would make me crazy, even though I wouldn't have even come if not to see one specific band.

I relaxed, knowing that at least for one show, I wouldn't need to fight the crowds. Theater of the Absurd would be head-lining tonight on one of the bigger outdoor stages, and I'd have an up-close experience.

Speaking of experiences, for the first time in my life, I got to stop at Will Call. The woman working the booth fingered her way through a stack of envelopes until she found one with my name in fat, black sharpie. She circled my map with instructions on where I should go since I no longer needed to follow the cattle herd of non-VIP regulars.

Inside the envelope, I found a plastic badge attached to a lanyard that I looped around my neck. I texted Shane to let him know I'd arrived. Then I headed toward a smaller gate around the backside of one of the stages. Flashing my badge gained me access to this more private area where the people rushing about had a totally different vibe from the front entrance. Roadies carried equipment. Apparent musicians lounged, smoking cigarettes or drinking beer. A smattering of folks like me dotted the landscape with their VIP badges, but they all came across as cool and collected. Like this was all normal. I was about to scream with joy.

I suddenly had the presence of mind to get out my camera and start snapping pictures. I'd need to document this at least for myself. Possibly for the blog.

"There she is!" An arm draped over my shoulder, and I reached up to take Shane's hand before turning and breathing him in.

"You smell like summer."

"Like a week on the road more likely." He tugged at me. "Come on, Star Shine. We're set up around one of the other stages."

The never-ending beating of drums pervaded the atmosphere. The music was loud, but somehow muffled or muted behind the stage. It was like listening to someone's stereo from a floor below. I could pick out the guitar licks and bass lines easily enough, but the vocals only came through sporadically. The occasional crowd cheers were loud and clear.

We had to weave around various obstacles and groups of people until we approached a safari tent behind yet another stage. Inside, I discovered air conditioning, food, drinks, and Noah asleep on a beach chair.

"Rick's gone into the city to do some kind of historical tour. Micah's sleeping on the bus. Noah and I had been planning to go listen to a few of the bands, but I guess he's out. What do you want to do?"

I looked around at the scene. It was so not rock-n-roll. I'd imagined getting backstage access for so long, but I'd pictured it like a scene from Spinal Tap where posh women and desperate groupies vied for attention. This looked more like summer camp.

"Who did you want to see?"

He pulled a folded-up guide from his back pocket and handed it over. "These are the bands playing right now."

I didn't recognize half the bands on the list. "You choose."

We spent the next couple of hours wandering aimlessly from stage to stage. Loyal fans had probably staked out a place by the stage, forced to sit through countless acts in anticipation for their own favorite, but plenty of people casually hung out like me and Shane, enjoying the moment for what it was, listening to the music, swaying along, entertained by the spectacle. I'd never experienced any concert or festival like this, with one hand in the pocket of a guy who made the moment feel special. Who made me feel special.

A couple of times, Shane ran into people who knew him, usually other musicians or the occasional tech he'd worked with. They had history, and the conversations were low-key small talk, observations about the lay out, differences to other gigs. It was fun to watch him light up on those occasions when a fan recognized him and asked for an autograph or a picture, but even they were usually cool, not squealing like they might with a real celebrity.

And he was mine, all mine.

As the sun began to set, we needed to think about food and the band's performance ahead. Back in the tent, Noah was awake, Micah and Rick had arrived, and it was time to get to work.

I took plenty of pictures of the preshow activities. It was surreal to see it all going down from a few feet away. Roadies bustled everywhere, mostly asking me to either move out of the way or to help carry some piece of equipment. I chose to fall back rather than screw something up. The sea of humans in front of the stage undulated like an ocean tide.

And then it was time. The final act of the night was announced to a deafening roar. The lights dropped. Shane gave me a kiss and crept to his drumkit. Micah, Rick, and Noah held back, and a spotlight hit Shane the first time he struck his drums.

Chills.

As Shane pounded out a rhythm, the crowd clapped along. Rick walked out and laid down the bass line. The crowd erupted in cheers at the unmistakable beginning to "Close Enough." Noah strutted out under his own spotlight, bowing and waving to screams. He grabbed his guitar and lit up the night with electricity. Finally, Micah walked out center stage, and everyone went nuts. He grabbed the mic and broke out in the first lyric.

> *The world spins and spins and spins*
> *Gravity pulling me back*
> *Back to you*

People crushed against the front barricade singing along, crying, losing their goddamn minds. I was losing my goddamn mind. The guys were so charismatic and talented. And I was so close, I could see drops of sweat flying off their hair. I could see the looks Noah and Micah shot at each other as they coordinated telepathically. I could see Shane's muscles as he relentlessly destroyed his drumkit. Rick stood still, nodding to the rhythm as he performed to perfection.

The whole show was brilliant.

Normally, at the end of a concert, I'd stand with the crowd demanding an encore, and after another song or two, the arena lights would come on, cuing the end of the show. The band disappeared into another dimension. Gone. Whisked away.

I hadn't expected the chaos on the other side. As soon as the guys stepped off the stage after the last encore, they were surrounded by people with various jobs. Techs shoved water bottles into their hands. Noah poured his over his head. Roadies began breaking down the instruments. I was jostled out of the way and fled to a less crowded spot behind the stage, near the safari tent, where Shane found me.

He was more sweat than man at that point. Rather than reach for me, he said, "Give me a few minutes to change. We have to head over to some afterparty for a little bit. You can come with us, or if you want, I can send you back to the hotel."

I chortled. Like hell I was going to miss out on a new experience.

"I'll wait for you here."

He smiled. "I was hoping you'd say that."

The pandemonium continued around me, and I suddenly felt incredibly awkward and out of place. There was no sign of Micah, Noah, or Rick either, so I attempted to slink back into the safari tent to hide out, but a muscular man in a black T-shirt blocked my path.

"Miss, you can't be back here."

I started to lift my VIP pass before it occurred to me that maybe Shane had been my true ticket into this area. "I'm with the band," I said, hearing how lame that sounded as it came out of my mouth.

"Well, you're going to have to wait out here."

He led me away from the tent toward a rope, behind which a group of twenty or thirty women and a few men craned their necks to peer around the stage.

When I joined the crowd, one lady said, "Nice try."

She had salon-perfect highlights in her straight blond hair. Her makeup had survived the heat of the day somehow, and her clothes weren't wrinkled, dusty, or moist from sweat. I'd avoided most of the festival filth, but she looked like she'd just arrived.

I looked around, wondering why they were all hanging out here. "What is this?"

"Um, it's the afterparty line?" By her tone, I assumed that was supposed to be obvious. "Are you VIP?"

I flashed her my badge, and she gave me a patronizing smile. "Must be your first time."

A second girl said, "It didn't used to be like this," in a world-weary tone. "They used to treat us better."

She was a brunette version of her friend, clean and neat, with caramel highlights threaded through a pair of braids. In comparison, I probably looked like a war refugee.

I texted Shane: *I'm in the afterparty line. I guess I'll see you when they let us in.*

I turned my attention back to the ladies. "You go to a lot of these?"

The blonde girl said, "I always get into the afterparties. I've been to so many, they all know me by now. They'll say, 'You again?'"

Brunette girl said, "I've become accustomed to getting a hug from Micah after the show. He's a huge hugger."

Blonde girl said, "If he comes out."

They nodded.

Blonde girl scanned me and said, "Just be sure to leave Noah for me."

They both laughed.

"Hey, isn't that Shane?" someone asked. Everyone turned toward the direction of the tent.

The blonde said, "That's totally Shane. I wonder why he's out here."

He kept heading toward us. "Layla!" He waved his hand in a come-on gesture.

"Who's Layla?" asked the brunette.

"That's me. I'll see you inside!" I savored their surprise as I stepped over the rope and met Shane halfway.

The afterparty was the lamest thing I'd ever seen. Granted, I wouldn't have felt that way if I hadn't hung out with these guys for longer than five minutes, but I couldn't unring that bell, and this scene just seemed pathetic to me now.

The huge tent was spacious and air-conditioned with an actual bar and some music pumping in the background. It reminded me a lot of a wedding reception, except that instead of couples dancing in pairs, women prowled in groups around two major destinations: Micah and Noah. Rick had found a folding chair and sat in a corner unnoticed, scrolling through his phone and occasionally pulling a drag off a cigarette. Shane and I parked ourselves near the bar and shared running commentary.

"Watch these two," he said, directing my attention to the girls I'd met before. "This should be good."

When a path cleared, they approached Noah and engaged him in conversation. Unlike Micah, who could maintain a sunny disposition in the face of a barrage of fans, Noah didn't even pretend he was tolerating any of this. His lip curled a little as the girls talked him into a picture. One of them handed a phone to someone, and each girl took a position on either side of Noah. At the count of three, as the impromptu photographer shot the picture, both girls turned their heads and kissed Noah on either cheek.

Shane chortled. "It's always something."

"They didn't even ask him first?" I was horrified. "What the hell?"

Shane just shrugged. "Whatcha gonna do? It's part of the job description."

"Assault?"

"Just remember this, Layla. If you ever see compromising pictures of me at an afterparty, question your eyes. Not that I've ever been the subject of a kiss attack."

I was shaking my head. "Gah. It's so inappropriate."

"At least they didn't grab for his crotch."

"Has that happened?!" I shouldn't have been surprised.

The blonde girl had lingered after the picture, and she was leaning into Noah now. She put a hand on his shoulder, but he lurched back.

"Shit. Here we go." Shane stiffened.

"What?"

"The come on." He pulled out his phone and checked the screen. "I think we've been here long enough. I'm gonna go grab your carry-on out of the bus. We can get an Uber to the hotel. Wait here."

I continued watching Noah who said something to the girl before striding directly toward the bar. When he saw me, he veered and made a beeline for me. He put an arm around my shoulder.

I drew away from him and backed up against the tent wall. "What the hell, Noah?"

He stepped closer and put one hand on a pole beside my head. "Layla, I'm sorry I was being a total dick to you before."

"You're kind of being a dick now. What are you doing?"

"Look. I just need your help for a minute."

"What are you talking about?"

He leaned close, whispering in my ear. "Did you see that girl earlier?"

I nodded.

"She's someone I got involved with once, and she will not leave me alone."

"So, why don't you just leave?"

"She'll follow us to the hotel."

"And? How's this my problem?"

"If she thinks I'm leaving with you, she'll find someone else to harass."

"There are perhaps a dozen other girls here who would happily leave with you. Why me?"

He looked into my eyes. His were bloodshot. "I'm completely exhausted. I haven't slept well in weeks, and I just want to get out of here without having to deal with any drama."

"Noah, what's Shane going to think if I walk out of here like that with you?"

Noah ran a finger through my hair. "Maybe I was wrong about you."

I was a microsecond away from slapping him. "Noah," I growled.

"I guess you think I'm a jackass. For what it's worth, the other day, I was aiming my anger at Shane and Micah because they're my brothers, and they have to put up with me. I didn't mean to get my assery all over you. Apologies?"

"I think Shane could use the apology more than me."

He nodded once. Whether he agreed or was just taking the unsolicited advice with a grain of salt, I had no idea.

"Will you just come with me? We'll find Shane and then we can all go to the hotel together. That's all. Okay?"

"Fine. But don't ever touch me again."

Chapter Twenty-Three

We caught up to Shane and grabbed an Uber to the hotel. Noah hooked a left for the bar as Shane and I waited side by side for the elevator.

Shane whispered, "I've got some very definite ideas about how to spend the rest of the night."

Going up to a hotel room with a rock musician felt like the ultimate cliché. I'd spent a decade deleting stories of hookups with these guys only to find myself on the cusp of becoming a groupie.

When the elevator doors opened, I grabbed both his hands and pulled him after me. Without even waiting for the door to close, he tangled his fingers in my hair and kissed me hard.

He drew back, one hand against the wall behind me, and it reminded me of the way Noah had pinned me at the after-party. Until that moment, I hadn't even thought about how I'd reacted to Noah Kennedy's face inches from my own. He was a heartthrob I'd once crushed on, but the reality of Noah did nothing for me. He'd shown me a level of self-centered disrespect I couldn't unsee. My response to him had been revulsion rather than attraction.

My response to Shane, on the other hand, was desperate need. I tugged on his T-shirt to better slide my hand up his muscled torso. "I'm dying to get you out of these clothes."

I fell back and hoped he'd take it for an invitation to possess me. He pushed me against the elevator wall, hands roaming down my body, reaching under my skirt, thumbs hooking the hips of my panties.

"May I?"

"Yes."

He slid my panties halfway down my thighs, then as he kissed me, his finger touched me and stroked, increasing the pressure until my voice escaped with an *Ah*, making my body feel like a bottle of champagne, bubbly, effervescent, tingly. He knew how to shake me up until I exploded.

He whispered, "I want every inch of you."

The elevator dinged, and he lifted me up without the slightest effort, hands under my thighs, my legs and arms wrapped around him koala-style.

He strode down the hallway like it was on fire, plucking the key card from his pocket and kicking open the door with urgency.

I lay my hands on either side of his face. Before I could utter a word, he crushed his mouth against mine and carried me to the bed, then dropped to the floor, tore my panties straight off, pushed up my skirt, and knocked my knees apart with his chin. He paused and looked up at me for approval.

"Shane."

"I've been thinking about this all day."

As his tongue touched me, we both *mmm*ed at the same time, his last words echoing in my mind. He'd been thinking about *this* all day.

Here was a man who knew what he liked.

And he took the time to learn what *I* liked. Soft, then hard, licking, then sucking, his mouth found my secrets. He slid a finger in and out, rubbing his thumb in places I'd never dreamed could feel such intense pleasure.

"There," I encouraged when he hit a particularly amazing combination. "Yes." He made me say *yes* a lot.

My back arched as I climaxed, but he didn't slow down, and I was so thankful, because my orgasm didn't end in a bang or a whimper. Rather, it grew more powerful, more delicious until it spread down my legs and around my back, like a wave of opium.

I jerked and stilled with a *wow*.

He broke away, laying one last kiss on the blast zone. "You make the most incredible face." He climbed up next to me, propping himself up on his elbow. "It's like you're filled with helium. Everything just goes—" He made a face of joy, smile widening, eyes unfocused, everything relaxing into bliss.

"You're one to talk."

"Why? What face do I make?"

"Shall we find out?" I trailed a finger down his torso.

He clamped his hand over mine and tugged me closer so I lay halfway across his chest, face to face. He brushed my hair out of my eyes and looked into my eyes. "I'd rather look at you."

"Like what you see?"

"So much."

He'd proven that through his actions, but it still felt nice to hear it. "It's only fair you count the ways."

"Every little detail is a world unto itself. I get a boner just looking at your lips." He winced. "Wow, that wasn't poetic."

"You're forgiven. Continue."

"Your body is like you were custom made for me. When I'm with you, I just want to look at you, touch you. I want to smell you and taste you. And I want to hear you. God, I love to listen to you talk. I love to hear you say my name."

"Shane."

"I've never met anyone like you." He smiled. "I can't believe you picked me."

"Well, Noah seems to hate me, and Micah's practically married," I joked.

"Yeah." He didn't laugh, obviously. It was a stupid thing for me to say.

"Sorry. I didn't mean that."

He lifted me off him and sat up. "Are you hungry?" Without acknowledging my lame apology, he picked up the room service menu and started to flip through it.

I was actually starving, but I took the menu from him and set it on the table.

"Shane."

"I'm sorry. I keep doing that."

He lay back down beside me, but his enthusiasm had gone from ready-and-willing to reluctant suitor in the span of a thoughtless comment.

I threaded my fingers through his. "We have to talk about this."

He let out a long breath. "I don't want to make a big deal out of it."

"Too late. You just shut down completely. It's already a big deal. Do you really think I'm secretly pining for Noah?"

"Of course not. I told you, it's my issue. It has nothing to do with you."

"It has everything to do with me."

"No, it's my personal history. You saw those girls tonight, right? That scene has played out every night for the past several years."

"That's only proof I should be the jealous one. You're surrounded every night by women who throw themselves at you."

"At Noah."

I rolled my eyes. "Would you be happier if they were throwing themselves at you? Should I worry you'll sleep with the first groupie who notices how hot you are?"

222 *Mary Ann Marlowe*

"Of course not." He furrowed his brow. "Have I given you any reason to think I'd do that?"

"Just making a point." I squeezed his hand. "We're going to have to learn to trust each other. Do you trust me?"

His thumb caressed my wrist. "You've never given me any reason not to."

"Except when I gawk at your friends."

"Only because when you do that, it reminds me that I'm nothing special."

"That's not true."

"But this is what I mean when I say it's *my* problem. *My* reaction is what's wrong."

"Yeah, but it's in reaction to me."

"Can you help it when you turn into a statue around Adam?"

"No."

"Exactly. And right now, I can't help how it feels when you stare longingly at Micah. How am I supposed to just get over a fear that lives in my bones? I know that you don't even *like* Noah, and yet this demon lurks, waiting for proof to the contrary. It doesn't care about facts or reality. It keeps whispering that you're going to figure out I'm not good enough for you and leave. Maybe not for Noah or Micah, but someone better will come along, and you'll realize I have nothing to offer you."

Ugh. All those red flags I'd been ignoring crystallized into my very worst nightmare. And yet, I wanted to run toward this particular danger. I wanted to douse the fire, or at least give Shane the chance to extinguish it himself. In the past, I would have already planned my escape.

Maybe I was foolish, but I geared up and entered the burning building.

"Shane, look at me." He turned his head. I gazed into his eyes, hoping our connection would survive this necessary dose of reality. "You never have to worry that I'm going to dump you for Noah or Micah. Or anyone, really." He started to answer. I laid a finger over his lips. "But you have to realize that what *will* come between us is this mistrust and jealousy."

His forehead creased, and he nodded slightly. I went on.

"I've had incredible role models who showed me how a good relationship works. My dad and brother each fell in love with their longtime best friends. They modeled respect and autonomy for me, so, mentally, I know that men can be rational, but I've run into my fair share of possessive guys who didn't know where they ended and I began. It was a total shock to me when every relationship turned into a shit show."

I paused to give Shane a second to catch up. "I'm listening."

"I understand you can't control how you feel, but I don't want to have to tiptoe around your fragile ego and worry that any stupid joke is going to trigger a freeze out. I need you to give me room to breathe."

"You don't have to tiptoe around me. You've done nothing wrong. This is something for me to work out, and I will." He kissed the tip of my nose. "I promise."

I knew it wasn't something he could promise. "It means a lot that you're trying."

"Maybe we could give each other time to get used to all of this? Like you said, things are changing so fast."

"Sure." It was a reasonable request. We both needed time to catch up to our new reality. I only hoped he wasn't counting on dealing with his jealousy by waiting for me to stop fangirling. Because I wasn't sure I ever would.

He nudged me so he could wrap an arm around my shoulder and pull me into him. "I'm sorry I spoiled the evening."

I kissed his neck. "Do you really want to keep talking when we only have tonight?"

His chest rumbled with soft laughter. "I really am a moron to have wasted our time dwelling on this."

"No. It's good we talked. But now I don't want to anymore." I dragged my fingers around his back and slipped his shirt off. "Mmm. This is the body I've been longing to kiss."

His shoulders relaxed, and the mood began to change for the better. I spent time getting to know his ab muscles which, for the record, were defined and fabulous. I unbuttoned and unzipped his fly, and he let me push his pants down. His boxers followed. And then he was in the flesh.

"You are the most beautiful man I've ever laid eyes on."

A sigh escaped him, and he laid me back down on the bed, whatever pity party apparently forgotten. He took control and began undressing me, slowly, as he kissed my skin wherever it became bare.

"Condom?" he asked.

"Do you need one? Has anything changed?"

"Just checking. Nothing's changed."

He wrapped his hands around my waist and dragged me to the edge of the bed. When he entered me, we both muttered oaths. His was more profanity, mine more prayer.

When he was in to the hilt, he dropped forward and kissed me. "I've missed you."

"Same."

"I didn't even know you existed, and now I can't live without you. How is that possible?"

"I don't know."

"It's like I was waiting for you." As he kissed me again, he drew back and slid in again, and color exploded behind my eyelids like fireworks.

"Don't stop, Shane. That feels so good."

"I love the way you feel. I love your body. I love being with you."

His words elicited emotion that mixed with the physical sensations to form a heady sense that I could only call love, though I had nothing to compare it with. I loved Shane's body. I loved being with him. Did I love him?

Did he love me?

This was stronger than a casual encounter, and although I didn't know if I could trust it, I gave in to the moment, to the glorious Hurricane Shane, taking what he needed from me and giving me exactly what I desired. And I came hard a second time, saying his name again and again.

At last, he dropped beside me, breathing hard. "Christ, Layla. I think I'm falling for you."

My hunger grumbles broke the moment, so we ordered room service and talked about where they'd be playing for the next couple of days. He promised he'd be home on and off and finally for a longer stretch in a month.

"I don't even know where we're playing anymore. It's always the same thing. Different view."

I stole one of his fries. "Do you ever get tired of it?"

"Parts of it are tiring. Seeing Noah's face gets old. But we worked so hard for this. It would seem ungrateful to find it tiring."

"But normal. It's grueling."

"It is. And if we get more successful, it will only be crazier. I know what Adam's life has been like. It's no wonder he's used parenthood to take an extended break to be with his family."

I didn't mention how much the fans hated that. I didn't mention why I would know that. After his mini freak out earlier, I just wanted to relax into him and have this lightweight conversation about the near future. I'd figure it out. Maybe I'd just hand the forum over to Ash and be done with it. I didn't think I could hang out in there like I once had anymore anyway. I'd seen too much. Fiction and reality had become divorced, and I couldn't pretend otherwise.

"So, when will I see you again?"

He grinned. "You're seeing me now."

But I'd be on a train back to New York in the morning. He'd be on a bus to Providence. "And after this?"

"I'll be home Wednesday for two days."

"Two days. Well, we'll have to make the most of our time together." I touched his hand. "How tired are you now?"

He ran his finger up my arm. "I can sleep later."

That was what I wanted to hear.

Talking Disaster Forum

Hipster101 wrote:
That's all my videos, guys. There are some better ones over on the TotA forum.

Sailor8 wrote:
Did you hear whether Noah's still moping around?

Hipster101 wrote:
Um, no.

CubbiesFan wrote:
@Sailor8 - There's some talk about him bringing a girl to the show. There's more detail on their forum— some pictures, too. Looks like he left with her.

Sailor8 wrote:
Thanks, CF. I guess it was only a matter of time before he'd move on. Wonder if that's a new girlfriend or if he's open for business again.

DeadFan wrote:
Guys, can we get back to talking about Hipster's videos?

CubbiesFan wrote:
Sorry, DF. On topic, did anyone notice whether they played any other new songs?

Chapter Twenty-Four

After such a killer weekend in which literally all my rock n' roll fantasies came true, I worried I'd lose the thrill of going to the office. But it would take me about a thousand years to fail to be awed every single time I came up out of the subway into Midtown Manhattan. The small-town girl in me couldn't even pretend to adopt an air of nonchalance about the big city.

Once I got to my desk, I settled back into my groove and remembered why I loved doing what I did. Ajit had helped me install coding software and showed me around the source files. It was better than constantly asking him what logic they'd used behind every feature or how they might implement something new. The code was a maze and a puzzle, and time slipped by much more quickly while I tried to navigate the complex web.

Suddenly it was time for lunch. I grabbed my purse and headed out where I got in line at a cart to buy my new favorite food: street meat. I carried it over to a ledge to enjoy the warmth and get some sun, legs stretched out.

"Can I join you?"

Without waiting for an answer, Gabe sat beside me with his own sandwich wrapped in the aluminum foil.

"It's a free country." I kept eating. Damn, the lamb was too delicious. I'd never be able to go back to Indiana where I couldn't get this right outside my workplace.

"You have a good weekend?"

"Indeed." I dragged a wedge of pita across the tzaziki sauce, sighing as I took another bite.

"You seem pleased. Your boyfriend didn't dump you?"

I choked. "What?"

"I figured he'd balk at dating someone who's so obviously using him."

I breathed in and counted to five. "Gabe, not that it's any of your business, but I'm not using Shane."

"So, he's okay with you upgrading?"

"What the hell are you even talking about? I haven't—"

"Friday. Aren't you sitting in with Walking Disaster? Wasn't that your goal all along?"

I shook my head, trying to ignore him. The rice had a spice in it that I couldn't place. Whatever it was, I loved it.

"You're going to sit here and pretend you aren't looking forward to a private concert with your favorite band, Pumpkin?"

I rolled my eyes at him. "Are you jealous, Gabe? Did they spurn you or something?"

He snorted. "You think I want to meet all these people? I have access to their contact info. I've been invited to their parties. But I keep it professional, Layla. That way I can write fair reviews."

"You mean, so you can pan musicians without having to look them in the eye."

Damn, my food was gone. I cracked open the can of soda that had been sweating on the ledge and took a long sip.

"Or so I can praise them without looking like a suck-up. Do you think Lars is going to want you writing these blogs if he finds out you're running a fan site?"

"He knows, and he approves. Got any more questions?" I snatched up my napkin and dabbed the corners of my mouth, ready to end this insipid conversation. Why was he even bothering?

"He might care that you're dating the musicians." He shaded his eyes which only gave him the impression of piercing me with his gaze. He was so off base.

"One of the musicians, Gabe. And so was Jo when he hired her."

That stopped him dead. "Right." He stroked his chin. "Though she works in a different medium."

I crumpled my trash and stood. My stomach churned. Street meat tasted great going down, but I hadn't figured out how to stop myself from overeating. "Are you done questioning my life choices? I'd like to get back to work."

"I'm hardly questioning your life choices. Well, not all of them." He glanced at his wristwatch. "Just the musician."

"Oh, my God. You *are* jealous!"

"Don't flatter yourself."

"That's it, isn't it? You think if I wasn't seeing Shane, I'd go out with you."

His eyes narrowed. "I've noticed the way you look at me. You can't deny you're interested."

I appraised him out here in the sun that really set off his light eyes and smooth bronze skin. He maintained his soft brown hair in a way I didn't mind at all. If I didn't loathe him, I'd find him cute. "You're attractive, I'll give you that. But looks alone don't cut it."

He laughed. "When I perused your fan site, you seemed to ogle the looks plenty."

His confession gave me a cramp. My forum was public, but his snooping still felt invasive.

"I don't mind a pretty face, Gabe. But like I said, it's not sufficient." I tossed my trash. "And besides, it's a moot point. I *am* seeing a musician. Sorry."

I turned and walked away before he could ensnare me in another dead-end conversation.

The first thing I did when I got back to my desk was to text Ash to say: *I think we need to talk about transferring the site to you.*

She took no time to respond: *Why?*

I didn't want to get into all the myriad complexities, so I just said: *I'm way too busy to keep up, and you're doing all the work anyway. You could ask someone to help. Maybe give the blog duties over to Jayhawk?*

On the one hand, it would feel weird to drop out and let her take over. On the other, it wasn't like anyone knew me. For that matter, I could tell Ash to log in as me and pretend I was still in charge. But that wouldn't solve my problem. My forum was starting to affect my real life, and I needed to make a break from it so people like Gabe wouldn't have ammunition to undermine my professional credibility.

Ash wrote back: *Let me think about it. I've never minded helping out, but I'm not you. I don't know if I could run the whole site.*

Fair enough. I could maybe build a team and distribute the load. But she was right. She wasn't me. She couldn't upgrade the software. She couldn't skip around the admin center or create banners or add widgets to the blog. If something ever went seriously wrong, she wouldn't know how to handle it.

Huge sigh. It wasn't important enough to worry about.

I turned back to a section of code Ajit had asked me to review so he could explain it to me later. This was what I cared about. The forum would wait.

Monday night, in Shane's empty apartment, I suddenly felt exhausted and alone. It made no sense. I'd seen him less than forty-eight hours before, and I was surrounded by proof of his existence. I poked around his things, trying to get to know him better, but his things weren't him. I found a super soft Arctic Monkeys T-shirt with holes in it that looked like he'd owned it since high school. I put it on.

On Tuesday night, Eden called to invite me to come over to hang out at Jo's for a while, saying, "I know you can start to freak out a little when they're on the road."

Freaking out. That was what I was feeling, not loneliness after all. Just a pent-up impatience and curiosity about where they were and what they were doing. I'd found fan video, but watching the band onstage wasn't what I needed. I'd talked to Shane on video chat, and that helped, but I was a pinball of anxiety. I'd only feel settled when he came back.

As I sat on Jo's patio sipping a beer, I explained, "It isn't that I don't trust him out there. It's just—"

"Tour widow."

"What?"

"You're a tour widow. You're living with a ghost while he's away."

"God, yes. That's exactly it."

She nodded. "Yeah, I hate it. But it's the life you're signing up for. Are you cut out for it?"

Her tone didn't convey judgment. More like warning. I didn't want her to worry. "Look. I've been alone plenty. I can do solitude. Everything's just so new. And I miss him."

Knowing he'd be home the next day only made it harder to fall asleep that night, but I finally drifted off. I woke to sheets lifting as a body slid in next to mine. A hand caressed my shoulder. Lips gently kissed my neck. I spun around.

"You're home?"

"We decided not to spend the night when we were just a few hours away."

He pressed a kiss to my forehead, and I rolled away, hand over my mouth. "You can't kiss me."

"What?"

I jumped up. "I have morning breath."

He started laughing. "I don't care."

"I do!" I ran to the bathroom and brushed my teeth. When I came back, he was stretched out, looking so delicious I could eat him alive.

He held a hand out. I climbed onto the mattress and walked on my knees back beside him. He played with the hem of my shirt, his shirt. "You look good in this." He lifted it up. "Can you take it off?"

I slipped it off, and he just stared. My nipples hardened under his gaze. I swallowed, imagining all the things I wanted to do to him first. It took all of a heartbeat to zero in on that mouth. More than anything, I needed to kiss him. I fell more than crawled the rest of the way to him, catching myself with one hand on either side of his head, an inch from his face. His lips turned up into a wicked grin.

"Why I believe you've missed me." He lifted his head and nipped at my lips.

I pulled back, teasing. "Maybe a little."

He tried again, and this time I let him catch me, losing myself in the sensual decadence of him. I slung my leg over his hip, grinding into his hardening cock. His hands wrapped around my waist before sliding up to thumb my nipples.

"Unfair," I whispered into his lips. "You're still wearing too much."

"You, too."

We sat up and took care of the barriers between us, then lay side by side, face to face, tracing each other gently, exploring slowly. I was torn between burning off my desire for him in a quick wham-bam-thank-you-ma'am, but this wasn't our first time together, and somehow we both understood there were other pleasures to be had. I discovered I could drive him insane by doing nothing more than running my nails softly down his spine. He could reciprocate by dragging his tongue down the nape of my neck.

After we'd worked ourselves into a state of heightened need, he slid his hand down my stomach, and with one touch, I nearly exploded in pleasure.

I pulled his hand back up and threaded my fingers into his, tugging him toward me. "Make love to me, Shane."

We rolled as one, me onto my back, him over me. He breathed out as he entered me, muttering something unintelligible. My eyes rolled back in my head at the sensation. As always, he started slow, but I wanted more.

I shoved his shoulder, and he followed my lead, turning us together, so he was under me. I sat up and began rolling my hips, taking him deep and then rocking forward until he was nearly free of me, then slamming back down hard. He gasped back an expletive. I set a punishing rhythm, pounding into him again and again.

All that foreplay had me so close already, that I only had to look down at Shane's face, twisted in ecstasy before the endorphin rush exploded, releasing a beautiful wave of pure bliss down my legs and up my spine in total satisfaction. I dropped my head onto his chest, breathing heavy.

Realizing I'd climaxed, Shane started to ease me off him, but he was ramrod straight inside me. I sat up, grinding back down on him again. I reached behind me until I found the apex of his legs and touched his balls with the tips of my fingers. They drew up tight, like walnuts, and he hissed out, "Holy fuck, Layla." I lifted my hips, fucking him while I played with him, and in another few moments, he came hard in me.

I dropped down beside him, and he pulled me over, wrapping his arms around me. I expected him to fall asleep, but instead, he said, "I've missed you. Tell me what you've been doing."

"Seriously? I should be asking you that. I've just been working."

"Have you gotten a chance to work on any of that, what did you call it, Python?"

"I can't believe you remembered I was working on that."

"You said you hoped they'd let you get some experience."

I'd mentioned it during one of our FaceTime calls, but I hadn't dwelled on it. I didn't think he'd find it that interesting. It touched me that he'd picked up on it. "Yeah, Ajit—that's my co-worker—is teaching me."

"And will they let you program?"

I sighed and turned to face him. "I doubt it. Ajit says I have a solid sense of the basics, but it's not enough." I bit my lip for a second before articulating the dream I'd begun to cultivate. "I think I want to take classes, maybe get a certification or two. Then I might be able to show them that I could join their team as a full-time developer instead of someone who comes up with ideas to pass along to them to code."

"So why don't you? There are probably summer classes. Have you looked into it?"

The wheels were spinning in my head. I was never going to fall asleep with all the possibilities. "I'm going to look into it tomorrow."

Chapter Twenty-Five

Tomorrow came a hell of a lot earlier than I ever thought possible. I nearly slept through my alarm. Shane didn't stir until I broke out of his stranglehold to turn my phone off. Then he grabbed me and pulled me back into him, whispering, "Stay."

"I can't."

"I know." He frowned. "Hurry back home. I'll make dinner."

"You cook?" This man would never stop surprising me.

"I'm an amazing cook. Just you wait."

I could not wait. But work also couldn't, so I got up, showered, and dressed, planting one last kiss on my gorgeous drummer boy before heading out for the day.

Fortunately, the day was routine. I had meetings. I put in my headphones and worked on a new proposal based on tools I'd found lacking while working on my blog post. I chatted in the breakroom with Ajit about his plans to take his kids to Dis-

236 Mary Ann Marlowe

ney for the first time. I got an email from Lars about setting up a rehearsal with Whiplash in a couple of weeks and nearly fell out of my chair. I texted the news to Ash and basked in her gushing.

At five, I yawned and stretched, closed my laptop, and made the mental trip from my cube, down the elevator, out to the street, into the subway station, through the tunnels, and finally up the stairs into Brooklyn where Shane waited for me. From there, my thoughts turned pornographic. Was it possible to wear him out?

Whatever hesitation I'd felt at the start of this fling or whatever it was, I'd only grown more attached to him. And he'd become more trusting. Everything was perfect.

I pictured him sitting in his apartment staring at the door, wearing nothing but a towel. My thighs cramped in agony.

When I opened the front door, Shane did sit on the sofa, elbows on his knees, staring at his open laptop on the coffee table. He so rarely cracked out the big tech, I wondered if he was writing music. My face broke out into the stupidest grin, thinking he might be writing me a love song.

"Whatcha doing?" I plopped beside him, expecting him to start talking a mile a minute about music or kiss me or jump up and cook me a sumptuous dinner.

Instead, he pegged me with narrowed eyes. "Do you happen to know Adam's middle name?"

"Joshua," I said without missing a beat, and then the universe expanded and collapsed in an earth-shattering heartbeat, and I understood. "I only know that because—"

"Because you're not just a casual fan. You're number one, president-of-the-fan-club level of fan. Right?"

"I'm what?"

"You literally have a fan club."

"Well, not exactly—"

"No, exactly." He lifted the laptop screen so I could see what he'd been looking at. The Talking Disaster banner was the one displaying the neck of a guitar with Adam's fingers fretting a C chord.

"Why are you looking at that?"

He frowned so hard, I didn't recognize him. " 'Noah's ass is a work of art.' " He gestured at the screen where those exact words stared back at me beside my username. Never mind it was dated two years ago.

I'd been posting on my fan site for years. It would take some digging to find specific posts where I'd said anything that could be construed as infatuation for any of the musicians. "How did you find that?"

"What does it matter? A better question would be, why didn't you mention that you were more interested in my band than you are in me? And oh, my God, are you interested in Adam! Was that your ultimate goal?" He laughed, a bitter nasty laugh. "Of course, it was. You got it, too. You played on Jo, one of the most trusting people I've ever known, and Micah, and me. Congrats. You got your invitation to hang with the band. Is that why you took a job at the magazine? How's it feel to be on the inside?"

I touched his arm. "Shane."

He jerked like I'd scorched him. I dropped my hand.

"How about this one?" He clicked on a tab along the top. Adam's face filled the screen. Shane scrolled until he reached my comment and read, " 'That's one of my favorites. Wouldn't mind trading places with that microphone.' "

"Shane. It's not like that. I had no intentions. Things just happened."

"Things just happened? That's a convenient excuse."

"I never planned to meet any of you. I swear." He was freaking me out. I'd never seen him angry, and he looked about ready to burst a vein.

His finger wagged at the laptop. "That comment is from the night I met you."

I pressed my fingers against my closed eyelids. "It doesn't mean anything, Shane. It's a fan forum."

"I have more. Shall I go through them?"

He clicked another tab. He had an ungodly number of web pages open. Had he been sitting here all day saving my past infractions for this confrontation?

I gave him a pleading look. "Are you telling me you've never been a fan? The Police. The Who. David Bowie. You can't tell me you wouldn't lose your mind if you met them."

"I admire those artists." He waved at the monitor. "I don't spend my time worshiping them. Lusting after them."

"I don't lust after anyone besides you, Shane, though you're making me reassess even that. I'm just a fan."

His cold eyes, barely visible through slits, cut toward me. "If that's true, then you won't mind staying away from Adam."

Boom.

My head felt like it was full of cotton. Had I lost my hearing? "Excuse me?"

"Don't go to their rehearsal Friday. Don't hang out with Eden while I'm gone. In fact, steer clear of Jo. Show me how little they matter to you."

Boom.

Every detonation blew a hole in my capacity to think logically. I had no name for what I was feeling. Confused, appalled, defensive, sorry, angry. It was new territory for me, and I didn't like it one bit. I didn't like the way he looked at me.

"Are you fucking crazy, Shane?"

He leaned in, uncomfortably close while wearing that sneer. "Me? I'm not the one desperately trying to sleep my way into a band's inner circle."

With that, my emotions crystallized into one single action: escape.

"Nope," I said and stood, intending to walk away from him.

"What do you mean, 'Nope?' " He followed behind me and tugged my elbow.

I wrested free and ran up the stairs where I shoved anything within grabbing distance into a suitcase. I didn't know where I was going. I just had to get out.

"Stop, Layla."

I stopped. "What?"

"What are you doing?"

"I'm walking away, Shane. You gave me an ultimatum, and I'm choosing not to play by your rules. You don't control who I do or don't see. I control that, and right now I'm choosing not to see you."

"You admit it then. This was never about me. You're done with me and now you just move on?"

I clenched my fist and fought back a scream. "This is about *you* being a dick to *me* right now. Nobody else. Just you and me."

"Where do you think you're going to go?"

"I don't know."

He pulled out his cell phone. "I'll call Jo and tell her not to take you in. Then I'll call Adam. He won't want you to come to the rehearsal after I share all this. Who do you think they'll side with?"

He was right about that. I sagged, hoping to make him relent. "It's my job, Shane. If you make that call, you'll jeopardize my career."

"Fine." He shoved the phone back in his pocket. "I won't make the choice for you, but I find it really hard to trust your motives, Layla."

"I find it really hard to give a shit, right now, Shane. You're behaving like a total asshole."

"Let's make it easy then."

I put my hand on my hip, acting tougher than I felt. "What are you talking about?"

"You got what you wanted. You don't need me anymore. So, let's just call it quits."

I sniffed and straightened my back. As if me packing a suitcase hadn't been a clue I'd already come to that conclusion. "Go on and paint yourself as a victim, used by everyone around you and discarded when they get what they want. Maybe you think people owe you their love in return for your magnanimous generosity and that justifies emotional blackmail. It's as if you think that's the only way to get people to love you."

He looked like I'd slapped him. My voice was too loud, and my finger was shaking, scolding him. I wasn't done.

"You know what, Shane? You set your own self up to be mistreated because you assume you will be. When you are, you're justified in your self-pity." I backhanded the tears from my cheek. "If you believed me capable of treating you that way, then this was never going to work."

I turned to go before the ramifications of what was happening hit me. I could cry in a taxi. For now, I needed to walk straight. I needed to keep to the high road.

Before I made it to his front door, he lobbed one last grenade after me. "Good luck with Adam. Try to remember he's married."

Fuck the high road. I spun back. "Call me when you grow up, Shane."

Then I rushed into the hall and slammed the door, so I wouldn't have to see his face.

Fortunately, Uber drivers responded faster than my ability to change my mind. I gave the driver Jo's address, hoping she wouldn't turn me away. For all I knew it was Jo who'd ratted me out, and if not, Shane may have already poisoned her against me. But I had nowhere else to go, so I texted her and breathed a sigh of relief when she replied:

Come on over. Eden's here and we're out on the patio staying out of Micah's way.

I was about to knock on the door when it swung open. As Micah went past shouldering trash bags down the steps, I slipped into the townhouse.

"Hello?" I called through the kitchen.

"Out here!" The patio door slid open a foot. From the darkness beyond, Jo waved me to join them. "Grab a drink from the fridge if you want. Micah bought beer."

A beer would have been perfect right about then.

I closed the door behind me and pulled up a chair. Eden had a beer, but Jo drank iced tea.

"We thought you'd be spending your few hours with Shane." Jo giggled with a salacious waggle.

"Did he chase you off so he could contemplate how sad his life was without you?" Eden was completely slumped down in her chair, practically sitting on her own back, with her bottle perched on her belly.

Just like that I burst into tears. "Oh, God." I turned my face away and pressed the hem of my T-shirt against my eyes.

A hand on my back, rubbing side to side, did not have the intended calming effect, and everything in me suddenly broke. The sobbing was embarrassing.

"Hey, everything's okay." Jo's subtle southern accent did the trick, and I managed to stop heaving. My breathing slowed, and I wiped my face one last time on my sleeve.

Eden had sat up, elbows on the table, concern in her dark eyes. "You want to tell us what's going on?"

"It's silly. I mean, we barely know each other. It's only been a couple of weeks."

"Oh. Well, if you don't feel you can talk to us." Jo twisted her lips into a frown.

I realized how they'd interpret what I'd said. "No. I don't mean you. I meant Shane. How can I be so upset about a guy I met two weeks ago?"

The two exchanged a look, then Eden said, "My mom once told me that time doesn't matter. She said that some couples take years to figure it out, but for others it's as obvious as night and day."

"Oh. I don't think—" I wasn't sure how to explain that things were as clear as mud with Shane.

"Then again, my mom has a lot of terrible advice."

I actually snort-laughed, and it felt great to find something funny.

Jo laid a hand on mine. "Did y'all have a fight?"

"I think what we had was a breakup."

"Are you sure?" Jo shot a concerned look at Eden.

Eden picked up on a signal. "Jo and I know a thing or two about musicians."

Jo nodded. "You wouldn't believe how close we both came to relationship-ending drama."

I looked up to the heavens for strength. They were going to hate me, but I had to come clean. "Oh, I know all about it."

"Sure." Eden tapped her finger against her bottle. "Did you know Adam wanted me to stay with him after the gossip articles came out, but I left him without giving him a chance to work things out?"

That wasn't in any papers. "No, I—"

"Yup. I could have saved myself quite a bit of pain if I'd just talked it out with him, but we both had some things to learn."

Jo leaned forward. "Did you know that Micah never broke things off with me? I needed the space, but then we dated in secret until the gossip about us blew over."

"What?" That wasn't the story anyone knew at all. "I thought—"

"I walked out on him because I couldn't take the pressure, but I realized he was worth putting up with all the scrutiny."

"I don't understand why you're telling me all this."

Eden stood and drained her bottle. "You and Shane started out at a breakneck pace."

"You just said—"

She dropped the bottle into the trash and pulled open the sliding door but stopped long enough to say, "What I said about time? It's true. Jo and I are telling you that you were in for a crash at some point. It happened faster than I would have predicted, but I'm not surprised. Shane's going on tour for a week. Take the time to step back and re-assess what you need."

As she disappeared into the kitchen, Jo squeezed my hand. "Eden's right, but you know, don't mind her sharp way of framing things. What she means to say is, things have a way of working out."

I sniffled. "Thanks. I appreciate that."

"Do you mind if I ask what you were fighting over?"

Shane's wish that I break things off with everyone might come true if I confessed, but it was going to all be out there sooner or later. Better if it came from me.

I covered my face with both hands for a few seconds, then peeked out through my fingers. "I run a fan site."

Eden stepped back out with two bottles in one hand. She held one out to me and sat. "You do what?"

Time to rip off the bandage. "Jo was asking why we fought. Shane found out about a fan site I run, and it upset him."

"Oh." Eden's mouth pinched ever so slightly. Or maybe I was imagining it. "What kind of fan site?"

I closed my eyes. Moment of truth. I took one breath, then a second, then opened my eyes. "It's a Walking Disaster fan site."

Her lips folded into her mouth, pressed together, like she was holding back her initial reaction, but then her chest shook, and I realized she was trying hard not to laugh.

"It's something I started when I was in college. Really, I just wanted to learn how to write the code, but then people showed up. Plus, I made some money on ads. Then it kind of blew up."

"You run Talking Disaster?" Eden looked more amused than I would have expected.

"Yeah." I decided to shut up and let her process it.

"Kind of blew up is an understatement. It's bigger than the official fan forum. By far."

"I know. I helped with the official fan forum when the label first set it up."

"Really? Are you responsible for how shitty it is?"

I cackled. "No, I fought with them to get better software. It's unusable. They had a platform for a bunch of musicians, so we were stuck with it. I did cheerlead and try to get people to move over. It would have been a bit of a relief to finally shut my site down. I mean, look at me. I'm gonna be thirty."

Eden was still chortling. For the first time she reached out and shook my hand in greeting. "Well, it's nice to meet you. You must be Pumpkin." Then she waved at my hair. "Another mystery solved."

"You know me?"

"Hell, yeah, I know you. You are an amazing site admin. How many times did I want to hug you for how you protect us from rampant fan speculation?"

I heaved a huge sigh of relief. "I'm sorry I didn't tell you any of this sooner. It's just. It's kind of embarrassing. Then Noah made such a big deal about being a super fan."

"Why exactly is Shane mad?" Jo's face was scrunched in genuine curiosity.

"I think he's partly mad I didn't tell him about it."

They both nodded, and I thought for sure they'd tell me he was right. Eden said, "Well, I'd be a huge hypocrite to chastise you for holding back on him. I nearly wrecked my relationship with Adam for hiding things."

"Same," said Jo. "You guys are in a new relationship. It takes time to trust that."

"Right. Still, I can't blame him for feeling blindsided." I picked at the hem of my shirt, uncomfortable with the rest. "But he also thinks I'm using him as a steppingstone to become friends with Adam." I nodded to Eden. "And you. And the rest of the band."

"Wow. That's about the stupidest man logic I've heard yet." Eden's eyes were wide with disbelief.

Jo's brows had permanently knit together. "Why wouldn't you have just used me, if that were the case? I could have introduced you to any one of them. And I did actually." She laughed. "I introduced you to Shane."

The thought of using her horrified me. I hoped she didn't think I had. "You know I didn't . . . I wouldn't . . ."

"I know that, silly. I'm the one who invited you here. I'm the one who dragged you to Eden's barbecue. Shane's the one who offered to walk you home. I assume he's the one who insisted you go to his rehearsal and the festival, and Adam's the one who invited you to *his* rehearsal."

Eden added, "Not to mention I've seen you in action. You're more like a manager at a daycare. You never fawn. You drop in and encourage others, mixing with them here and there. You know you could have used your own position to gain access, but you've never once even asked."

"I *have* posted some appreciative comments about the band. I mean, before, when they were single."

"See? Most people don't even bother to make that distinction. Girls drooling over Adam is kind of baked into his existence. And mine." She duck-lipped a look of resignation.

My entire body sagged in relief. "So, it's not weird that I'm a dorky fan geek of your husband's band?"

Eden shrugged. "If that's weird, add me to the club. I'd have to question your judgment if you weren't a huge fan of my super talented husband."

Silence settled, but I still had a problem. I blew out a breath. "Shane doesn't seem to share your point of view."

Jo rubbed my forearm. "I'm sure he's overreacting. He'll realize that and come around."

That wouldn't solve the fact that he'd been a total asshole to me. "I'm not sure I want him to come around. He was so jealous and—" I stopped myself. Shane was their friend more than I was. It felt wrong to speak ill of him and possibly undermine his relationships, especially since he was more likely to stick around than I was. I had no connections here.

"And?" Eden cocked her head. "You can speak your mind. Those guys are bozos most of the time."

"Well, I like him. I do." I bit my lip, trying to think how to phrase this. "This jealousy seems so out of proportion for where we are in our relationship. He's rushing everything, and I haven't even unpacked my suitcases."

Jo nodded. "Micah moved wicked fast, and I wasn't really ready for that. We sorted it out, of course." She patted my hand. "Go on."

Her confession made me less anxious than I had been about opening up with them. "I mentioned it to him, but he's so charming, he put me at ease. I mean, he was acting possessive, but in a way that felt safe and okay." I grabbed my beer and took a long swallow. "Then today, he demanded I don't go to the rehearsal Friday. He ordered me to stay away from you all."

Eden arched one eyebrow. "Excuse me?"

"That was my reaction exactly."

"Well, obviously he's wrong."

I let myself fully relax for the first time in hours. "Oh, thank God."

"You didn't think you deserved that, did you?" Jo crossed her arms, and I was loving the girl power solidarity.

"No. That's why I told him he couldn't dictate my choices and grabbed my suitcase and left."

Eden jumped to her feet. "Oh, hell no. This will not stand."

"Where are you going?" I made to follow her, but Jo held up a hand.

"I'm going to have a little talk with my brother." Eden tossed her hair defiantly and slipped into the townhouse.

Jo turned back to me. "So, have you considered starting a website for a photographer? She'd pay you. Asking for a friend."

I choked on my beer, laughing.

Then her expression shifted to concerned. "You stay here as long as you need."

A weight lifted.

Ten minutes later, Eden rejoined us, saying, "Okay. I've let Micah know what's going on, and he's going to talk some sense into Shane."

"Thank you. I don't know what I've done to deserve such friendship. I'm sorry to have brought this drama here."

She sort of punched my shoulder. "I should apologize. I always meant to reach out to you on the forum and send you tickets or flowers or money. It always passed through my mind and then escaped me. Maybe I can make it up in the future."

How could she not know that just the offer was better than anything she could have given me? Knowing that I'd made her and Adam proud of my site was worth more than any compensation they might give me. Then I had an idea.

"You know what would be huge?"

She cocked her head. "What?"

"If you could come on the site sometime and do a Q&A."

"I don't think your fans would want to talk to me." She stuck out her tongue, like she'd eaten a bug, imitating the imagined fan disgust.

I chuckled that she'd called them *my* fans. "Oh, but they would. Really."

She didn't look convinced but said, "However, I think I could convince Adam to do it." She laughed at my sudden shock. "He loves talking to fans. I think he might have volunteered if it wouldn't have made him look like the attention-seeking fan whore he innocently pretends not to be."

"God. The server might go down."

"Why don't we arrange something to coincide with whatever you get Friday. You can give Lars some video. Keep some as exclusive to your site. Then Adam will hang out on the forum for an hour."

I was speechless. "That—" I couldn't finish. I just grabbed her in the biggest bear hug I could, and for the first time, I heard her really laugh. It was a truly gorgeous sound.

"My boobs are gonna explode. Adam's probably going insane alone with the baby." She grabbed her purse and shot me another glance. "I still can't believe you're Pumpkin. How crazy is that?"

The Rock Paper

Fly on the wall: Walking Disaster
By Layla Beckett

I'm going to confess something right up front. I'm a huge dork for Walking Disaster. I'm not an overnight fan. I didn't discover them after they hit the pop charts. I don't forget about them between albums, and I never have something better to do when they pass through the town where I live. I love a lot of bands, but I obsess over Walking Disaster.

Proof?

I have every one of their albums plus recordings from back when they were called The Pickup Artists. I own a T-shirt from every single tour. My ultimate cred is that, as someone recently told me, I'm literally the president of the fan club. I run a fan forum called Talking Disaster, and it's one of the most popular fan sites for Walking Disaster.

To say I was thrilled to sit in on their rehearsal in a quiet Brooklyn suburb would be a quantum understatement. Lucky for you, the band let me record everything, so you don't have to take my word for how incredible they were.

To be honest, this wasn't the first time I've met Adam. In fact, it was the third time. However, I'd initially gotten to know private citizen Adam, backyard barbecuer, diaper-changing dad, and super nice guy. But the man in the rehearsal studio was all rock star. His white T-shirt bunched up around the waist of his black jeans, and his tattoos peeked out below his sleeves. He strode over and gave me a hug like we were old friends. He smelled like heat and mystery. And dryer sheets, honestly.

Some of the video is below the fold, but with the blessings of the band, there will be another blog with extra bonus videos posted on the Talking Disaster fan forum later today.

Chapter Twenty-Six

Over breakfast Thursday, Jo reminded me I could talk to Zion about rooming with him over in Williamsburg. She said, "He spends half his time over at Andrew's anyway."

But I didn't want to take advantage of Jo and her friends anymore.

It had been foolish of me to slide into cohabitation with a guy I just met. I should have at least set up an alternate residence in case things didn't work out.

Like exactly right now.

I started combing through craigslist, calling people, finding out I couldn't afford any place in this area of Brooklyn. I estimated how much Shane was paying from a real estate site. No idea if he owned or rented, but either way: *Yowza*. I hoped for his sake the band didn't break up and wondered why he wasn't kissing Noah's ass to make sure things stayed solid.

Friday morning, a tour bus pulled up in front of the town-house, purring loudly as Micah and Noah loaded up the things they'd taken out to the sidewalk. I watched from the window and wondered if Shane was aboard. If he was, he didn't make his presence known.

As the bus rolled away, leaving Jo a tour widow again, she called for her driver and, on her way to the art gallery, dropped me off outside Shane's to pack up the rest of my things. I prayed the security code he gave me would work.

On the street outside that paint-chipped green door, she scrawled out directions to drummer Hervé's house for the Walk-ing Disaster rehearsal, then gave me a hug, saying, "Are you sure you don't want me to stay with you?"

But there was no need. I only had a few things at Shane's, and I wanted to be alone when I confronted the space we'd shared, even if only briefly.

Once inside, I went on the hunt for anything I'd left be-hind. It all fit into a duffel bag Jo had lent me. Toiletries mainly. A pair of socks. Some dirty clothes in his hamper. Such a small imprint I'd left on his world, but his apartment dredged up so many fond memories. Memories of him playing his guitar for me, calling me Star Shine, feeding me cinnamon croissants, and making love to me passionately and gently. I honestly thought he'd fallen in love with me. How stupid was I?

I was tempted to squat while he was away, deal with my lodging problems later. Shane would be gone until next Sunday. He had weird food in his fridge and a bookshelf full of books I should have already read. I grabbed *The Little Prince* and climbed into his bed with a sidelong glance at his empty pillow. Where was he? Was he thinking about me? I tried to stoke my anger at him, but mostly what I felt was sad.

But then I remembered how he'd asked me to distance myself from the only friends I'd made simply because they happened to be the same people I'd fixated on for years. Okay, when I thought about it that way, I could kind of see his point, but it hadn't been an issue until his jealousy reared its ugly head. And I hated the thought of giving in to bullying even once. What a slippery slope toward total subjugation.

I took out my phone and checked my calendar. I only had a couple of hours to kill before I was expected at the Walking Disaster rehearsal, an event that should have given me nothing but endless joy, and here it was colored by guilt and self-doubt. Fuck Shane. I was going to go, and I was going to enjoy every second of this once-in-a-lifetime experience.

With my duffel bag in hand, I started to drop his key off on the funky table I'd admired the first time he'd shown me his extra cool lair, but I couldn't let it go. I might never use it again, but it was a link I needed to hold onto a little while longer. I locked and closed the door, hoping it wasn't metaphorical. I still wanted to find some way to work things out, but I didn't know how. Not with his attitude. Not with my refusal to be someone other than who I was.

And with that, I left Shane's world behind, summoned an Uber, and headed to the address Jo had given me. I got out a block early to grab a cup of coffee, then with nerves flipping over in my stomach, walked up the front steps to the home of the legendary drummer, Hervé Diaz.

Hervé opened the door with a massive grin. "You must be Layla. Jo said such lovely things about you." I grabbed the hand he'd extended, expecting to say hi and shake, but he tugged me into a hug. "Any friend of Jo's has to be all right. Come on in. The guys are setting up downstairs."

He whisked me down to his basement, which was completely decked out with a couple of sound booths and all kinds of production recording equipment. I may have wiped the drool from my chin.

Charles McCord and Mark Townsend both greeted me with a wave and a salute respectively. My eyes bugged out. Stay cool, Layla.

"And I don't think I need to tell you who that is."

Adam was sitting on an amp, walking an octave up the neck of a guitar. Fucking sexy as hell. "Layla! You made it!"

He crossed the room and gave me a hug, and I didn't even think about sniffing him. "Thanks so much for inviting me to do this. It's such a great honor."

He chuckled. "Well, I hope it works out for you."

And right then, it was evident that he was doing this as a favor to me, not because his band needed the exposure it would bring. They didn't need it. But I needed them, and he was okay with that. I felt humbled that he'd extend his powers of good to someone like me.

Hervé showed me where to set up my equipment, then I lived every fan girl's fantasy. Again.

The guys played for a couple of hours, and they made it more show than rehearsal. In fact, it wasn't the fly-on-the-wall experience I'd expected at all. It felt planned out, almost scripted. There was no bickering. They didn't squabble over songs. They weren't putting together a setlist for an actual tour. The band wasn't even touring, which made me wonder: What were they rehearsing for?

They did play some unreleased material, and that would be the gold in my article and a huge hit at my forum. But they mainly played songs off their latest album, all super polished and professional.

I couldn't help but compare the experience to the rehearsal with Shane's band, a band I hadn't followed as closely, and yet, they'd set a bar no other band would reach. And the reason for that wasn't the music or the performances or even how welcome they made me feel. It was simply Shane's joy at having me there.

And for the first time, I almost regretted choosing this over the boy who'd given me those shy smiles when Noah had first accused me of being a super fan. Turns out maybe Noah had been right. Maybe my priorities were completely out of whack.

What was I doing here? Was this really worth losing Shane over? Surely Lars would understand if I didn't follow through. This wasn't even my real job.

Everyone I knew online would be eating their hearts out with jealousy if they knew where I was sitting, but all I could think about was how lonely I was going to feel when I walked out with a camera full of videos and nobody to go home to.

As the band wrapped up, I thanked them for giving me such an incredible opportunity, hoping my gushing sounded as sincere as it would have been just a month earlier. I did appreciate them donating their time, especially since they didn't need to at all, kicking myself for having mixed emotions on a day like today.

What the hell was wrong with me?

Once I got back to Jo's, I set to work writing the blog and editing videos. Once Lars gave me the go-head, I posted the article on the *Rock Paper*, then went over and stared at a blinking cursor on my own site, trying to figure out how to word my unmasking.

At Adam's suggestion, and cleared by Lars, I planned to write an exclusive for Talking Disaster to coincide with the magazine article. By mentioning my site in the magazine, I'd already given the game away. My fans didn't need to be spoon-fed clues on the worst of days. They'd connect the dots in a heartbeat. Still, writing it out on my own blog felt like a huge confession. One that would invite a ton of questions and open the door to the kind of scrutiny I'd tried to protect the band from.

But it was time to come out from behind my moniker and own my double identity. It was time to be Layla.

Talking Disaster Forum

AdamAnt wrote:
Hey, she mentioned our forum.

Di$a$ter wrote:
She didn't just mention it. She said she runs it.

AdamAnt wrote:
Shit, is that Pumpkin?

Talking Disaster wrote:
Gotta be. Hey, Pumpkin! Say something!

Wannabe wrote:
Did you guys hear the new song?

DiazRules wrote:
What did she mean by more to come? Do you think there are more videos, or is she going to come give us a recap?

ADAMate wrote:
Pumpkin!! Bravo! I love seeing our community mentioned in the ROCK PAPER! OMG!

InTheMood wrote:
Wow, what a bounty of WD goodness.

AdamFannnn wrote:
Thank you Pumpkin/Layla for making me almost feel like I was there. It sounds like it was a most wonderful time. I love the new songs! I also loved Adam's between song banter.

JacksMom wrote:
Pumpkin, what kind of camera did you use to record with.

Delusion wrote:
and Mark's guitar skillz are CRAZY good.!!

Knope4Prez wrote:
PUMPKIN! You are FAMOUS!!!

AdamAdamAdam wrote:
On the internet.

Chapter Twenty-Seven

*W*hen I got to the forum, someone had already started a thread with the link. I blew a raspberry. Why did I bother updating my blog?

As I expected, they immediately honed in on who'd posted the article rather than the actual content. I was tickled at how happy they were that the forum itself got name dropped, like it made them famous, but I wasn't surprised when one of the more cantankerous posters said I was a hypocrite for moving in on Adam in that way. Another poster who balked at commercial influence suggested that maybe I'd been friends with them all along. *What if she set this site up for them?* He was met with a chorus of *So, what?* Even if the label had set it up, there'd been no interference. It had always been a welcoming environment.

That didn't stop them from speculating.

RetiredNurse wrote: *Pumpkin's always quick to stop conversations that get too invasive. Like she's got a personal stake.*

Shy Guy wrote: *Don't forget she did the Theater of the Absurd thing too. Maybe she's been an insider all along.*

Ouch. Nobody could claim they held back on their opinions. I'd be lying if I said it didn't sting a little to hear them question my integrity so openly.

Thankfully, CanadaFan was the voice of reason. *Why would she just now make herself public then? You all are grasping at straws. Let's wait and hear from her.*

Sounded like a call to make my entrance.

I cracked my knuckles and started writing a post on the thread.

Hi, guys. To answer your questions, no I haven't been working for the label all this time. The truth is, I got a job at the Rock Paper. *The whole rehearsal idea came about organically, and I feel super fortunate to have been able to participate.*

Also, you guys should be making plans to be online later today, because in addition to some more exclusive video, Adam has agreed to come by the forum and do a Q&A around five. Start posting questions here now. I'll pick out a few and post them in a new thread. And check out the blog for an exclusive video of "Hurricane Warning."

That should get them off my case. I'd be a hero for all this content

I took a break to steal a bottle of San Pellegrino from Jo's fridge. I missed Shane's pretentious water. I missed him. I'd written the entire article with him riding on my shoulder. I could picture him grousing at all the gushing I had to do.

I didn't regret anything I'd written though.

First because it was honest. My admiration for the band was legitimate, but Shane's jealousy was misplaced. I had no interest in any of those guys romantically, and my comments about Adam's sexiness didn't change that.

Second because, truthfully, I wanted Shane to hurt. Shitty of me, I know. He clearly had issues that went beyond me, but if I was going to be accused of something, I might as well get the enjoyment of the crime. I laid it all out there. If he was ever going to come to terms with me, he'd have to take me with all of my wide-eyed fascination with rock musicians.

As if he wouldn't have jumped at the chance to sit in a room while Keith Moon had rehearsed with The Who. I made a mental note to ask him exactly that.

If I ever had a chance to.

As questions rolled in, I called Eden. She passed the phone to Adam so I could walk him through the registration. I made his account unavailable to private messages, because come on.

"Can you get Eden to record you sitting at the computer with the fan site up? Some idiot's going to think you're an impostor."

As I'd expected, someone called bullshit on the authenticity of Adam's participation, so as soon as I got the video from Eden, I posted it at the top of the answer thread. That ought to shut up the majority of them. There'd always be some spoil sport.

The next hour was amazing.

I started the Q&A with a softball lob. AdamFannn asked: *Describe yourself in three words.*

Adam took forever to write a response, but eventually he wrote:

Hard-working, loyal and uh . . . I've always wanted to be referred to as erudite. Can I go with that? Eden is sitting here saying nobody will believe that, so I'll say kind. I like to think I'm kind.

Thankfully, the Q&A was a madhouse that demanded my attention and pushed Shane from my mind. We ended up going over the hour, and Adam allowed us to go on another thirty minutes, promising to come back and do it again some time.

Once I knew he was done, I called Eden back to thank her for getting Adam to do the Q&A.

"No need to thank me or Adam. Really, it was long over-due. He was just going to sit here and veg out flipping channels anyway."

I laughed. "Please don't ever say that to the fans. You're killing my image of him."

"I'm pretty sure he'll do that himself over time." It amazed me that she seemed to assume that there would be time for me to come to that conclusion. She snickered, probably aware that despite how normal he was, he was still sexy as fuck. "I'll see you at Jo's tonight, right? Rom com night?"

"Oh, yeah. See you then!"

In a million years, I never would have thought I'd one day be friends with them. If I had, my fantasy of it wouldn't have met at all with the reality. I would have imagined myself as a totally different person first of all—witty and cool, clever and interesting. The first night I'd met Adam, I was wearing a bor-rowed T-shirt and I told him about my dad's band. Yup. uber cool.

I should have been over the moon, but everything was a fucking mess.

It would have been easier if I could have stayed mad at Shane, but after a couple of days apart, my initial outrage had subsided, and I remembered little things about him that I missed already. His laugh. His smell. His rock-hard body. His endear-ments. I wanted him to come home and call me Star Shine and I'd tease him with Cuddle Rock. Or maybe Star Shane. For once, I'd have a real-life relationship that didn't turn to shit.

Except it already had. Unless he could suddenly morph into someone who didn't try to take control of me, I was ratio-nalizing away some major flaws to allow myself to accept less than I deserved. My parents had taught me to value myself and trust my gut.

They were wrong about that though. My gut was a stupid traitor. No, I needed to listen to reason and carry on with my plan to move out and move on.

To do that, I needed to ignore my heart, though it was breaking.

It was around one or two in the morning. Eden had long since gone home, but Jo and I had moved to her backyard patio to enjoy the cool night air and talk. After watching a romantic comedy where everything went south, but then despite all the odds, the couple had worked things out again, I was wallowing in my own despair, wondering if Shane and I might find our way through.

"I don't know what I'm hoping for. An apology? A declaration of love?" It felt easy to talk into the darkness. Jo was kind enough to listen. "I'm beginning to wish I never met him."

"I doubt that. But—"

As if I'd conjured it, my phone rang with an incoming call from Shane. I hesitated. "Should I answer that?"

"Up to you." She started to stand, but I held up a finger. I wanted solidarity.

I hit Answer and put it on speaker. "Hi, Shane."

Silence.

"Hello?"

Nothing. Then some scratching sounds, muffled.

A voice came through, "—but he chickened out." It sounded like it came from several feet away. There was a heavy rumbling sound beneath the other sounds, like they were on the bus.

"I didn't chicken out." That was Shane, much closer. Much clearer. "It's complicated."

I looked over at Jo, eyebrow raised. She put her hands over her mouth. "Butt dial."

"Should I hang up?"

She shook her head and scooted closer to my phone when a different voice that sounded like Micah said, "It's not complicated. Do you want the girl?"

Shane: "You know I do, but—"

Micah: "But nothing. You do realize you're the one who fucked up, right?"

Shane: "Did you read what she wrote today? She got what she wanted."

The other voice. Noah? "You know, Shane. I tell you this all the time, but you are your own worst enemy."

Shane. "No, you are."

Micah: "Stop it, both of you, or I'll turn this bus around right now."

Jo and I just stared at each other, eyes wide, as we listened in. "Should I hang up?" It seemed obvious I shouldn't be eavesdropping on them. "I should hang up."

My thumb hovered over the End button, but she lifted a hand. "Wait a second."

She took out her phone and typed something. A ringtone sounded through my speaker, and she grinned. "That was my text to Micah."

A second passed before we heard Micah saying, "Shane, check your phone."

The ruffling sound increased, and then Shane's voice came through, loud and clear. "Layla? What the—"

"I think you accidentally called me."

"What? When? How long ago?"

"Just a second ago. I couldn't hear much. Are you on the bus?"

"Yeah, we just left Baltimore. It's only a couple of hours to D.C., so we're pressing on. I guess we get to sleep in tomorrow for a bit once we get to the hotel."

"How was your show?"

Jo stood and patted my back.

Shane's voice continued out the speaker. "We had a good crowd."

Jo pointed toward the house with a tilt to her head, clearly wanting to give us privacy. I nodded, and as she slipped through the sliding door, I switched the speaker off and held the phone to my ear. I wanted to listen to his voice like he was right there with me.

"Glad to hear it." The hitch in my voice gave away the emotion I wanted to hide.

Maybe he heard it because he added, "To be honest, it wasn't as fun without you here."

Should I tell him I missed him, too?

"So, does that mean you're no longer mad at me?"

"I'm not mad, Layla. I'm hurt. There's a difference."

"You're overreacting."

"Am I? I told you I needed more time, and not three days later, I get this email with links to pages filled with every single thing I've told you freaks me out."

"What do you mean you got an email?"

"It doesn't matter. It should have come from you. You could have warned me."

He was right about that. "I know. And I'm sorry." I sighed. "But you also said you were going to try and trust me. At the first bump in the road, you demanded I sever all ties with your friends. That's not an overreaction?"

"I shouldn't have asked that of you, but at that precise moment, I needed some certainty that you wanted to be with me. Only me."

"And it wasn't enough for me to tell you that?" I leaned back and stared at the pitch black sky, repressing a scream. "What did I tell you about your own mistrust being the very thing that was going to break us apart?"

"I know." His exhale came through, matching my own pent-up frustration. "But do you know how many times my mistrust has been well founded?"

"You're projecting your fear onto me, and I don't know what I can do to convince you that you're delusional, short of acquiescing to abusive demands."

"Abusive? I'm not—"

262 Mary Ann Marlowe

"Yes, Shane. You wanting to control me is abusive."

"I'm trying to convince you I'm *not* delusional. I've had girlfriends dump me the minute they thought they had a chance with Noah."

"Noah stole your girlfriend?"

"No. Not exactly. Noah's just . . . Noah."

"What does that mean?"

"Well, you've met him. Imagine having him come tell me that my girlfriend tried to seduce him."

"That's awful, Shane." I understood where he was coming from, but that didn't solve our issues. "Still, I'm not the girl who broke your trust. I didn't try to seduce Noah. Whatever I said about him on a fan forum years ago isn't reality. I never wanted to actually *be* with Noah."

"What you wrote about Adam wasn't years ago. That was today."

I wanted to throttle him. "That was an article for fans. I wrote it as a fan."

"There's a magnitude of difference between being a casual fan and running a fan site."

"Not really. It's just a hobby. It's not a criminal enterprise."

"It's more than just a ringtone of your favorite song. It's an obsession."

"Says the guy who collects specialty bacons."

"Funny."

"Come on, though. Guys get football and comic books. You get to actually *be* in a band. I wanted to learn how to code and talk about music. Where's the sin in that?"

"I didn't say there was anything wrong with it. What I said was it's impossible not to wonder if you might want to parlay your connection to me into a chance to get closer to Noah or Adam or . . . I don't know, absorb the atmosphere of the band. Or maybe gain some notoriety. Can't you see this from my point of view?"

"Do you honestly think I'd be talking to you right now if I'd already gotten what I wanted? Wouldn't I be done with you?"

"How the hell should I know? I could still be your permanent connection to the world you've been watching from afar for so long. I don't want to be that person."

Ugh. "Shane, it's not my responsibility to make you trust people. I don't want to spend my life trying to prove myself to you. You want assurances that simply don't exist outside of a dictatorship. Is that really the kind of relationship you want to have?"

"Of course not." His voice dropped low. "I want you, Layla. I've never felt like this about anyone before. But I'm afraid."

"I'm afraid, too, Shane. I've never experienced anything like this with anyone. For what it's worth, I have doubts and trust issues, too, but I was hoping time might be the key."

He sniffed, and I realized he was crying. Shit. "That's what I've been asking you for. Can you give me that?"

"I don't know." Even if he got over this incident, I'd always have an uneasy feeling he was watching over my shoulder, checking up on me, questioning me. Where that might lead, I didn't think I wanted to know. I needed him to be someone else. I needed him to stop making me feel like an opportunistic maneater, and he hadn't managed to.

"I'll be back next Sunday. Can we talk then?"

What more was there to say? I didn't want to have this argument over and over. "I've moved my stuff out of your place. I'm looking for someplace permanent to live."

"Right. You don't need me anymore."

"Jesus, Shane." I welcomed back the anger. It was an easier emotion to endure. "Goodnight."

"Night, Layla."

Chapter Twenty-Eight

Throughout the weekend, I kept getting nice messages from people reaching out to remind me of times we'd interacted.

Jaclyn, the Theater of the Absurd fan site admin sent me a message titled: *Congrats and a question.*

> *Hey Pumpkin,*
> *Now that you're a big celebrity, it might be fun if you'd be willing to come over to my board and do a quick Q&A. I understand if you're totally busy, but maybe when you get some free time. Everyone over here has tons of questions they'd love to ask you.*
> *Let me know,*
> *J*

It cracked me up that she thought I was suddenly an interesting enough person that anyone would want to interview me, but then again, if our positions had been reversed, I probably would have done the same thing. The fans would be happy to talk with anyone who had connections to the band.

A couple of people I'd never spoken to in my life directly, though their screen names and avatars were familiar, contacted me with invitations.

Hey, I see that you're friends with Adam. My band will be playing a gig in Queens tomorrow night. It would be awesome if the two of you came. Let me know and I'll send you the deets.

As if I could drag Adam out to see any random band perform. Nice try though.

On my way into work on Monday, my Walking Disaster notification went off, and I checked the text from Ash.

I've got to be in NYC this weekend. Can we meet up?

I stopped and pondered her question. NYC was a long way from Portland. Especially on such short notice.

What's going on? Business?

Family thing, actually.

Sure. I can swing by wherever you'll be staying. I'd love to finally meet you.

Actually. I don't know where I'll be staying yet . . .

I couldn't exactly invite her to stay with me since I didn't have a settled place myself. The housing search had stalled, but I felt the pressure to figure things out. Shane would be home Sunday, and I couldn't be homeless when he got back. I didn't want to be at a disadvantage when he'd already shown a willingness to coerce me.

Speaking of my strange online relationships, my private message queue on the site had become untenable. No matter how many times I cleared it out, I'd come back to dozens more. I'd stopped trying to read them and instead skipped over anything with *Congratulations* in the subject which meant almost everything I read was an invitation to hang out or a request for a favor. Was every single poster going to try to contact me now?

Apparently so.

Most of the messages were innocuous. It wasn't until mid-morning, after my developer meeting that I received the first private message that really creeped me out.

Subject: Sneaky

I met you at a show in South Bend. I can't believe we didn't figure out you were *the* Pumpkin before with that hair. Very sneaky of you. Do you think you'll be able to get the band to come this way again?

What was going on? How would anyone know what I looked like?

I started scrolling through the forums until I saw a thread titled: *Fan Blogger article you guys should see.* I'd heard that name recently.

I didn't bother scanning what was copied in the forum and went straight to the source. The article was titled *Rumor Mill.* It was dated Friday and had several paragraphs of random gossip about different minor celebrities. I got halfway down the page and saw why it had made it to my forum. Right in the middle of the article were four pictures, side-by-side.

They were photos of me.

A couple of weeks ago, I took a walk through an area of Brooklyn where the band Theater of the Absurd rehearses, trying to get some pics of Noah Kennedy after his girlfriend left him for front man/guitarist Samuel Tucker of Whiplash.

I noticed this girl (see photo #1 below) heading into the rehearsal with Shane. I pegged her for management, agent, sister, groupie, or girlfriend.

No big deal and not noteworthy.

Except.

Curious, I staked out Shane's apartment, and guess who should emerge? (See photo #2).

But what really sparked my interest was the discovery of a couple of photos an anonymous source sent me from Boston Calling last week. That same redhead can be seen fraternizing with Noah Kennedy. (See photo #3 and #4).

Draw your own conclusions about the relationship status of this apparent groupie, but I can confirm that the redhead in all of these pictures is a certain Layla Beckett of the Rock Paper *and newly admitted fan forum admin at a prominent* Walking Disaster *fan site.*

I'd never had to defend my own relationships online, and I understood now why Eden had been so thankful for my protection of her. Objectively, I knew this was just par for the course when dealing with adjacent fame. But Jim Bone—his actual name—had stalked me and exposed me. It made me feel vulnerable, and it hurt. He'd gotten close to the truth, but I hated that everyone always immediately assumed I'd been using Shane, just like he feared.

I thought about my parents reading that, or what few friends I had, or the forum denizens. With no recourse to fight back and deny it, a story like this should have reduced me to tears. Fortunately, I did have experience. I knew that almost nobody paid attention to fan forums except the hardcore fans themselves. I thanked my lucky stars I only had to deal with this backwater bullshit.

Plus, I did have recourse. I had an army at my disposal. And a blog which gave me a voice. I could have fought back if I wanted to. I could have asked my posters to flood this *Fan Blogger* with angry comments and force him to take it down. I could have contacted him myself and worked out a deal. I could have even run a blog series about a certain stalker who hung out spying on the apartments of private citizens instead of providing anything useful.

None of it seemed worth the trouble. So what if my identity was blown? The only person that information could hurt had already assumed the worst. What more damage could be done?

We still had rules on my site, though. I texted Ash. *Could you go into the forum and remind the posters not to bring over gossip even if it's about me. Thanks.*

Everything was under control, but it left me with a low-grade depression. I remembered how cavalier I'd been about Gabriel's reaction to the attacks from my posters and felt a pang of remorse. Who was I to decide how someone else should feel about being targeted online?

I leaned back in my chair and swiveled around. I nearly jumped out of my skin when I saw Gabriel standing right in front of me, like I'd conjured him.

"Shit, Gabriel. Sidle much? You gave me a heart attack."

He held a mug of coffee in a way that made him look like he was at a cocktail party, mingling. "I read your article on Friday."

"Yeah, I can guess your reaction. My enthusiasm has no place in a serious magazine. Yadda yadda yadda." I spun back toward my laptop. "We've had this conversation already, Gabe."

"Actually, I came to apologize. I was wrong."

Interesting. I faced him again. "Do tell."

"After I saw you here with that drummer—"

"Shane."

"—Shane, right. I thought you'd written a puff piece based merely on your infatuation with him. In my own writing, I have to search for the good and the bad, so I was holding you to the same standard."

"This is starting to feel like a back-handed compliment."

He shook his head. "Not at all. I'm trying to contextualize."

"You're pointing out the lack of critical thinking in my article."

He held up a hand. "Stop. I'm telling you that I understand now what Lars is after. What you wrote about the Walking Disaster—"

"Walking Disaster."

"What?"

"It's just... Never mind. Go on."

"What you wrote reminded me of how I felt when I used to actually love a band, back when I first started writing." He looked behind him and hooked a chair with his foot, rolling it over. He settled in with his elbows on his knees and started back in, hands moving, reminiscent of Shane. "When I was about fifteen, I heard Metallica for the first time. Do you remember when you first heard them?"

I thought about it. "Not exactly."

Wouldn't have pegged him as a heavy metal fan if he hadn't spammed my blog with Metallica-based sock puppets.

"Well, I do. I was—"

Pete, at the cube next to me, stood up and said, "Guys. Normally, I don't care if you want to hang out and chat, but I'm on a deadline. Could you take it to the breakroom?"

Gabe checked his watch. "Want to go for a walk? No funny stuff. I'll tell you the rest of this."

My gut said no, but my brain said he was offering an olive branch, and I probably owed him an apology of my own for starting the online war. "Sure."

He held the glass door open for me and said, "I feel as though we got off on the wrong foot."

His willingness to let go of a valid grudge mollified my own attitude. A little. It was more than Shane had done.

The elevator doors opened, and we waited side by side, surrounded by strangers from other floors. How could there be such an infinite supply of strangers? After a week working in a small building in Indianapolis, I at least recognized everyone. Every day in New York was a total reset. Gabe was beginning to feel like an old frenemy in comparison.

As we exited the building, he steered me around the corner, away from the crowds.

"So, you were telling me about Metallica."

"That can wait. What's troubling you?"

I sagged. "I guess I owe you an apology as well."

"What for?"

"First for the cyberbullying. I thought I understood what it would be like to be on the receiving end."

He laughed. "It's not fun, is it?"

"Not in the least."

"But that's not what's wrong, is it?"

The truth slipped out. "You were right about Shane."

"How so?" He stopped walking and turned to face me.

"He kind of proved your point."

"Do you mean—?"

"We seem to have what they call irreconcilable differences. He wants me to have no interest in musicians, and I want him to have a little faith in me."

He pressed his lips together, more sympathetic than I would have expected given the circumstances. He reached over and touched my arm. I nearly jerked back, but he said, "Layla. I'm sorry. I mean it."

"Yeah, well." I shrugged. "Whatcha gonna do?"

"I'm serious." His fingers tightened. "You deserve better."

Clearly, he meant himself. His eyes softened, and those pretty lips curved. I could objectively see that he was attractive. And attracted to me. He'd apologized. If we'd only just met, I might have given him a chance.

It wasn't like I'd be cheating on Shane either. Shane had thrown away his shot.

But Gabe and I hadn't just met, and there was too much water under the bridge. He sent my spidey senses into overdrive, and my heart revolted at the thought of him.

"Gabe."

I turned to walk back toward the office, but to spare us any awkwardness, I changed the subject. "Thanks for listening. Tell me about Metallica."

Chapter Twenty-Nine

Sometime during lunch, Ash called and left a voicemail message.

"Circumstances changed. I'm flying in tomorrow. I know it's super short notice, but I'd still love to get a chance to meet up. My flight arrives around two, then I've got to find a place to stay somewhere in the Brooklyn area. I don't really know my way around. I looked on Travelocity for a hotel, but damn, they're so expensive. Maybe you could give me a recommendation. Anyway, I don't know if I can go all the way into the city. Maybe I could come find you tomorrow night. I don't want to inconvenience you though." She finally took a breath before awkwardly signing off. "Sorry for the long rambling message. I'll talk to you later."

I knew I should offer to put her up, but I didn't know how Jo would feel about it. Plus, I had no idea how long Ash was planning to stay. For all I knew, she was moving here indefinitely. For all I knew, she was moving in on my new life.

272 Mary Ann Marlowe

That thought twisted my gut. It was unfair, and I chased it away. She'd done nothing to warrant my suspicions. Yet there they were. Lately so many people I'd rarely spoken to were finding reasons to message me for favors.

I fought creeping doubts and decided to trust her intentions. After all we'd known each other for years.

I texted Jo: *A friend is coming to town for some family emergency tomorrow. Do you mind if I let her stay on the sofa/ floor/bed for a couple of nights? I promise to get my living situation squared away asap.*

She shot back a short *No problem.*

It felt weird inviting someone from the fan world into my little musician bubble, but hopefully Ash would be cool about it.

Jo can put you up for the night.

The incoming text from Ash didn't settle my nerves.

So, you really are staying with her? That's incredible. But Micah won't be there right? They're on tour still?

Yup. Until early next week. I'm not staying permanently anyway. I'm looking for a new place.

So, you're not Shane's girlfriend?

I rubbed my eyelids. Is this what fame was? Just a million people knowing your business? Then again, if they were so interested in me, they'd have figured out we broke up. Thankfully, Shane's antics didn't generally make the gossip pages.

Nope.

That's too bad. He looks like a cutie. Maybe I'll bump him up in the pretend boyfriend list.

She meant it as a joke. I didn't like it one bit though. I wanted to text back: *Hands off! Mine!* But that wasn't true. It brought home how I'd eventually watch him find someone who wasn't me. I'd watch him move on.

I had to keep telling myself we weren't right for each other. He *should* find someone else. As should I.

On Tuesday, Ash texted just after three to let me know she'd arrived. I told her how to get to Jo's, then left work early to meet her there.

The first few minutes were spent hugging and saying how great it was to see each other. She insisted we take a photo together to put up on the site. She said she was going to title it: *Fearless leader and her acolyte.*

I didn't protest. My cover had been blown. Why deny her a little fun?

She gawked at Jo's townhouse. "I'd kill for a place like this, even in Portland. Must be incredibly expensive, huh?"

I shrugged. "You want some water? Or we could go out and get coffee?"

"Water's fine. I don't want to put you out. If you have work to do or whatever. Go on about your business. I'm gonna jump online for a few, if you don't mind. I need to touch base with my family."

While I went to get her a bottle out of the fridge, she made herself at home on Jo's sofa. I still didn't know what family she had here. Why wasn't she staying with them?

I set the water on the coffee table. "Is everything okay?"

She didn't answer. I glanced over to find she'd shoved in her headphones. Her laptop was opened to the fan site, and she'd gone first to post our picture instead of checking in with her family.

I opened my own laptop and logged in. I had enough work to do that I could forget about Ash for another hour, but then my stomach started to rumble. As if she was reading my mind, Jo texted: *Are you hungry? I'm on my way home and can't stop thinking of tacos. There's a little place around the corner where we could meet.*

Starving. But Ash is here now. Can I invite her along?

I'd love to meet her. Zion just texted too. Andrew's out of town, still. It will be the four of us.

Perfect. Send me the coordinates. I'll meet you there.

I waved to get Ash's attention. "Hey."

She glanced up and pulled out an earbud. "Yeah?"

"I'm going out to meet Jo for dinner in a bit. You're welcome to come."

Her entire face lit up. "Seriously? That would be amazing."

"You don't need to meet up with your family?"

She dismissed the question with a dramatic eye roll. "You'd think. I've got some time."

"Is someone sick?"

"No. Nothing like that." She didn't elaborate. I narrowed my eyes at her, expecting her to give me something, but she jumped up and rummaged through her bag. "Do you mind if I change?"

Without waiting for an answer, she climbed the stairs, and the next thing I heard was her exclaiming over pictures of the band upstairs. She yelled down, "Is this Micah's guitar?"

I held my breath and tried to remember that I hadn't been any less excited a few weeks earlier.

Ash came back down the stairs wearing an actual Theater of the Absurd concert T-shirt, ripped jeans, and she'd put on serious eyeliner and lip gloss. I had to say, "The T-shirt might be a little much."

She looked down at herself. "It was this or a Walking Disaster T. Considering the circumstances, I figured this was less offensive."

I wanted to tell her, first of all, Jo wouldn't be offended by a Walking Disaster T-shirt. Second, I wanted to know what possessed her to fly across the country with nothing but concert T-shirts.

Then I remembered my own suitcase. If I hadn't brought professional clothes, I'd be wearing pajama pants and concert shirts. "One sec."

I went upstairs and dug through my own meager wardrobe until I found a plain black knit top that would probably fit her. I took it down and tossed it over. "Try this on."

Like a pouty teen, she exhaled. "Fine."

"You don't have to wear it. I figured you'd want to meet Jo as a person rather than a fan."

"But I am a fan. What's the difference?"

"Do whatever you want, but we need to get going."

On our way down the outside steps, she asked, "Who else will be there?" She was practically bearing down on me.

"Just Jo and one of her friends."

"Eden?"

"Not Eden." Before she could ask, I added, "Or Adam." At least I doubted it. With the baby to watch, they seemed to spend most of their time socializing at home or where they could bring the kid, but what did I know? I'd only observed them for a little while.

"How did you get to meet them?"

I'd already explained it, but as soon as I said, "Jo introduced us," I could already follow the leaps of logic that Ash might make. If she met Jo, she might also meet Adam.

I still found it incredibly annoying that she'd somehow managed to glom this experience off me. For the first time, I considered the suspicions that had been growing. I let myself imagine that maybe she'd made up the family emergency.

We didn't speak again until we'd walked a few blocks. Then she started asking questions. "What part of Brooklyn are we in? Where does Adam live? Are we close to where Shane lives? Do you know where they rehearse?"

"Who?"

"The band."

"Which band?"

This went on the entire way over. Finally, we arrived. The restaurant wasn't much to look at, but Jo had picked it, so I figured it would be fine. Zion waited outside and waved as we approached.

Ash's motor mouth restarted. "Who's that? Is he in a band?"

"That's Jo's friend, Zion. And no. He's a photographer like Jo."

Her shoulders sagged, and I felt like I'd had to tell her the Ferris wheel was closed. "Sorry. But he's a really nice guy."

Jo came running up from behind us. "Layla! Wait up."

We stopped, and Ash reached into her back pocket for her phone. Before it hit me what she was doing, she clicked a photo of Jo rushing up the street, in sweats and an old T-shirt. If Jo noticed the invasion of privacy, she didn't say. She caught up, out of breath, and I worried for a minute about her health. I knew nothing about diabetics, but I'd seen the whole tribe surround her when she'd gotten lightheaded before.

"Are you okay?" I asked.

She smiled. "Yeah. Thanks for asking. Just running late as always. Is this your friend?" Her hand was already out. "I'm Josie Wilder."

Ash said, "Yeah. I know. I'm Ash." Her eyes were moons. "Do you mind if we get a picture together?"

I couldn't take much more. "Not right now, Ash. Let's go eat."

Jo said, "If you don't mind me looking like a wreck. I've been working at the studio and lost track of time until Zion texted."

"You don't have to." I wanted to smack Ash, but she'd already swung around and held the camera up, oblivious to Jo's hints that she wasn't exactly presentable for a picture.

Jo said to me, "Really. I guess I should be flattered. I don't get this kind of attention much anymore."

Zion gave me and Jo each a hug and shook Ash's hand. "I've been here forever. Let's eat!"

At least for the time it took to order and eat, Ash stopped behaving like she was starstruck. I tried to imagine how she'd behave if she actually met Adam and remembered I'd completely lost the ability to stand normally when I'd first met him. Adam and Eden seemed to roll with it. I figured I needed to learn to do the same thing, but then Ash blurted out, "You're so lucky to have snagged Micah. He's amazing."

Jo laughed. "He really is."

Zion tried to wrestle the conversation back to a common topic. "Have y'all seen the latest Star Wars?"

Instead of volleying back, Ash asked, "Where are you from, Zion?"

He pressed his lips together, but the corners lifted, and I could tell his controlled smile threatened to erupt into laughter. "Georgia."

"Oh, is that how you know Jo?"

"As a matter of fact."

Jo caught my eye, and I saw something there that made me wonder if she felt pity for me that my friend was behaving like she'd just ridden into town on the dumb-ass train, or if she was starting to wonder why she'd ever thought I was cool.

Unaware that Jo's demeanor had grown unusually chilly, Ash turned toward her, elbow on table, back now to Zion, and began to question her about how she'd met Micah. "I mean, I know about what the papers said, but how'd you first get introduced?"

Zion said out of the corner of his mouth, "Looks like Jo has a new best friend."

I realized what was going on, what Ash wanted. I could see her moving in on Jo, trading me in, trying to follow the same path I had to make friends and get in. Unlike her, I hadn't premeditated the whole thing. I'd become friends with Jo because I'd befriended Jo as Jo and not Jo as Adam's wife's brother's girlfriend. Did she count the degrees of separation? Did she think she'd hang out with me until she could make the jump?

I didn't want to make a scene, so I didn't interfere with her misguided attempts to draw Jo out. Jo shot a glance to Zion once, looking for an escape. Zion made a valiant attempt to change the topic by asking how my apartment search was going.

I sighed. "I want to be settled by Sunday, before Shane gets home. I checked out a place in Jersey City, but—"

Zion shuddered. "Why haven't you come over to check out my place yet?"

"Uh." I winced. "I got the feeling you weren't really looking for a roommate."

"What? No. I'm just worried it might be too busy for you there. But you'd be welcome to take Jo's old room. Why don't you come over after dinner?" He cast his eyes at Ash with a head-shake, then added, "You can bring your crazy friend along, too."

Before I could go through the motions of Midwestern protocol, thanking him, refusing him, making him insist, then finally accepting, Zion took my hand. "Don't even try to say no. It's settled."

He might have just been looking for a way to rescue Jo, but I was so grateful. I tugged his hand so I could bring him in for a hug. "Thank you, Zion. You're a lifesaver."

Jo looked over with a curious eyebrow lift, and I filled her in. "Looks like you're losing your house guests a little early."

As soon as dinner was over, Ash and I walked back to Jo's to gather our stuff up, once again. Zion went on home ahead of us to make sure the apartment was presentable, and I prayed this was my last big move so I could finally unpack.

We called for an Uber, and as we waited on the front stoop, I thanked Jo profusely for her hospitality and friendship. She insisted I was welcome anytime. She shook Ash's hand and bid her farewell. "Well, it's been nice meeting you. How long are you in the city?"

"I'm not sure. A few days I should think. Possibly into next week."

Even though Jo seemed exhausted by Ash, she gave her a hug and said, "I hope you'll be in town when Micah gets back. I'm sure he'd love to meet you."

Ash must have read that as potential for a future encounter. "I would love that."

It astounded me that Jo could be so gracious, though I understood why she had to be. I'd seen what happened when a musician or anyone associated with a band disrespected a fan. It was blood on the walls for days, weeks, years—sometimes forever. Jo probably knew better than to be rude to Ash when their time together was ticking down with the seconds.

When Jo leaned in to hug me goodbye, I said, "I'm so sorry. I had no idea."

She squeezed extra hard. "It happens. Not your fault."

It was a relief not to be painted by the same brush as Ash, though I'd shown enough clues that I was in the same family of art supplies. Jo took me at face value.

I had no requirement to treat Ash with such polite good humor, and the minute we climbed into the Uber, I let it all out.

"What the fuck, Ash? Did you lose your mind?"

"What are you talking about?"

"You just spent the entire dinner grilling Jo like you were a reporter. Or a crazed fan girl."

She crossed her arms. "I'm not ashamed of being a fan. I had no idea you were such a snob."

"What are you up to, Ash?"

"Excuse me?"

"Did you set out to use me to meet Adam? Do you really think you can use Jo as your next steppingstone? After all, that's probably what you think I did, huh? Make friends with Jo so I could end up on the inside?"

"Didn't you?"

"No!" This argument was making me think of my fight with Shane. "I didn't intend to. I didn't invite myself out to dinner with Jo. I didn't invite myself along to stay at her place. It just happened."

"Neither did I, Layla. You invited me." That was technically true, but she'd given me little choice apart from being rude.

"You never had any interest in meeting me, but then I met Adam. Isn't that right? You flew out here on some make-believe family emergency so you could climb over me and get to Adam. Admit it."

She leaned against the car door, glaring at me, sucking on her teeth, and I thought I had her. She'd have to confess. "My brother's having a baby."

That wasn't what I expected her to say. "Your brother's having a baby?"

"Well, no. My sister-in-law is. Obviously. She went into labor yesterday, and we thought she'd have the baby by now, but the doctors put her on some drug—Turbo Lean or something like that—and it stopped the labor. They did some tests and want to evaluate her for a few days. If everything's okay, they'll induce her."

My eye twitched.

It sounded like a convenient excuse. It still didn't add up to me. "Why didn't you just stay with them?"

She exhaled a growl of irritation. "First of all, my sister-in-law hates me. Apart from that, she's on bed rest. My brother doesn't want anyone stressing her out. I was only supposed to be here a few days."

"Where do they live?"

"In Williamsburg. You might know that if you ever spent time on the site getting to know anyone rather than just managing people and sharing news about the band. You think I'm the spastic fan? You don't even bother to talk to people unless we're talking about what goes through Adam's head when he writes songs."

I felt gutted. "You're not hoping to meet Adam?"

She threw her hands up. "Of course, I'm hoping to meet him. You think I'm insane? This almost famous shit's really gone to your head, Layla. You know they don't belong to only you."

"Are you expecting me to introduce you? You don't expect Jo to introduce you to Micah?"

"Put yourself in my shoes for a minute, Layla. I mean, I know you've been an insider for the breathtaking span of a month, but if our roles were reversed, wouldn't you harbor the possibility of meeting him?"

Then I remembered that I'd had that exact hope when I'd first met Jo. It was an innocent desire. I didn't really expect to meet Micah or Eden or Adam, but by virtue of knowing Jo, the door had opened.

"Cause if you think you wouldn't have wanted to, you're fucking crazy, Layla."

Her last words hit me, hard, right in the heart. It was exactly what I'd said to Shane.

"Oh, my God." My head began to spin, and I laid my forehead in the palms of my hands. "Oh, shit."

Bless her, Ash didn't ask the Uber driver to stop and let her out. She laid a hand on my knee. "Are you okay? What's happening?"

"I'm sorry. I'm so sorry." I lifted my face from my palms, unsurprised to find them damp. The dam threatened to break, and my voice cracked. "I'm such an asshole."

She took my hands, despite the tears. "I hadn't ever thought so before today. What's going on?"

"Everyone crawled out of the woodwork. People I'd never talked to before. They all started wanting something from me. At first, it was nice. But then it kept happening, and—"

"—it got creepy. I can imagine. I've had a few people hitting me up to find out if we could set up a site-level meet and greet for one of their New York shows. I told them not to be presumptuous wankers. Ever since Adam came by for the Q&A, they all feel closer to him."

"To be honest, I did feel like you. Exactly like you. Only I hid it. I pretended I wasn't a huge fan. I didn't tell anyone about the site. I thought it would scare them off."

"Well, that seemed to work out then."

"Except it didn't. Not with the one person who matters."

She cocked an eyebrow. "Little clue here?"

"Shane." My breathing sped up with the mention of his name, and the sobbing kicked in for real. "Now I get it. I get what he meant."

"Hello? You want to get me up to speed?"

"If I'd spent years like this instead of days . . ."

"So, I guess you're just going to talk to yourself now. You need a minute alone?"

Her words registered, and just like that I started laughing. "He wanted me to prove it was always him. How could I do that? He'd never believe me."

"A one-sentence summary would probably suffice. Otherwise, I'm not gonna be much help."

I blotted my face with the hem of my shirt. "When Shane found the site, he jumped to conclusions. He thought I was only dating him to get to the other guys—Noah or Adam."

"But Adam's married. Wait." Her mouth dropped open. "You're dating Shane?"

"Was."

"Holy shit. Good on you!" She twisted her mouth and muttered, "Mental note to cross him off the list."

"Ash, I really am sorry. I should have just asked you instead of exploding all over you."

She leaned forward and wrapped her arm around my shoulders. "You know I love you, Layla."

"Love you, too, Ash."

"Not as much as you love Shane, though."

I smacked her. Then I looked into her eyes for some hope. "Help me figure out how to prove I'm not this super fan, that I'm not just using him."

She shrugged. "Shut down the site."

The core of the earth could have detonated at that moment, and it wouldn't have held a candle on the extinction-level event blowing my brain like a fiery comet.

"Shut down the site? My site?" The site I'd built from scratch, cultivated, maintained, marketed, grown, and loved like a best friend. It could be as irritating as a needy toddler, but in the absence of any real friends, the site had been my sole companion. I tried out the suggestion again. "Shut down the site."

"You keep saying that."

I was back to talking to myself. "What would it prove? What if I give it all up for nothing?"

"You know, if you have to ask that question, it makes me wonder if Shane might be right. What do you want, Layla?"

It would be a huge gesture, and not one Shane had asked of me. But it couldn't be for him. It couldn't just be about winning his trust because I wasn't sure he could win mine. This would have to be for me. I closed my eyes, sucked in a breath and held it.

Delete my fan site. Of course.

I wouldn't stop being a fan. I wouldn't let Shane's jealousy chase me completely away from the life I'd started to build. But I would prove the fandom didn't define me. I didn't need to be Pumpkin39 anymore.

The tears welled again. "If I shut down the site, what about you? What about everyone else?"

She rubbed my knee. "Layla, I hate to be the one to tell you this, but there's this place called Facebook . . ."

Would they all find each other there? Would life go on elsewhere? Would I matter to them anymore?

There it was. I realized it had always been a little bit about me. Okay, a lot. I'd thought by remaining anonymous, I was proving I didn't care about the notoriety, but that wasn't exactly true. I'd miss the ass kissing even though I'd demurely told them not to treat me special. I'd miss the feedback on my blogs. I'd miss cracking skulls from time to time and having people do what I said because I was the one who said it.

Everything crystallized around one brilliant realization.

"I need to shut down the site." It was so obvious. I jumped out of the Uber the second it stopped in front of the address Zion had given me. "Come on. We have an empire to destroy."

"Whatever you say, Fearless Leader."

Chapter Thirty

Zion buzzed us up, then gave us the tour, such as it was. Unlike Micah and Shane, Zion apparently lived on normal wages because his place was a small two-bedroom all on one floor. His kitchen and living room overlapped in the same space, like on *Friends*. He showed me to Jo's old room where she'd left behind her enormous bed that took up almost the entire space. It was perfect.

With a handshake, we worked out a loose agreement. He insisted on paying more than half the rent owing to a couple of factors. One being that his boyfriend would often come and go. Two being that he expected I might be spending more time away from home once Shane got home.

I explained that we'd broken up already. With a dramatic, "Oh, my God," he dropped onto his sofa and started grilling me for details.

Ash said, "But she has a plan to get him back."

I shook my head. "I know it won't change anything really. Maybe it will make me feel good to show him he was wrong. He might never even know I did it."

"You're not going to tell him?"

Zion looked back and forth between us. "Tell him what?"

"She's going to delete the fan site." Ash looked perversely happy, considering she'd invested as much time as I had in that community. "Isn't it romantic?"

Zion beamed. "It's insane. I love it."

"This is ultimately for me, not him. Even if it made him trust me, there's still the issue of my shattered trust in him. He acted like a big bully."

I didn't mention how he'd left a Shane-shaped hole in my heart in the process.

"When are you planning on doing this?"

I looked at Ash and took a breath. "Tonight, at midnight."

He clapped his hands together. "I want to be there when all this goes down. I positively live for drama."

We camped out in his kitchen discussing how to go about the destruction of the site and prep the users for what was to come. We decided it would only be fair to post a statement on the site to warn the posters of the impending collapse of civilization. That would give them time to collectively freak out and then come up with their own plans to reconnect elsewhere.

While Ash jumped on the forum, I banged out a blog post. We'd post them simultaneously.

I typed furiously.

Dear friends,

It is with sadness that I am announcing Talking Disaster will cease to exist at midnight EST tonight. I realize that many of you have made this place a regular stop on your Internet rounds, and some of you have made this your home. I'm so grateful for this amazing community and for what you've all given me over the years in laughs and friendship. It's time for me to close this chapter on my life and begin another.

You may be asking why I don't just hand over the reins to the website to someone who could run it in my stead. That's a valid question, and one I would have considered if my motives were simply to move on. You may be thinking that something negative happened with Adam or the band to make me want to abandon them, but don't go there. Adam has been incredible, and I'm going to encourage him to find you guys wherever you might go and continue to interact. I will always love the band. It's just that Adam and the band aren't the center of my world. And they haven't been for a very long time. Too long.

Trust me. This is about me and my need to cut this habit cold turkey. If you hate me for doing this, so be it. I hope that you will understand though and continue to count me among your friends.

Where do we go from here? I'm sure any one of you could spin up your own website if you wanted to go that route. You could make a group on Facebook as well. Hit up DeadFan (Ash) as she might have some ideas. If anyone is worthy of picking up the Fearless Leader moniker, it would be her. She's been my rock for the past few weeks as I transitioned to my new job.

Best wishes!
Pumpkin39

Ash had written something similar and pointed to the blog for more info. We both hit Submit and stared at each other in disbelief. She made a nuclear explosion with her hands and laughed. "This is kind of awesome."

"I think I might throw up." What was I doing? I pressed my hands to my face, wondering if I'd made a terrible mistake. I hit refresh and saw comments flooding in on the blog.

So sorry to see the site go, but you've been doing this for a long time, and it's been obvious for a while that you haven't been as engaged as you once were. I think this move has been a long time coming. I wish you the best of luck in everything. You were the shit, Pumpkin.

I posted a thank you and read the next comment.

Is this because you're friends with the band now? You said you're not mad at them, but is there some conflict of interest thing where they're afraid you might let state secrets slip or people might no longer see you as an impartial fan?

I hit reply.

Honestly, this has nothing to do with the band. They told me they love the site. I'm not exactly friends with the band. I'm just lucky enough to have gotten to know them a bit more.

More comments came in. Mostly supportive. Some were angry at the short notice. Soon, they were no longer directed at me. Instead, they began talking about what to do. The same was going on in the forum. Fans making plans to move their campsite to another location. That's when I knew we could leave them to it.

As we waited for midnight, we sat on Zion's sofa watching entertainment news and speculating about the fallout. I started to have serious second thoughts about bringing down the board, but I reminded myself I wasn't wiping the site out of existence. It would still be there in code and data, at least for now. For all intents and purposes, it would be gone. Nobody would be able to login. Nobody would be able to share pictures or videos. Nobody would be able to read my old reviews and leave nasty comments. Nobody would be able to private message me.

Speaking of my private messages: Oh, my God.

I logged into the forum one last time and opened the queue. There were so many messages. At first they had varying subject headers, but around ten, a trend began to take shape. Message after message had the subject: *To Layla*. Not *To Pumpkin*, like they saw me as a real person. Like they'd coordinated their effort to say goodbye or beg me to reconsider. I couldn't even start to open them, or I might cry.

When midnight struck and we convened at the kitchen table again, I pushed the laptop over to Ash.

"I can't do this."

She opened up the admin panel to the page with the link to disable the site. "You can."

"Holy shit." I waited for her final nod of approval, then raised my finger and slowly lowered it like a bomb in slow motion, complete with the whistling sound. As I clicked it, she said, "Boom!"

I copied my blog post onto an index.html file, added my contact email, and uploaded it to my public_html directory. That would force anyone coming to the main page to see my message. Then I redirected all traffic to the front page. To be extra thorough, I changed permissions to make the rest of the pages inaccessible and I renamed the database.

"Well. That's that."

I blew out a lungful of air. I thought I might cry after we were done, but Zion handed me a beer, and tilted his bottle toward me.

As we clinked, he said, "Vive la révolution."

I suddenly did feel like celebrating, relieved and proud of myself for walking away on my terms. It really had been a long time coming.

Ash got word that her sister-in-law was back in the hospital, so she rushed off first thing in the morning to meet her brother there. Zion insisted on cooking me some breakfast before I left for work.

"I miss Jo sometimes. We had a rhythm. And Andrew doesn't eat breakfast, so . . . Can I make you some eggs?"

He set a plate on each of our placemats, then started interrogating me. "Do you want someone to tell Shane what you did?"

"Not really. No." The eggs were perfect. I tried the toast and bacon. I could get used to being treated like this. It would be like being home with Mom again.

"Have you talked to Adam or Eden?"

That was a good question. "No. Do you think this will make them want to have nothing to do with me now?"

He shrugged. "I couldn't say. Eden's a tough read, but I've only known her to bristle over invasions into her privacy. Not sure how she'll react to a complete embargo on free publicity for her husband. Adam probably won't even notice."

"Did you talk to Jo?"

"I'll let you do that." He studied me a minute and added, "Can I give you some advice?"

"Of course."

"Not everyone is who they appear to be."

That wasn't what I was expecting to hear, but I chewed on my bacon and mulled it over. I figured he meant Shane. "I've already begun to figure that out."

"Sometimes people hide in plain sight. Sometimes they wear disguises to protect themselves. You have to give people time to reveal themselves."

I sat on that a minute, wondering if he was warning me that the Shane I'd first met had been hiding someone much more sinister. If that were the case, then why did they all seem to want things to work out? Was he saying I should give Shane more time to show me who he really was?

Or was he talking about me? Had he somehow understood the double identity I'd only just shed?

"Thanks, Zion. I'll think about that."

On my way in to work, it occurred to me that I'd simply fall into obscurity for most of the fan site people. I had no plans to join whatever group they set up elsewhere, and the only way they had to reach me would be through the admin contact email, which would continue to work until I let the domain name lapse. I'd been afraid to check it, but I logged in on my phone before going up to the office. My inbox was filled with multiple emails with the subject *To Layla* just like the private messages. I nearly opened one up, in case they were simply kind farewells, but I didn't know if I could resist a sustained effort to get me to bring the site back up. I'd read them later. In a week or a month. Once they'd had a chance to move on.

As soon as I got to my cube, Gabe appeared. "That was a bold, Napoleonic move. What made you go and pull the plug like that?"

Why wasn't I surprised he'd noticed?

"Just time to move on."

"Good riddance to bad rubbish is what I always say." He leaned his elbow on my cube wall. I used to think it looked elegant, but now it was bordering on creepy. "I'm curious, though. You trying to win back little drummer boy?"

Shane was anything but little. I pulled out my chair and dropped into it, intending to swivel away from him without giving him any more explanations.

"I don't know what you're talking about."

"Because you do realize that ship has sailed, right? Once he saw how you felt about Noah, even once, he'd never trust you again."

Now that was a piece of information I hadn't shared with anyone but my closest friends. Curiosity won out. "How did you know—?"

"That Shane would drop you over something so small? You forget. I've been covering these guys for a long time. Shane's so obviously insecure about his position in the band, always in the shadows, never the one who gets the girl." He grinned, and he might as well have been holding a flashlight under his chin for all the malevolence in his expression. "Kind of ironic that he had the girl but chased her away out of sheer jealousy. Pretty stupid of him."

"How did you know he'd seen what I wrote about Noah?"

His breath hitched, but he must not have thought I noticed. "What else would make him blow it with you?"

"Gabe, did you—" He had said he could get anyone's contact info. And he'd been all over my fan site. "You sent him the link, didn't you?"

"I thought he should know." He grabbed the chair from the cube that was perpetually empty. "Layla, it's time you stop leading me on and give me an answer."

"Leading you on? What are you even talking about?"

"I'm not going to wait around forever."

"Well, you're gonna have to."

"Come on, Layla. That drummer isn't going to give you another chance."

"No, Gabe. Understand this. My response to you never had anything to do with Shane. You're a pompous, self-involved twat. Since you also more or less confessed to sabotaging my relationship with a guy I really could have seen myself with, I guess what I want to say is: Fuck off."

He had the audacity to look stunned. Like he'd really thought I was stupid enough to fall in line with his plans. He stood, straightened his shirt, and said, "Bitch," before walking away.

I waited for him to get out of earshot before I let the tears fall. Gabe may have orchestrated my breakup with Shane, but he'd only precipitated the inevitable. If I didn't hate Gabe so much, I might have to thank him for saving me the time. Shane would have eventually discovered my history of ranking the boys in the band. He would have seen that he hadn't rated anywhere in my list of pretend boyfriends. He would have figured out Micah gave way to Noah at some point. Then he'd do the math and come up with the same wrong conclusion.

Gabe was right. Shane and I didn't stand a chance. He might see that I blew up the website, but he'd also know that I was staying with Zion. Nothing substantive had changed. In his eyes, I'd gotten my way. I'd insinuated myself into the band. One of the last comments I'd read on the blog suggested I no longer needed the board because I had the band. Shane would no doubt say the same.

I stopped to assess where I was at with my life.

I had my job. Ajit had let me code a small piece of one of my solutions, and Byron offered to let the company pay for any training I wanted to take to get more up to speed.

I had my new writing gig. An email from Lars listed a series of bands who wanted to volunteer to be a part of the *Fly on the Wall* series. The *Rock Paper* gave me a lot of cred. I might get to travel some. I'd be meeting more bands. Things looked like they might take off.

I had friends. Ash would go back to Portland, but we'd stay in touch. Even if I never saw Adam or Eden again, I had Jo and I had Zion now.

I had my family. Mom and Dad wanted to come out to visit soon. I couldn't wait to show them around. My brother had set a date for his wedding, and I'd get to fly home and bask in hometown comfort.

And I had myself. I'd come to the city split in two. Real me and Internet me were separate and secret from one another. I'd found a way to merge them together, and I came out the other side whole. I no longer felt the need to hide who I was.

The world would go on. If I could go back a month and see myself now, I'd be impressed and excited about my future. If I'd never met Shane, I'd be more or less in exactly this same spot. Once I worked him out of my system, I'd reclaim the excitement I had at the start. I could do that. It would take some time and focus, but I'd get there.

Chapter Thirty-One

I didn't see much of Ash for the next several days. Despite her sister-in-law's dislike of her, Ash offered to stay with the couple to help them transition into parenthood. But on Sunday, when Jo sent her an invitation to come out for an outdoor party, she jumped at the chance. "I need to get away. Just tell me when and where."

Jo offered to send her driver to pick her up, and I got in on that ride, too. I wanted to be with Ash when she arrived. Of course, she realized the minute we pulled up where we were going. She recognized the front of Adam's townhouse from the gossip pages.

"I'm impressed," I confessed. "These places all look the same to me."

"You don't remember that video of Jo passing out in the sidewalk right here?" She pointed at a tree, and then I did remember it. In my defense, it had been ages ago. Plus, it was a pretty nondescript tree.

She grabbed my elbow. "Oh, my God. Come the fuck *on*."

I had to laugh. "Be cool, okay?"

"Are you fucking kidding me? Is he here?"

"Yeah. I think so." She slipped off a yoga wrap to reveal that, of course, she had on a Walking Disaster T-shirt. I sighed.

We rang the bell, and Eden answered. She had the baby cradled in one elbow. "Hey! You must be Ashley. I'm Eden. This is Joshua."

Ash didn't freak out. She touched the baby's hand and said, "Are you a big boy?" She looked up at Eden and asked, "Does he sleep through the night yet?"

Eden moved out of the way and let us in, answering, "God, I wish. Though what you call night varies . . ."

They went on ahead of me, talking about babies like they were picking up a conversation they'd left off before. I guess having spent days with her brother's baby had left Ash wanting to talk about nothing else.

Zion was behind the kitchen counter, but Ash already knew him, so she waved and said, "Hey, Zion!" Like it was no big deal. I laughed at how easily she'd managed to adjust to all this.

That was before we went out back. I decided to sit back and watch her transform into psycho fan. Adam stood in the yard, hammering together some kind of small wooden swing set for babies. Ash walked straight up to him, and said, "Oh, my God."

I held my breath, but she shocked me.

"Where did you find this? It's perfect!"

She got down on her knees and studied the instructions laid out on the ground. Adam dug out the front page, with the manufacturer information and held it up. "I ordered it from here."

Next thing I knew, she was holding a complete conversation about how hard it is to find quality children's play equipment. "I was just looking at those little musical chairs for my nephew—he's only three days old—but they seem too advanced for any baby."

Adam paused and scratched his chin. "Oh, yeah. They're okay for nap time, but forget about using them to entertain the baby for any length of time."

I sat in a chair on the porch, absolutely mesmerized by her ability to do that. Jo placed a lemonade in front of me and sat. "Taste this. It's amazing and low in sugar."

I took a sip. "Is that strawberry?"

"Strawberry and lemon. Good, huh?" She followed my gaze out to the yard. "Your friend seems to have made herself at home."

"Yeah. I'm quite shocked."

"What about you?"

I turned to face her. "Me?"

"Have you made yourself at home? Do you like it at Zion's?"

Eden joined us. "Did you ask her about Shane?"

Jo shook her head. "I wasn't sure if I should."

"You guys can ask me about Shane. I don't have anything to say, but I'm an open book."

Eden dropped her chin on her palms, elbows on the table. "So, did you ever respond to him?"

Jo said, "It's okay if you don't want to. We can be friends with both of you, whatever you do."

"Respond to him about what? I haven't heard from him in a week."

They exchanged a glance. "You haven't heard anything from him?"

"Not since he butt-dialed me."

Jo called, "Zion?"

He stuck his head out, and she asked, "Has she seen it?"

"Why are you asking me?"

"Because you live with her!" Jo jumped up with a shimmy. "Oh, my Lord. She hasn't seen it."

"Seen what?" I seemed to be the only one who didn't know.

Jo came back with a tablet and began typing. Then she set it down in front of me, out of the glare. "Watch." She had YouTube pulled up.

The title of the video: *To Layla.*

The image opened shaky, blurry with blobs of light broken by blobs of shadow that occasionally coalesced into people on the stage. The sound was loud, and the speakers sounded blown out. Jo hit stop. "Let me find a better one."

She minimized the video and returned to the search results. The entire page had the same video. Or the same title anyway. Every single one said, *To Layla,* but the thumbnails were different. The next video Jo clicked on was clearer and from a different angle. Micah stood on stage, talking. The camera zoomed in on him. Jo made sure the volume was up and the screen maximized.

Micah was already talking.

"Come on, everyone. Cameras out. We encourage you to record this and share it far and wide. This is a brand-new song. Never performed anywhere. Hell—" he chuckled "—we've barely practiced it."

The video panned around. Phones were out everywhere. Little iPhone Micahs floated above the crowd below the real Micah, who announced. "Now, this is important. When you upload this, please give it the title *To Layla.* This message is for her."

I hit the screen to pause it. "When was this recorded?"

Jo frowned. "Uh."

Eden said, "Tuesday."

Tuesday? That was the day Ash came to town. This concert would have coincided approximately to the time she and I were moving over to Zion's, posting on the forum, and getting ready to hit the detonator on the site. If the site had been up all week, this video would have been posted there, and I would have seen it. But I'd been avoiding all the fan sites all week.

Then I remembered the messages.

The emails.

I took a shaky breath and blinked back tears.

"You guys should put it on the TV," Adam yelled from the yard. Ash was no longer beside him, and I noticed she'd snuck up behind us to watch over Jo's shoulder.

Eden said, "Ooh, good idea! Go!"

We all raced into the house, and within minutes, she had the video on a widescreen TV. My curiosity was killing me.

"Everybody comfy?" she asked, settling into a leather love seat, next to Jo, who now hugged a pillow.

Ash and I shared a sofa directly in line with the screen. I nodded. "Play it."

Micah lifted the guitar strap up and over his head, then said into the mic, "This requires a change in personnel."

For the first time, I could see Shane as he stood and came around the drumkit. He wrapped his hand around the neck of Micah's guitar, and as he ducked his head under the strap, Micah took his place at the drums. Ash said, "I didn't know Micah played drums."

Jo laughed. "Not really."

He must have known enough because he began to tap a simple four count rhythm. Shane stepped into the spotlight. Someone had brought out a stool, and he hooked it with his ankle, sitting before the microphone. As he adjusted it, he said, "This is going to be interesting. I've never played in front of more than one person at a time before." The crowd cheered. "I might be about to make a total fool of myself here, but it's worth it. I need to apologize to a girl in a pretty big way. Do you think this will work?" The roar brought the speakers to their limit, and they started to crackle.

Ash took my hand. "This is for you?"

I nodded, but I couldn't tear my eyes away from Shane. I hadn't seen him in over a week, and my soul hurt from wanting him. I'd missed his face, his ever-changing expressions, his manic energy, and mostly, the way he'd looked at me before he'd lost all faith in me.

I prayed he'd found it again.

He lifted his knee and rested his foot on the bar, and then he began to play. First a C, then an E, an F, then a C.

"I know this song."

Sure enough, he began with the same first verse he'd sung to me before.

> *Another tequila sunrise/misty and gray.*
> *Empty house*
> *Empty bottles*
> *And the sun sets*
> *On another lonely day*

As he sang, Micah managed to keep a steady beat going. Rick worked in a simple bass line between the verses, and Shane continued as he had once before. That first verse had made me sad when I'd first heard it, picturing broken-hearted Shane, but now he was describing the house he'd be coming home to, tonight probably. Dark and empty. I'd left it that way.

> *Hope glints against the darkness*
> *Pinpricks of light*
> *Fill the night sky*
> *Moonage daydreams*
> *And the time comes*
> *For her star to burn bright*

Ash said, "Damn, girl."

Shane looked up, and the entire stage exploded in tiny pinpricks of light everywhere, like stars shining. The crowd ate it up. The rhythm transformed, picked up as he sang the chorus.

Constellations turn
Turn around in flight
Stars shine
Shine against the night
Wish I may
Wish I might
Find my one true love's light.

That was the extent of the song as far as I knew. I expected him to simply repeat the chorus and end there. He proved me wrong. Yet, again.

The key changed, as did his strumming pattern. Noah came in with the melody from the chorus, but it played against the bridge in a way that gave me unexpected chills.

I'm a star man
waiting in the sky.

Another cheer erupted at the nod to David Bowie.

Show me a sign
A flicker of ginger-haired star shine
Beguiling beacon
I think she'll blow my mind

I was chewing on my knuckles to keep from squealing. With the Bowie throwbacks and the references to my hair and his nickname for me, not to mention the incredible sexiness of him playing that guitar, I was ready to take him back. If that's where this was headed. I hoped it was where this was headed. Who could resist a love song serenade? Then he started the second verse.

Her star shoots across the heavens
A wondrous sight

> *Touch the sky*
> *She falls to earth*
> *And I catch her*
> *'Mine,' I say, holding tight*

On this last line, he looked menacingly from right to left across the audience, his impact clear: He knew he'd been wrong. The whole band was jamming out. Noah started playing in earnest, a whole crazy show-off guitar solo. Then all at once, every instrument but Shane's guitar went silent, and the guys all froze. The lights dropped except the single white beam on Shane.

I don't know if he'd ever played for so long, and he'd started making some mistakes, but he kept going. He strummed that original set of chords and leaned in.

> *Her spirit burns too hot to hold*
> *Though souls align*
> *I set her free*
> *And gaze above*
> *For her star shine*
> *To ease my worried mind*

The last line sucker-punched me, in a good way. If I hadn't known the song was for me, that last line, stolen from Eric Clapton's "Layla" sealed the deal. He sang the chorus once more, now with all the guys joining in. And then as he wrapped it up, he said one time. "Forgive me, Layla. I was wrong."

The lights dropped, and after a beat, the crowd went insane. The video shut off right after, and every head swiveled toward me.

"Well?" asked Jo. "What do you think of that?"

Eden reached down to the lower shelf of an end table and came up with a box of Kleenex. She nudged Ash with it, and Ash held it out to me. I plucked out a few and pressed them to my cheeks. It took me a minute to find my voice.

"That's been up since Tuesday?" Tears fell unchecked. "Why didn't you say anything, Ash?"

She put her hands up in defense. "I've been busy with the baby. I had no idea."

I looked from Jo to Eden. "We assumed you'd seen it. Don't you run a fan site? We figured you're all over concert videos. Didn't your posters send you links?"

My eyes closed. "They did." They'd probably posted it to the forum before I took it down. Shane hadn't shot me a link. He'd waited, and I'd said nothing. For nearly a whole week.

The front door opened, and a voice called, "Eden? You here?"

In walked Micah and Noah. I tilted my head, trying to see between them, watching for Shane, but the door closed. Micah came in and hugged Eden, then slid in next to Jo. "We figured you guys would have food."

Noah waved at everyone and wandered straight out back to the grill where Adam now reigned supreme. I caught Ash's head bobbing back and forth, trying to watch both the new guys at once.

"Micah, this is my friend Ash."

He leaned forward with his hand outstretched. "Hi! Any friend of Layla's."

I butted in. "Micah?"

"Layla?"

"Where's Shane?"

"Ah." He licked his lips. "He's gone home."

Jo ran her fingers through his thick blond hair. "She never saw the video. We just played it for her."

His eyes widened. "Are you shitting me?"

Without realizing I'd stood, I found myself on the other side of the sofa grabbing my purse strap. Then I remembered Ash.

"Ash, I'm gonna—"

"Go! Go! I think I'll be okay." She poked her head twice in Noah's direction, and I had to laugh. Poor Noah.

"Micah, is your driver here? Can I borrow your car?"

"It's a service. One can't be too far away. Give me a minute."

I weighed out how long it would take to walk and agreed to wait. Everything was a blur until I stood outside Shane's front door. When had I punched in the security code and climbed the stairs?

I put the key in the lock and pushed open the door. His living room and kitchen were empty. No sign that he'd even come home, yet. I quietly climbed the stairs and emerged in a deserted bedroom. His rectangular black duffel bag sat at the foot of the bed.

The bathroom door was ajar, and the light was out, leaving one place he could possibly be. I squared my shoulders facing his music room/office. I'd never gone in there before. I tapped on the door, and it flew open.

Shane.

A myriad of expressions crossed his face. Wide-eyed surprise melted into relief that blossomed into that gorgeous smile I'd missed like the sun in winter. Tears filled my eyes, and I took a tentative step forward, hoping that everything I'd interpreted from his song, from his message meant what I wanted it to. I swallowed, searching his eyes for the forgiveness he'd promised me through ten thousand videos.

Without words, he swept me into his arms, mouth on my forehead, fingers in my hair, lips on my lips. "You're here."

"I'm here."

"When you didn't respond, I didn't think I'd see you again."

"I never saw your song, Shane. Your brilliant, heart-wrenching, loins-on-fire, beautiful love song."

His eyebrow arched. "Loins on fire?"

I shoved his chest, then grabbed the fabric on his shirt and pulled him back. "I deleted my website."

"What?" It came out as a laugh. "Why?"

"Because I don't need it. My friend Ash reminded me there's nothing wrong with fandom, but for me, that site had become an unhealthy substitute for real relationships."

"Your friend is very wise."

"It wasn't worth losing you over."

He held up a hand. "No, you weren't in the wrong there. I shouldn't have reacted the way I did."

"You shouldn't have." I laughed. "But still. I'm sorry. I understand how finding that site would play into every one of your worst fears. You had valid concerns. I'm sorry I walked away instead of trying to work it out."

"It's true. Finding that site hit every single button, but I reacted poorly. I can't believe I was such an idiot. Micah told me every day I was an idiot, and one day, I woke up and realized he was right. I did the one thing that you'd told me would wreck our relationship. I wanted you so much I chased you away. How dumb is that?"

My stomach flipped. "Do you still want me?"

"Is it possible to want you even more?" His strong hands grasped my waist, and he hoisted me up. My legs wound around him.

I needed to touch him and slid my fingers behind his neck, tracing the skin under his collar, but I wanted to make sure he wasn't going to freak out again every time I turned into a gawking fan girl. I needed to know we weren't going to have this fight until the end of time.

"And if I want to sit in on Whiplash's rehearsal next week?"

"Whatever you want, Layla. That will always be your choice."

I hugged him. "Thank you."

"So you forgive me?"

"You are forgiven, Shane. Just—"

"Just what?"

"Give me a little room to breathe."

"I know. That was the point of my song. I—"

"No. I mean, right now. You're squeezing me too tight."

His chest rumbled with laughter, and he carried me to the bed and laid me down. "I promise I'll treat you like a butterfly. I'm so fucking glad you came back."

He laid down beside me, and we rolled on our sides, fingers gently touching any exposed skin. I said, "I don't know how I was so lucky to find you."

"You didn't find me. You plunged into my life like a comet."

I smiled. "Leftover song lyrics?"

"So busted." He rested a palm on my cheek, gazing into my eyes. "I'm the one who's fallen. I've fallen so hard for you. I've been obsessed with you. I'm head over heels in love with you."

My gut reaction—to balk at the possibility of his love—met a stone wall of resistance, and I remembered what Eden had told me about time not mattering. "I'm pretty sure I love you, too, Shane."

And then we stopped talking. I needed more than words. I needed to possess him if only for a moment in time. And I needed to be possessed.

Epilogue

A cool breeze stirred against my exposed shoulder, waking me. I felt around on the floor for my T-shirt and threw it on, then stumbled over to shut the front window. The building across the street blushed pink and orange with reflected sunrise. The summer nights had been warm, and we'd sat out on the fire escape every night since Shane had gotten home from his west coast tour.

The light crept across the wooden floorboards, illuminating first his fingers and arm that hung over the side of the bed. Those arms had held me at our ballroom dance lessons. They'd hugged me when I'd signed up for computer classes. They'd wrapped around me in that very bed as we made love or as I slept.

I tiptoed over and touched the skin the morning sun revealed. His face, beautiful and sweet. His shoulders, broad and strong. His back, smooth and inviting. I slid the covers down and down, and he woke, turning toward me, exposing another impressive part of himself to the day.

"Morning," he said, snatching my hand and pulling me to him. "You're up early."

My hand found him and brought him fully erect. "So are you."

"I was dreaming about you."

That made me smile. I straddled him, rubbing our sexes together just to watch his face melt into serene happiness. "What did you dream?"

"I planned an elaborate scheme with secret rooms and a hot air balloon, I think." He pushed his hands up my torso, and my shirt bunched up. I lifted my arms and let him take it off.

"What kind of scheme was this?"

He groaned in response, but in his defense, I was soaking wet now and grinding against him. He was so massive, I loved to use him like a sex toy, and he'd let me. I leaned down to suck on his lips while I stroked myself with his anticipation.

He whispered, "It was a proposal."

My head jerked up. He lifted my hips easily and let his erection defy gravity. I wanted him in me as desperately as he wanted it. The words hung there. "A proposal."

"Yeah. I was asking you to marry me."

"In your dream."

"Right."

"And what did I say?"

The tip of his penis breached my entry. I wanted to slide down. I wanted him to fill me up, but I waited.

"You said 'yes.' " His blue eyes dilated, and he tilted his hips up, gaining some ground.

"So, we're dream engaged?"

"I'd marry you right now. You can't hold out forever."

I didn't know if he meant against engagement or against his cock now definitely in the zone. He was right on both counts. Despite my insistence that time didn't matter, I'd discovered it did, on the four-week anniversary of the night we'd first hooked up, when Shane surprised me by proposing. He'd gone the traditional route: Dinner, nice suit, on his knees with the ring in the box.

We'd only been back together a few days.

I'd said, "Shane."

That's all it took for him to sigh and put the ring away. I thought we'd have a fight, but he understood. He said he'd try again.

He did. A whole month later, he took me out of town to a bed and breakfast. We rode horses. He planned a picnic. The ring was hidden, and I was supposed to find it, but then he'd misplaced it, and he had to expose his plan. We spent thirty minutes digging through the basket trying to find the missing ring.

I'd said, "You know I love you. But it's way too soon."

Now it was August, and he had me at a complete disadvantage. I loved him. I loved being in his bed with him under me. I never wanted to leave his side, and I mourned like a grieving widow when he left for weeks on tour. All that held me back was a traditionalist's view of a proper timetable.

In his arms, time stood still. All that mattered was where our bodies met.

I bore down and relished his satisfied moan as our hips connected. With him deep inside me, I bent forward and lay a kiss on his pretty lips.

"Mmm. There." He thrust upward, hitting me in that spot that shattered planets. "Yes, *yes*, Shane."

His eyes lit up. "When?"

How could I resist him? If I said *now*, I was afraid he'd toss me over and start making calls. "Christmas?"

He flipped me onto my back and pulled out far enough to make me sigh. "Next week."

With him inside me, I'd agree to nearly anything. "Mmm." He hit the place that made me think of sugar. "Keep going."

"Saturday."

My back arched, and he picked up the pace, bringing me closer and closer. I rasped out, "Anything you want."

"Today."

I crashed around him. "Yes. Yes."

He exploded in me and all I saw were stars.

Acknowledgments

This series of book owes its existence to fan forums. Back in the day, I was working on a doctorate in French lit when I heard the siren call of computer programming and made a complete U-turn. Even after I changed careers and started working in development, I couldn't stop tinkering with my own websites. I'd been involved in forum communities when I found myself with a domain and some software and asked, "Hey, would anyone want to join my little fan site?" To my great surprise, that community grew fast and furious. I built another. I spun up fan sites so fast, people used to joke every time I'd find a new musician I loved, "Hey username, when can we expect the fan site?" And while I loved hanging out and chatting with other like-minded fans, I got a huge kick out of writing blogs, especially when I had a partner in crime to share the load.

So thanks to sidekicks like McLovin and dozens of other usernames I could rattle off—friends I've never met and people I've traveled the world with.

I am indebted to my writing circle for all the support and encouragement they give me every single day. This book had fallen off my radar when I picked it back up, dusted it off, and started working on it again. I wouldn't be anywhere without Kelli Newby, Elly Blake, and Kristin Wright, who generously read all my words, sometimes multiple times, and courageously offer up improvements. They make my books a little better with every suggestion. As always, I have to thank my cheer section: Jen Hawkins, Summer Spense, Kelly Siskind, and Ron Walters. You guys make the writing world go 'round.

If you enjoyed this book, please consider leaving feedback on goodreads or on whichever ebook retailer you buy books from. Reviews help authors reach readers.

And check out my other books:

Some Kind of Magic
A Crazy Kind of Love
Dating by the Book

Find out more at maryannmarlowe.com

Do not miss Eden and Adam's story in

SOME KIND OF MAGIC

by Mary Ann Marlowe
Now available in bookstores and online!

In this sparkling novel, Mary Ann Marlowe introduces a hapless scientist who's swept off her feet by a rock star--but is it love or just a chemical reaction . . . ?

Biochemist Eden Sinclair has no idea that the scent she spritzed on herself before leaving the lab is designed ot enhance pheromones. Or that the cute, grungy-looking guy she meets at a gig that evening is Adam Copeand. As in *the* Adam Copeland— international rock god and object of lust for a million women. Make that a million and one. By the time she learns the truth, she's already spent the (amazing, incredible) night in his bed . . .

Suddenly Eden, who's more accustomed to being set up on disastrous dates by her mom, is going out with a gorgeous celebrity who loves how down-to-earth and honest she is. But for once, Eden isn't being honest. She can't bear to reveal that this overpowering attraction could be nothing more than se-duction by science. And the only way to know how Adam truly feels is to ditch the perfume—and risk being ditched in turn . . .

Smart, witty, and sexy, *Some Kind of Magic* is an irresistably engaging look at modern relationship—why we fall, how we connect, and the courage it takes to trust in something as myste-rious and unpredictable as love.

Read on for a preview. . . .

Chapter One

*M*y pen tapped out the drum beat to the earworm on the radio. I glanced around to make sure I was alone, then grabbed an Erlenmeyer flask and belted out the chorus into my makeshift microphone.

"*I'm beeeegging you...*"

With the countertop centrifuge spinning out a white noise, I could imagine a stadium crowd cheering. My eyes closed, and the blinding lab fell away. I stood onstage in the spotlight.

"Eden?" came a voice from the outer hall.

I swiveled my stool toward the door, anticipating the arrival of my first fan. When Stacy came in, I bowed my head. "Thank you. Thank you very much."

She shrugged out of her jacket and hung it on a wooden peg. Unimpressed by my performance, she turned down the radio. "You're early. How long have you been here?"

"Since seven." The centrifuge slowed, and I pulled out tubes filled with rodent sperm. "I want to leave a bit early to head into the city and catch Micah's show."

She dragged a stool over. "Kelly and I are hitting the clubs tonight. You should come with."

"Yeah, right. Why don't you come with me? Kelly's such a—"

"Such a what?" The devil herself stood in the doorway, phone in hand.

Succubus from hell played on my lips. But it was too early to start a fight. "Such a guy magnet. Nobody can compete with you."

Kelly didn't argue and turned her attention back to the phone.

Stacy leaned her elbow on the counter, conspiratorially talking over my head. "Eden's going to abandon us again to go hang out with Micah."

"At that filthy club?" Kelly's lip curled, as if Stacy had just offered her a *non*-soy latte. "But there are never even any guys there. It's always just a bunch of moms."

I gritted my teeth. "Micah's fans are not all moms." When Micah made it big, I was going to enjoy refusing her backstage passes to his eventual sold-out shows.

Kelly snorted. "Oh, right. I suppose their husbands might be there, too."

"That's not fair," Stacy said. "I've seen young guys at his shows."

"Teenage boys don't count." Kelly dropped an invisible microphone and turned toward her desk.

I'd never admit that she was right about the crowd that came out to hear Micah's solo shows. But unlike Kelly, I wasn't interested in picking up random guys at bars. I spun a test tube like a top then clamped my hand down on it before it could careen off the counter. "Whatever. Sometimes Micah lets me sing."

Apparently Kelly smelled blood; her tone turned snide. "Ooh, maybe Eden's dating her brother."

"Don't be ridiculous, Kelly." Stacy rolled her eyes and gave me her best *don't listen to her* look.

"Oh, right." Kelly threw her head back for one last barb. "Eden would never consider dating a struggling musician."

The clock on the wall reminded me I had seven hours of prison left. I hated the feeling that I was wishing my life away one work day at a time.

Thanh peeked his head around the door and saved me. "Eden, I need you to come monitor one of the test subjects."

Inhaling deep to get my residual irritation under control, I followed Thanh down the hall to the holding cells. Behind the window, a cute blond sat with a wire snaking out of his charcoal-gray Dockers. Thanh instructed him to watch a screen flashing more or less pornographic images while I kept one eye on his vital signs.

I bit my pen and put the test subject through my usual Terminator-robot full-body analysis to gauge his romantic eligibility. He wore a crisp dress shirt with a white cotton undershirt peeking out below the unbuttoned collar. I wagered he held a job I'd find acceptable, possibly in programming, accounting, or maybe even architecture. His fading tan, manicured nails, and fit build lent the impression that he had enough money and time to vacation, pamper himself, and work out. No ring on his finger. And blue eyes at that. On paper, he fit my mental checklist to a *T*.

Even if he was strapped up to his balls in wires.

Hmm. Scratch that. If he were financially secure, he wouldn't need the compensation provided to participants in clinical trials for boner research. *Never mind.*

Thanh came back in and sat next to me.

I stifled a yawn and stretched my arms. "Don't get me wrong. This is all very exciting, but could you please slip some arsenic in my coffee?"

He punched buttons on the complex machine monitoring the erectile event in the other room. "Why are you still working here, Eden? Weren't you supposed to start grad school this year?"

"I was." I sketched a small circle in the margin of the paper on the table.

"You need to start applying soon for next year. Are you waiting till you've saved enough money?"

314 Mary Ann Marlowe

"No, I've saved enough." I drew a flower around the circle and shaded it in. I'd already had this conversation with my parents.

"If you want to do much more than what you're doing now, you need to get your PhD."

I sighed and turned in my chair to face him. "Thanh, you've got your PhD, and you're doing the same thing as me."

When he smiled, the corners of his eyes crinkled. "Yes, but it has always been my lifelong dream to help men maintain a medically induced long-lasting erection."

I looked at my hands, thinking. "Thanh, I'm not sure this is what I want to do with my life. I've lost that loving feeling."

"Well, then, you're in the right place."

I snickered at the erectile dysfunction humor. The guy in the testing room shifted, and I thought for the first time to ask. "What are you even testing today?"

"Top secret."

"You can't tell me?"

"No, I mean you'd already know if you read your e-mails."

"I do read the e-mails." That was partly true. I skimmed and deleted them unless they pertained to my own work. I didn't care about corporate policy changes, congratulations to the sales division, farewells to employees leaving after six wonderful years, tickets to be pawned, baby pictures, or the company chili cook-off.

He reached into a drawer and brought out a small vial containing a clear yellow liquid. When he removed the stopper, a sweet aroma filled the room, like jasmine.

"What's that?"

He handed it to me. "Put some on, right here." He touched my wrist.

I tipped it onto my finger and dabbed both my wrists. Then I waited. "What's it supposed to do?"

He raised an eyebrow. "Do you feel any different?"

I ran an internal assessment. "Uh, nope. Should I?"

"Do me a favor. Walk into that room."

"With the test subject?" It was bad enough that poor guy's schwanz was hooked up to monitors, but he didn't need to know exactly who was observing changes in his penile turgidity. Thanh shooed me on through the door, so I went in.

The erotica continued to run, but the guy's eyes were now on me. I thought, *Is that a sensor monitoring you, or are you just happy to see me?*

"Uh, hi." I glanced back at the one-way mirror, as if I could telepathically understand when Thanh released me from this embarrassing ordeal.

The guy sat patiently, expecting me to do something. So I reached over and adjusted one of the wires, up by the machines. He went back to watching the screen, as if I were just another technician. Nobody interesting.

I backed out of the room. As soon as the door clicked shut, I asked Thanh, "What the hell was that?"

He frowned. "I don't know. I expected something more. Some kind of reaction." He started to place the vial back in the drawer. Then he had a second thought. "Do you like how this smells?"

I nodded. "Yeah, it's good."

"Take it." He tossed it over, and I threw it into my purse.

The rest of the day passed slowly as I listened to Kelly and Stacy argue over the radio station or fight over some impossibly gorgeous actor or front man they'd never meet. Finally at four, I swung into the ladies' room and changed out of my work clothes, which consisted of a rayon suit skirt and a button-up pin-striped shirt. Knowing I'd be hanging with Micah in the club later, I'd brought a pair of comfortable jeans and one of his band's T-shirts. I shook my ponytail out and let my hair fall to my shoulders.

When I went back to the lab to grab my purse and laptop, I wasn't a bit surprised that Kelly disapproved of my entire look.

"I have a low-cut shirt in my car if you want something more attractive." She offered it as though she actually would've

316 Mary Ann Marlowe

lent it to me. Knowing I'd decline, she got in a free dig at my wardrobe choices. We were a study in opposites—she with her overpermed blond hair and salon tan, me with my short-clipped fingernails and functioning brain cells.

"No, thanks. Maybe next time."

"At least let me fix your makeup. Are you even wearing any?"

I pretended she wasn't bothering me. "No time. I have a train to catch."

She sniffed. "Well, you smell nice anyway. New perfume?"

"Uh, yeah. It was a gift." Her normally pouting lips rounded in anticipation of her next question. I zipped my computer bag and said, "Gotta go. See ya tomorrow, Stacy?"

Stacy waved without turning her head away from whatever gossip site she'd logged on to, and I slipped out the door.

As I stood on the train platform waiting for the 5:35 Northeast Corridor train to Penn Station, I heard someone calling "Hello?" from inside my purse. I fetched my phone and found it connected somehow to my mom, whose voice messages I'd been ignoring.

Foiled by technology and the gremlins living in my bag, I placed the phone to my ear. "Mom?"

"Oh, there you are, Eden. I'm making corned beef and gravy tonight. Why don't you come by before you go out?"

I didn't know how to cook, so my mom's invitation was meant as charity. But since she was the reason I couldn't cook, her promise of shit on a shingle wasn't enough to lure me from my original plans.

"No, thanks, Mom. I'm on my way into the city to hear Micah play tonight."

"Oh. Well, we'll see you Sunday I hope. Would you come to church with us? We have a wonderful new minister and—"

"No, Mom. But I'll come by the house later."

"All right. Oh, don't forget you've got a date with Dr. Whedon tomorrow night."

I groaned. She was relentless. "Is it too late to cancel?"

"What's the problem now, Eden?"

I pictured Dr. Rick Whedon, DDS, tonguing my bicuspid as we French kissed. But she wouldn't understand why I'd refuse to date a dentist, so instead, I presented an iron-clad excuse. "Mom, if we got married, I'd be Eden Whedon."

Her sigh came across loud and clear. "Eden, don't be so unreasonable."

"I keep telling you you're wasting your time, Mom."

"And you're letting it slip by, waiting on a nonexistent man. You're going to be twenty-nine soon."

The train approached the station, so I put my finger in my ear and yelled into the phone. "In six months, Mom."

"What was wrong with Jack Talbot?"

I thought for a second and then placed the last guy she'd tried to set me up with. "He had a mustache, Mom. And a tattoo. Also, he lives with his parents."

"That's only temporary," she snapped.

"The mustache or the tattoo?" I thought back to the guy from the lab. "And you never know. Maybe I'll meet Mr. Perfect soon."

"Well, if you do, bring him over on Sunday."

I chortled. The idea of bringing a guy over to my crazy house before I had a ring on my finger was ludicrous. "Sure, Mom. I'll see you Sunday."

"Tell Micah to come, too?"

My turn to sigh. Their pride in him was unflappable, and yet, I'd been the one to do everything they'd ever encouraged me to do, while he'd run off to pursue a pipe dream in music. So maybe they hadn't encouraged me to work in the sex-drug industry, but at least I had a college degree and a stable income.

"Okay, Mom. I'll mention it. The train's here. I have to go."

I climbed on the train and relaxed, so tired of everyone harassing me. At least I could count on Micah not to meddle in my love life.

Chapter Two

At seven thirty, I arrived at the back door of the club, trailing a cloud of profanity. "Fuck. My fucking phone died."

Micah exchanged a glance with the club owner, Tobin. "See? Eden doesn't count."

"What the fuck are you talking about?" After two hours fighting mass transit, I'd lost my patience. My attitude would need to be recalibrated to match Micah's easygoing demeanor.

Micah ground out his cigarette with a twist of his shoe. "Tobin was laying a wager that only women would show up tonight, but I said you'd be here."

I narrowed my eyes.

Micah's small but avid female fan base faithfully came out whenever he put on an acoustic show. His hard-rock band, Theater of the Absurd, catered to a larger male following and performed to ever-increasing audiences. But he loved playing these smaller rooms, bantering with the crowd, hearing people sing along with familiar choruses.

Before Tobin could get in on the act, I blurted, "Can I charge my phone in the green room?"

I made a wide berth around Tobin's plumage of cigarette smoke and followed Micah down the shabby narrow back hall. Dimly lit eight-by-eleven glossy posters plastered the walls, advertising upcoming bands and many other acts that had already passed through. Nobody curated the leftover fliers although hundreds of staples held torn triangles of paper from some distant past. A brand-new poster showing Micah's anticipated club dates hung near the door to the ladies' room. That would disappear during the night as some fan co-opted it for him to autograph, and Tobin would have to replace it. Again.

The green room was actually dark red and held furniture that looked like someone had found it on the curb near the trash. And it smelled like they'd brought the trash, too. God knew what had transpired in here over the years. I tried to touch nothing. Micah flopped down on the sofa and picked up a box of half-eaten Chinese food. His red Converse tennis shoes and dark green pants clashed with the brown-gold hues that stained the formerly whitish sofa.

I plugged in my phone, praying I'd remember to fetch it before I left. I fished out some ibuprofen and grabbed Micah's beer to wash it down. I waved off his interest in the drugs I was popping. "Birth control," I lied.

Without looking up from his noodles, he said, "Oh, good. I was starting to worry you'd joined a convent."

When Micah finished eating, he led me to the front of the club and put me to work setting up his merch table. His band's CDs wouldn't sell, but his self-produced EP of solo work would disappear. Mostly for girls to have something for him to autograph. They'd already own his music digitally. A suitcase filled with rolled-up T-shirts lay under the table. I bent down and selected one of each design to display as samples.

Micah moved around onstage helping the club employees drag cables and whatnot. Not for the first time, I envied him for inheriting some of Mom's Scandinavian coloring and height, while I got Dad's pale Irish skin and raven hair. Micah repeated "one-two-three check" into the mic a few times and then disappeared around back to grab one last smoke before he had to transform from my sweet older brother into that charismatic guy who held a crowd in the palm of his hand.

Right before the doors opened to the public, one of the guys I'd seen setting up the stage stopped by the table and flipped through the T-shirts and CDs. He picked up Micah's EP and then raised dark brown eyes. "Micah Sinclair. You like his music?"

He wore faded jeans and a threadbare T-shirt from a long-forgotten AC/DC concert under a maroon hoodie. His black hair fell somewhere between tousled and bed head. I saw no traces of product, so I assumed he came by that look through honest negligence rather than studied indifference.

My quick scan revealed: too grungy, probably unwashed, poor. I resisted the urge to pull the merch away from his wandering fingers. But I wouldn't risk the sale, so I leaned in on my elbows, all smiles.

"He's amazing. Will you get a chance to hear him perform?"

"Oh, yeah. Definitely." He set the EP down and held out his hand. "I'm Adam, by the way."

I wrapped my hand around his out of sheer politeness and proper upbringing, but I couldn't help laughing and saying, "Just so you know, my worst nightmare would be dating a guy named Adam."

He quirked his eyebrow. "That's kind of discriminatory."

"My name's Eden." I waited a beat for the significance to register, but I guess any guy named Adam would've already dealt with such issues of nomenclature. His eyes lit up immediately.

"Oh. Seriously?" He chuckled, and his smile transformed his features. I sucked in my breath. Underneath the dark hair, dark eyes, and hobo wardrobe, he was awfully cute. "I'll rethink that marriage proposal. But could I get you anything? You want a beer?"

This was a new twist. Usually, the ladies were offering drinks to my brother. I loved getting the attention for a change. "Sure. Whatever lager or pilsner they have on tap."

He walked off, and I snickered. *Maybe some guys like pale brunettes, Kelly.* As he leaned against the bar, I assessed him from the rear. Tall enough, but too skinny. Questionable employment. Either an employee of the club, a musician, a wannabe musician, or a fan. Shame.

Micah strolled up. "Is everything ready?"

I forced my gaze away from Adam's backside. "Are you?"

He scratched his five-o'clock chin scruff. "That's the thing. I may need some help tonight. Do you think you could maybe sing backup on one song? I was hoping to harmonize on 'Gravity.'"

"Sure." What were sisters for? I had his whole catalog memorized, even the music from his band, although that music ran a little too hard rock for my tastes.

Micah left me alone at the merch table, and Adam returned with a glass. "Did I just miss Micah?"

He'd pulled his hoodie up so his face fell into shadow, giving him a sinister appearance. With the nonexistent lighting in the club, I could barely make out his features. This odd behavior, coupled with his interest in my brother, made me worry maybe he was in fact one of the crazy fans who found ways to get closer than normal, and not, as I'd first thought, an employee of the club. How had he gotten inside before the doors opened?

Before I could ask him, a woman's sharp voice interrupted. "Will Micah be coming out after the show?"

I looked toward the club's entrance, where people had begun to stream in. I took a deep breath and prepared to deal with the intensity of music fandom.

"I assume so. He usually does."

She didn't move. "It's just that I brought something for him." She held up a canister of something I guessed was homemade. I'd advised Micah not to eat whatever they gave him, but he never listened. And so far he'd never landed in the hospital. I knew his fans meant well, but who knew if those cookies had been baked alongside seven long-haired cats?

"I could take it back to him if you like." I made the offer, knowing full well it wouldn't do at all.

"No. Thank you. I'll just wait and give them to him later. If he comes out." She wandered off toward the stage.

I spotted one of Micah's regular fans, Susan something-or-other, making a beeline for the merch table. She looked put out that I was there before her. "Eden, if you like, I'm more than happy to man the merch."

I never understood what she got out of working merch for Micah. He didn't pay except possibly in a waived cover charge. And she was farther from the stage and possibly distracted from the performances. Perhaps it gave her status. Whatever it was, it made her happy, and I was glad to relinquish the duty to her.

"Thank you, Susan."

She beamed. "Oh, it's no problem." She began to chatter with the other women crowding up to the merch table. I overheard her saying, "Micah told me he'll be performing a new song tonight."

Adam caught my eye, and we exchanged a knowing smile. So okay, he wasn't a fan. He stepped beside me as I walked to the bar to get a seat on a stool. "So you're not the number one fan, then?" he asked.

I smiled. "Of course I am."

Before we could discuss our reasons for being there, the room plunged into near-total darkness, and Tobin stepped onto the stage to introduce the opening act, a tall blond whose explosion of wild hair had to weigh more than the rest of her.

She pulled up a stool and started into her first song without further ado. Out of respect, I kept quiet and listened, although her performance was a bit shaky, and the between-song banter didn't help. It pleased me that Adam didn't turn to me to say anything snarky about the poor girl to me or talk at all. I had to glare over at the women hanging around the merch table a few times, though. They'd shut up when Micah came on, but they didn't seem to care that other musicians preferred to play to a rapt audience, too.

In the time between acts, Adam ordered me another beer. At some point he'd dropped his hood back, but with the terrible lighting in the club, I had to squint to see his face. Normally, I wasn't a big fan of facial hair of any kind, but Adam's slight scruff caused my wires to cross. On the one hand, I worried he couldn't afford a razor out there in the cardboard box he lived in. On the other hand, I had a visceral urge to reach up and touch his cheek. And run my finger down the side of his neck.

He caught me staring when he leaned closer to ask me how long Micah had been performing.

I wasn't sure what he was asking, so I gave him the full answer. "He's been singing since he was old enough to talk. He started playing acoustic when he was eleven, but picked up electric when he was fifteen. He formed a metal band in high school, and the first time they performed live anywhere beyond the garage was a battle of the bands."

Adam's expression changed subtly as I recounted Micah's life history, and I could tell he was reassessing my level of crazy fantardness. I laughed and said, "I told you I was his number one fan."

His smile slipped, but he managed to reply politely. "He must be very talented."

Something about the timbre in his voice resonated with me, almost familiar, and I regretted my flippant sarcasm.

Before I could repair my social missteps, the lights faded again, and the girls near the stage screamed in anticipation. A spotlight hit the mic, and Micah unceremoniously took the stage. He strummed a few notes and broke directly into a song everyone knew. The girls up front sang along, swaying and trying to out-do each other in their excitement.

Adam twisted around and watched me, eyebrow raised. Maybe he expected me to sing along, too. I raised an eyebrow back and mouthed the words along with Micah. Wouldn't want to disappoint him. Finally, Adam straightened up to watch the performance, ignoring me for several songs.

Micah performed another well-known song, then a new one, introducing each with some casual-seeming banter. I knew he planned every word he said onstage, but the stories he told were no less sincere for that. He controlled his stage presence like a pro.

Before the fourth song, he announced, "This next song requires some assistance. If you would all encourage my sister, Eden, to come join me, I'm sure she'd hop up here and lend me a hand."

The audience applauded on cue. As my feet hit the floor, Adam's eyes narrowed and then opened wide as he did the math. I curtsied and left him behind to climb up onstage to perform—Micah's support vocals once again. Micah strummed a chord, and I hummed the pitch. Then he began to play the song, a beautiful ballad about a man with an unflagging devotion to a woman. The ladies in the front row ate it up. Micah knew I got a kick out of performing, and I suspected he asked me up so I could live his musician life vicariously.

When the song ended, I headed back to the anonymity of my stool. The hard-core fans all knew who I was, but if they weren't pumping me for information about Micah, they didn't pay much attention to me. There was a fresh beer waiting, and I nodded to Adam, appreciative. He winked and faced forward to listen to Micah. That was the extent of our conversation until Micah performed his last encore and the lights came back up.

Then he turned back. "You were right. He's very talented." He tilted his head. "But you held out on me. Your opinion was a little bit biased."

"I was telling you the truth," I deadpanned. "I am his number one fan."

"You two look nothing alike. I'd never have guessed."

"We have a crazy mix of genetics."

As we chatted, the area behind us, near the merch table, filled up with people waiting for a chance to talk to Micah, get an autograph, or take a picture with him. The lady with the cat-hair cookies had nabbed the first place in the amorphous line. I scanned the rest of the crowd and discovered that Tobin had lost his bet. A pair of teenage boys holding guitars stood on their toes, trying to get a glimpse of Micah over the heads of the other fans, but he hadn't come out yet. They were most likely fans of his edgier rock band, taking advantage of the smaller venue to meet him, pick his brain about music, and have him sign their guitars. They'd still be competing with at least thirty people for Micah's time.

If I wanted to go home with my brother, I'd be hanging out a while. I could still catch a train back to New Jersey, but Micah's place in Brooklyn was closer. I decided to stay. It had nothing to do with the cute guy paying attention to me. I just didn't want to navigate Manhattan alone and drunk.

Adam leaned in and asked, "So what do you do? Are you a musician, too?"

"Actually, no. I'm a biochemist."

"Finding cures for Ebola?"

That caught me off guard, and I snorted. "No, nothing like that." I didn't know what to tell him about what I actually researched, so I half-lied. "My company's developing a perfume."

"What's it like?"

I scooted over. "I'm wearing it. Can you smell it?"

He met me halfway, eyes dilating black. I knew I shouldn't be flirting. He didn't appear to meet a single one of my criteria and, in fact, actively ticked boxes from the "deal-breaker" list. I didn't want to lead him on only to have to give him the heave-ho in the next thirty minutes.

He took my hand and kept his dark eyes on mine as he lifted my wrist up to smell the fragrance Thanh had given me. "Mmm. That's nice."

Without dropping his gaze, he brushed his lips across my skin, and an electric current shot up every nerve in my arm. I drew my hand back, shrugging off the shiver that hit me like an aftershock. "And you? What do you do?"

326 Mary Ann Marlowe

He laughed and scratched the back of his neck. "Well, I'm a musician."

I blinked back my disappointment. From Adam's appearance, I hadn't had high hopes, but he might've been dressed down for a night out. Way down.

On my list of suitable professions for my prospective mate, musician wasn't at the absolute bottom. There were plenty more embarrassing or unstable career choices. I wouldn't date plumbers or proctologists for obvious reasons. Salesmen either because, well, I didn't like salesmen, but also because their financial situation might be uncertain. Plus they tended to travel. My ideal guy, I'd decided, would be an architect. But there weren't many of those swimming around my apartment complex in Edison, New Jersey.

I had nothing against musicians. On the contrary, I loved them. I'd supported my brother in his career, but the lifestyle was too precarious for my peace of mind. Even the most talented had a hard time making ends meet. Traveling and selling merchandise became a necessity.

Which is why I never dated musicians.

Unfortunately, all the doctors, lawyers, and architects I encountered were usually not interested in jean-clad, concert T-shirt wearing me. This train of thought brought me around to the realization that I'd judged Adam for dressing exactly the same way.

Micah saved me from sticking my foot in my mouth when he appeared at our side. "Adam! I'm glad to see you here. I see you've met my sister." He turned to me. "Eden, do you mind if I steal him for a few?"

Adam threw me a glance. "Will you be here when I get back?"

The jolt of butterflies this simple question gave me came wholly unexpectedly. "I'll be here. I'm leaving when Micah does."

He flashed a crooked smile at me, and I traced his lips with my eyes. He was going to be trouble.

They headed toward the green room, leaving me as confused as Adam must've been when I went onstage. I didn't know who he was, or why my brother wanted to see him.

I weighed the possible options.

Option one: The most logical explanation was that Micah was hiring Adam to temporarily replace his bassist, Rick, who was taking time off to be with his wife after the birth of their first child. I congratulated myself for solving the mystery on my first try.

Option two: Maybe Adam was a drug dealer. No, other than smoking and drinking, I'd never known Micah to try a recreational drug. And surely, this wouldn't be an ideal location for such a transaction. Besides, Adam already said he was a musician. Option one was looking better and better.

Option three: Or maybe Adam was a homeless man Micah was going to take in out of charity. A homeless man who'd just bought me three beers. I rolled my eyes at myself, but then felt awash with guilt. He probably wasn't homeless, but it did seem like he might be struggling to get by, and I'd accepted three drinks I could've easily afforded. *Good job, Eden. Way to drive a man to starvation.*

Every new option I came up with to explain Adam's presence here defied logic and stretched the imagination. I gave up and watched the crowd thin. When Micah and Adam came back out, the bar was empty, save me and the staff.

Micah poked me. "We're going over to Adam's. You can come or just go straight back to my place." He bounced on his feet. I looked from him to Adam, standing relaxed up against the bar. From the looks of things, Micah had a boy crush. I might be interrupting a bromance if I tagged along.

Adam stepped toward me. "I have a fully stocked bar, and I don't like to drink alone." His smile was disarming. The whole situation seemed so contrived, and I had to wonder whose idea it was.

Micah stifled a yawn. "Come on, Eden. Just for a drink. Let's go see how the other half lives."

Did he know what that expression meant? "Okay, but let's get going. Some of us have been awake since this morning."

Mary Ann Marlowe lives in central Virginia where she works as a computer programmer/DBA. She spent ten years as a university-level French professor, and her resume includes stints as an au pair in Calais, a hotel intern in Paris, a German tutor, a college radio disc jockey, and a webmaster for several online musician fandoms. She has lived in twelve states and three countries and loves to travel.

CPSIA information can be obtained
at www.ICGtesting.com
Printed in the USA
LVHW040548140620
657964LV00003B/619